Praise for

NATALIE C. ANDERSON

"A twisty-turny, chock-full-of-secrets, so-exciting-you-have-to-force-yourself-to-take-breaks-and-breathe kind of novel."
                    —*The New York Times* on *City of Saints & Thieves*

"A gripping journey of vengeance."
                    —*Us Weekly* on *City of Saints & Thieves*

★ "Anderson . . . breathe[s] ferocious life into a story that needs to be told. This is one of those tough but invaluable books with the power to increase a reader's awareness of and empathy for teens who have lost the right to be young."
                    —*Booklist*, starred review of *Let's Go Swimming on Doomsday*

"A teenage Congolese refugee (a blend of *The Girl with the Dragon Tattoo*'s Lisbeth Salander and X-Men's Storm) in Kenya seeks revenge for the killing of her mother."
                    —*The Hollywood Reporter* on *City of Saints & Thieves*

"[A] linguistically beautiful murder mystery tale that will have you tearing through the pages, all along its twist and turns."
                    —*Bustle* on *City of Saints & Thieves*

"A riveting account . . . [where] greed, guilt, and redemption are layered in a sober yet tender narrative showing the lengths one will go to for loved ones."—*Kirkus Reviews* on *Let's Go Swimming on Doomsday*

"This nail-biting murder mystery set in Kenya follows Tina, a Congolese refugee, as she tracks down her mother's killer in the midst of corrupt businessmen, a master thief, and a street gang."

—*Seventeen* on *City of Saints & Thieves*

★ "[I]n this fast-paced thriller . . . Anderson adeptly uses language to bring Tina's world to life as she carefully traces her heroine's history to reveal a shocking truth."

—*Publishers Weekly*, starred review of *City of Saints & Thieves*

"An intriguing examination of ways familial loyalty and guilt can lead anyone to make desperate choices. Anderson uses the exploration of manipulation and coercion to craft a thought-provoking narrative."

—*School Library Journal* on *Let's Go Swimming on Doomsday*

★ "[A] wonderfully twisted puzzle of a murder mystery."

—*Booklist*, starred review of *City of Saints & Thieves*

"*Ocean's Eleven* meets *Blood Diamond*: Natalie C. Anderson's *City of Saints & Thieves*, a gripping tale of revenge and redemption, tracks a murderer through the jungles of Congo and the far reaches of cyberspace, shining a light on the importance of family and friendship along the way—a perfect cocktail of suspense, action and heart."

—Tara Sullivan, critically acclaimed author of *Golden Boy* and *The Bitter Side of Sweet,* on *City of Saints & Thieves*

★ "[A] solidly plotted, swiftly paced international murder mystery that's laced with just a hint of romance. . . . Highly recommended for teens looking for a gritty, suspenseful, immersive read driven by a tough, smart, realistic heroine."

—*School Library Journal*, starred review of *City of Saints & Thieves*

"[Anderson] makes it clear how difficult it is for even children to survive this faith-based and historically rooted conflict unscathed."

—*The Bulletin of the Center for Children's Books* on *Let's Go Swimming on Doomsday*

★ "[B]y setting a fast-paced crime drama with compelling characters in this fraught region, Anderson does the good service of interesting young readers in this ongoing human conflict and the tragic toll it continues to take on the people of the region."

—*The Bulletin of the Center for Children's Books*, starred review of *City of Saints & Thieves*

"*City of Saints & Thieves* will pull you from the very first page into a rarely seen world, violent and beautiful, where the only rule is survival and the only weapons are a young woman's courage and love."

—Francisco X. Stork, award-winning author of *Marcelo in the Real World* and *The Last Summer of the Death Warriors*, on *City of Saints & Thieves*

★ "Natalie C. Anderson's breathtaking debut is deep, dark and— remarkably for the subject—quite funny at times. . . . Pages will fly by as readers root for Tiny and her loved ones."

—*Shelf Awareness*, starred review of *City of Saints & Thieves*

"In prose as tenacious as her vendetta-driven and irresistible protagonist, Anderson interweaves personal and national tragedies, answering legacies of loss with the promise of family and friendship. *City of Saints & Thieves* is a world opener of a debut, one worth reading and remembering."

—Ashley Hope Pérez, Printz Honor–winning author of *Out of Darkness*, on *City of Saints & Thieves*

"A story full of twists and turns, proving nothing is ever as black and white as it may seem."   —*Kirkus Reviews* on *City of Saints & Thieves*

"Anderson's dark thriller will appeal to readers who prefer their mysteries political and their stakes high and who will feel rewarded by solutions in shades of gray rather than black-and-white."

—*The Horn Book* on *City of Saints & Thieves*

LET'S GO
SWIMMING
ON
DOOMSDAY

ALSO BY NATALIE C. ANDERSON

City of Saints & Thieves

LET'S GO SWIMMING ON DOOMSDAY

NATALIE C. ANDERSON

WITHDRAWN

PENGUIN BOOKS

PENGUIN BOOKS

An imprint of Penguin Random House LLC, New York

First published in the United States of America by G. P. Putnam's Sons, 2019
Published by Penguin Books, an imprint of Penguin Random House LLC, 2020

Visit us online at penguinrandomhouse.com

THE LIBRARY OF CONGRESS HAS CATALOGED THE G. P. PUTNAM'S SONS EDITION AS FOLLOWS:
Title: Let's go swimming on doomsday / Natalie C. Anderson.
Other titles: Let us go swimming on doomsday
Description: New York, NY: G. P. Putnam's Sons, [2019] | Summary: "Forced to become a
child soldier, sixteen-year-old Somali refugee Abdi must confront his painful past"
—Provided by publisher.
Identifiers: LCCN 2018023326 | ISBN 9780399547614 (hardback) | ISBN 9780399547638 (ebook)
Subjects: | CYAC: Child soldiers—Fiction. | Refugees—Fiction. | Spies—Fiction. |
Islamic fundamentalism—Fiction. | Terrorism—Fiction. | Brothers—Fiction. |
Somalia—Fiction. | Kenya—Fiction.
Classification: LCC PZ7.A528 Let 2019 | DDC [Fic]—dc23
LC record available at https://lccn.loc.gov/2018023326

Penguin Books ISBN 9780399547621

Printed in the United States of America

Design by Jaclyn Reyes
Text set in Cartier Book Std

1 3 5 7 9 10 8 6 4 2

For the troublemaker of Cairo

ONE

I float, I float, I float.

I open my eyes and for a second they sting, and then nothing. I look around. Underneath me the floor of the ocean swells up pale and solid. Above, the sun is broken on the water's surface into a million shining pieces.

By now I can hold my breath for almost two minutes if I'm relaxed like this. I've carried a stone in from the shore, and the weight is perfect. It anchors me, and I am very still. Fish like slivers of glass sail by, too small for eating. Through the drone of water in my ears I can hear a crackling noise that my father once told me was the sound of tiny shrimp breathing. A jellyfish rides the current.

I think I'd like to be a jellyfish. This is what it would feel like to be brainless and transparent.

One minute and fifteen seconds. My vision is starting to

pulse. I can feel my blood surging in my temples, telling me to breathe.

I wait.

One minute and thirty-eight seconds. Lungs burning, something animal in me screaming, Decide! Live or die!

I look up at the shards of sun and tell it, Not yet. I want to live, of course I do, but it's so tempting to stay. As soon as I break for air, there's no pretending to be anything other than a boy who must swim back and put his feet on the ground. A boy who will feel his weight again, surprisingly heavy on his bones.

For as long as I can, I resist. Two minutes and four seconds.

I don't want to be the boy who will walk out of the waves, water sluicing down his black arms, falling from his white fingertips. That boy will walk past the fishermen's boats, past the fishermen. He'll walk from the beach onto the tarmac. He'll pass old, shattered buildings that remind him of dogs' incisors. He'll pass new buildings wrapped in scaffolding like ugly gifts. He'll disappear into Somalia's capital city, the White Pearl: Mogadishu.

Two minutes and sixteen seconds.

My head breaks the surface and I gasp. Air and water sting my throat.

I tell myself I've chosen to live, but the water knows the truth. Waves brush my arms, soft as shroud linen.

The water knows I have to die.

TWO

By the time I get back to the hotel, I am completely dry.

"Where have you been?" Commander Rashid says, closing the distance in two big strides and grabbing me by the collar. The others look at me from the floor, eyes shining in the gloom.

"Swimming," I say, pointing toward the water. "Just swimming, sir."

"Swimming?" His eyes bulge. "*Swimming*? What do you think this is, a holiday?"

"I'm sorry, sir."

I am not sorry.

He looks me over, and I can tell he's searching for signs that I'm cracking. Or that I'm having second thoughts, or that I've done the unthinkable and sold him and the Boys out.

"I needed to bathe," I tell him. "Like a . . ." I pretend to search for the word, even though I've thought long and hard about what to tell him. "A purification."

Commander Rashid's voice is low and soft—a knife glinting in the dark. "That was a long bath, boy. Hakim Doctor has faith in you, but if it were up to me . . ."

He's interrupted by Bashir jumping up from the floor. "Commander," he says, "I apologize, but can I please have your assistance with these connections? I'm not sure if the wires go here or to the other panel." He holds up a tangle of plastic and metal to demonstrate.

Rashid makes a strangled noise and lets me go. "Not that one, *doqon*! Do you want to kill us all now?"

The commander should know that Bashir could make a bomb out of two mangoes and a shoestring, but my friend's ruse is lost on him. Maybe we're all just that tightly wound right now. Bashir winks at me over the commander's head and I creep away, slip into the adjoining room of the half-built hotel. It's empty except for my brother, who is lying on the floor. One whole corner of the room is gone, like something has taken an enormous bite out of it. A mortar, probably. A hot breeze rummages through the rooms, but the smell coming off Khalid is still heavy and foul.

I pick up the bottle of water and tip it into his mouth. I try not to gag. Is it the smell or my guilt that makes me want to throw up? "How are you?" I ask.

"Fine," he grunts, after taking barely a sip. "What do you

think you're doing, wandering off?" He's trying to sound tough, but his voice is a rasp.

"I just went for a last swim, that's all."

"A swim? Now? Da'ud, you know there's no time to—"

"Shh." It barely even registers anymore when he calls me the new name. "Hakim Doctor said you aren't supposed to talk. The stitches will open."

The bandage across his stomach is a muddy red brown and needs changing, but we're out of clean cloth. Only the Doctor would know for sure how bad the wound really is, but he's not here. He gave Nur and Commander Rashid instructions over the phone and Nur stitched my brother up as best he could, but what Khalid really needs is a hospital, antibiotics. But he's not getting any of that, not now that his face has been circulated across Mogadishu as a Most Wanted Jihadi.

Whether he lives or dies is all in God's hands now, according to the Doctor. I get it: I know what would happen if we took him to the hospital. The doctors would turn him in for the money. I know that. But doing nothing is making me crazy. I try not to think what my mother would say if she saw me just sitting here watching him die.

If she knew that this was all my fault.

The soldier's bullet didn't hit where it was supposed to. Instead it sliced right through him, just under his ribs, tearing through his intestines, from the smell of it. "Septic," I heard one of the guys whisper when he thought I couldn't hear. I'm not

5

sure if the shot really was an accident or intentional, but either way, looking at Khalid sweeps away all my remaining doubts about what I'm about to do.

My brother gurgles when he breathes, and his skin is the color of old *canjeero* bread. I pour a little water on a rag and wipe his face. He's burning up.

"When do you leave?" Khalid asks.

"A couple of hours."

He nods. It looks painful. He closes his eyes. "It should be me there, not you."

"You should be here. Getting well, *Inshallah*."

"I don't want to be well," he says very softly. His eyes stay closed. "It wasn't supposed to happen this way."

I don't answer for a few seconds. I'm not sure which part he's talking about, but it doesn't matter. He's right. None of it should have gone down like this.

I'm going to fix it, I want to tell him. I'm going to fix everything.

But I don't say that. Straining for sincerity, I say what I know will make him feel better. "It was God's will." I must be a good enough liar, or Khalid's a good enough believer. The crease in his brow smooths.

"God's will," he agrees.

I squeeze his shoulder gently, but I think he's already asleep again. I wait until his breathing is regular. For a moment, he is Dahir again, just my big brother. Khalid the warrior fades away.

"Please, God . . ." I trail off. It's all the prayer I can manage.

I stand and go to the others.

Commander Rashid is waiting for me. The thing he carries is bulky and awkward. Wires spring from it like insect legs. The commander's mouth is a narrow, angry slash. He's still watching me, still suspicious. But the Doctor has given his orders, and the commander will follow them.

He places it carefully in my arms and steps back. "Let's see if it fits."

THREE

NOW: NOVEMBER 4
SANGUI CITY, KENYA

"So . . ." the social worker says as she checks her papers, ". . . Abdiweli. How exactly did you end up here?"

The sinking sun through the bars on the window doesn't show much of the police holding cell I've been dumped in. Not much you'd want to see anyway. The walls are unpainted concrete blocks, and the corners are furry with grime. There's an army cot with a suspicious brown stain, and a bucket, which, from the smell of it, is where I'm supposed to relieve myself. Geckos cling to the wall and lick their eyeballs.

The woman watches me with sharp blue eyes. She told me her full name, but it was just a long jumble of syllables. I must have looked confused, because then she said, "Just call me Sam." Which I think is a boy's name, but I don't ask. She's from the UN refugee agency, and she says she's here to help, but I'm not sure what that means. I'm still handcuffed to a table leg.

Sam frowns. "Do you need an interpreter?"

I shake my head and pick at a scab. The table between us is decorated with years of prisoner graffiti. Initials, verses from the Bible and the Koran, variations on "fuck the police," penises. I wonder how the prisoners did it. With their fingernails? It's not like anyone let them have knives.

The social worker begins to stand. "I think you might. Let me just see if I can call Sayid . . ."

"No, Madam Sam," I say, the words coming out rusty but clear. "I speak English. I understand you."

She lowers herself slowly back into her chair. She's as white as a plucked chicken except for her nose, which is red. On her wrist a beaded Maasai bracelet announces "KENYA." Maybe she forgets where she is sometimes and has to remind herself.

"So tell me. What's your side of the story?"

I shift in my chair, tugging my too-short sleeve over the knobby bones of my wrist, like I can hide my hand. The stumps where my fingers once were are pulsing again, and under the grubby bandage I know the skin is angry, stretched tight against ugly black scabs. The whole mess is taking way too long to heal. It's hot and it's itchy—God, is it itchy. The handcuffs aren't helping.

"I couldn't pay."

The police wanted a five-thousand-shilling "fee" to set me free. I must have pissed one of them off when I asked if they were stupid or just crazy, because I've been locked to this table for at least six hours. I wonder if the UN has to pay "fees" to get me out of here.

Sam's eyebrows pinch. "I'm not talking about that."

I shrug. "They told you why."

"I want to hear your side. I'm trying to get you out of here." Lowering her voice, she leans forward. Her loose brown hair sways into her face. "You're lucky they even called us. You know how they're treating Somali boys these days."

I have been shifting, turning my good ear toward her without even realizing it. Does she know something? Why did the UN send a white American lady, not a Kenyan? Is she really from the UN? A shiver crawls up my spine. This is a trick. She's trying to get me to slip up and say something.

After a long silence Sam says, "They tried calling your uncle first, but the line was disconnected."

My mind goes blank. Uncle? Then I remember. That's right, that's what I told the police when they brought me in, that I stay with my uncle. I gave them his real name but a phony number.

"Where is he?"

My uncle Sharmarke died when I was ten. "I don't know." I scratch at the scab again.

It's getting late in the day. All the good sleeping spots are going to be taken in the alley behind Kenyatta Street if I don't get out of here soon. *If* I get out. Would sleeping in jail really be so bad? It couldn't be any worse than the street. I resist the urge to lay my head on the table and ignore Sam until she goes away. Instead I say, "Maybe Uncle Sharmarke is at work." *Or dead. Probably dead.*

"Do you have a different number? I can call him right now."

I don't answer.

"Don't you want to go home?"

I've come to realize that with most adults, if I just don't say anything, usually they give up. Eventually, I am rewarded with a sigh. "Did you steal that mobile phone?"

I shake my head no.

"The policeman says you did."

I don't try to set her straight. What's the point? His word against mine. Guess who wins that argument. The first I heard of a stolen phone was when the officer grabbed me. Never mind that all they found in my pockets was a ratty wallet, empty except for a single business card that I can't bring myself to throw away. No phone. But what am I supposed to say? I thought I saw one of the Boys walking down the street and freaked out? When I ran, the shopkeeper must have thought it was because I'd stolen something. He shouted for the cops. Cops grabbed me. And here I am.

Sam sighs. "Come on, kid, throw me a bone. You need to tell me whether you took it or not, so I can get you out of here. This will all be a lot easier if I know the truth. Being a thief is better than being a . . ." She stops herself. But I know what she was going to say. It's on the lips of everyone in Sangui City:

Terrorist.

My toes curl up in my sandals. I stare at the trash in the

corner. My bad ear starts to do that ringing thing, like it's underwater.

Sam tries again. "Look, the police and the UN don't want you to stay here; you're sixteen, underage. That hand needs a doctor. Did you steal the phone or not?"

I shiver at the word *doctor*. Sam sounds annoyed, but maybe like she's telling the truth. Maybe she does want to get me out. "No," I say. "I didn't steal it."

"Then why did you run from the officer?"

"Because he chased me."

Sam presses her lips together. She watches me for a long time. I find myself staring at her hands. Her skin is so pale that I can see blue veins under it. Finally she stands up, gathering her papers. "I'll be back," she says.

I watch the sun shift angles behind the window bars. This cell isn't so bad, really.

I've been in worse.

It's sort of a relief to leave my fate to Sam. Either she'll persuade them to let me go, or she won't. Being a white *muzungu* from the UN has got to help.

Sam seems a little better than the *muzungus* I've met at the Glory Christian Life Center. I've been there a couple of times because they give out free lunch. Those white girls are just a few years older than me, all big eyed and soft. They think because they've been in Sangui City for five minutes that they "get" Africa. That fixing poverty or elephant poaching or whatever is just a matter of rolling up their sleeves and getting to work. They say things like, "Africa calls to me," as if Africa is a beautiful smiling woman beckoning from a doorway.

Wallahi, they're annoying.

At the Glory Christian Life Center they're always trying to talk to me about Jesus—that's the price for food. The first time one of them started in with the whole "Do you know Jesus Christ, the redeemer?" thing, I almost told her to shut the hell up. Doesn't she know talk like that can get her killed? But then I remembered I wasn't in Mogadishu anymore. I've found myself spacing out like that, ever since that night. Getting confused, seeing things. So I calmed down and just listened politely, waiting until I could slip away and get my plate without seeming too rude.

Sam returns after maybe half an hour, looking flushed but victorious. A fat, grumpy police officer follows, keys in hand, and unlocks my cuffs. When he bends over me, I see spots of stew he's spilled down the front of his uniform.

"All right, let's go, Abdiweli," Sam says.

I rub my wrists. They sting, but unlike my fingers, they'll be fine.

"It's just Abdi," I say, like just Sam, but she's already heading out the door.

This is good, I tell myself as I follow. *Getting out of here is a good thing. You don't want to be in jail.* The words slide through my brain, failing to rouse any sort of response, good or bad. All I feel is nervous about being out and exposed again.

As we're leaving, the police are bringing another guy into

the station who's bleeding from a pink gash on his scalp, his head bobbing around on a neck as useless as a rubber band. The officers have to pick him up under the armpits and drag him inside. He's missing a shoe and smells like beer and pee. We keep walking.

My eyes automatically sweep over the people in the yard, but I don't notice anyone suspicious. Ladies in bright *kangas* wait to bring food to locked-up family members. They sit under the palms with the patience of saints. Their kids scuffle in the sand. Men with somber faces and ill-fitting suits line up at an office window for something.

The white Land Cruiser Sam aims for stands out like an elephant in the parking lot, its antennas bristling importantly.

She sits up front with the driver, and I get in the back. They talk in muted voices while I look out the window. An officer has just come out and told the waiting women that they can queue up to bring food to the prisoners. They jostle for position in line, and a fight almost breaks out.

"Is this right? Your address?" Sam asks, twisting around in her seat.

I look at where she's pointing on the form. The address I gave to the police was 100 percent fake. The driver, a Kenyan, looks at me and seems to see more than Sam can. "We want to take you home," he says. "What neighborhood? Eastleigh?"

"No," I say quickly. Definitely not Eastleigh, the place in Sangui City most people refer to as "little Mogadishu." But I can't tell them to take me to Kenyatta. That part of town is just office buildings and lunch restaurants. Nobody lives there. Well, no one but street kids anyway. So I say the first thing that comes to mind: Mbagani area, Jogo Road.

That satisfies them, and they both turn around and the driver pushes us out into the press of metal and glass that is Sangui traffic. The sun is setting and I hear the *adhan*, the call to prayer, start up from somewhere in the leafy-green neighborhood. I lock my door.

The car windows are cracked only a fraction, tinted so no one can see inside, but still, I keep scanning. Looking for what, I don't know. That little sign that something is off, the tickling sensation in the back of your brain. That primal instinct that tells you when someone is looking at you, lining up their sights. The same people who taught me to listen to that part of my brain are here somewhere. The Boys are walking these streets, ready to slice me up. Because I'm their little traitor.

I try desperately to keep my eyes open, but it's like my body has decided, *Enough. You're safe enough.* I will close them for just one second. Just one.

FOUR

Like I said, I've been in worse cells.

At some point while I'm lying on the damp concrete floor with my hands and ankles tied, I have a revelation. Here's what I think: My family and I weren't actually abducted from our beds in the middle of the night by soldiers. My mother, grandmother, little sisters, and brother are not in a nearby cell, broken or in the process of being broken.

I think that maybe, in fact, they have been abducted by aliens.

Wait. I know how that sounds, but just hear me out. Let me explain. It makes a lot of sense, actually. Why haven't I been allowed to see them? Why won't these soldiers tell me where I am?

Because they're scared, that's why. They don't want me to know the truth.

I'm not talking about a bad abduction. I'm talking about one like in *Close Encounters of the Third Kind*. We showed it on repeat about a year ago at Salama Cinema Palace, the backroom DVD hall where I used to work. The movie was old as shit, but awesome. Isn't it actually possible, *totally* possible, that right before the soldiers broke into our compound, Hooyo, Ayeyo, Hafsa, and the twins were just beamed up? I saw the light. It was blinding. Knocked me right out, didn't it?

I close my eyes, open them, see the same thing: nothing. It's that dark. I warm to the thought that in the chaos, child-like aliens with gentle little hands saw what was happening and stopped time, came down, and led my family away to their spaceship. They intervened at exactly the right moment and protected Hooyo and the others from the men who have me now. Maybe the aliens didn't see me, or they thought I was dead. That's why I got left behind. The soldiers only managed to get me.

I can picture it all so clearly. My family is sitting up there in space, and they are all fine. Ayeyo is complaining that the aliens talk too softly while she nods off in her comfy white space chair. And maybe instead of a little dog, like in the movie, there's a cat up there for Hafsa to play with. One that looks like the tabby that ran away during the long rains last year. Faisal and Zahra play with silver alien LEGOs. Maybe even Aabo and Dahir are there. They found Aabo and beamed him straight up from whatever construction site he was working on in Saudi, and Dahir has escaped from the Boys. The little aliens are friendly, and when the time is right, when everything is safe again, they'll rescue me from this pit and we'll all go zooming off into space, to a better world.

I want to tell my captors that I've figured it out. I know what they don't want me to know. But I can't seem to make my body take on the task of sitting up. I tell it to move and nothing happens. My head and face are sticky and swollen, and my mouth won't form words. I smell copper and urine, mildew and dirt.

Thoughts flit through my head in the dark like pale butterflies.

FIVE

"Hey, boy, *kaalay,* get up."

Big hands grab me under my arms and haul me up off the floor. By the time my head clears enough to think about struggling, I've been dragged into another room and flung into a chair. My body is a symphony of pain: I hurt in too many ways to count or separate. I finally get one eye open, and the world swims at me in the shape of a man's silhouette. I can't see his face. The room is dark, and the only light comes from a bulb behind his head.

I try to figure out where all my limbs are. My hands are tied behind my back. My ankles are shackled together. It finally clicks that I've been like this for a long time. Days. I feel a tug at my feet. The soldier who put me in the chair is binding them behind me, attaching them to my wrists, hobbling me. The word *helicopter* pops into my head. It's what they call this position:

feet tied to hands behind your back. Every once in a while a body will show up on the street, still tied up like this, tortured, dead, dumped for the seagulls to peck at and the people to learn a lesson from.

Comforting thoughts.

"What is . . ." The garbled words in my head won't come out right. "Where am I?"

The man doesn't reply. He is smoking, a gray cloud pooling around his face in the stagnant air.

I shake my head, trying to get my vision to work. Bad idea. Hurts like hell. I can't make the man's face out, but the hand with the cigarette is white. Not good. There are no white guys in Mogadishu you want to run into. Especially not in . . . wherever I am. The cell has no windows. No way to tell where I am or how much time has passed. I don't even know if I'm still in Mogadishu.

"Who are you?" I manage. "Where's my family?" I feel something hard in my mouth and spit it into my lap. A piece of tooth.

The man exhales. "So many questions." The words are Somali, but his gravelly voice isn't.

Was there a white guy with the soldiers who grabbed us? I have no idea. When they burst into our house, I thought the men were thugs who'd come to rob us. It happens all the time in our neighborhood. But it didn't take long to figure out that these guys weren't your average pack of *khaat*-high looters. They had body armor and big guns and moved in an organized pack. They'd been trained. They were taking orders. They shone lights in our eyes so we couldn't see. And all they said was "Be still! Stop talking!" again and again. The whole thing probably took less than two minutes. The last I remember I was being separated from my mother and grandmother, my sister and the twins, and tossed into a truck. I woke up here. Alone.

My best guess is that I've been here two, maybe three days. This guy is the first person to actually talk to me. The soldiers come to visit, but it's just to beat me into a bloody mess every couple of hours like they're on a schedule. Electrical wires whipped against my bare feet until they're fat and oozing. Fists cracking against my face and ribs. It hurts to breathe. It hurts to be alive. They haven't questioned me. They haven't said anything. It's like I was brought in just for the pleasure of beating the shit out of me.

The man continues to smoke and watch me. A soldier brings a cup of water and holds it to my lips. It runs down my neck as I try to swallow.

I think I might be in the Hole.

People don't come out of the Hole.

That's all I can figure, that I'm in the underground prison that's been passed from president to occupier to warlord—whoever's in charge of the capital—over the years. But the thing is, you have to be someone special to make it into the Hole. And not to be all humble about it, but seriously, I'm nobody. Ask anyone. I've worked hard at it. Abdiweli Mohamed, total nobody. Kid who does okay in school, keeps his head down, runs from trouble. Family as poor as anyone else's. My dad's not a politician; he's in Saudi working construction like half the dads in my neighborhood. No one in my family is a troublemaker, unless you count my eighty-year-old grandma, my *ayeyo*, whose potty mouth would make a soldier blush.

The man pulls a chair out of the shadows and sits in front of me. I can see his face now. He's definitely white. Shit. The only white guys in Mogadishu are the occasional journalist with a death wish and European and American military. They're supposedly training the Somali army and the AMISOM troops from Uganda and Kenya. AMISOM—the African Union Mission in Somalia—and the army are everywhere, but the white guys stay out of sight, on bases near the airport. Whispered rumors are always going around about night raids by American Navy SEALs, bombs dropped by drones. If you're smart, you don't ask. You don't want to know. You don't want to have anything to do with it.

And you definitely don't want to be stuck down in the Hole with one of them.

AMISOM and the army are supposed to be the good guys, and we cheer when they march down the street, and yeah, they're better than Al Shabaab, but I follow one simple rule, hammered into me by my father before he left to find work in Saudi: Don't trust guys with guns. Any of them.

I look around the cell again. Both guards have AK-47s trained on me. I may not have gone looking for trouble, but it doesn't seem to have mattered, Aabo. It came looking for me.

"Are you hungry, Abdiweli?"

Hungry? That's what he asks, after his friends have spent the last couple of days tenderizing me like a side of meat? The man waits for my answer. I shake my head no. I can see him better now. He has thin glasses and a beard. He isn't in fatigues, just normal clothes, simple pants and a button-down shirt like a schoolteacher. He's looking at me, but something about his gaze seems like he's not really seeing me. Like he's inspecting the engine of a broken-down car. As if I'm something mechanical that will work if he can just figure out which screw to turn.

"I need to ask you some questions," the man says.

"Who are you?" I ask again.

"You can call me Mr. Jones."

"My family . . ."

"Your family is fine."

"Where are they? I need to see them." I try to stop it, but my voice cracks. "Please."

He cocks his head. "Maybe. My questions first, though. Then we'll talk about your family." Mr. Jones has a folder in his hands, which he opens. "I need you to be truthful with me. Can you do that?"

I look from him to the folder. I know where this is going. "I'm not a terrorist."

"No," he agrees, like he knows everything there is to know about me already. He holds up a photo of a man walking down a street. "Do you recognize him?"

23

At first I don't. It's the beard, maybe, and something about his eyes. He's older, obviously. But then I do, like a slap across the face. For a second I don't move. Then I lick my lips. "No."

"Are you sure?" Mr. Jones flips the photo around, as if to be sure he's shown me the right one. He lets me look again.

I shake my head. A bead of sweat rolls into my eye, and I blink. A thousand thoughts rocket through my brain, one after another: *he's dead he's not dead that's not him it is him where did he get that photo where is he is it really him it can't be him—*

Mr. Jones looks past me and nods. A signal. It snaps me out of my head. I start to turn, but feel my feet being yanked back, my toes scraped against the concrete, old wounds reopening. "No!" I shout, trying to shake free.

But the hands hold my ankles tight. I hear the telltale whistle and the electrical wire slices against the soles of my feet like a lick of blue fire.

Like all the other times this has happened, I scream.

"Oh, come now, it's not that bad," Mr. Jones says to me.

I let myself moan, high and soft like a girl. I am so beyond caring about how I look to these soldiers. I watch a string of my drool roll down my bloody shirtfront.

"Come, look again."

I don't lift my face.

"It's your brother, isn't it?"

When I still don't answer, I hear the whistle, and I'm already screaming before it hits.

"It's your brother Dahir. Okay, that's enough."

At first I think he's talking to me, but then I realize he's telling my torturers to stop. For a second I don't believe it. I wait, but nothing happens. Choking a breath, I feel a sudden surge of relief. None of them have ever stopped once they start, no matter how I beg or cry or scream. Not until they're good and ready. This man, he can control them. I feel words bubbling up, and I nearly let them slip. *Thank you,* I almost say.

What is wrong with me? Suddenly I feel worse than I've felt at any point so far and I gag, but nothing comes up. It's like my eyeballs have come unhinged from my head and I'm seeing myself from a high, far corner of the room.

"We'll take his identity as a given," Mr. Jones says. "Dahir Mohamed, age nineteen." He picks up my chin and forces me to look at him. His eyes are calm. Up close, I can see that Jones is older than I had thought at first. His face is wrinkled, blotchy. White hairs sprinkle his beard. "Where is he?"

"I don't know," I say.

"You don't know."

"No."

He shakes me by the jaw. Not hard, just enough to make me look at him again. "We do. We know where he is."

"Where?" I can't help asking, even though I know he's not going to say.

But Jones replies, "About seventy kilometers south of here. At an Al Shabaab training camp on the coast. You know who Al Shabaab are, right? *The Youth, the Boys?*"

I nod slowly.

He smiles, flashing stained teeth. "Of course you do."

And suddenly I know that *he* knows. He knows that the last time I saw my brother was three years ago. Dahir was being driven away in the back of one of Al Shabaab's battle trucks. I don't know how Mr. Jones knows, but it's there in his eyes.

My thoughts start flashing in pieces:

We thought Dahir was dead.

If the Boys take you, that's the best you hope for.

But here is a photo of my brother. Alive. Walking down the street. In Mogadishu, it looks like.

Which can't be. It's impossible.

If he were here, he'd run away.

He'd come home.

My brain refuses to even consider any other possibility.

Jones stands up, walks to one of the walls, and stares at it, like he's looking out at a beautiful vista. "How old are you, Abdiweli?"

"Sixteen," I say, wary at the change in topic.

"And are you in school?"

Do I go to school? What does that have to do with anything? "Yes. Hamar Secondary."

"Your mother teaches there."

Why is he asking all these questions when he already knows the answers? "Yes," I say.

"Is that where Dahir was abducted from?"

An old, familiar guilt starts to rise up inside me like a black tide. I don't reply. I'm not sure I could speak right now, but it doesn't matter. Jones nods, like I don't even need to be here to hold up my end of the conversation. "You're lucky to have escaped being recruited yourself. Al Shabaab say they're here to drive out the foreign invaders and restore order, to bring back the Islamic caliphate, but they're extremists, terrorists, plain and simple. They're ruining this place, Abdiweli, this beautiful homeland of yours. Your government and your army are trying to exterminate them, but I have to be honest: your government and army are weak."

Lucky. Luck had nothing to do with it.

"You're American, aren't you?" I ask. Suddenly all of this seems totally surreal, like maybe I've stepped into a second-rate action movie. He sounds like he's repeating a memorized script. He's playing the part of Shady Government Dude.

He smiles, like he's impressed that I know he's full of shit. "Does it matter? I'm not wrong about your country, am I? Al Shabaab has killed twenty-seven people in the last two weeks. Eight of them were children. Somali, all of them. Muslims. There was a suicide bomb at a park here in Mogadishu just the other day. They killed regular people taking their kids out for a stroll."

I don't answer. He's telling me things I already know. Everyone knows what they do. My head starts to pound again. I realize my gaze has slid from his face and I have to wrench it back. The way I'm feeling, if I'm not careful, my thoughts will come untethered and fly away. I need to stay focused. I still don't know where my family is. Or why this man is showing me pictures of my missing brother.

I force myself to speak clearly. "I have nothing to do with any terrorist stuff, I swear. I don't know anything about my brother. I haven't seen him since he was taken. What do you want from me?"

"It's not what I want, Abdiweli; it's what you want. I'm only here to help you, the Somali people, take charge of your city and your country and make them strong again. To turn this place into a democracy." He walks over and sits back down. "So. Tell me. What do you want? Do you want your country back? Your home? Or, how about this: let's not talk politics. Let's keep it simple. Do you want your family to be safe? Your mother? Little Hafsa and the twins? They're just innocent children."

When I don't answer, I feel a sharp slap against the back of my head. "He asked you a question, maggot!" the Somali soldier spits.

Mr. Jones raises his hand. "Shh, no, no," he says softly. Then to me, "I can make them stop hurting you, Abdiweli. We can fix all of this. All you have to do is tell me you want to keep your family safe."

I feel myself unraveling. His question sounds simple but I know it's not. What is he asking? My voice is barely a whisper. "I want them safe."

Mr. Jones puts a comforting hand on my shoulder. "What would you do to get them back? Would you be brave? Strong?"

I nod limply. I am so confused, so tired, so wracked with pain. I think about my father. Stay away from the men with guns, he said. But he also told me to keep my family safe.

"I . . . Yes. I'd do anything."

Mr. Jones squeezes my shoulder and stands. "Good boy." He nods at the man behind me. "Cut him loose and bring him upstairs."

SIX

NOW, NOVEMBER 4
SANGUI CITY, KENYA

You see only the street, scabby and brown. You're in the third-floor window looking down onto broken asphalt and sand. It's empty and quiet because you emptied it. Those pockmarks on the wall above the sign advertising Nido Powdered Milk are yours. That body lying on the ground—he's yours. A trail of black drops go around the corner. Except they're not black, they're red. And they're not yours, they're still his, because he's still alive.

So you watch the street, because it's your damn job, and if you think about anything else other than this one small piece of real estate—if you think of your mother or your brother, or even scratch the place where a fly is crawling on your neck—you won't see the bullet that the still-alive AMISOM soldier will send flying at Samir's head. Samir with the Dumbo ears who sucks his thumb at night when he's asleep. Samir, who's creeping down your street, trying to get to the next safe spot. Samir, who's knocking on doors, pleading, but nobody will let him in because to them he's the bad guy, and he can't shoulder the doors open because his shoulder's hanging all weird and bloody. So he creeps on, and you sweat into your sandals and watch for a wink, a flicker, anything that will show you where the guy you've shot has gone and where his next bullet will come from.

And Samir throws up his hands. It looks like he's saying, Screw this, I give up, but then you hear the shot, and you can think all this before you hear the shot because that's where your head is, taking everything in like you're seeing it amplified through crystal, and Samir hits the wall and slides down in a red streak and you spend one full inhale, exhale looking at it, and then you move on because he's gone.

You swing your muzzle toward where you think the shot came from, and you're whispering, "Come on, you sonofawhore," even though you should be praying, and you spray all over the wall, wasting ammo now, veering toward losing control, breaking what glass there is to break, and then you stop and you take a breath in and you see him. You squint back at your sights and breathe out, and for a split second before your finger chokes the trigger, time slows and you feel like the exploding center of a thousand-pointed star. There is no difference between you and the gun, and you hear your name shouted but you don't respond.

Da'ud, Da'ud, Abdi, Abdi—

"Abdi. Abdi."

I jerk awake like a sprung trap.

"Hey, easy," a funny voice says.

31

I blink, heart pounding, sinuses full of adrenaline.

Sam has her hands up, like *I'm safe, see?* She exchanges a look with the driver. "We're here."

Not Mogadishu. A city street. Some other city. Sangui City, Kenya.

"This is Jogo Road. Where's your place?" the driver asks.

I look around, wiping drool off my chin. Samir is dead. Long dead. It's dark now; the sun set while I slept in the back seat of the cruiser. "Over there," I say finally, choosing a direction at random, pointing with a finger that still shakes.

I roll the window down a little. I'm covered in sweat. I take deep breaths through my nose, trying to stay quiet. I can smell the ocean from here, mixing with the smoke of charcoal cookstoves and sweet-rancid wafts of garbage. Everything is dark and yet too bright. We pass kiosks selling neat rows of dry goods lit with fluorescent bulbs—sugar, long-life milk, cooking oil, children's shoes, bras. Butchers and charcoal sellers are doing a tidy business with the day workers coming home. The cars around us lurch and press like a herd of cattle. I feel my pulse start to slow.

"When we get there, I want to talk with your uncle," Sam says.

"Okay. That way." The street I've chosen is dark. Light from the shops shows only the first few meters of the space between buildings, and the ground is a chewed-up mud track, the kind that would swallow a sedan whole.

The driver eyes it skeptically, like I'd hoped.

"I can walk from here," I say.

"No, I want to talk to your uncle," Sam repeats.

"He's not home. He's working."

"Let me try calling him again."

She dials, and I overhear the inevitable chime and a pleasant voice saying, "*Samahani.* Sorry, the number you are trying to call is not available."

I put a hand on the door handle.

"Not so fast." Sam looks around, thinking. "Your uncle. Where does he work?"

"He's a porter," I say. "In the market."

"Which market?"

"Um, the big one."

Her eyes narrow. She looks back down the dark street. "Which flat is yours?"

I point vaguely. "There."

"The one with the lights on? With blue curtains?"

"Yeah, that's it."

People on the street are starting to stare at us. The big white UN car, Sam's white skin. I open my door, slide into the muggy night. If I just go fast enough, Sam and the driver will watch me vanish into the dark, and that will be the end of it. I'll steal some food, find a corner to tuck into, and . . . A car door opens behind me.

"Abdi, wait."

Is she serious? Our audience of passersby doubles instantaneously. People stop to gawk at her. *Muzungus* don't come to these sorts of neighborhoods after dark. Even I know that, and I've only been in Sangui a couple of weeks. I hear the driver trying to convince her of the same, but she tells him two minutes, and to stay here with the car, and then she's following me down the road, the idiot.

I walk faster, and my senses go on automatic alert as we leave the light. *It's fine,* I tell myself as my eyes skip around the shadows. *It's fine. No snipers here. Nobody watching. No one here recognizes you.*

But still, I move quickly, not waiting to see if Sam is following me. My feet only stutter as we reach my "home." I lead the way up the filthy, trash-covered stairs onto the apartment building's landing, to the flat with the blue curtains.

I have no idea what I'm going to do next, and I'm starting to think I should just run, but then Sam puts one hand on my shoulder and reaches past me to rap on the door. Before I can quite get myself to move, it's flung open and there's a woman glowering at us. A tumble of children freeze in the middle of play behind her. They stare.

"Yes?" The woman's eyes flick from Sam to me, suspicious.

"Good evening—sorry to bother you. Does this boy live here?" Sam asks.

"Eh? This boy?" The woman gives Sam a look like she's playing at something. "No."

Sam's grip tightens. "That's what I thought. Thank you."

And I should run, I know I should, but I just can't find the energy it will take, or the enthusiasm for the effort, and then we're walking back down to the street, back toward the cruiser, and I don't know what I'm doing, I'm simply walking down the road. Watching myself walk down the road. Letting Sam steer me. My legs feel like they weigh a thousand kilos each. Then I'm getting back in the car. I shouldn't.

But I get in and buckle my seat belt.

When I glance back at the apartment, the big lady and her kids are still watching us from their doorway.

"We go?" the driver asks.

Sam buckles her seat belt too and nods. "*Twende*, back to West Ring." As we part the sea of cars and people, she asks, "You don't have an uncle, do you?"

I see her in the rearview mirror. I shake my head no.

"You don't have a place to stay."

Shake, no.

The driver eyes her.

She sighs, looks at her phone. "Are you hungry?" she finally asks.

I glance up. "Yeah."

"Let's stop by Kuku Express," she tells the driver. She puts her phone to her ear. "My boss is *not* going to like this."

"No," the driver agrees.

I sit very still, low in my seat, and stare out the window at the lights of the city. I try to find stars in the sky, but the electric glow of buildings is too bright. It's like stars are something ridiculous I dreamed up one time. Like it's totally possible that they never existed at all.

SEVEN

THREE YEARS EARLIER
MOGADISHU, SOMALIA

I was thirteen and it was an almost normal morning.

"Dahir! *Dahir!*"

My mother stood in the doorway to the courtyard and glowered toward Dahir's room. "Quit doing your hair and come on! Don't you make me late, not today!"

At her ankles two-year-old Faisal fretted and tugged, like he knew some plan was afoot that would leave him at home alone with Ayeyo and his twin sister while the rest of us went off to do something exciting. Hooyo scooped him into her arms and swept back into the house, her skirts snapping. She sounded angry, but it was clear that she was as excited as any of us.

Ayeyo, propped up on cushions in her favorite corner, was feeding Faisal's twin, Zahra, doughy bits of *canjeero* and banana. BBC Somalia blared on the radio next to them. My grandmother never missed the morning news. As loud as she played it, our neighbors never missed it either. Though she'd never admit it, she was pretty deaf. The whole neighborhood could probably hear her radio.

"Dahir is going to go bald as an egg," she predicted, taking Faisal from my mother. "Combing his hair every five minutes."

"I think he's checking out his beard." I winked at my sister Hafsa, who was standing next to the front door, impatience in every muscle. "Maybe a sixth hair came up overnight."

She grinned. Ribbing Dahir for how much time he spent preening in the mirror was one of our favorite hobbies. When he wasn't around to hear and beat us up, of course.

Hafsa pulled her backpack straps up on her shoulders for the millionth time. It was as big as she was, stiff with newness. Her school uniform practically sparkled. It looked like Hooyo had carried on the tradition with her third-born of buying our uniforms two sizes too big, so they could be worn for longer. Even though she was a teacher at our school, Hooyo didn't get a discount on stuff like uniforms and supplies. In my case, she usually just mended the holes in the armpits and knees of Dahir's hand-me-downs. "You want a new uniform, you buy it!" she'd shout and give me that look that said, *I dare you to complain.*

You did not complain to my mother unless you wanted to get smacked with her sandal. My mother wielded that sandal like a djin with a sword: so fast and mercilessly, you'd swear she was magic.

So old uniforms for me it was. It wasn't so bad; most of the kids at my school were in the same boat. If you had enough money for new uniforms every year, you went to private school. Lucky for Hafsa, she couldn't very well wear her big brothers' old uniforms, so hers was new for her first day of school. She'd been dressed and ready with her backpack on since the call to *Fajr* prayers before dawn, clomping around the house in her also-too-big shoes to accidentally-on-purpose wake us all up.

Hafsa was seven and should have started school already, but last year the schools were closed most of the time because Al Shabaab Boys kept storming in and rounding up kids, carting them off to join their rebel movement. The Boys treated schools like an open candy jar. Just reach in and take whatever you want. Even Hooyo, who normally wouldn't have let us miss school even if an asteroid was headed straight for Mogadishu, decided that at fifteen and twelve, Dahir and I were just too likely to get snatched up. Instead she left us at home and went to school alone, refusing to stop teaching. But most days no students showed up to her biology and English classes.

"If I don't go, I don't get paid!" she would protest when my father would try to persuade her over the phone to just quit. He was already in Saudi working construction by then.

"You're a woman and you teach *English*," he would say, never quite managing to keep the pride out of his voice. "You're basically begging them to come after you. Maybe you should leave the city . . ."

"And do what? Go to the filthy camps in Kenya where we'll live in tents with the animals? Al Shabaab Boys are there too, you know. Do we go to Saudi? With what money?"

She would wave his worry off. "If I see those Boys coming, I will run and hide and pretend to be a cleaner. *Inshallah,* God will keep me safe from brainwashed *ciyaalsuuq* hooligans."

Or she would lie and say to him, "You're not here. You don't see it. The news makes it look much worse than it really is."

She would change the subject. "Zahra has that cough again. I'm going to have to take her back to the clinic. Can you send money? *Wallahi,* they charge too much for medicine."

Aabo told her he would take more jobs, find some way to make up for the money lost. But what Hooyo didn't say was that it wasn't actually about the salary. I overheard her asking our auntie Nafisa, who owned a small shop, to borrow money. I heard her tell Auntie what she hadn't told my father. The truth was that none of the teachers were being paid. The government was broke, or at least that was what the politicians said from behind their tinted Land Cruiser and Mercedes windows as they went hurtling through the streets from one guarded compound to another.

Auntie Nafisa told Hooyo she should come work for her. It was safer. But my mother just shook her head and said, "Someone's got to teach these kids. If they grow up ignorant, who's going to fix this country?"

It wasn't until the school headmaster finally stepped in and told my mother to go home because they were locking the school up that she finally did. She was the last teacher to leave. That was six months ago. Since then she'd turned her sights on Dahir, Hafsa, and me, and she was as brutal with her homework loads as she was with her sandal. I'd almost cried with relief when we heard that the Somali army and AMISOM had finally kicked the Boys out of Mogadishu, and schools would open again.

Of course, my excitement was nothing compared with Hafsa's.

"Dahir is ready!" Hafsa screamed, announcing my brother as he stepped out of the old servants' quarters. He'd taken over the little room when he turned fifteen, long after we couldn't afford a maid anymore, saying, "I need my privacy!" Which, of course, didn't stop Hafsa and me from sneaking in to poke through his stuff and stare at the Pepsi-branded posters of football players that he'd scavenged from neighborhood cafes.

Scowling into the sun, he strode toward us on gangly legs. He'd grown taller over the last months and looked a bit like one of the storks that stalked Lido Beach. His hair was meticulously arranged into curls so oily, they practically dripped. My mother called this look, currently popular among all his friends, Wet Sheep.

Dahir ducked through the low doorway in a wave of cologne and immediately went to the small mirror in the hall to adjust his shirt collar. Hafsa and I watched him silently.

"You smell," Hafsa said finally.

Dahir turned on her, nostrils flaring. "I smell?"

We went still. For a second it looked like Dahir was going to shout at her. His temper was as short as his legs were long these days, a fact all of us complained about. Even my mother would tell my father, "That boy is such a *teenager*," shuddering like he had some gross disease. Aabo would laugh through the phone and say he was glad that at least there was a man at home to take care of us, to which Hooyo would snort, "Ha! Please. I said teenager, not man. My mother would be more use in a fight."

(To be fair, she might have been right. My *ayeyo* was as scrappy as an alley cat.)

"I smell?" Dahir asked again, bending closer to Hafsa.

I shifted nervously.

"I smell like"—he lunged for her—"a Ladies' Man?" Grabbing Hafsa by the waist, he pulled her into a biceps curl. Her initial scream of terror quickly turned to giddy squeals.

Ladies' Man, as I knew from snooping in Dahir's room, was the name of his cologne.

"*You* smell"—he held her squirming to his face—"like you've been sleeping with the chickens!"

"I do not!" she screeched. "Stop!"

"Pshew, when did you last have a bath, chicken girl?"

"Last night! You're mussing my uniform!"

"Some impression you're going to make on your first day of school!" Dahir lifted her again and again until Hafsa was breathless from laughter, putting her down only when he realized he'd forgotten his new pen in his room. He was about to get it, but at that moment my mother came out of the kitchen like a hurricane, shooing us all out the door, shouting about how the headmaster was going to beat us all if we were late. Ayeyo yelled to not forget to buy milk on the way home. Faisal started crying again. The BBC jingle blared.

There was no such thing as a normal morning anymore, but on that first day of school we were close. Almost there.

Dahir was sixteen.

If he'd known he would never see our home again, my brother might have lingered. He might have breathed in the smell of dew rising off the packed-dirt yard of our compound, of wood smoke from breakfast and the yeasty tang of bread rising in the kitchen. Maybe he would have stopped to look at the family photograph that Hooyo wanted taken at a proper studio before Aabo left. He might have smiled at how high she hung it on the wall, just below the age-faded photograph of the Kaaba that her grandfather had brought back from his *hajj* in the 1950s. Smiled at how starched and stiff we looked in that photograph she was so proud of, all of us together in front of the soft-focus background. He might have paused to pick up small, ordinary things. A favorite chipped cup. A spoon that all of us had, at one time or another, put in our mouths.

But he didn't know. How could he have?

The morning might not have been totally normal, but we all expected to make it home that night.

Everyone did. Except him.

EIGHT

NOW: NOVEMBER 4
SANGUI CITY, KENYA

"Slow down, you're going to choke." Sam offers me a napkin with a look like she's afraid I might bite her hand.

It takes all of my willpower to put the chicken leg back on my plate while I chew. I wipe grease off my face. *Lovely, lovely grease. It has been too long since I've seen you.*

Sam's apartment is huge, but there's nothing in it. Maybe she's just moved in. She at least has a TV and an uncomfortable-looking sofa. Books lean against the wall in stacks. In front of the balcony doors a potted plant has died in a crunchy heap. Maybe she's been here a while. It's hard to tell. There's nothing on the walls but a calendar over the kitchen table I'm sitting at. The top half is a photo of yellow puppies in a basket, and the calendar half shows two months: November and December. The days up through today, November 4, are marked off with big slashes of red marker. The sixteenth of December is circled heavily.

I can tell she doesn't want me here, but she's told me about fifteen times to make myself at home.

After leaving my fake home on Jogo Road, she made a bunch of phone calls in the car in a low voice, one after another that went like, "Hi, this is Sam, I'm calling from the UN. Is this Halima? [Or Kadijah or Mohamed or Kamal.] Yes, I'm sorry to call at dinner [sorry to call so late; yes, I know it's late; sorry, did I wake you?], but I have a boy with me, a minor, and he needs a place to stay, and I'm wondering if you have space for him to sleep . . . ? He's sixteen . . . No, a boy . . . Um, I'm not sure . . . Oh, but you were on the list of families that— Oh. Okay— No, of course. I understand . . ."

And on and on and on like that, glancing over her shoulder at me while I pretended I couldn't hear until she ran out of numbers to call. Finally, as we pulled up in front of Kuku Express, she turned to me and said brightly, "So just for tonight, you might have to come and stay at my flat. I have an extra room."

Then, not waiting for an answer, she jumped out and went inside, phone glued to her ear again. After putting in our order, she paced the sidewalk and waved off beggars and talked to someone in a tone that sounded like she wanted to shout but was trying to be polite. Maybe it was her boss. I heard her say, "It's just not professional . . . Not a babysitter . . . Why not a hotel?" and the driver and I sat in uncomfortable silence, each pretending like we couldn't hear her, until he finally got the bright idea to turn the radio on and drown her out with pop songs.

And that's how I ended up here. In her house. Sitting at her table eating chicken and chips like it's the most normal thing in the world. Like last night I wasn't fighting three other kids and a dog for garbage scraps. She made me wash my hands really well before I ate, and she's checking out my messed-up hand while I eat with the other. I shouldn't be eating with my left hand like this; left hands are "dirty" hands, reserved for bathroom business, but I'm starving and I can't stop myself.

She frowns at the two missing fingers—stumps, I guess you'd call them—and the scabby scarred mess that surrounds them and scatters up my arm.

"How did this happen?" She swabs gently at the dirt crusted into the scabs.

I see other hands swabbing gently in my mind, and I have to resist the urge to pull away. "Accident."

"What kind of accident?"

I've already told the lie several times, so it comes easier now. "I was cooking and the propane tank exploded."

"You lost both fingers like that?"

I frown. No one has ever questioned my story. "They were burned badly. They had to be cut off."

"It's infected," she says. "We'll need to have it looked at tomorrow and maybe get you some antibiotics."

She busies herself putting goo on the wounds, and then wrapping clean gauze around the open bits. "Where is your family, Abdi? Are they still in Somalia?"

I have another bite in my mouth, a big one, which I try to swallow, but I can't. The chicken suddenly tastes like shredded newspaper. My eyes water with the effort of getting the lump down. "Gone."

She pulls off the rubber gloves she's been wearing, *snap, snap*. She balls them up and tosses them into an overflowing wastebasket. Then she leans toward me over the table, past the shoved-aside clutter of papers and envelopes and pens and old coffee cups and take-out menus. Her voice is soft, but her eyes bore into me. "Where?"

I shrug, not meeting her gaze. "I came back from school one day and they were gone."

"They just up and left?"

Up and left. I put the chicken leg back down, looking at it as if for the first time. Now that I'm no longer starving, the lumps of fat and gristle against the bone make me feel a little queasy. What do I say? If I tell her the truth, it'll lead to all sorts of other questions I don't want to answer. "I don't know where they went," I say. "I went to school in the morning like always, but when I got back . . ."

"Is that why you came here to Sangui?"

Up and left. Up into the air and gone. I see my mother hovering in a doorway, looking straight at me. It takes me a second to come back from that night. I nod to Sam's question.

46

"Where do you think they went?" she asks.

"I don't know," I repeat.

"What did your neighbors say? Didn't someone see them leave?"

I take a big gulp of soda. The bubbles burn my throat. "No. Lots of people were gone. There was shelling in our neighborhood that day."

"So it was your mom, dad, and siblings who went missing? You have siblings?"

She sounds so formal. I wonder suddenly if I'm being interviewed, if she's working now. And then I realize, *Duh, Abdi, of course she is. She's a social worker for the UN. She looks concerned, but that's her job. It's not real.*

I pull my bandaged hand off the table and put it in my lap. She's not going to be satisfied with simple answers. I realize I have to pay attention, or I'll end up locked up in a police cell again. I have to be careful about what I say. Very careful.

Meeting her eye, just for a second, I tell her, "My *aabo*—my dad—is in Saudi Arabia. He went a long time ago to work construction. It was just my mother and my little sister and the twins and my *ayeyo*. My grandmother."

"You were the man of the house."

I swallow, nod.

"That's a lot of responsibility."

"I don't know. I guess."

"Do you want to try family tracing? If they've registered with the UN somewhere else, we might be able to locate them."

47

I don't answer, but the idea curdles in my stomach. *No, I want to shout. That's the last thing I want. I know where they are, but no one else can know. Don't go looking them up.*

She waits. I can tell she thinks that I don't understand. "There are these databases where you can type in names—"

"Can I go to sleep now?" I cringe as soon as the words are out of my mouth. I sound rude, but I feel like ants are crawling up and down my back. Sweat prickles under my arms.

Her eyes widen. "Sure, of course. We can talk about it tomorrow. You're full?"

I nod. My stomach has started to gurgle ominously, not used to food like this, and so much of it so fast.

The guest room she opens up for me is just as bare as the rest of the apartment. There's a single bed with a mosquito net and another door leading to a bathroom that she tells me is just for me.

She says there are linens and towels and soap, but my mind stops registering her words. I'm alone on the beach at a moment when the waves are soft and the sky just seems to melt into the water.

"Abdi?"

I come back to myself and look up. She seems to be asking me something. She has a funny expression on her face. "Okay?"

I nod and smile. "Okay." I have no idea what she's said.

I've got to stop spacing out like that. I haven't been around people enough to realize how weird it makes me seem.

"Just knock on my door if you need anything, okay? I know

this is a little strange, sleeping here. But at least you're safe, and in the morning we'll sort out where you'll stay tomorrow."

When she leaves, I close the door behind her. *Safe.* I hesitate, then slowly turn the key in the lock. I'm careful, but it's loud. I press my good ear against the door and hear her footsteps fade. I listen until her door closes. I wait. It takes a second, but I hear a clunking echo—her door locking—across the apartment. It's only then that I notice I've been holding my breath.

I get into bed with all my clothes on, and wait for sleep that I know won't come.

NINE

THEN: AUGUST 17
MOGADISHU, SOMALIA

Mr. Jones gets straight to the point. "Al Shabaab are planning something big. And I want you to infiltrate them and find out what it is."

The room we're sitting in is three stories above the Hole, and I feel like I can finally breathe again. A breeze tugs the window curtains, and I catch glimpses of Mogadishu's rooftops, a hint of ocean.

I've washed the worst of my wounds at a tap in the courtyard. I've prayed. I've had food and water. Coming out of the Hole was like opening a door onto another planet. The compound is nicer than any I've ever seen in real life. It must be some sort of government property, invisible from the street behind a bomb-proof wall and razor wire. There are flowers and trees, and the house is huge, recently whitewashed. But the fact that it's nice just makes my stomach twist up when I know what's below. I can't help wondering if the buckets of blood that have soaked from the Hole into the ground over the decades helped fertilize it and make these trees and flowers so . . . lush.

I thought about yelling for help while I was in the courtyard, but it would have been useless. No one was going to leap over the wall and save me. Not from a government compound, not from my guard with his AK-47. If I shouted, all that was going to happen was that I'd get a mouthful of gun-butt and more broken teeth.

Everyone here seems to be in a hurry. Lots of soldiers. Somali army mostly, but some AMISOM too. Cars going in and out of a big metal gate with a concrete blockade outside, the kind they put up in front of hotels so suicide car bombers can't get close.

Jones, on the other hand, looks relaxed. He's seated calmly behind a desk, waiting for my reply.

"You're crazy." It's all I can think to say. He wants me to get information out of a bunch of super-religious thugs who'd just as soon shoot me as say hello? "Why would Al Shabaab tell me anything?"

Mr. Jones just smiles. "You can speak English, right? Can we speak English? I so rarely get that luxury these days."

"I speak English," I say cautiously, switching from Somali.

The smile grows broader. "Excellent. Your mother taught you, I suppose. You're a smart kid, Abdiweli, anyone can see that. So, to your question, I think what you should be asking is, why *not* you? You're intelligent and motivated."

"Motivated?"

"You know the word, right?" When I nod, he asks, "Where do you think your family is, Abdiweli?"

My hands start to tremble. "What have you . . ."

"Don't worry. I'm taking care of them."

The trembling travels up my arms. "What does that mean?"

"It means I'm keeping them safe while you and I talk. Your mother, your grandmother, your two little sisters, and your little brother."

He identifies each of them slowly and clearly, pushing their faces deep into my brain.

"Safe." I swallow. "They're prisoners."

"They're my insurance."

"You mean if I don't help you, you'll . . ."

"Abdiweli," Mr. Jones says, leaning forward. "Let's focus on the positive. I'm offering you an opportunity. If you're able to get us the information we need, I can get them passports and visas. Plane tickets. Think about it. They could go somewhere safe. South Africa, maybe even Europe."

My head throbs. "And if I can't?"

He leans back. "Look, I wouldn't go to all the trouble of getting you here if I didn't think you had a shot." He pulls the photo of my brother out and sets it on the desk between us, where I can see it. I can't help but stare. "The thing is," Jones says, "Dahir isn't just a foot soldier. He's a leader, part of Al Shabaab's inner circle. We think he might know things. Important things. Things you can find out from him."

"Dahir?" I balk. "Inner circle?" My brother loved movies like *The Fast and the Furious* and sang along with American hip-hop: stuff Al Shabaab says is *haram*. Stuff they've killed people over. He wasn't super-devout; Hooyo used to have to chase him out of the house to get him to Friday prayers on time. I mean, Al Shabaab kidnapped him at gunpoint, for God's sake. Why would he turn around and join them? "That's not . . ." I fumble. "There's no way . . ."

Jones continues, "And the base where he's stationed is strategic. One of the nerve centers for Al Shabaab, run by General Idris."

I feel myself go cold, despite the heat. "General Idris? The Butcher?"

"Also, we know that Al Shabaab's spiritual leader, the man they call the Doctor, is a frequent visitor."

I stare at Jones. He's got to be joking. The Butcher and the Doctor are legendary. The Butcher used to lead one of the biggest clan-based militias in Mogadishu, and he was known for . . . well, you don't get the nickname "the Butcher" for nothing. Then he went jihadi, joined up with Al Shabaab, and brought a bunch of his soldiers with him. And if the Butcher is Al Shabaab's sword arm, then the Doctor is its brain. He *was* actually a doctor years ago, but supposedly all the terrible stuff he saw during the American-backed Ethiopian invasion a few years ago made him militant. There are crazy rewards out for both of them, but the Doctor is the real prize. He's worth, like, five million US dollars or something. Because of that, he's kind of a ghost, the Osama

53

bin Laden of Somalia. No one knows where he is, or if they do, they're not dumb enough to tell. Five million's a lot, but you can't spend it if you're dead.

And Dahir is in with *them*? Jones must be lying. Or he has Dahir confused with someone else. It doesn't make sense. But the photo glares up at me. I want to look away from it but can't. It's like seeing Dahir through cracked glass, all bent out of shape and distorted.

It's been three years. Three years living with those guys, if what Jones is saying is true. How did my brother survive so long? What sorts of things would he have seen?

What sorts of things would he have done?

In my mind, Dahir's face in the photo turns, stares straight at me. His lips move: *Whatever I am now, it's your doing.*

I start to shake.

I make myself say, "They're forcing him. He's not like that."

Mr. Jones sighs, like he's the teacher and I'm a student who's just being stubborn and not learning the lesson on purpose. "Abdiweli. I know it's not easy to find out that someone you care about has changed so drastically, but hear me out: it's terrible, yes, but you're in a position to make something good come of it. You can turn this into an opportunity to make a difference, to save lives. We may have pushed Al Shabaab out of Mogadishu for now, but they still have other territory under their control. They're still a threat. They're still powerful, and if we don't take them out, they could come back, even worse than before. You can help us."

I press my knuckles into my eyes. What is this "doing good" bullshit he's peddling? How can he talk about doing good when he's holding my family hostage?

"All I'm asking is that you get close to your brother. Talk to him. Find out about the attack they're planning."

Everything he says swirls in my aching head. I try to sift through it and understand what he's told me, what he's asking me to do. First, I'm supposed to accept that my brother has gone militant, that he's chosen to stay with the same guys who abducted him off a schoolyard at gunpoint. That he *is* one of those guys. The same guys who kill people in the street for smoking or not wearing veils. Then this Jones dude—who's probably CIA or something—wants me to infiltrate Al Shabaab and get my brother to tell me Al Shabaab secrets so said CIA man will let my family go. And then we get to all go off and live happily ever after?

"But . . ." I say, "you have drones and bombs. Why the spy stuff? Why aren't you just blowing them all up?"

Mr. Jones raises an eyebrow and I want to scream, *Don't give me that look! I'm not the monster; you are! Everybody knows you Americans bomb Al Shabaab bases all the time! Don't act all holy!*

"The base where your brother is stationed is a training camp for young men your age," Jones says. "Would you rather we do as you suggest and kill a hundred or more of them, including your brother?"

"No, but I—"

"Even if we did, there are other training camps, other

bases," he goes on, waving a hand to dismiss the idea. "Killing these few militants doesn't necessarily accomplish our mission. The attack could be staged from anywhere. What we want is to stop whatever they're planning. And ultimately we'd like to bring the Doctor and the General in. Alive. They have connections to other terrorist organizations. We need to know what they know."

"I don't even . . . How would I . . . ?" I ask, my voice limp.

"We'll embed you. We'll get you in front of Al Shabaab and you'll ask to join them. They're always looking for recruits. You'll say you want to be in the unit with your brother."

"Won't they wonder how I even know Dahir is one of them?"

"You know Al Shabaab took him, don't you? Where else would he be?"

Dead, I think darkly. Like most of the kids who get abducted and sent to the front lines to be human minesweepers. "And what if they don't believe that I really want to join them?"

"You'll have to be very convincing, I suppose."

I feel myself slipping. "You don't understand!" I shout, unable to keep my voice calm. "You make it sound so easy. They'll kill me right there on the spot if they think I'm a spy. They're always killing people they think are working with the government as spies!"

Jones doesn't reply for a while. When he does, his voice is cold, practical. "Believe me, I do understand. You think you're the first guy we've tried sending in? You probably have a fifty-fifty shot at being accepted."

Great. I put my fists back up to my temples.

"Think of your family, Abdiweli. They could be far away from here."

My voice cracks. "How do I know you haven't already killed them?"

I hear footsteps and then a digital camera is being shoved under my nose by one of the guards. I take it, blink. On the screen is my family, sitting in a huddle in an unfamiliar room.

I feel a burning in my chest and throat, like I'm going to split down the middle and blow away on the wind in a thousand pieces.

"That was taken this morning," Jones says.

"What did you do to my mother?" I whisper.

"She wasn't cooperating. Her face will heal."

"Let me talk to them." The image is starting to blur in my trembling hands.

"That's not possible. Maybe later."

On the tiny screen my mother holds Faisal in her lap and Zahra sits tucked up against her, small and wide-eyed. My grandmother scowls. Hafsa looks strange, her eyes dull. The whole left side of my mother's face is swollen and lopsided. She still manages to glare, but there is blood all down the front of her dress. Finally the guard wrenches the camera from my grip.

"They're fine, Abdiweli. But it's up to you whether they

stay that way. You know firsthand what my men are capable of. Do you really want your little sisters to suffer like you did? Do you want that for your grandmother?"

My helplessness and fear start to boil in my gut. "If you touch them . . ."

"It doesn't need to be that way, Abdiweli. Not at all. All you have to do is get me the information we need."

I clench my jaw, feeling like if I don't, it will all come exploding out. "And what about Dahir? If I help you, you can get him out too?"

"Dahir has made his choice," Mr. Jones says. "Now it's your turn to decide what happens to the family you have left."

"Will you kill him?" I ask quietly.

"That's up to him."

My mind feels woolly, like I'm being smothered. Like if I could just pull the strands apart, I would see some solution, but I'm too tired, too broken. I force my brain to crank into gear and think. What if . . . The sharp edge of an idea slides through me. What if I'm looking at this the wrong way? Maybe Jones is offering me an opportunity. What if once I'm inside, I can get Dahir alone and talk to him? Can't I just tell him exactly what's going on? Faced with that, what else can he do? Didn't he already prove once that he's willing to give up everything for his family? He'll have to come with me. We'll bust out of wherever he is and go rescue Hooyo and the others. Maybe Dahir knows how to get in touch with Dad. Aabo will know what to do. We can make everything right again.

The plan warms in me. Sure, it's full of holes—like, *how*, exactly, we find and rescue Hooyo and the others—but still, it feels like there's some glimmer that it's possible, right? Dahir will listen to me. He'll help me. He'll help his family. We can all get out of this somehow.

I look up, forcing myself to keep my face blank. I can't agree to go along with Jones just like that. He'll get suspicious. I have to work the angle he's expecting. "You can get my family somewhere safe?" I ask.

For a second Jones's eyes shine with victory. Then he's composed again. "Yes, Abdiweli. I can."

My disgust for him is as thick as bile in my throat. "I want them to go to *your* country. To America."

His mouth curls in a smile. "There's the spirit I knew you had. We'll see. South Africa, maybe Europe. America is difficult."

"What I'm doing will be difficult." I hold my breath, waiting.

"I'll see what I can do," he finally says. "So you're in?"

I think of the blood spattered down my mother's dress, Hafsa's blank stare. The men standing just outside the photo's edges. Do I have a choice? Saying no means leaving my family to this man to do whatever he wants to them. I feel the cuts and bruises all over my body. The thought of the same thing happening to my mother, my little sisters and brother, my grandmother nearly makes me vomit.

And then there's Dahir. I see him frozen halfway over a schoolyard wall, hanging forever in my mind between Before and After. Is this fate? In some twisted way it feels like God is giving me an opportunity to save him. To make right everything I let go wrong that day.

I take a deep breath. "Yes."

"All right." He stands, all business now, getting things started. "We don't have much time. We need to get you tagged and up to an AMISOM outpost a few hours' drive from here. Our source tells us that Al Shabaab fighters from your brother's base are going to attack it early tomorrow morning. They'll succeed, and they'll release the prisoners AMISOM is keeping there. You'll be one of those prisoners, and you'll need to persuade the Boys to take you back with them. They've taken over an old fort on the coast. Very secure. Very picturesque, actually. Right on the water. Talk to your brother. Once you know something, get yourself put on a mission into the city. Someone will make contact. They'll use a keyword so you'll know it's us: *lightbulbs.*"

His words wash over me, barely finding purchase in my brain. Tagged. Prisoners. Fort.

Jones stops talking, studies me. "Abdiweli?"

I look up. The light from the window plays weird tricks on his glasses; I can't see Jones's eyes. I don't know what he's thinking.

"Are you ready?" he asks.

I look around the empty room, catch a glimpse of the ocean through the window bars before the curtains obscure it again. "Does it matter?"

He takes his time answering. "No," he finally says. "I suppose it doesn't."

TEN

NOW: NOVEMBER 5
SANGUI CITY, KENYA

I can hear Sam on the phone before I'm even fully awake. She's talking about me. Her voice is low, but she must not realize how much her empty apartment echoes. I slip out of bed and stand beside the door to listen.

". . . He's really out of it," she says. ". . . half starved. He's got this bad wound on his hand . . . Yeah, missing two fingers. He says it happened in a cooking accident, but I don't know . . . No, he seems like a good kid . . . I mean, quiet, and obviously traumatized, but . . . mmm . . . Mmm-hmm."

She listens for a while. "No, I haven't had luck getting anyone on the phone who might be able to take him. I went through the whole list last night. Shockingly, nobody wants to take in a sixteen-year-old homeless Somali boy. But I'll keep trying. I mean, it's not like he can stay here . . . Yeah, okay, that's a good idea . . . I'm going to drop him off at Maisha on the way to work . . . No, I know, but Mama Lisa owes me a favor. She'll take him, at least for the day . . . I know, I know, but what else am I going to do? Dump him at public school? He'll bail. And I'm not leaving him here alone in my home. At least there the nurse can look at him and they can keep an eye on him . . . No, I'm not taking him to that place, not after last time. They're wackadoos. Believe me, I know their kind . . . Besides, he's Muslim; they'll spend all day trying to convert him, and then we'll have another Somali Christian on our hands and he'll be *impossible* to find a foster family for . . . Uh-huh. Okay, see you soon, bye."

I creep backward and stand in the middle of the room. In the bright morning sun, I feel bleached and empty. I look at my hand. I can't see much under the bandages, but it isn't pulsing like it was last night. I can't figure out how to feel about the situation I'm in. I try caring, but it just makes me want to crawl back into bed. I think I fell asleep sometime before dawn, but the regular round of nightmares didn't exactly make the little sleep I got restful.

After some fiddling I figure out how to turn the shower on. I've never actually taken one. It was all bucket baths back home. It's nice. I make sure my bandaged hand is outside the spray and stand unmoving for a long time with the hot water pouring onto my upturned face. I can't remember the last time I was clean all over.

When I'm finished, I put back on the same clothes I've been wearing for a month. They're filthy, but it's that or nothing. I look at myself in the mirror over the bathroom sink and find my face jarringly unfamiliar. It's sun-darkened and seems longer. I need a haircut. My cheeks aren't fat anymore. I run my fingers over my jaw, tug the few hairs there, stretching my skin.

When I can't avoid it any longer, I leave the room. Sam is in the kitchen, dressed for work. She puts on a smile when she sees me, and I put on a smile when I see her. I wonder if we both know we're fakers.

"Did you sleep okay?" she asks.

"Yes, thank you." Then I don't know what to say. I finally sit down at the kitchen table.

"Breakfast? I've got porridge and . . ." Sam opens one kitchen cabinet after another. They're all basically empty. "And tea?"

"That's fine, thank you." I look around the apartment again while I wait, but there's not much to see. It looks even more empty and neglected in the morning light. "Did you just move into this place?" I ask.

"No, I've been here for a year." She bangs cupboards more loudly.

"It's a big flat. Does somebody else live here? Your husband?"

"No," she says. "I'm not married."

"Why?"

She peers around a cupboard door at me. Her brown hair is tucked behind her ears, and she wears no makeup. She doesn't wear any jewelry other than the Kenya bracelet either. Her nose, long and a little crooked, is beginning to peel under the sunburn.

"I'm not ready," she says simply. She takes a container of milk from the fridge, sniffs it, and makes a face. "Black tea okay?"

I nod. "What's on December 16?" I ask, looking at the calendar over the table again with the big red slashes.

"Hmm? Oh, that. Uh"—she turns off the singing kettle—"nothing. Just a family thing." Before pouring water into the bowl of dry porridge, she peers into it and picks something out. I swear it wiggles.

"A holiday?" I ask.

I hear her snort. "Sort of."

She comes to the table with mugs of tea, sugar and a bowl of porridge for me. It's lumpy, not exactly cooked, and possibly infested, but I'm hungry. I dump four spoonfuls of sugar into my tea and four into my porridge. Then add another spoonful to each for good measure. Just in case they taste like bugs.

Sam watches with raised eyebrows but doesn't stop me. "I'm going to take you to a girls' center today while we get your, um, your living situation sorted out," she says.

I pause, spoon halfway to my mouth. "A girls' center?"

"It's a boarding school. And they do skills training. I talked to the head teacher, and she said you can come and hang out today while I'm at work. Their nurse can look at your hand too. They won't bite," she assures me. "And it's just until we find a family for you to stay with. Then you'll start school somewhere else."

Just me and a bunch of girls? And then it hits me. Just me and a bunch of girls. That sounds like the last place the Boys would come looking for me. Something small and knotted loosens in my chest, just a little.

Sam holds her tea and watches me eat. "So . . . Did you go to school in Mogadishu?"

"I was in secondary school."

"That's where you learned English?"

I almost tell her about my mother, but then I stop. I'm not even really sure why. For some reason I can't make my brain go there, like it would take some stupendous feat of strength just to open the iron lid on the subject. Instead I nod again and stick to the easy stuff. "And I've seen a lot of American movies. I worked at a cinema."

"Really? In Mogadishu?"

"Not an actual cinema. It was just the back room of a teahouse. They had a TV and a DVD player. I've seen all the *Fast and Furious* movies, James Bond, *Jason Bourne, The Avengers, 24, CSI: Miami, Law and Order*." Talking about Salama Cinema feels weird, like it was a thousand years ago and some other Abdi who worked there.

"Al Shabaab allowed them to show American movies?"

"It was only open about six months. The Boys smashed it all up when they found out about it."

And dragged the owner, Mr. Fuad, off to God-knows-where. No one ever saw him again. But I don't say that. It's too early in the morning to get that real.

"So what's your favorite film?" Sam asks.

I have to think about it. "You know *CSI: Miami?*"

She shakes her head.

"It's a TV show, not a movie. I've seen all of seasons one through five. One hundred and twenty-one episodes."

"Wow. That's . . . a lot of TV."

"Yeah."

I'm not sure it's my favorite, but it's the first thing that comes to mind. I thought a lot about *CSI: Miami* those first few nights after I got to Sangui, when I didn't sleep, when I just sat in that doorway and tried to look mean so nobody would mess with me. It helped calm the jangling in my head, picturing those clean laboratories, the officers' careful cataloging of evidence. Each tiny hair or fiber examined, cherished like a jewel. Every fragment a critical clue, leading to a rational conclusion. And unlike in the real world, after forty-five minutes there was always a clear picture of what had happened and a bad guy in handcuffs. Sunglasses on, roll credits.

I realize I'm staring off into space again. I shake myself, scrape at the last of my porridge. "You've never seen it?"

Sam takes my empty bowl and dumps it and our mugs into the kitchen sink. "Let's hit the road. I'm going to be late for work." She comes back to the table and starts shoving files into her satchel. I think she hasn't heard my question, but then she says, "I didn't start watching TV until I was an adult. I don't know about all sorts of pop culture things."

I nod, even though I'm not exactly sure what she's talking about.

"All set?"

I look down at myself. I have nothing to grab, no books, no bag, nothing. It's just me, the clothes on my back, my sandals. The closest thing I have to possessions is the near-empty wallet in my pocket. I could disappear off the face of the earth and barely cause a ripple.

"Sure," I say, and follow her out the door.

ELEVEN

A truck, rattling like death over the sand and through dry river-beds.

A bargain made.

Zip ties around my wrists.

A promise.

Stopping only once to let me piss into the sand. Sand sucks it up like me and my water never happened.

We're there. Wherever *there* is. Out of the truck, into the police station, into another cell, meant for two, holding ten.

Don't scratch the scab. If you pick the chip out, we'll never find you again.

From now, fourteen hours.

Wait.

Wait.

Wait.

Sun falls and rises.

No one talks to you. You could be a spy, after all.

An explosion on the north wall. Gunshots. Get ready.

They will come, they will be fast, they will scream and beat you.
They will ask if you are a spy. Are you a spy?

No, I am only Dahir's brother.

Say it again.

Only Dahir's brother.

(Chances they'll kill you: 50-50.)

You must ask for your brother by name. It might save your life.

His name, our lineage: Dahir, his father, his father's father,
on and on . . . Dahir-Mohamed-Abdullahi-Kulane . . . Only his
brother would know all the names.

Don't scratch the scab.

Don't worry if you look frightened.

You're supposed to be frightened.

Blindfolded (again), tossed in a truck (again), taken to the
Fort, tossed in a cell (again). Beaten (again).

Keep the faces of your family in your head, in the place
where the fists can't follow.

Hooyo, Ayeyo, Hafsa, Faisal, Zahra

Are you ready?

Dahir-Mohamed-Abdullahi-Kulane

Are you ready, Abdiweli?

It's time.

TWELVE

NOW: NOVEMBER 5
SANGUI CITY, KENYA

Sam drives us in her own car through Sangui's morning traffic. I spend most of the ride glued to the window. I can't seem to shake the instinct to keep vigilant, as if I'm still riding around through the scrub in the back of a *technical*—one of those armored pickup trucks all the militia groups in Somalia use.

Back there we were on watch for an ambush: herders paying too much attention could be lookouts for the Somali army. A bend in the road or high brush could hide soldiers. But we also had to check the sandy road itself. Disturbed ground might be nothing but an animal scratching around looking for grubs. Or it could be a buried bomb, powerful enough to take out our vehicle. If it was a particularly bad day, you could get both the bomb *and* the ambush. Blow up the technical, sweep in and take out the survivors. A boom and bag.

But today we're driving through a leafy green neighborhood,

the Ring, where all the rich people of Sangui City live. There are no roadside bombs in the Ring. No one is hiding in the bush, ready to shoot up Sam's car. The Ring is as safe as Sangui gets. Here, at eight in the morning, there are only air-conditioned cars driving kids in uniform to private schools, houses like castles that I glimpse behind walls topped with electrified barbed wire.

The asphalt of the road we zoom down is as smooth as a river, and the medians are full of neat rows of flowers. Occasionally the ocean glints through the trees. Unlike most of the rest of Sangui, everything in the Ring is clean, orderly. Women in green jumpsuits sweep the curbs with grass brooms. Billboards advertise body lotion and new housing estates.

I wonder if parts of Mogadishu would look like this if the fighting had never started. My dad loved to remind us that our hometown was once called the White Pearl, that tourists came from all over the world just to stroll on our beaches and broad, tree-lined boulevards. That you could sip cappuccinos and mango juice under umbrellas in cafes, or go listen to the greats like Sahra Dawo crooning about love and medicine at Al Uruba Hotel. He'd take me out in his boat and point at the coral-block buildings that hugged the beaches. *"Squint and imagine, Abdi. Repair the facades, re-glass the windows, stucco the walls and paint them pearl white and shell pink. It will be beautiful again one day."*

Sam pulls into a driveway almost hidden in a cascade of purple bougainvillea, and honks. Through a small window in the metal gate a guard's face appears. When he sees it's Sam, he smiles and lets us in.

"*Habari za asubuhi!*" Sam calls good morning to him in Swahili as we drive into a dark tunnel of fig and palm trees. The wheels of the car crunch over white gravel and shells.

Sam parks in front of the biggest house I've ever seen. *This* is a girls' center? It looks more like a movie star's mansion. Walls and columns sprawling, it seems to go on forever, red-tiled rooflines disappearing one after the other, windows like eyes on a spider—too many to count. Another guard greets us with a smart little salute from the edge of a yard filled with flowers. Hibiscus glows gem-red, and iridescent sunbirds dart between the trees.

We're met on the path to the house by a sturdy-looking Kenyan woman. She holds a clipboard authoritatively against one hip, a pudgy baby on the other.

"Abdi," Sam says, "meet Maisha's director, Mama Lisa. Like Mona Lisa! But with a better smile."

"Who?" I ask, confused.

Mama Lisa looks like someone's grandmother, soft around the middle, with kind, crinkly eyes, and coils of gray at her temples. She wears a simple T-shirt and slacks with a well-worn apron on top. "*As-salamu alaykum.* Welcome, Abdi. I hear you will be staying with us today."

"*Wa-alaykum salam.* Yes, madam." I'm surprised. I haven't been greeted with a *salam* by someone who's obviously not Muslim since I came to Kenya. But Mama Lisa doesn't give me much time to think about it.

"How are you with children?" she asks briskly.

"Excuse me, madam?"

Without warning she deposits the baby she's holding into my arms. I stare at it in horror. "Madam?!"

She smiles. "You'll be fine, Abdi. Just hold her like you are carrying a sack of *posho*. On your hip. Not that tight. Good."

Mama Lisa and Sam smile at me as I try to get a better grip on the baby's warm squishiness. They don't even seem to care that my hand is only half useful in its bandage. I can't remember the last time I held a baby. Maybe when I was a kid, dragging Hafsa and my twin siblings around. The baby smiles at me and crams her fist into her mouth.

"She likes you! So. Do you know about this place, our Maisha Girls' Center?" Mama Lisa speaks swiftly, like she has a long list of things on her clipboard to accomplish today. I start to wonder if maybe she's not so soft and grandmotherly after all.

"No, madam," I say, trying to talk around the slobbery fingers the baby's taken out of her mouth and shoved into mine. I taste mashed peas and try not to gag.

Mama Lisa does not come to my rescue; instead she puts the clipboard behind her back and rocks on her heels, inspecting me. I shift the baby a little, trying to stand up straighter without risking dropping her.

"Mmm-hmm," she says. "Well then, come. I'll show you around."

Not knowing what else to do, I follow her to the veranda, where three girls sit at a table in the shade. They're doing

73

something with a big bag of fabric. Two are wearing Western clothes. They're probably South Sudanese, but the other girl wears a modest dress and a headscarf and looks Somali. They all look at me and then the baby in my arms, and I feel my face go warm. Why did this woman give me this child? Why give it to me, the boy, and not these girls? I scowl at the baby. She laughs, clapping my face between her hands. My frown slips. She does look sort of like my sister Hafsa when she was little.

"Here."

I look up and freeze. The Somali girl is right in front of me, holding her hands out for the baby. I can now see that she's ridiculously beautiful, like a girl in a movie, with smooth high cheeks and liquid black eyes surrounded by lashes like fine lace. The kind of girl who doesn't give guys like me a second glance.

"You look confused," she says.

My cheeks grow hotter. "I'm fine," I say.

The girl gives me a hint of an amused smile. To my dismay she withdraws her arms and crosses them over her chest. "Fine."

It's only now that I notice her pregnant stomach, and like an idiot I find myself doing a cartoonish double take. She notices and immediately her expression goes dark, like shutters being slammed shut on a window. She returns to the table, fluffs her dress over her belly and attacks her work again without a second glance at me.

"This is beautiful, Muna," Sam says to the pregnant girl, picking up a red-and-blue tie-dyed scarf out of the bag. "Will you save it for me?"

"Of course, Madam Sam. Maybe you need two? One for a friend?"

Sam laughs. "Ever the entrepreneur! Fine, save me two."

"Our girls are getting their wares ready for sale," Mama Lisa tells me. "They make the scarves here, and the co-ops in town sell them to tourists."

Sam starts asking Muna how she's feeling. I am sort of listening, but most of me is now concerned that my ear is going to be ripped from my head by a chubby claw. Seriously, this baby is much stronger than she looks. As I wince, I feel the weight shift in my arms and my eyes pop open in terror, thinking I'm letting her slip. But it's just one of the other girls taking the baby from me. She doesn't look at me or get any closer than she has to. As soon as she has the baby, she's back on the far side of the table again.

"Come," Mama Lisa says, and Sam and I follow.

I glance back at the little baby, but she only has eyes for the girl who has her now. Traitor. My gaze shifts to the Somali girl, but she's still ignoring me.

Mama Lisa leads us into the dark foyer of the home. There must be a dozen rooms I can see just from here. Polished mahogany floors sprawl.

"The house was donated to our organization by the Swedish royal family," Mama Lisa says, watching me gape at my surroundings. "And the girls who stay here are refugees. Most are from Congo, Somalia and Ethiopia. You are from Somalia too?"

A group of girls with books in their arms pass by. Some of them stare at me and giggle, but most act like I don't exist.

Starting to sweat, I try to remember the last time I was around this many girls. I forgot how they move in packs. I forgot how good they smell, like gum and perfume. I forgot how utterly terrifying they can be. Give me a dozen militia Boys over a whispering, giggling cluster of girls any day of the week. Forget bullets. Girls can rip you to shreds with nothing more than a raised eyebrow.

"Yes," I say, finding my voice. "I'm Somali. The girls don't stay with their families?"

Mama Lisa leads us down a hall into a bright kitchen. A woman is scrubbing pots from breakfast, humming loudly along with the radio, but otherwise it's empty. The windows look out onto gardens and a play area for children. I can hear girls' chatter and laughter from one of the rooms nearby, and a teacher telling them to settle down, get out their books and turn to page ninety-three.

"Most of the girls don't have families here in Sangui City," Mama Lisa says, to my question. "Or they can't stay with them."

"They've been in difficult situations, Abdi," Sam says, in a pointed way that brings the Somali girl's full belly to mind.

Mama Lisa begins to make tea for us, stirring milk in a saucepan on the stove. "The places they come from are war torn, dangerous. Well, you probably know, don't you? Some of them were kept as soldier's wives and escaped. Or they were sold. Sometimes by their own families." She cocks her head. "Do you understand me?"

I swallow and nod. I understand. Better than I'd like to.

She adds tea to the milk and stirs it. Beyond the woman scrubbing pots at the sink, in the garden, two girls are bringing a dozen small children into the yard. The kids waddle toward the brightly colored slides and swings.

"They are survivors," Mama Lisa goes on. "They want to go to school and get jobs and take care of their children. Those are their babies out there. But most of them are still children themselves. Bring mugs, please," she says, nodding to a cabinet above my head.

I pull three mugs down, fumbling a little with my bandaged hand.

"What I'm explaining is not for you to repeat," Mama Lisa says. "It's not so you can ask the girls questions. I'm telling you because I want you to understand that you need to be on your best behavior here. A gentleman. Men, boys, are not normally allowed at Maisha. But Sam has assured me that you will be respectful and bring us no trouble." She cuts her eyes at Sam, who shifts, looking a little like a schoolgirl being warned by her teacher. "*Sawa sawa?* We understand each other?"

"*Sawa,* madam," I agree quickly.

Looking at Mama Lisa's serious face, it suddenly hits me that she and Sam don't know what they're asking. They're telling me to be good as if that is the most logical, possible thing in the world. I almost want to laugh. Sam barely knows me; she doesn't understand what she's promised Mama Lisa. She has no clue who I've been, what I've done. She can't see all my old sins, the ones I wear around my neck like an anchor.

But what if . . .

A tingling feeling starts in my chest.

. . . What if I wasn't that boy?

What if I was someone else entirely? Or, better yet, what if I was *only* Abdi? No one else, ever again.

Maybe it doesn't have to be complicated. Maybe I can just start over. Am I crazy? Could it be that easy? No here one knows me. No one knows that other kid who's been walking around in my skin for the last few months, doing those things. I don't have to be him anymore. All I have to be is good. When I say it to myself like that, it seems so simple.

The feeling grows and stretches out tentatively, like something new and green straining for sunlight.

Just Abdi.

"All right, then," Mama Lisa says. The milk is hot enough for her to pour into mugs. "Drink your tea and then we shall have a look at that hand. And afterward, you will start classes with the girls."

THIRTEEN

THEN: AUGUST 20
THE FORT, SOMALIA

Roosters are crowing when the Al Shabaab Boy opens the door to my cell.

For a while he just stands there looking at me. Finally he waves a hand over his nose. "Eh, you smell like a crusty asshole."

I want to tell him that there's no stinking toilet in the cell they've locked me in, so what's it supposed to smell like? Jasmine and sunshine? But I'm too tired. I am one big bruise on top of a bruise. And besides, I'm used to the smell after a full day and night.

"Stand up," the Boy says, and holds out a scarf that he wants to put over my eyes. I catch a quick glimpse of a broad, sandy compound dotted with acacias. The Boy himself is short and dark and skinny, but that's all I see before the fabric is over my eyes. It smells faintly of gasoline.

"Are you Al Shabaab?" I ask. "Is my brother here? Dahir?"

"No questions. Shut up. Go."

It takes me a second, but I stumble out and he turns me in the direction I'm supposed to walk. I feel a sting on my calves and realize the boy is switching me with a stick like he's driving sheep. Maybe it's better than the gun butts and electric wires I've been getting hit with lately, but still. It kindles what little anger I have left. I am sick and tired of being beaten by strangers.

Everything happened like Mr. Jones said it would. The Boys rolled up on the AMISOM outpost in their technicals. The guards scattered. After pulling us all out of the cells, they killed two prisoners. For no apparent reason they shot the guy beside me. Maybe just to scare the shit out of the rest of us. Mission accomplished.

The Boys knew Dahir's name when I was shouting, "Don't shoot! I'm Dahir's brother! Dahir Mohamed Abdullahi Kulane . . ." etc., etc., naming my father, grandfather, great-grandfather, great-great, and on and on like I'd been practicing for hours, names dredged up from my memories of when Aabo used to make me repeat them, our whole lineage, all the way back to the first Somali brothers God put on the earth. Of course, the Boys didn't know if I had them right or not, but maybe it helped. Test me, I was telling them. *I am who I say I am.* I held my hands up over my head, shouting like a madman as I waited for the bullets to slice me up.

But instead the Boys blindfolded me, threw me in the back of a technical, drove a couple of hours, marched me straight to this tiny cell and tossed me in.

And here I've sat in my stink for nearly two days.

Guys came in twice to beat me up and shout in my face—"Why are you here? Who told you about us? You are a spy! Admit it!"—but somehow I managed to just keep insisting that I know nothing. It wasn't that much different from the Hole. In fact, the Hole was probably good practice. I began to wonder if maybe Jones had put me down there and had his men beat me just to make sure I was prepared. What a sick, efficient bastard.

The rest of the time I've been here I've just been staring at the wall, feeling fear and guilt wrestle like eels in my stomach. Fear, because I can't stop myself from imagining worse and worse scenarios for what Jones will do to my family if Dahir and I can't rescue them. Guilt because it's my fault Dahir is even here in the first place.

It wasn't like it was a surprise when the Boys pulled into the schoolyard that morning three years ago, midway through second period. Still, I don't think anyone really expected them to show up on the very first day of school. It was stupid, but I remember thinking, They can't come back *today*; we just got here. As if they were supposed to politely follow some sort of schedule. Like later we'd be ready or something.

Kids jumped out of second-story windows and tried to climb the compound walls. One boy broke his ankle, which at least made the Boys think twice about taking him. But in the end we were pretty well trapped. The school walls became our prison. The Boys got to pick and choose.

They chose Dahir.

He could have gotten away. He almost did. He was already halfway over the wall. A bitter taste that has nothing to do with my wounds swells in my mouth. For the thousandth time since I've been here, a voice in my head mocks me: *What kept him from running, Abdi? Why didn't he escape?*

Lost in old, worn-out memories, I trip on something and almost fall. The sudden movement makes me feel all my wounds fresh again, and I chomp my teeth in pain. I need to get out of my own head and start paying attention to what's around me. That's what a spy like James Bond would do, right?

The Boy hasn't tied the blindfold very well, but still, all I can see are the sand and rocks we're walking over. We pass through a space that feels open like a field. I hear people shouting. It's some sort of drill, but they're far away. There's a food smell too, a scent like heaven that makes my stomach sit up and roar, but we walk away from it. Eventually the Boy opens a metal door with screaming hinges and pushes me through. The sound of waves and the smell of salt and seaweed are unmistakable. We're on a beach.

"Stop," the Boy says. He finally yanks off my blindfold, and I'm left blinking out at the ocean, bright as hammered silver. We're in a small cove surrounded by rock cliffs. They form part of a wall behind us, which the metal door is fixed into. Razor wire is looped all over the top.

"Hey, stinker, here."

A knife flashes and I wince, but the Boy just cuts the zip ties away from my wrists. Suddenly my hands feel all wrong, like after so many days tied together they've forgotten how to live apart.

He points the knife at the water.

"Get in. Wash off good. Put these on." He drops a nubby black *khameez* and trousers onto a rock. I finally look at the kid and have to keep myself from lurching back. He only has one real eye. The lid of the other is split in half like the hull of a nut.

"Can you swim?" he asks.

I nod.

"Good. I won't have to lifeguard your ass. But don't go too far, and don't even think about trying to get away. If the current doesn't get you, the sharks will." He raises a lazy finger to the wall behind us. "Or the guys sitting sniper."

I have to assume there are Boys with guns up there, on lookout, ready to nail me if I make a wrong move.

"Where's my brother?" I ask, feeling sick.

The Boy only grins. "Better hurry. Can't be smelling like shit when you meet the Doctor."

FOURTEEN

My first class at Maisha Girls' Center is algebra. I'm normally okay at math, but halfway through class I realize I'm totally lost. I can't keep focused on what the teacher is saying. It's hard to hear. It's hard to sit still. Plus the teacher's voice is soft and calm, and it makes me sleepy. Then there's my hand. Holding my pencil with only three fingers makes it cramp. My numbers look weird, like a little kid wrote them. I find myself staring at the marks I've made on the page until they jitter around like ants. Little noises find their way into my good ear and distract me: the girls breathing and scratching their pencils, a rooster crowing somewhere outside.

My head is still full of x and y squared when I walk outside into the garden for break. I stretch my back and try to ignore two girls who are watching me and whisper-giggling.

"Mrs. Bota is tough, huh?"

I start. The pregnant Somali girl stands a few feet away.

She's watching a group of toddlers tumble in the play area next to their nursery. It takes me a second to remember her name. Sam called her Muna. I try not to stare at her belly. "I haven't done math in a while."

Muna considers this, like she's thinking about asking why. It's a relief when instead she just says, "I could help you study. But Sam says you're only here for the day."

"Yeah." We watch the other girls file out and find places to sit in the grass. "Thanks anyway."

"You're from Mogadishu?"

"Yeah. You?" I risk a look up at her face. Her cheeks are as smooth as the inside of a seashell.

"Me too."

"Really? What neighborhood?"

She looks away. "It doesn't matter."

I don't press. Of course it matters. But Muna's face tells me to keep my mouth shut. Maybe she doesn't want to say because it would probably tell me what tribe she's from, and then I could make all sorts of assumptions about her because of it. Maybe she's from one of the minority clans and she thinks I'll be an asshole because of it. Or maybe—

"What happened to your hand?" Muna asks, interrupting my thoughts.

I automatically put it behind my back. The nurse has cleaned the wounds and put a new bandage on it. She gave me pills to take every day that she says will clear up the infection. "Nothing," I say.

"Nothing took two of your fingers off?"

"Accident," I say after a pause.

"Kinda like this is an accident?" She waves her hand over her protruding belly.

I glance at her, then back down at my feet.

"Don't act like you didn't notice or something. I'm pregnant, not stupid."

I do my best not to react to the way she speaks, so matter-of-fact. We watch a toddler walk bow-legged out of the play area, chasing a red ball that has escaped into the grass. He comes at it like a little zombie, arms wide.

"In Mogadishu people like us just minding our own business are always getting into one sort of 'accident' or another," Muna says, her brow creasing. "Beat up, blown up, cut up, knocked up."

I don't know what to say. I watch the little boy. Isn't anyone going to go get him? He's making for the edge of the yard, ball forgotten, toward some rocks. My ear starts to ring. He's going to fall.

Muna stands there a little longer, then takes a deep breath like she's made her mind up about something. She walks across the grass and scoops the little boy up from behind. She swings him high in the air and he squeals with laughter, his little feet kicking out sharp and strong. She says something to him and he grins around the finger he's put in his mouth. She picks up his ball, and carries both of them back to safety.

FIFTEEN

THEN: AUGUST 20
THE FORT, SOMALIA

After my ocean bath I dress in the *khameez* shirt and trousers. It's the same uniform the one-eyed Boy is wearing. He blindfolds me again and takes me back through the compound and into a cool dark space. A building.

After stumbling up two flights of stairs, I'm pushed into a kneeling position on the floor and my blindfold is pulled off again. I blink. The room is stifling and dark, and worse, there's a giant standing over me. Is this the Doctor? He doesn't look like a doctor. He's dressed in fatigues like a soldier, and his rough face looms above me like the side of a mountain. It's hard to guess his age. Old enough to have seen some shit. Young enough that he can clearly still kick some ass.

"Thank you, Bashir," the man says to the one-eyed Boy. "That's all we need for now. You can go back to your work."

"I'm almost finished, sir. Do you want to see it when I'm done?" Bashir asks.

"Yes, let me know."

"Thank you, General."

General Idris. The Butcher. Shit. Holy shit. Don't faint. Don't piss your pants.

Before he leaves, Bashir gives me a look that's almost sympathetic. It says, *Sorry, stinker. You're done for. Nothing I can do about it.*

The General continues to stare at me after the door closes. Sweat prickles under the cheap fabric of the *khameez*. The air in the room is stale, and I feel like panting; I can't get a full breath. There are windows, but they're covered with heavy blankets, so there's hardly any light and no breeze. It doesn't seem to bother the Butcher.

"Why are you here?" he finally asks.

I lick my scabby, dry lips. "Your men brought me here."

"But you asked to be brought. Isn't that right?"

"I— Yes. My brother is here."

"Your brother is here, *sir*."

"Yes, sir. My brother Dahir. I—"

The Butcher cuts me off with a flick of his hand. "Who sent you? How did you know your brother was here with us?"

I hear a voice in my head: *Don't worry if you look frightened. You're supposed to be frightened.* "I— No one. What I mean is, I didn't know he was here; I just knew he was a soldier for Al Shabaab. I took a chance that maybe one of your men knew him . . . sir."

No response.

So much for my bath. I'm drenched in sweat now. "If you just talk to my brother. Please, sir. He'll tell you who I am. His name is Dahir. Is he here?"

The General hasn't taken his eyes off me, and I have to force myself to shut my mouth. To not fall on the floor in a blubbering mess and confess all my sins. What was I thinking, agreeing to this? How am I supposed to go up against the most feared dude in Somalia? I get that hot-cold feeling like I'm maybe going to throw up. Maybe I'm going to throw up, like, *on the Butcher*. I am so dead.

"Why were you in that outpost prison?"

I take a deep breath, pray that whatever's in my stomach stays in my stomach. This question I am ready for. *Stick with a version of the truth.* "The AMISOM soldiers arrested me at a checkpoint. They don't trust any boys my age. They must have thought I was with you—that I was Al Shabaab . . . sir."

A pause. "And your brother's name is?"

They'll ask you the same questions over and over again, to try to trip you up.

"Dahir," I repeat. "Dahir Mohamed."

Sweat drips into my eyes. Is he even here? Or is the Butcher just playing with me? I look around the room like an idiot, like maybe my brother's hiding in a corner, laughing at me.

Dammit, Dahir, you'd better be here.

"You are nervous."

"You're a warlord," I blurt, before I can stop myself. *Abdi, you* doqon.

89

But the General's face splits slowly into a grin. "Not a warlord. Not anymore. Now I am a Mujahid. A soldier for God. But you shouldn't be nervous. You have nothing to fear from us, if you're telling the truth." He steps away. "Your brother, eh? He is not Dahir anymore, you know. He has been given a new name: Khalid. A warrior name, which he earned. He is the youngest unit commander here. He has a strong faith, and is humble before God and Prophet Mohammed, peace be upon him."

"*Alayhi as-salam*," I repeat. Somewhere in the back of my brain, under all my terror, I find myself thinking, *Humble? Dahir?*

"Do you want to see him?"

I put a hand to the ground to steady myself. "Please . . . sir."

The General looks at me for a few more heartbeats. Then he shouts at someone in the next room, making me jump, "Send him in!"

I turn slowly, my breath starting to hitch.

A boy walks forward to stand in the doorway. He doesn't look at me. He looks at General Idris. His sandaled feet are wide, army-style. He is taller now, and wears a *khameez* in military green with a red-and-white *keffiyeh* around his neck, like jihadis from the Middle East. His face is thin, and his eyes above his beard are sunken and hard.

But there's no doubt. It's him.

"Dahir?" I croak. And then I can't stop myself. I jump up, throw my arms around him.

He doesn't move.

His body is stiff, all muscle and bone like a rope pulled

tight. He's still not looking at me. He doesn't even blink. I step back, my arms awkwardly falling to my sides. Confusion crawls over me like a rash.

"Dahir," I say again, desperate to hear him speak.

The General chuckles behind me. "He won't answer to that name. Try Khalid."

"K-Khalid," I say, and immediately it feels wrong, like trying to put your shoes on the wrong feet. How can I call him that? He isn't *Khalid*. He's Dahir Mohamed Abdullahi. Mohamed is my father's name. Abdullahi is my father's father. Who is Khalid? Who are his people? Khalid isn't a person I know. He doesn't exist.

But when I say the name, I'm rewarded with my brother's gaze, and a small upturn of his lips. Almost a smile.

"*As-salamu alaykum,* brother," he finally says to me.

I let out a wheeze like I've been punched. It's Dahir's voice. He's still in there. It's been a long time, he looks different, he's got some weird new name. He probably hates me, but it's still him, right? I've found him. He's alive—that's what's important. It doesn't matter what he looks like or what he's calling himself, or what Jones says he's become. I just need to get him alone so we can talk. I have so much to tell him that it's practically bubbling out of my mouth, a river overflowing its banks. I want to blurt that a crazy American guy is holding Hooyo and Ayeyo and the twins and Hafsa hostage. I want to confess what I've done to get here. I want to tell him that not a day goes by when I don't think about that day. I want to beg him to forgive me. I want to tell him he looks like an idiot in his jihadi outfit. I want to ask him why

91

he didn't come home. I want to hit him for not coming home so he'll hit me back and then we'll fight until we both feel better. And then he'll forgive me and everything will start to be right again. We'll leave here and we'll fix things. We need to go.

Together.

Now.

But I feel the eyes of the General burning into the back of my neck, and so I just swallow at the dryness in my mouth. All I can whisper is *"Wa-alaykum salam."*

"Is this your brother, soldier?" the General asks.

Dahir's eyes travel over my face, as if he doesn't know me, as if we didn't come from the same womb, sleep under the same roof, side by side on the same mat for most of our lives. *Say yes, asshole!* I want to shout.

"Yes," he finally says. "The son of my mother and father." He looks away from me.

"He was being held at the Baarde checkpoint," the General says. "He was asking for you."

Does Dahir's face change? I can't tell. "Yes, sir."

"Did he know you were here with us, Khalid? How? Have you talked to him?"

"No, sir, not at all, sir."

The General frowns.

My brother's voice is firm. "I swear it, sir. I haven't had contact with any of my family in three years, sir."

The General looks back and forth between us. Finally he says, "He wants to join us, Commander. What do you think?"

I suddenly feel as much as see Dahir's eyes twitch toward me. His chest starts to rise and fall, and for one second a veil is lifted from the face of the soldier before me, and my brother's eyes appear. *Dahir's* eyes. Hope sparks in my chest. He blinks. He starts to speak.

And then behind him, a shadow appears in the doorway. A hand falls on Dahir's shoulder. "My brothers," a man's voice says.

Dahir stiffens.

And my brother is gone.

He steps aside to let the man pass. Head bowed, Dahir-now-Khalid returns the greeting, "Hakim Doctor."

The man who comes in the room isn't as tall as the General or as broad across the chest, but there is no mistaking the shift in power. The Doctor is in charge. He moves slowly, with precision. He looks straight at me, his eyes bright and full of curiosity, and for a second I can't breathe. I look into his eyes and it's like all the air gets sucked out of the room.

"Welcome, Abdiweli," he says. "I am Dr. Mohamed Warsame. My brothers just call me Doctor." His voice is melodious, clear, like he's about to begin reciting a poem.

He comes closer, raises a hand to my face, and I wince. He stops. "I won't hurt you." He holds my chin gently, looking at my face. It takes me a second to realize he's examining my bruised cheek and the cut on my lip.

"You are lucky," General Idris says stiffly to me. "Not everyone is honored by a meeting with Hakim Doctor."

I try to still my shaking, but my breath rattles.

The Doctor frowns. "The men were too rough with the boy." To me, he says, "I am sorry."

"I'm fine, *Alhamdulillah*."

I'm fine? Some of my senses start to come back to me. What am I talking about? I'm fine like a run-over turd.

"I'll talk with these young brothers for a while, General. Tell Safiya to bring my bag."

"Yes, sir."

The Doctor leads us onto a veranda shaded by *neem* trees. It feels like an oasis after the stuffy, dark room. I get my first real view of where I am. The building is one of four or five set in a large, sandy compound. The compound itself is circled by the high walls of the old fort, made of massive coral blocks. To the west, beyond the walls, I can see the shine of tin roofs in a distant town. To the east, the ocean.

And below the veranda, *them*.

The Boys. At least a hundred. They are drilling under the dappled shade of acacia trees and camo netting. They all sprout AK-47s on their shoulders. As I follow the Doctor and Dahir to a carpet on the veranda floor, I see a line of Boys rush at a newer building. They sling their guns forward and pepper the side of it with bullets. *Ta-ta-ta-ta-ta-ta-ta!*

There are human-sized figures painted on the wall. Some of them with smiley mouths.

As soon as we're seated, a girl with a covered face comes out bringing tin cups of water, and then a red backpack with a white crescent on the side for the Doctor. She puts everything before us with bright green gloves that disappear under the arms of her dress.

I realize how thirsty I am when I take my cup and can't stop drinking until it's gone. Water sloshes down the front of my shirt. The Doctor motions for the girl to bring me more. As she does, he methodically pulls out his supplies from the bag and spreads them on a clean towel. Dahir/Khalid sits cross-legged next to us, but a little apart, his back straight, eyes averted.

The Doctor leans toward me and dabs rubbing alcohol on my face. "Again, I am sorry about the poor treatment. We had to be sure you were not sent here as a spy."

"I'm not a spy," I say. I'm a little surprised at how easily the lie crosses my lips. Especially seeing as how my insides feel like jelly. Careful, I remind myself. If they think for one second I'm lying, I'm as good as dead. Dahir won't be able to save me. I sneak a look at him.

He'd try. He would.

"It happens," the Doctor says, wiping softly at the dried blood. I can see it coming away on the gauze, old and then fresh, brown then red. "People have come here claiming they want to join our struggle." Red and then clean. "When in reality, they have been bought, and will betray us. We must be vigilant."

I start to sweat again. It trickles down the nape of my neck.

"These cuts look old. Did the AMISOM soldiers harm you at the checkpoint as well?"

"Yes." I swallow. "They questioned me. Everyone has asked me so many questions. The soldiers, then your men . . ." The same urge to blurt everything out hits me again, and I have to bite the inside of my mouth. "I'm not a spy," I repeat.

Do not start crying, Abdi.

The Doctor discards the gauze and begins applying ointment to my cuts. It smells faintly of eucalyptus, a smell that reminds me of the ointment my mother would swab on our chests when we had coughs. It makes me feel a little calmer.

"I know," the Doctor says. "You're not a spy. Your brother has told us. You're a good boy. You're strong." He cocks his head. "You seem more like a Da'ud than an Abdi. Do you know the story of Da'ud?"

I force myself to think back through my lessons at *duqsi*. "He slew the giant Goliath when he was a boy."

"Yes, and he grew to be a king. Do you hurt anywhere else?"

"My feet. And here." I lay my fingers against my ribs.

"Your ribs will have to heal on their own, I'm afraid." The Doctor motions for me to show him my foot and says, "Does your family know you are here?"

"They . . . No." I glance at my brother. Nothing. I wince as the Doctor twists my foot in his hands. I realize I'm actually a little embarrassed about how dirty my feet still are, even after my ocean bath. "I left everyone in Mogadishu."

"If you join us, you will not be able to communicate with them. Are you prepared for that? You must start new here."

Gunfire pops behind us. *Ta-ta-ta-ta-ta-ta-ta!*

"I have my brother," I say.

Dahir/Khalid still doesn't meet my eye. I take another big gulp of water, fighting the urge to throw it in his face, cup and all. Why can't he at least look at me?

"If you join us, we will all be your brothers, one and the same." The Doctor finishes cleaning the wounds on one foot and moves on to the other. "Why do you want to fight with us? It shouldn't just be because your brother by blood is here."

"I want to free my country from the godless oppressors." The words sound hollow, flat. The Doctor glances up from my foot. He doesn't look convinced.

I dig deeper, my heart starting to pound, trying to find the right way to put it. "I don't want to live like this for the rest of my life, in a war zone," I tell the Doctor, which is true. "I want to be safe. I want my family to be free." Also true. I look at my brother. "I want my family to be proud of me for fighting for them." True.

The Doctor watches me. "Those are good reasons to start with," he finally says. Done with my feet, he washes his hands in a basin the girl has silently set beside him. "Here we fight for divine justice."

Relief begins to drip through my veins. I seem to have passed a test.

"There is no true law in our country anymore, Da'ud," the Doctor says. "There are no righteous leaders. You have seen it. The rulers of our country have let themselves be bought by foreigners who do not have the common people's interests at heart."

Da'ud, he calls me.

"The politicians have abandoned us," he goes on. He shakes water off his hands and then zips up his bag in one swift, decisive motion. "Either they live like sultans in exile, or they colonize their own people here. They grow fat on our country's resources while we starve. They're parasites. Do you know what a parasite is? They're the worms that make children's bellies look full, when actually they are eating them from the inside. They call themselves Muslims, but no true Muslim can turn a blind eye to the suffering our people face every day. It is up to us to make things right. Do you know why?"

I shake my head slowly.

His voice is a warm hum now, low but strong. "Because God calls us to it. And we know we must answer. He asks much of us, it is true. He asks us to shed the mantle of our tribe, our family, our vanity. To lay down our pasts and become part of something greater. It is not an easy thing He asks. If you commit to the fight, He will test you in His flame, and flame burns. It burns away all that is not pure and strong. Some do not survive. You must have faith as hard as steel to withstand it."

I can't look away from the Doctor.

"We will bring God's law. We will bring His order, *Inshallah*."

"*Inshallah*," Dahir murmurs.

"The people will see," the Doctor continues.

I hear the Boys resume their exercises outside, rhythmic, sure.

"Those who do not follow God's law will not be able to hide. God is merciful, but He is just. The wicked will be punished according to His law. They cannot hide from God." He's looking at me like he can see straight into my stained, guilty soul. "No one can."

Am I shaking? Yes. No. I don't know.

The Doctor goes on, "Justice. That is what our people need."

"God is great," my brother says.

"We will overthrow the government oppressors." The Doctor's voice fills my chest, like I am a drum and his words are the mallet. "We will restore peace. We will bring order."

"God is great!" Khalid says again.

"We will make His kingdom on earth."

"God is great!"

"Peace and order can only come from the one true, merciful, righteous God."

"God is great," my brother murmurs a final time, his eyes closed, voice thick with emotion.

I stare at the Doctor, terrified, transfixed, bewildered. His eyes are black pools like deep space, stars shining in a void. I barely hear the next round of gunfire. Maybe I'm getting used to it.

"Don't be afraid, Da'ud," he says, gripping me by the shoulders. "Abdi was afraid, but not Da'ud. You are safe. We are your family now. You're home."

SIXTEEN

NOW: NOVEMBER 6
SANGUI CITY, KENYA

Foster families are apparently harder to come by in Sangui City than Sam had counted on. I overhear her talking to Mama Lisa about it when she drops me off at Maisha the next day.

". . . they only want little kids," Sam tells her in a low voice.

I duck down to listen, pretending to tie my laces.

"Why do you think we started this place?" Mama Lisa asks Sam. "They don't even want to take teenage girls. And if they are pregnant, absolutely not."

"Well, don't worry," Sam assures her. "We'll find a family for him today, I'm sure of it. And then he'll be out of your hair, I promise."

"Mmm," Mama Lisa replies politely.

I finish fiddling with my laces and walk inside. The shoes are new. Everything I'm wearing is. "You're going to have to spend another night at my place," Sam told me when she picked me up from Maisha yesterday, "so I bought a few things I thought you might need." She pulled a bag out of the back seat of her car and shoved it at me, her cheeks bright pink. "Nothing fancy."

As we drove away, I pulled out two white shirts and two pairs of khaki trousers. Underwear. A toothbrush, toothpaste and deodorant. A shaving razor, and something I didn't recognize.

"What is this?"

She looked at the bright yellow thing in my bandaged hand, and realization flickered over her face. "Oh, I didn't even think about your hand . . ." She swallowed. "It's a yo-yo."

I swiveled it between my remaining fingers. "What's a yo-yo?"

"Um . . . it's a toy." She seemed flustered. "I should have thought about . . . but maybe it will still . . ."

"What do you do with it?"

"We can try later. Maybe you can do it left-handed. It's a little juvenile, but I always wanted one when I was little and I wasn't allowed, so I thought I'd get you one."

I put all the things back in the bag, careful not to wrinkle the new shirts. I wanted to tell her she shouldn't have bought me anything, but looking down at myself I realized just how dirty and worn out my clothes were. I ducked my head. "Thank you," I said.

"It's all okay? It'll all fit? We can take it back and get different stuff if you want. I don't know how boys your age dress. And the yo-yo was dumb, I'm sorry. Just ignore it."

"It's all great," I assured her.

When we got back to her place, I handed the yo-yo to her. She hesitated, then showed me how to loop the string around my finger and flick the body out so it would wind out and back. She showed me how she could make it "sleep" and did a trick called walking the dog.

After I was finished with my homework, I messed around with the yo-yo while we watched *Survivor*, a TV show I'd never seen before. I tried throwing it with my left hand at first, but it didn't feel right, so I switched to my bad one. It felt better that way. Sam watched me out of the corner of her eye. By the end of the show I had sort of gotten the hang of it. I liked the way it thunked solidly back into my palm.

When I couldn't sleep later, I got up out of bed and stood in the middle of my empty room, flicking the yo-yo out with my bad hand, bringing it back in the dark.

ALGEBRA PASSES IN a blur this morning. It's better than yesterday, but I still can't seem to focus. Twice Mrs. Bota calls on me, and twice I find I have no idea what she's just asked. Not because I don't understand, or even because I don't hear her; it's that I hear the question and then it's gone, evaporated. English is a little better. I even sort of like the book Mrs. Otieno's assigned to us, *Things Fall Apart. You got that right,* I'd thought when I heard the title. At the break I have my nose in it, trying to catch up to chapter twelve, where the rest of the class is. I'm just reading a sentence I really like: . . . *silence returned to the world. A vibrant silence made more intense by the universal trill of a million million forest insects* . . . when a finger jabs me in the back. Hard.

"Hey, you. Boy."

I turn around to find a large girl in a cartoon kitten T-shirt. The kitten smiles. The girl does not. "What are you still doing here?" she demands. "This place isn't for boys."

"I . . . uh . . ."

"When are you leaving?"

She's about my height, but built like a rugby player. I'm pretty sure that even if I wanted to fight her, she'd win. I look around, but no one seems to be paying any attention to us. "I don't know," I say.

She inches closer, narrowing her eyes. "You scared of me, boy?"

"Er . . ."

"You should be. I don't really like your kind."

I decide not to ask what my kind is. Somali? Male? "Look, I'm just here until—"

"I saw you looking at my girl Muna," she interrupts. "You better watch yourself. You lay a finger on her, I'll cut your dick off, hear?" She steps closer and reaches for my crotch.

"Hey!" I yelp, jumping back. "I haven't done anything! Are you crazy?"

Her eye twitches. "What did you call me?"

"Alice! Stop!"

I look up, expecting to see a teacher intervening, but instead find Muna striding toward us. Heat swooshes up my cheeks. The kitten T-shirt girl, who must be Alice, backs up a step but continues to eye me like I'm something sticky she found on the bottom of her sandal.

Muna grabs Alice's arm. "You're going to get in trouble again for starting fights."

"This punk wants to jump your bones, Muna," Alice says, jutting her chin at me.

"What? I didn't— No, I d-don't!" I stutter. "You're insane!"

Muna rounds on me. "Don't call her that," she snaps.

I throw my hands up, backing away.

"And I can handle myself," she tells Alice, who looks at her toes like a scolded child. "He's not going to mess with any of us, are you?"

I feel a pitching mix of anger and embarrassment churning in my stomach. I glower at them both, not answering.

"Are you?" Muna demands.

"Of course not!" I finally say.

Alice doesn't stop glaring, but Muna squeezes her arm. "It's fine, really. Will you save me a seat in biology?"

She doesn't seem to notice she's being steered away until she's already walking back across the garden.

"I'm sorry," Muna says, once she's gone. "Alice is really protective, and—"

"I didn't need your help," I interrupt.

Muna looks startled for a second, and then her expression

hardens. "That's what you think. Fine. Next time I won't bother."
She starts to walk away.

I watch her go, wrestling with myself. "Wait!" I blurt. "I— I
didn't— I *don't* want to jump your bones. I never said anything
like that."

When she turns back, she lifts her chin. Her perfect cheek-
bones become a fortress wall. "You'd better not have."

"*Wallahi*, I swear. You're the only person I've even talked to
since I got here. Well, you and now Alice, I guess."

She doesn't move, but something passes over her face that
I can't quite read. Finally she says, "I'm going to swing. You can
come if you want."

Lost, I ask, "Swing?"

She nods toward the children's swing set. "My feet hurt."

She turns to go without waiting for me to respond. I shift
from foot to foot. The yo-yo Sam gave me is in my pocket, and
I close my bad hand around it, my fingers nestling into the
groove between the disks. I follow her.

We have about half an hour until the next class. Girls are
scattered over the lawn, talking, braiding one another's hair,
catching up on homework. On the patio three of them tug
newly dyed scarves out of a plastic washbasin and open them
up to hang on the laundry line. They wave softly like the flags of
undiscovered countries.

The swings are low and I put my hand out to help Muna
settle into one, but I'm too slow, or maybe she's ignoring me because it's the hand covered in a bandage and she doesn't want

to touch it. Or maybe it's because I'm a guy. Or maybe it's just me. Once her feet are stretched out before her, Muna allows herself a sigh of relief. I sit on her right, so my good ear is toward her. The swing is so low that my knees feel like they're up around my neck.

She tilts her face up to the sun. "I don't want a boyfriend, okay? Just to be clear."

"Sure, of course not," I say, quickly averting my eyes from her belly.

For a while we just sit there, watching the sun warm the flowers in the garden. Muna is the kind of girl who, all other things being normal, makes me feel like my feet are three sizes too big and worry that my breath stinks. I don't know why she's even talking to me. But maybe it's the calming rhythm of the swinging, or the way she's already told me exactly where I'd stand if I even tried to make a move on her. Maybe it's because she doesn't seem like the sort of pretty girl who will expect me to entertain her with witty banter. Or maybe it's just that nothing is normal anymore. Whatever it is, I find myself relaxing.

"Alice isn't that bad, really."

I pull the yo-yo out of my pocket and start wrapping the string around my finger. "She's terrifying."

Muna laughs. It's a big, throaty laugh, and even she seems surprised to hear it. "She's got a point, though. What *are* you doing at a girls' center?" Muna's tone is nicer than Alice's, but still mildly accusing.

I open my mouth, but find I don't have an answer. I haven't

stopped to think about it, I realize. Not really. For the first time, it truly hits me that I shouldn't be here. That I'm an interloper. That probably some of these girls are here precisely because of what boys like me did to them.

Without warning, the image of a girl, broken and bloody, fills my head. I fumble and drop the yo-yo.

"What is it?" Muna asks, seeing my face.

"Nothing." I grab it back up and wind the string, trying to close my mind before more images rush in. But it's too late to stop the familiar feeling of shame from rolling over me like an oily black wave. I let my toes drag in the dirt. Maybe I should leave. It's not like I couldn't walk out the front gate. I doubt anyone would try too hard to stop me. But where would I go? My guilt fights with a familiar feeling of numbness. It all seems too hard to figure out. I put the yo-yo in my pocket. The only thing I can think to tell Muna is what I told Alice: "It wasn't my idea. Sam brought me here."

You sound like a five-year-old, Abdi. Like I have no choice in the matter. Like lately it hasn't even occurred to me to weigh in on my own life. Because it hasn't. Because just thinking about trying to decide what happens to me is starting to give me a headache.

"You don't have anywhere else to go?" she asks.

That question's easy to answer. I shake my head no.

She purses her lips, rocks back and forth in the swing. Finally she nods at my hand. "Did Al Shabaab do that?"

I twitch.

"What did you do? Steal something?"

For a second the question's almost funny. Almost. "Something like that."

Back and forth. The swing's chains creak. "Were you one of them?"

It shouldn't surprise me; somehow I knew the question was coming, but it still catches me off guard. "N-no," I say. "No, I hate Al Shabaab. They're murderers."

The lies still come so easily. I can't tell if she believes me or not. She doesn't say anything like, *Oh, no, of course not, sorry I even asked. Yeah, you don't seem like that kind of person.* She knows better, I guess. Maybe she knows all too well that all sorts of people get caught up in all sorts of things. For a while we're quiet, but then she makes a noise that I almost don't catch, like a grunt.

"Are you okay?" I ask.

"Yeah, just . . ." She puts her hand on her middle. "She's stretching out."

"It's a girl?"

"A big girl. Heavy." Muna shifts restlessly on the swing, like she can't find a comfortable position. "I was watching a program on TV the other day about astronauts," she says. "They just float around in space. Weightless. I'd pay a million shillings to feel like that right now."

"Weightless," I repeat. It does sound nice. "Like swimming."

"Hmm. Like swimming? Is it?"

I look at her. "Sure. You said you're from Mogadishu, right? You never swam in the ocean?"

She tilts her head, suggesting the tiniest hint of a smile. "You ever see any girls swimming at Lido Beach?"

I frown. Now that I think about it, no. Sometimes girls would come to the famous beach in giggling packs and wade up to their knees, or mothers would walk their toddlers into the small waves, but I can't remember seeing any of them really go for it, out past the breakers.

She sees the answer on my face and shakes her head. "Men and women swimming together? Al Shabaab would shit themselves."

My knees lock for a split second, and then I hurry to keep swinging, forcing a laugh. "Yeah, I guess so."

"Actually, we're supposed to go to Paradise Island in December on a field trip. It's a mall with a water park called Splash Land. There's a pool there; some of the other girls were talking about it." Her forehead wrinkles. "But I can't go in."

"Why?"

"Splash Land rules. You have to pass a swim test. I don't know how to swim."

"You don't?"

She shrugs. "When would I have learned?"

"You have to know how to swim. It could save your life."

The corner of her mouth tugs up again. I'm not really sure why, but I persist. "The beach is close, right?" I know it is; I could just barely see the water from our algebra classroom on the second floor. "Do you ever go?"

"Some of the girls go with a teacher in the afternoons," she says cautiously. "If it's nice."

"I'll teach you!" I blurt, unable to help myself. I suddenly feel buoyant, almost giddy. "I'll go with you! I'll show you how to swim."

She presses her lips together in a frown. Just as quickly as the good feeling comes, it disappears. I've pushed too hard. She's going to say no. It's not appropriate. I'll make her uncomfortable.

I start to tell her never mind, it's okay, but before I can, she looks up and asks, "Can Alice come too? She doesn't know how to swim either."

I open and close my mouth. "S-sure. Of course. Absolutely."

"Okay," Muna says, after a pause. She leans forward and puts her hands on her belly. The little smile comes back. Then she whispers, "Hear that? We're going to learn to swim."

SEVENTEEN

Dahir is dispatched to take me to my new unit, the 106s. There are five units: 101, 102, 104, 105 and 106. Dahir is in charge of the 102s. I'm not sure what happened to 103, but I have other, more important things to figure out right now.

The General's let me go without a blindfold, and I hurry down the stairs after my brother, who's moving like his pants are on fire. I hold my ribs, wincing. I wait until we're outside, away from the guys guarding the front door of the building, and then snatch his elbow. "Dahir! We have to talk."

He shakes me off. "Don't call me that. My name is Khalid."

He leads me through a part of the Fort that's straight out of *The Mummy*. Or *Lara Croft: Tomb Raider*. The new buildings, mud brick and topped with tin roofs, look flimsy and poor next to the old walls made of massive coral block. We pass a tiny mosque painted green. A kitchen block where the same girl with the gloves who served us earlier is bent over a charcoal stove. She doesn't look at us as we pass. Another girl pulls sun-stiffened uniforms off a laundry line nearby.

Once we're past them, I try grabbing my brother's arm again. "Look, I get that you probably hate me. I would hate me too. But can you please just listen for one second? This is important!"

Dahir/Khalid's feet slow slightly. "I have orders to take you straight to your unit."

"Unit? I'm not going to a unit!" I look around to make sure no one is watching us. "Da— Khalid, listen, I came here to find you, not join these nut-jobs!"

"Hey!" Khalid says, stopping abruptly and whirling on me so fast I almost run into him. He holds a finger up at my nose. "That's blasphemy! Watch out or God will cut out your tongue! I knew you were bullshitting back there about wanting to fight for our country."

My mouth opens and closes like a fish. I grab his finger and try to keep from shouting. "Of course I was! Don't you hear yourself? Are you brainwashed or something?"

He grunts, like the question is too stupid to deserve an answer.

"What are you even still doing here?" I ask. "Why haven't you run away?"

Dahir/Khalid's face twitches. He glances up at the building we've left, and then grabs me by the collar and drags me around the side of a crumbling shed, out of view. Among an assortment of rusty machine parts that have been brought back here to die, he finally looks at me. "Listen," he says, "it may sound crazy to you, but being recruited was the best thing that ever happened to me!"

For a second I can't even respond. Then I splutter, "You didn't get recruited, you got taken at gunpoint!"

He shakes his head, frustrated. "It was God intervening, bringing me here. Didn't you hear the Doctor? Don't you know what the government is doing to our people? The politicians say they're Muslim, but they work with the Americans and Europeans. Those nations are always meddling like they know what's best for us, like we're too stupid and backward to decide on our own! But look what they did to Iraq and Afghanistan!"

"Dahir," I say shakily, "you're talking crazy. That doesn't have anything to do with—"

"Crazy?" He barks a laugh. "Don't you remember what happened to Uncle Sharmarke?"

"That's totally different. He got killed by Ethiopian soldiers."

"Because he was a soldier with the Islamic Courts Union! Killed by Christian Ethiopians who were funded by who? The Americans! Al Shabaab is what's left of the Courts, and the Americans haven't stopped trying to wipe us out!"

I try to speak, but Dahir goes on, talking like he's onstage and I'm not even here anymore. "They do the same thing to innocent Muslims around the world. They bomb whole villages, whole city blocks, not caring who they kill—old people and children! Aabo was wrong; there's no such thing as staying away from guns. You can't be neutral. You have to choose sides, and if you don't, you're just letting them win. I'm not going to sit around anymore and let them try to destroy Somalia too. I'm going to—"

"Hooyo is gone!" I blurt out. "I didn't leave them. Ayeyo, Hafsa, the twins—they're all gone! *That's* why I'm here. You're right. I'm not here because I want to fight; I'm here because I need your help! You have to come with me. We have to rescue them!"

Dahir's eyes narrow. "What do you mean, gone?"

I feel sick with everything that I came here to tell him boiling inside of me. But now that I'm in front of my brother, finally able to speak . . . the words won't come. My voice sticks in my throat. Now, listening to him, there's also a curdling, babbling fear in my gut. Dahir isn't thinking straight. He's talking like one of them. I swallow, my brain churning like wheels through sand. What will he do if I tell him about Jones, one of these murdering Americans he's talking about? Will he believe me? Will he help me?

Or will he tell the General?

And if he does, then what?

What happens to Hooyo and the others?

"Dahir," I say, trying to keep calm, choosing my words carefully. "You never should have ended up here in the first place. It's my fault, I know that. But now you can leave, you can get out of here, and we can go find our family. I know I don't have the right to ask you to help me, but think of them. Think of Hooyo and Hafsa and the twins. They need you. They've been . . . taken. We have to get them back."

He eyes me. "Taken? What are you talking about? Who took them? A gang? AMISOM?"

"I . . . I don't know," I finally say. "Just men. With guns. They came in the middle of the night. I . . . I ran away. I haven't seen them since then."

"When?"

"A few days ago."

He looks past me, his eyes skating over the compound. Hope pulses through me. Is Dahir actually listening now? If I can just get him to come with me, then I'll tell him the full truth of everything later, when we have time, when we're far away from this place. "We have to find them," I say, gripping his arm. "We can figure out how to get in contact with Aabo. He'll know what to do. We can get them back. Come on, Dahir, please. Let's get out of here," I beg.

I can see some sort of struggle going on behind my brother's eyes. What is he waiting for? Why is he even hesitating? "They took all of them?" he asks. "Even the twins? Hafsa?"

"All of them." I wait, blood humming in my ears, holding my breath until it's about to explode in my chest. I'm ready to jump up and go the second I know he's finally heard what I'm telling him. Long seconds pass.

"They're trying to get to me," he finally mutters. "They did the same thing to Rashid. Those AMISOM bastards kidnapped his wife, dangled her in front of him."

I don't know what he's talking about, but it doesn't matter. "Help me, Dahir," I beg. "Help me rescue them."

He digs his knuckles into his eye sockets and stands like that for what seems like forever, minutes ticking by, his lips moving faintly like he's having some internal conversation. I don't know if he's praying or what, and it takes everything in me not to reach out and shake him. But finally his brow smooths. He straightens the *keffiyeh* around his neck and looks up.

I'm already starting to move. "Let's get—"

"I can't go."

The chill in his voice stops me dead. I reach out, my fingers fluttering at his sleeve. "Dahir—"

"I have to stay here." With every word, he straightens, pulls away. "I made a vow to fight. If I leave, then they get what they want. They win."

I can feel myself starting to shake again, a howl of frustration building in my throat. "Who cares?" I demand. "It's our family. What about fighting for *them*? *That's* what you need to do! Not play warlord here with these people!"

"They're not warlords," he says. "They're my brothers."

"*I'm* your brother!"

He looks at me with something like pity, and it makes me want to punch him in the face as hard as I can.

His voice infuriatingly calm, Dahir says, "Staying here and fighting is the only way to help Hooyo and the others. Once we defeat AMISOM and the puppet politicians, we'll set all the prisoners free."

"But—they need us now! Not in some fairy-tale future when everything is better!"

"I'm sorry," he says, stepping back. "I can't. I vowed to fight with the Boys. The Doctor is counting on me to lead my brothers. I'm staying." He looks away from me, like he's already back with his unit in his mind.

"I need you," I say, my voice cracking. I grab his arm. "Our family needs you, Dahir. Please, you're Dahir, you're not this Khalid person! You're—"

I hear the blow before I feel it, right on top of the old ones, ripping the Doctor's bandage off my cheek. I find myself on my knees, the ground reeling.

For a few moments nothing moves except the bandage, flapping on one piece of tape as I sway.

Then, softly, "Abdi . . ." Dahir slowly crouches down next to me. "Shit. I'm sorry." He rubs his hands over his face.

I sniff, trembling in fury.

He sighs. "Look, try to understand. I do care about Hooyo and the others, of course I do, but I can't abandon my brothers now. When they brought me here, I was a child. I was younger than you. I didn't know anything. I thought they'd kill me, but I was wrong. The Doctor showed me my path. He made me a new person. A better person. I made a promise to him and to God to fight for all of us, all the *Ummah*, not just our family. God is testing me, and I know what I have to do. Fighting for control of Somalia is the best—the only—way to win freedom. For everyone. This is the path God has laid out for me, and I can't waver. I know you want to go do something, but what? You don't even know who took them or where they are."

I look up, begging him to understand somehow without me speaking. No. He's wrong. I *do* know who took them.

Show me my brother. Show me Dahir, the Dahir I remember, the Dahir who gave his life for mine, and I'll tell him everything.

Show me I can trust him.

But all he says is "I'm not leaving."

His words are as final as hammering the lid onto a coffin.

My already reeling head starts to spin, faster and faster. I feel myself floating, untethered, a speck on a vast ocean with no land in sight.

I look out at the barren compound. The Boys are milling under the trees, on break from training. Ever since I made this bargain with Jones, all I've let myself think about is finding Dahir. I would find him, he'd come back with me and we'd find some way to rescue Hooyo and the others. He'd know what to do. Or he'd tell Jones whatever he needed to know. Because how could he possibly be more loyal to the Boys than to us? He's talking about the government and politics, all of it vague and far away, when what's happening to our family is blisteringly real and urgent. Who is this person in front of me who can't see that? What happened to my brother?

I try to pull myself together, swipe at my running nose. I need time. Time to figure out what to do. Maybe I can keep talking to him, trying to make him see. I can't just give up, give in to this feeling of total helplessness. I owe that much to Dahir. And what other choice do I have? Without him, how do I even begin to rescue Hooyo and the others? He has to help me.

And if I can't convince him, then, well, I don't know.

"Look," Dahir says, "what if God led you here to be a warrior, like He did me? What if that was what He intended all along? You got here late, but it doesn't matter. You're here. Stay. You're being offered a chance. Let Him work through you."

My brother pushes himself up off the ground and extends a hand to pull me up. His eyes are bright and focused, their brown depths the exact color of our mother's.

I stare at his hand.

And then, what else can I do? God help me, I take it.

EIGHTEEN

NOW: NOVEMBER 8
SANGUI CITY, KENYA

Day four since Sam picked me up from the police station and guess what? I'm still homeless. Shocking, right?

Sam says it's not because people don't want *me*, it's just that they're scared. It's a weird time right now in Sangui City. I know what she means. People are jumpy about terrorists after Al Shabaab hit that resort up the coast near the Somali border a few weeks ago. Three Kenyans and a tourist died. A Somali kid with no history and no family and exactly the right age to be trouble? Who might have seen and done things you wouldn't want to expose your family to? People think teenagers are trouble regardless, just like Mama Lisa said. You throw terrorism into the mix? I wouldn't want to take me in either.

Nights at Sam's are quiet. It's actually pretty nice. I do my homework. She does the work she brings home. We eat takeout in front of the TV.

When they flash pictures of Al Shabaab on the seven o'clock news before *Survivor*, my heart stops for a second. But you can't tell who anyone is—everyone's face is covered with *keffiyehs*, and anyway the footage looks old. The news anchor says that the number of Al Shabaab recruits is up, that there may be close to a thousand members now in Somalia and northern Kenya.

"Three thousand," I correct.

Dammit, Abdi. Keep your mouth shut.

Sam looks up. "You think?"

We're on separate ends of the couch, and she's typing on her laptop while I stare at my yet-to-be-started algebra homework. She's changed out of her work clothes and is wearing her at-home uniform: an old blue T-shirt with the UN logo on it and men's trousers. Her feet are bare, and her hair hangs down around her shoulders like fraying ribbons. It's so different from how my mother would dress to feel comfortable, and for the first couple of days Sam's bare feet and loose hair made me sort of uncomfortable, but it got normal fast. We've settled into a routine of sitting here on the couch at the end of the day, feeling the breeze grow cooler as it comes in through the open balcony doors, listening to nightjars call and geckos bark, bathed in the comforting light of the television.

"That's what I heard." I lean over my book, studying question number one hard enough to burn a hole in the paper.

"Did you ever run into them in Mogadishu?"

"Um, no. They were around, but I stayed inside most of the time."

She seems like she wants to ask more questions, so I say, "Do you know how to solve linear equations?" and she says, "Sure, let's see," and turns off the TV even though *Survivor* is just about to start, which is kind of a bummer because I wanted to see if Tammy, the evil white girl with dreadlocks, or Marcus, the guy who can actually build a fire, is going to get voted off at the tribal council. But no *Survivor* is better than being asked more questions about Al Shabaab, so I let her explain how to solve for *x*.

"You're a better teacher than Mrs. Bota," I say, after she lays it all out in really simple terms. "I didn't understand at all this morning in class."

"Thanks. Try solving the next one."

"Were you good at math in school?" I start reassembling the equation like she showed me. I like how she explained it; it's all about balance.

"Uh, yeah," she says. "I was pretty good, but I wasn't at a school."

I look up.

"My mom taught me algebra," she explains. "I was home-schooled. In the United States, parents can keep their kids at home and teach them if they want."

"Why? Did your school close or something?" I ask, thinking of those long months when Hooyo would teach us at home while gun battles raged in the streets.

She picks at a spot on the sofa cushion. "We never went to public school. My parents wanted to supervise what we learned." She pauses, like she's considering something, then adds, "And to give us more religious instruction."

"Like, Christianity? The Bible and stuff?"

Sam shifts. Her eyes dart to the calendar with the puppies on the wall. "Yeah, Bible study, and listening to recorded sermons from my parents' church."

"Oh. That part sounds kind of like *duqsi*."

"What's *duqsi*?"

"Quranic class," I say. "I mean, all the kids in my neighborhood went to learn the Quran, but some of the kids in my neighborhood *only* went to *duqsi*—if their parents were really religious, or they couldn't afford school fees or something. Are your parents really religious?"

"Yeah . . . My mom is."

I start to ask about her dad, but then I see the look on her face. She isn't sad, exactly; it's like she's got the same numb feeling I get sometimes. Like she could just keep picking that spot on the couch forever. Like maybe that's what she would be doing if I weren't sitting here watching her.

She clears her throat and nods at the question in my textbook. "Do you see how to solve it?"

I look back down. "Yeah, you subtract three from this side first, right?"

"Mmm-hmm. And then?"

When I'm finished solving the problem, she says, "Keep going. I'll check your answers with you."

She tucks a strand of hair behind her ear absently, then gets up and goes to the kitchen. I roll my pencil between my three fingers, trying to figure out how to hold it in a way that doesn't make my hand cramp. The stumps wave like little blind things, trying to help. Stupid fingers. They don't seem to understand they're not there anymore.

From the kitchen Sam says, "Speaking of family, remember what I was saying about tracing yours? I tried today at work through the Red Cross registry."

I freeze. "You did?"

She peeks around the corner. "Nothing came up," she says, her eyes soft. "I'm sorry."

I look down at my homework, feeling both relieved and crushingly disappointed. Nothing. Of course she didn't. *You gave her fake names, dummy. What did you expect?* It seemed like the right thing to do at the time, but now I'm not so sure. What would she find with their real names?

"Sometimes it just takes a while," Sam goes on. "I'll keep checking. Hey, how about some ice cream?"

"Yes, please," I say, after a second. Then, "Thank you. For trying."

I put my pencil down, totally unable to care what *x* equals. I turn the TV back on. Sam comes to the kitchen doorway, looks over like she wants to maybe say something about finishing my homework. But then she doesn't. Instead she hands me a bowl and sits down. We watch *Survivor* and eat ice cream.

NINETEEN

FIVE YEARS AGO
MOGADISHU, SOMALIA

The day before Aabo left for Saudi, he took Dahir and me out in his boat. He was selling it that evening, and he wanted to sail one last time. We set off from the beach taking all the normal fishing nets and gear, but when we were far enough out, Dad didn't cast them. He didn't use the motor that day, just the sail, and when we were out past the breakers, he let the sheet luff. We sat looking back at the buildings that rose from the white sand. From there, Al Uruba Hotel was as pretty as a wedding cake sitting on the point. The cafes and restaurants were too far away to see the cracks and broken plaster. It looked like what it had been: the White Pearl.

"Why can't you stay, Aabo?" I'd asked. "I don't have to go to school. I'll help you fish."

I was eleven then, Dahir fourteen. He punched me. "Don't," he warned. I must have asked that question a thousand times over the past week, enough so that the night before, I'd over-heard my parents whispering that maybe Aabo should have just slipped away in the night without goodbyes. Maybe it would have been easier.

"It's okay," my father had told Dahir, and reached out to rub my hair with his callused hand. "And of course you have to go to school. Your mother would kill me." His eyes crinkled and he sighed. "You know how much I wish I could stay, boys."

"Then why don't you?"

Dahir was bent over a net, knotting it back together where it had frayed apart. "Because there are no more fish," he said, plucking viciously at a thread.

I looked to Aabo. How could there be no more fish? He came home with fish every day.

He frowned, but after a moment nodded in agreement. "Not enough," he said. "Not enough to send you kids to school so you won't be out here like me when you're my age."

"But why are there no more fish?"

"Because the damn Chinese have stolen them all," Dahir said, scowling.

"Son."

"Sorry, Aabo, but it's true! That's what everyone says. The Chinese, the Europeans, all of them."

"Really, Aabo?" I asked. "That's not fair."

A little smile tickled Aabo's lips. "No, it's not." He looked from us out to the sea, like he could read answers in the rippling waves. "Dahir's right. It used to be that there were so many fish that they'd be bumping shoulders just to swim." He mimed a fish, blowing his lips out big and knocking into me to get a laugh. "They'd jump out of the water and into your hands, saying, 'Just take me already, I can't stand how crowded it is down there!'"

I giggled, but Dahir said, "And now you barely catch enough for us to eat."

I looked from my father's rough hands to the ragged hems of his trousers. He was sea worn but strong from years of hauling nets. He'd never wanted to be a fisherman like his father. He'd gone to university and had a degree in history. But by the time he'd graduated, there were no jobs for history majors, and he had a new family to provide for.

"We should blow them all out of the water," Dahir said. "*That* would be fair." In a barely audible mutter he added, "Then you wouldn't have to go."

Aabo's smile slipped away. He turned from the shore to look at each of us in turn. Dahir kept his eyes stubbornly fixed on his net, even though now he was just picking at the threads, ripping them, making things worse. Maybe he realized that it didn't matter what shape the nets were in anymore. Aabo reached out and stilled his hand.

"I want you boys to listen to me, okay?"

Dahir's mouth was a hard twist. He didn't look up.

"One day all of this will be different, *Inshallah*," he said.

"Things will get better for the city and for us. I have to go tomorrow, but I won't be gone forever. A year, eighteen months at the most."

Our father put his hands on both of our shoulders and pulled us toward him, so that all of our foreheads bumped as the boat bobbed in the waves. It hurt a little, but Aabo didn't let us go. "While I'm gone, you have to be brave, okay? And strong, and smart. Especially smart. Help your mother. Protect the little ones. And stay away from the men with guns, hear me? Soldiers, warlords, pirates, all of them. It might sound like a good idea right now to blow them all out of the water, but that way of thinking is what's had us all fighting each other for thirty years. Don't get caught in that trap."

Dahir's mouth pinched, and Aabo squeezed his shoulder. "Promise me?"

"Promise," I said quickly.

Dahir took a little longer to reply, but when he did, I could tell that unlike me, he'd actually thought about it. "I promise," he told our father.

Aabo smiled. "You're good boys. I'm proud of you."

He turned back to look at the shoreline again. We looked at it too, and pretended we never saw him swipe water from his eyes.

TWENTY

No one's got a watch. Instead everything's organized around prayers.

I try to be a good Muslim, pray five times a day and all that, but if I'm being honest, I probably average more like two or three. And I've never been one to pray *Fajr*. Never been one for anything that happens before dawn, but rolling over, thinking about praying, and then deciding to go back to sleep and make up for it later at *Dhur* just doesn't fly here.

The days go like this:

Still Dark: Get shoved awake to pray *Fajr*.

Try to get my head right for *Fajr*. Intentions are important, our unit commander, Yusuf, reminds us.

Fall asleep standing up in *Fajr*.

Get slapped on the back of the head by Commander Yusuf for falling asleep during *Fajr*.

Dawn: Push-ups and a 5k bush run, presided over by Commander Yusuf, who is going to give himself hemorrhoids from screaming at us so much. Highlights of the run: thorny bushes, scorpions, snakes, mongoose and territorial, grumpy-as-hell, cute-sounding-but-seriously-misnamed honey badgers.

Sunup: Porridge and chai for breakfast. Nurse scorpion stings and blisters.

Too Soon: "Tactical"—jumping in and out of holes, climbing over piles of rocks, rolling on the ground, crawling between strings of razor wire. (Try not to be like that kid Jalil, who got it in the face from a carpet viper and died within hours when all his insides turned to mush.)

Sun-Boil, or, a Couple of Hours after Too Soon: Religious studies. (DVDs played on a laptop powered by a generator—mostly in Arabic, so no one really gets it, but is anyone going to admit it? Please. We're just glad to be sitting down in the shade.)

Midday: Better intentions to pray properly. Pray *Dhur.* (Hope praying *Dhur* covers the sound of stomach growling.)

Second-Best Time of Day: Lunch. *Canjeero* and lentils or mystery meat stew. Pasta if we're lucky.

Sweaty-Balls O'Clock: Passing out for an hour after lunch because even Commander Yusuf can't move in this heat.

Too Soon Part Two: Commander Yusuf shouting us awake. Marching and jumping jacks, more scrambling around in the dirt. Learning fast that if you don't get up quick enough, you get latrine duty.

Best Time of Day: Ocean time. Guys who can't swim get

lessons from a kid named Liban. The rest of us swim to the point and back. Turns out I'm one of the best swimmers. Way better than Liban. After a couple of days I start teaching lessons to my unit and the 102s.

Afternoon: Pray *Asr.*

Post-Asr: Weapons training: AK-47s, RPGs, MP5s (mostly without ammo since they can't spare the expense, so how we're supposed to know if we can actually hit anything is beyond me). Sometimes driving instruction, which is pretty cool.

Pre-Maghrib: Confession time. Before we pray, we're supposed to come up with three sins we committed that day. There's plenty to choose from: thinking impure thoughts, losing focus during prayers, slacking during exercises, and so on. One by one we confess to Commander Yusuf, promising ourselves that tomorrow we won't have to include "impure thoughts" again, like we have every day this week, which all of us know means jerking off in the latrine or behind D-block. He tells us to do better, and to pray for strength at *Maghrib.* Note: I think I'm getting an ulcer from holding in my real sins: lying, betrayal, doubt.

Pray Maghrib: Pray to do better. Pray for strength.

Dinner

Pray Isha

Sleep

Wake Up

Pray Fajr

Repeat . . .

TWENTY-ONE

"Um, no. It is not possible to learn how to swim without getting wet."

Alice folds her muscular arms over her chest and gives me a look like I'm just being difficult.

I'm standing knee-deep in gentle turquoise waves, waiting for Muna and Alice to join me. Neither seems ready to accept the fact that swimming involves, you know, water.

"Are you sure there are no sharks?" Muna asks, not for the first time.

She's fully dressed, like she's ready to go to school. Alice is wearing a skirt and a T-shirt over her swimsuit. When we got to the beach and I took off my shirt and they took off nothing, it took me a second to get it that they were going to swim in all their clothes. It's weird, but I've never really thought about how girls—even Alice, who's not Muslim—have all these modesty rules that mean they can't wear whatever they want. It's actually kind of a problem. And come on, I'm not worried about it because I'm desperate to see them half naked. It's because clothes get in the way. They're heavy when they're wet and can tangle and drag you down. Of course, it doesn't look like either girl is going to be getting in deep enough for that to even remotely matter.

"Well, there *are* some sharks, but they're out deep."

Alice backs up two paces.

"Sharks are more scared of you than you are of them," I say, echoing what my father told me when he taught me how to swim when I was a kid. "And most of them are tiny."

"How do you know? You've never swum here!" Alice protests.

"It's the same ocean," I say, waving up the coast. "Somalia's just right there. I swam all the time! How different can it be?"

I decide not to mention that Mogadishu is notorious for its shark population because there used to be a camel slaughterhouse up the coast. Some trivia is best saved for dry land.

"Come on, it's nice!" I say, splashing warm water at them.

"Don't!" Muna squeals, which actually makes Alice come closer, just to scowl and kick water back at me.

"That's it!" I say, grinning at Alice.

Behind Muna and Alice, Maisha girls are sitting on *kangas* they've spread out on the sand. The bright colors of the cloth look like slices of rainbow. The afternoon sun is roasting. A few girls are in the water too, but most just watch us, or lean their heads together to gossip. Mama Lisa has volunteered to accompany the girls to the beach today, and I'm almost sure it's because she knew I was coming. She sits talking with another teacher, relaxed but keeping a eye on me. Yesterday, when I asked her if I could give Muna and Alice swim lessons, she acted all suspicious, like I was going to kidnap one of her girls. "You know you need to keep a healthy distance, right, Abdi?" she said. "You'll be leaving here soon, don't forget."

"I know," I said quickly. I promised her I'd be a gentleman, and eventually she said yes, but it's clear she's ready for me to move on.

Leaving, however, is looking more and more distant all the time. I thought I'd be at Maisha only a couple of days, but it's been a week, and no family has jumped up to welcome me with loving arms into their home so I can start school in a new place. I'm still staying at Sam's and she's still super-nice, but how long can I really live with her? She tells me not to worry about it.

I worry about it.

If I'm being honest, I don't actually want to move to a new place, or to a new school. I like Sam. I like staying at her apartment. I still have nightmares that I'm back sitting sniper, trying and failing to keep my friends from dying, but at least I wake up somewhere that feels safe. And Maisha is pretty cool. The teachers are good; the girls are nice. Even Mama Lisa's surveillance isn't that bad. She doesn't do it because she's mean, she's just protective. I get it.

I back up, the water surging around me. The waves are

calm, and it's clear enough that I can see my toes against the sand. It feels so good, and the sun is so hot, that I can't resist any longer. With a whoop I jump and twist around, diving into the coolness.

It's weird swimming with my injured hand, but not bad. I've taken my bandages off. The flesh around my nubs is stretched tight and pink, but the infection is pretty much gone, and the nurse says it's healing just fine. And underwater, I barely even notice the ringing in my ear.

After swimming five or six meters I turn around, swim back and burst up. Alice and Muna still look skeptical when I rub my eyes and grin in their direction, but while I've been under, they've both come farther out. Alice is up to her knees, and the tiny waves lap Muna's thighs.

"It's nice, huh?" I ask.

"What do we do now?" Muna runs her fingertips over the surface of the water nervously.

"The first thing is to get comfortable," I say. "That's how I taught my br . . . little brother how to swim."

I *did* teach my brothers, just not my real little brother, Faisal.

I taught them like my *aabo* taught me. Most of the Boys had grown up in or near Mogadishu and could splash around fine, but few could do more. The best of them could dog-paddle. Poorly. To really be good in the water, they had to first learn not to flail. You can't be afraid of the water, but you have to respect its power, my dad would say. And then he'd tell me to go fetch a shell, pointing at the bottom. He'd make a game of it. I'd bring him little pink ones the size of twenty-shilling coins, or a certain kind of conch we would pry out with a knife and eat right there in the dhow. Some people, like my mother, think eating raw sea snails is nasty, but my dad loved them, and so I made an effort to choke down the slippery meat without gagging. He would close his eyes and grunt with pleasure as he chewed.

The best was when I'd find little pieces of broken china among the rocks and coral, because Aabo would get really excited. He said they were precious, remnants of an older age when wooden ships would sail to Somalia with loads of goods from India and China. He'd tell me in his history-major voice about how the captains would put rubble—including broken china— in their hulls to weigh them properly, and when they got to Mogadishu, they'd dump it in the port to make room for the things they were taking back.

Muna splashes me. Has she been calling my name?

"Um, okay. Do like this," I say, shaking myself.

I lean over until my face is underwater, stay that way until I can concentrate again. I come up with water beading off my hair into my eyes. "You have to blow bubbles out of your nose. That way the water won't get up it."

Both girls look at me like I'm crazy.

"Do you want to learn how to swim or not?"

Muna puts her hands on her hips, eyeing the surface. "Can I hold my nose?"

"Sure," I concede.

Alice watches Muna with a deep frown of worry. Muna starts to bend forward, her nose tightly clamped between her fingers, but doesn't make it very far. "My stomach is too big," she mumbles.

So we move in a little toward the shore, and she sinks down and steadies herself on her knees. "Hold my hand," she demands. She clenches my fingers in a grip like iron. Her skirts swirl around her. She pinches her nose shut and slowly puts her face in. She stops when the water is just below her scrunched-shut eyes.

"Your whole face." I try to ignore how intensely aware I am of her hand in mine. I've never held a girl's hand. My little sister's doesn't count. "Don't be scared," I say, as much to myself as her.

Her eyes pop open momentarily to glare at me, but then she keeps going, until the water covers her eyelashes and soaks the edge of her headscarf. Then she pulls up and lets out her breath in a huge *powah!* She wipes her eyes and grins at both Alice and me. "I did it!"

And even Alice smiles.

"I'M STARVING," Sam says, plunking down our take-out bags on the coffee table. I turn on the TV while she pulls Ethiopian food out.

"Me too," I say, inhaling the steam coming off the dishes. I'm extra hungry today after our swim lesson.

We dig in. Ethiopian's not Somali food, but it's close, and the smells are almost enough to make my eyes water along with my mouth.

"My mom made the best *canjeero*," I say, without thinking.

Dammit, Abdi. Nothing like thoughts of lost family members to make you suddenly and completely lose your appetite.

They're always coming out of nowhere: little snippets of my old life. It's like nothing is safe; everything reminds me of them. Stupid stuff like brushing my teeth or hearing a bird's call can knock me over. La-dee-dah, boom, here's a nice memory of your *hooyo* to punch you in the face.

Sam gives me a sympathetic smile. Her nose wrinkles, the old sunburn still peeling. "My mom was a terrible cook. She passed it on to me, as you can probably tell. My dad was okay, for never having set foot in a kitchen until they divorced." She goes quiet too.

"Sam?"

"Mmm?"

"What's the calendar for?"

She takes her time finishing the bite in her mouth. Pushes food around in the Styrofoam container. She doesn't look up at the photo of the basket of puppies or the days scratched off in red. "It's a countdown," she finally says, without meeting my eye.

"To what? You don't have to tell me if you don't want to," I add, when she hesitates.

"No, it's okay. It's kind of hard to ignore, huh?" She looks around her apartment, as if noticing for the first time that the calendar is the only thing she's hung on the walls. She tears off a tiny piece of *canjeero* but just holds it, thinking. "Remember how I said my mom was really religious? Well, when I was a kid, my parents followed a man who convinced them—all of us—that the world was about to end. Fire and floods and plagues and all that." She nods at the calendar. "On December sixteenth, this year. The beginning of the Apocalypse. Judgment. Doomsday."

I look from her to the calendar. "But do you believe . . ."

"No, I don't," she says firmly. "Not anymore. But I did."

I must still look confused, because she says, "He had everyone believing that the only way we would be saved from going to hell was if we did exactly what he said. Which included some very bad things. Or, well, letting him do some very bad things. To all of us."

I lower my eyes. I don't need her to tell me what. Her voice is steady, but I can tell it's because she's forcing it to be.

"My father took me away from that church when I was fifteen," she says. "But my mom stayed. And my brother. I haven't seen them in twelve years." She takes a breath, letting it out slowly. "I started counting down because . . . It's hard to explain, exactly, but I guess the best way to put it is that I'm counting down until it's *not* doomsday. If that makes sense."

She's rolling the *canjeero* between her fingers, making a sticky mess of it without really noticing. The look on her face says she's somewhere far away, in a different life.

"I want that day back," she finally says. "And I guess I'm hoping that once it comes and goes and the world doesn't end, maybe my mother and my brother will wake up. It's important to me, that day. But not for the reason *he* wanted it to be." She sits there for a second completely still, and then sort of shudders all over, like she's just woken up. She looks at me almost like she's surprised to see me sitting there. Half smiling, she says, "I shouldn't be telling you all this."

"Why?"

"Because it's unprofessional." She looks at the ball in her hand and puts it down. "Maybe don't mention it to anyone at Maisha, huh?"

"No, I won't," I say.

I look at the bright red circle on the sixteenth. Doomsday. One of the videos we watched at the Fort was of this imam who talked about Judgment Day, that it was close upon us, because doesn't the *hadith* say that it will happen at a time of great corruption and chaos? And wasn't that exactly what the world looked like at this very moment? We should be ready, unless we wanted to burn in hell. A lot of the guys were totally into it, especially those who sort of flirted with death anyway, the ones who maybe liked the idea of dying and joining their dead families.

I want that day back.

"What will you do?" I ask. "On the sixteenth?"

"I don't know, actually." She smiles a little. "The plan is just . . . to not die, I guess."

TWENTY-TWO

THEN: SEPTEMBER 1
THE FORT, SOMALIA

"Brother Da'ud!"

The shout comes from behind. I turn to see a lanky, big-toothed kid named Weli jogging toward me through the shadows of the acacias. He's out of breath and has to pause to grab his knees and pant asthmatically before he can talk.

"What's up, Weli?" I try not to sound impatient. I'm headed to lunch and I'm starving. Already guys are swarming the kitchen block, the food queue fifty deep.

Weli holds up a small knife and smiles like a kid who's won a prize. "I found this for you!"

"Uh, okay?"

He wipes sweat off his face and gestures with the knife at my feet. "Now you can . . . you know . . ." His expression is almost bashful.

I look down at myself, shake my head. "I can what?"

He lays the knife in my hand and leans forward to whisper, "Your trousers."

I look again. What? Am I not zipped up? Weli's face gives me no clues. Is this some sort of joke on the new kid? But Weli doesn't really seem like the joking sort.

His smile is starting to look strained. He rubs his sweaty hands together, shifting from one foot to another. I look at his trousers and realize his are cut high, the cuffs a good hand's width from the ground.

"You want me to cut my pants?" I ask, confused.

Just then a hand reaches out and takes the knife. "Hey, Weli, thanks for this, brother. Don't worry, I'll help him."

I turn to see the kid with one eye who brought me to see General Idris on my first day. He's in my unit, but I haven't seen much of him in the two weeks I've been here. He spends most of his time running errands for the General, and the rest of it in the garage, churning out IEDs. It takes me a second to dredge up his name. Bashir.

"Are you sure?" Weli frets. "I should—"

"No, go," Bashir says.

Weli's smile surges. "Thank you, brother." He bobs his head. "I just noticed his trousers were . . . and I wanted . . ."

"It's okay, man." Bashir gives Weli a friendly shake on the arm. "Go ahead to lunch. Peace be with you."

Relieved, Weli wishes us the same and walks toward the kitchen, his smile bright again.

Bashir watches him go, taking a drink from a soda bottle filled with water.

"What was that about?" I ask.

"He wants you to cut your pants off at the ankle, 'cause *'Whoever trails his garment on the ground out of pride, Allah will not look at him on Judgment Day.'"*

I look around and for the first time notice that most of the other guys are wearing their pants high.

"It means that you should take care of your stuff, you know, be grateful you have a garment and don't let it drag in the dirt. It's not supposed to be a guide for how to tailor your trousers, but . . ." He hands the bottle of water to me. I take a grateful swig. "But that dude would lick the Doctor's sweaty balls with a please and thank-you if he thought that's what God wanted him to do."

I spit up the water, glance around quick to see if anyone else has overheard.

"He'd make sure they were halal first, but yup."

I shake my head at him, trying not to laugh. "Man, how can you say shit like that? Aren't you all, like, here for the cause and stuff?"

Bashir scans the lunch crowd like he's looking for someone. "Sure," he says casually.

I watch him. The way he's said it makes my radar buzz. Something's off.

"Why are *you* here?" he asks.

Buzzing turns to alarm bells. "Um, the *Ummah* . . . and, you know, freedom. And stuff."

Nice, Abdi. Real slick. I'm opening my mouth to try to salvage my fumble when without warning, my stomach growls, loud as an angry lion. Bashir watches me clutch my belly and grins. He claps me on the shoulder. "Come on, I can get us lunch."

Not sure what else I can do, I let him steer me to the back of the kitchen shed, into the shade under the trees.

"You're Commander Khalid's brother, right?" Bashir asks.

"Yeah."

"Pretty lucky you landed here in the same place with him."

"I guess."

At the door of the shed Bashir shouts in, "Hey, beautiful, it's your backdoor man!"

A girl comes to the door, wiping her hands on a cloth. I'm pretty sure she's the same girl who served the Doctor and my brother and me that day, but it's hard to tell. She was wearing a *niqab* then, a full face veil. Behind her, two other girls bustle around steaming pots and piles of *canjeero*. The heat blasting out of the little concrete kitchen is enough to make me step back.

"Hey, ugly," the girl says. "Cutting line?"

"You bet," Bashir says. "Can I have a plate for two starving soldiers?"

"Look at you, asking special favors. When you gonna bring me that thing you've been promising?"

"It's coming, it's coming, sunshine. Patience."

She grunts but turns back into the dark and heat of the

kitchen, returning a few seconds later with a heaped-full plate of *canjeero* and stew. Two hard-boiled eggs, a treat, float in the juices. My mouth waters. It's twice the rations we normally get.

Bashir starts to reach for it, but she pulls back. "Don't play, ugly. It's really coming?"

"Would I play with the most beautiful woman on earth? Come on, we're starving."

"Who's your friend?" she asks, still not relinquishing the plate. "Is he going to tell on me and get me in trouble?"

"Don't be crazy, *habibi*," Bashir says. "You know I'm watching out for you."

She looks unconvinced, but lets Bashir take the food from her. "You're my sun and moon, Safiya."

"Kiss my ass," she replies, before disappearing into the kitchen again.

Still smiling, Bashir leads us to a spot under a tree, away from everyone else. He sets the plate down on the ground before us. He's still got me feeling all off balance, but I haven't seen this much food in ages. My hunger wins out, and I join him in the attack.

"You wanna know how I got this eye?" Bashir asks after a little while.

I pause, a bite halfway to my mouth.

"Come on, you know you're curious."

It's true. "How?"

Bashir takes another bite, swallows, then says, "The Doctor's my cousin."

145

"Oh?" I say, noncommittal. Great. That's the last thing I need, the Doctor's cousin taking an interest in me.

"Soldiers came looking for him at my house a couple of years back," Bashir says, talking and chewing at the same time.

"AMISOM?"

"Somali army, or special police or some shit. Anyway, he hadn't been home in ages, but they weren't hearing it. 'Where's the *hajji*? Where is he?!' Like they've got a hot tip that he's currently taking a dump in our outhouse. And we're all, like, 'Man, how are we supposed to know?' And when they can't find him, they get pissed. They decide to take my sister instead." He takes a sip of water. "Asha. Twelve years old."

I feel the food in my stomach start to harden.

"My brother tried to stop them, and they shot him cold dead. Bam. And then I get the brilliant idea that I can save Asha, so I jump on one of them. I'm all of, what, fourteen then? Dude puts his rifle up to knock me out of the way and the bayonet goes right into my eyeball, like chopping an onion." He holds a greasy finger up to his eye to demonstrate. He sits that way for a second and then drops his hands, chews thoughtfully. "I don't think he meant to do it. I think it probably freaked him out." He looks at the messy plate of food. "But they took Asha anyway. Never saw her again."

I can't stop staring at the scar over his eye. I have no idea what to say.

"That's why I came here," Bashir says. He takes another

piece of *canjeero* and scoops up more stew to shove into his mouth. "Have you been out on a mission yet?"

I shake my head. "Commander Yusuf says soon."

"You're excited about going."

No, because that's when Mr. Jones will find me, I think. But I can't say *that,* so instead I bob my head and say, "Yeah, man. I'm ready to actually get out there and kick some ass."

"You are, huh?"

I would have thought the answer would satisfy him, but his face stays blank. I can't read him at all.

"You come find me when you get back," he says. "Let me know how it goes."

"How it goes?"

"You'll see. You might not totally understand why you're here and how you feel about all this, but don't worry." He sucks oily red sauce off his fingers one by one. "You will."

TWENTY-THREE

"Abdi—a word, please."

Mama Lisa catches me between classes, the halls of Maisha echoing with chatter. Muna, who's walking with me from algebra to English, says, "I'll save you a seat," and I follow Mama Lisa back to her office.

"Come in and shut the door," Mama Lisa says, sitting down.

The office is small and cozy, wood paneled with a window overlooking the playground. On her desk is a computer, a tray stacked high with papers, pens and pencils in a mug, and a glass ball the size of a fist with swirly colors inside.

I take the chair opposite her, trying to keep from appearing nervous. "Yes, madam?"

"I wanted to check in on you," she says, folding her hands together and placing them on the desk. "How are you finding it here?"

"It's very good, madam."

She nods, agreeing. "Your classes? Are you understanding everything?"

"Yes, most of it. Algebra is hard, but I'm doing okay."

"And your classmates?" she asks, her eyes never leaving my face. "You seem to be making friends."

"Yes, madam."

"Sam tells me they haven't had much success in finding a foster family for you."

I drop my eyes. "No."

"It isn't your fault, Abdi. You know that, right?"

"Yes, madam," I say, the response a reflex more than anything else. Sam's been telling me the same thing for days.

Mama Lisa watches me for a moment longer, and then says, "Abdi, let me be honest. I was not happy about the prospect of Sam bringing you here."

I feel myself shrinking into my chair.

"But I agreed because the UN is an important partner for us, and because we thought it would only be for one day. And now it has been almost two weeks. You have kept your promise to be a gentleman, and I appreciate that. The UN is paying your tuition here, just like they do for all these girls, and until they find a home for you, we are glad to have you come to classes. But gentleman or no, I feel it is time we talked again. We must be clear on some things."

Her face is both kind and serious, and for the first time I

realize that Mama Lisa isn't really that old; it's just that her eyes make her seem that way.

"The mission of Maisha is to help girls," she says. "I realize that it is not just girls who suffer in war, but girls suffer disproportionately."

"Yes, madam." I find myself turning my good ear toward her.

"Maisha is a safe haven. For some of these girls, it is the first safe place they have ever known. Many of them have spent their whole lives just doing what they needed to do to survive, but here they can finally let their guard down a little. One day they will have to go back out into the world, which, as you and I both know, is not always a safe place. But for now, safety, peace and calm is what they need to heal. Do you understand?"

I nod again.

"Healing is a process, Abdi. A delicate one. It doesn't take much to disrupt it, to send someone back into a bad place—mentally, I mean."

"Madam, I . . ."

She lifts a hand to stop me. "I'm not accusing you of anything, Abdi. I just want to remind you that even friendship can be complicated. Sometimes it is difficult to keep a friendship from growing into . . . something else. Especially at your age."

Is she talking about Muna? She must be. But I don't like her like that. Muna's face appears very clearly in my mind, the way she looked under the sun with water beading on her cheeks. I mean, I'm not an idiot. I can see she's beautiful. Of course Mama Lisa assumes I'm into her. But I'm not sure I even know how to think about whether I like Muna like that. It's like that part of me that would have cared about wooing girls has gone missing. It's lost out there, somewhere in the desert between the Fort and Mogadishu, a scrap caught on a thorn bush.

What I do know is that the idea of not hanging out with Muna and Alice anymore feels like a kick straight to my gut. "Do I have to stop the swim lessons?"

Mama Lisa's face softens. "No, I don't think so. The swimming lessons have been good for the girls. But you must be very careful to remain appropriate."

"Madam, I swear it's not like that. I—"

"Again," Mama Lisa says, "I'm not accusing you. But my first duty is to these girls, and I would be remiss if I did not make myself one hundred percent clear." She leans across the desk. "Our girls have been through hell, and somehow, against all the odds, they have survived. They deserve a safe place to heal where, for a while, they don't have to worry about every interaction they have with a man. Do you understand me, Abdi?"

"Yes, madam."

"So be careful," she says. "Especially with one girl in particular that I think you're growing close to. Can you promise me that? Because if you can't, it may be time for you to leave."

"I promise," I tell her, searching her face for some sign that she believes me.

Mama Lisa settles back in her chair, watching me with those old, all-seeing eyes. "Thank you, Abdi. You may go."

"YOU'RE QUIET today," Sam says on the way home from Maisha.

She nudges her car forward a few inches. The traffic is terrible, and we're stuck at an intersection near a new shopping plaza. Six lanes of cars plus a steady throng of pedestrians are all trying to push through a haze of construction dust. In the middle of the road a sweating traffic cop bleats stubbornly on his whistle and waves his hands like he's trying to put out a fire. A fine white powder has settled into the wrinkles of his shirt, and everyone ignores him.

It's hot, and kids are selling soda in plastic baggies and Chinese folding fans and groundnuts in twisted paper funnels. They step easily through the press of metal, trot alongside slow-moving cars' open windows to make deals, dodge between bumpers to scout for customers, always a hair's breadth from getting squashed. I recognize a couple of them from sleeping in the alley near Kenyatta Street.

"Sorry, Sam," I say.

"It's nothing to be sorry for," she says, glancing over. "Everything okay at Maisha?"

I think of Mama Lisa's warning, and how after the talk I couldn't quite convince myself that I *don't* like Muna, not like that. Why did Mama Lisa even have to bring all that up? It's like she put the idea of liking Muna into my mind. It's her fault I'm all confused now. "Yes," I lie.

We creep forward half a meter. A boy appears suddenly at my window, and I lurch back. Then I see he's just offering me a banana. "Ten shillings," he says, his voice muffled through the glass. By the time I catch my breath and shake my head, he's already gone, alert for a better customer.

"So," Sam says brightly, like she's trying to ignore my twitchiness, "no new news about a foster family. You're going to have to put up with me for a little longer."

I keep looking out the window, scanning the other faces, one by one. Not a Boy. Not a Boy. Possibly a Boy. "I like staying at your place," I say.

She darts a look at me, her cheeks going pink like she's almost embarrassed, but maybe a little bit pleased too. After a second she says, "Hey, I know what we should do instead of sitting like dummies in this traffic."

"What?"

"Let's stop at Paradise Island and get pizza. It's the new mall they're adding onto over there," she says. "We can hang out until rush hour is over. Yeah?"

I straighten in my seat to see where she's pointing. "Paradise Island. That's where Maisha is going next month for a field trip." I think about telling her that I'm teaching Muna and Alice how to swim, but then I wonder if she'll react like Mama Lisa. I decide not to.

"Well, let's go check it out," Sam says, turning the wheel and looking for a way out of the traffic. "Bet we can even find a DVD of . . . what was that show you like?"

"*CSI: Miami*," I say. It takes me a second to realize that a smile has snuck onto my face.

Paradise Island is like nothing I've ever seen. It's so clean, so enormous, so full of color and lights and sound that when we walk through the door, I just stand there, staring with my mouth open until someone behind me pushes past, grumbling.

"This way," Sam says, once we're through the metal detector. She takes her bag back from the security guard, who's riffled idly through the contents.

We pass shops that twinkle with goods: jewelry, made-in-China fashions, a wall of televisions, high-end trinkets and beads for the tourists. In the center courtyard under a glass atrium is a man playing piano and a brand-new Land Cruiser that people observe solemnly with their hands fisted behind their backs. Looking up, I see that there are two more levels above this one. A big blue sign points toward "Splash Land! The most fun under the sun!"

Sam leads me in the opposite direction, down one of the broad halls with shops lining both sides. My yo-yo is in my pocket, and I find myself gripping it. The mall is crowded with shoppers: mothers on their phones dragging their uniformed kids on after-school errands, kids on their phones looking bored. Along with the Kenyans, there are Europeans and Asians. Even though they're obviously of different nationalities, they all seem similar. There's something in the way they walk, the sparkle of the rings on their fingers, a pudginess around the waist: it's a sheen of wealth. They take it for granted that they are entitled to be here. Like this is the most natural state of being imaginable.

The Doctor would hate this place.

"Let's sit outside," Sam says when we get to the food court, pointing at the terrace.

The table we find overlooks the ocean. A metal gate surrounds the dining area, separating Paradise Island from the beach and the rest of the real world. The sea is a strange color in the afternoon light, some mix between gray and pink and green, and as soon as I set eyes on it, I realize how tense walking through the mall has made me. All those people. All those lights and sounds. I let go of my death grip on the yo-yo and take my hand out of my pocket. I try to relax my shoulders.

Glancing around, I see a guy standing on the beach beyond the gate. His hands are thumbed through the loops on his waistband, and he watches people eat on the terrace. He looks Somali, thin face, paler skin. Something about him tugs a thread in my memory. I stare. Do I know him? Have I seen that face before?

He catches me looking at him, and a slow smile spreads over his face.

Oh, shit.

A waiter materializes at our side, blocking my view.

I try to peer around him without being too obvious as Sam orders pizza and sodas. By the time she's finished and he moves, the boy has disappeared. I look up and down the beach, twisting in my chair, but it's no use. He's gone.

"Everything okay?" Sam asks.

It's nothing, Abdi. Just some kid.

But that smile. It was so familiar.

"Yeah," I say. "I'm fine. Just hungry." It's a lie. All my appetite is gone.

It wasn't one of the Boys. He probably wasn't even looking at me. He was probably looking at the hot girl two tables over. I've mistaken seeing familiar faces on Sangui City's sidewalks before. That's why I ran and got caught by the police last time. *You're being paranoid,* I tell myself. But I can't shake the creeped-out feeling the guy's given me.

Sam leans back in her chair, sighing happily. "This certainly beats traffic."

I try to breathe normally, to copy her and lean back, but my body keeps going rigid. I can't keep myself from eyeing the beach, and now the waiters, the customers. I scan the mall's rooflines, where a sniper would sit.

"Sure you're okay?" Sam asks.

"Sorry."

She pushes her sunglasses up onto her head so she can look me in the eye. "You've got to stop apologizing for everything, Abdi."

I open my mouth, but catch the *sorry* before it slips out.

"It's safe here," Sam says, after a beat. "There are guards at all the entrances and on the beach. Metal detectors, the works."

I cut my eyes at her. How does she know I'm worried about stuff like that?

"One day, if you want to, you can tell me about what's making you nervous," she says. "Sometimes it helps to talk."

I fiddle with the edge of my shirt. Because I don't want to be rude, I nod.

"I mean, only if you want to. But it does help."

I take another look around. Sam's right. There are walls surrounding the mall. There's a gate before the beach, guarded by a man in uniform. But I can still see at least five places where the security is lax, where a group of guys moving fast and with purpose could get through easily.

"A cafe outside like this wouldn't be safe in Mogadishu," I say. My ear starts to ring. I look back out at the ocean while I wait for it to stop.

Sam puts her hand on my arm above the missing fingers. "You're safe, Abdi," she says softly. "You really are."

I try to force a smile again, but it's no use. "People would want to attack it. Rob it."

She waits for me to keep talking. I pull my hand away slowly and lay it flat on my thigh, my three remaining fingers making a sort-of peace sign. Which is ironic, to say the least.

Sam puts her hands back in her lap too. She watches me for a little while. "Did you ever see anything like that?"

I feel the old fear again, like a shell coating my arms and chest, making it hard to breathe. "Yes," I say, barely a whisper. Sam keeps watching me, but I can't meet her eye.

"You don't have to talk about it, Abdi. Not if you're not ready. But . . ." She frowns, looks out at the ocean. "I know what it's like to be scared of something for so long that it seems like it's all there is. And I know how much it helps to talk about it, even if it's embarrassing or painful. Sometimes telling another person what's bothering you can be like taking a weight off that you didn't even know you were carrying. If you ever want to talk—about anything—there are people whose job it is to listen. Counselors. People who wouldn't judge you. Or you can talk with me if you want."

"They have counselors at Maisha," I say.

"Exactly. Someone like that."

I look at her from the corner of my eye. "You talked to a counselor about your family and the religious stuff?"

"Yeah, I did." She's turned to face me squarely. "Shitty things happen to good people, Abdi. For no good reason at all. And it's not your fault. Sometimes it's easy to forget that. Sometimes we need to be reminded."

I look out at the ocean. Sam says she wouldn't judge me. But she doesn't know what I've done. It's one thing to have stuff done to you. It's another to be the one who does it. If I told her everything, would she really still let me stay in her house? Eat her food? Watch TV with her on her couch?

No way.

I hunch down in my seat, cross my arms over my stomach. Once my father told me that the way to keep from getting queasy in a boat is to watch the horizon line. I stare out at it, a separation of water and sky that stretches out to infinity, and wait for the ache to pass.

TWENTY-FOUR

THEN: SEPTEMBER
THE FORT, SOMALIA

Days go by.

Soon a week, then two, three.

I see Dahir only at mealtimes, but he sits apart, with the other commanders. We sleep in different bunks. He's always with his unit, and I'm always with mine. It's not like we have free time. There's no opportunity to get him alone and talk again. Even if we did, I'm not sure what I'd say. He looks at me like I'm a stranger.

Thoughts of my family are always with me, like a low buzzing in my ears, but I just can't figure out how to turn that feeling into something productive. When I'm doing the exercises, the prayers, the buzz sometimes even goes away.

And I hate it, but every day it becomes a little easier to answer to the name Da'ud, a little harder to remind myself why I'm here. Or even where I am. Most of the kids here are teenagers, and sometimes this place just seems like some sort of demented boarding school.

The guys here aren't at all what I'd expected. For boys who are supposed to be hard-core extremists, they are extraordinarily . . . well, ordinary. At least in my unit, which has the newest soldiers. There's pudgy mama's boy Ahmed, and giraffe-kneed Gari and toothless Toothless. Samir with his big ears and Jabir, who farts when he laughs. I'm not sure if those are their real names or not. Some of them I swear I've seen before, maybe even played football in the streets or swum at Lido Beach with. I'd ask, but we're not allowed to talk about where we're from, or what our clan is, or any of that stuff, because apparently we're all one big, happy Somali nation. Tribal politics have no place here. We're supposed to be focused, a brotherhood. Just Somali. All equal. Good Muslims who love our country. To suggest that we're here for any other reason is blasphemy.

You hear things, though. Some guys were rounded up like Dahir. Some chose to join after their families were killed or went missing—at least as a jihadi you know you'll get fed, and you might even get revenge. A handful signed up because they're super-religious. They want to make sure they blow their noses exactly like the prophet did, and get stomachaches if they can't figure it out: was it the left nostril first or the right? They don't question orders; they just obey.

Some of the guys saw people they loved die and now they want to kill. Some of them saw people they loved die and now they want to die. Those ones seem relieved when none of the commanders try to talk them out of it, when they get pats on the back, assurances of heaven. We have a couple of guys like that in our unit, and you have to treat them carefully. They're as unpredictable as the white powder Bashir puts in his bombs. One second they're hugging your neck and calling you "dear brother." The next they've got a knife at your throat, spittle flying, eyes rolling, wanting to know why you're looking at them like that. It's like whatever horrible shit they saw has turned into a virus inside them. It makes their heads fuzzy, and it's just itching to jump from the point of that knife into the next warm body.

The Doctor comes and goes. When he's around, we gather together after dinner and build a fire, and it almost feels festive. He talks to us. Not like we're children, like most adults do, but like we actually have brains between our ears.

"When I was a teenager," he says, the fire crackling and dancing, "the fighting was all along clan lines. That was after the government was toppled in the early nineties. Majority clans kept their own militias and they'd fight back and forth for territory, killing anyone who got in their way. They were the warlords. They ruled by the gun and the fist, and cared only for making themselves rich. There was no government to speak of.

"It was into this chaos that the Islamic Courts Union was born. Good, brave men who were fed up with bloodshed banded together and began fighting back against the gangs." His eyes sparkle in the light. "Fighting and *winning*, *Alhamdulillah*.

Ten years after the chaos began, they put an end to the age of the warlords. They brought peace to the streets. They punished the wicked and upheld the righteous in the name of God."

He stops. His forehead creases.

"But this, an Islamic State, made the Western powers nervous. The Americans couldn't abide an Islamic government. Even if the Courts were bringing peace and justice, protecting widows and orphans. They could not stand the idea. So what did they do?"

We wait. I know what happened; my father told me all this history, but still I find myself leaning in, hanging on every word.

"The Americans joined up with the Somali government in exile, the same men who were too afraid to even set foot in their country, and instead 'ruled' it while living out of luxury hotels in Kenya. Then they all joined up with the Ethiopians, our Christian neighbors who have hated Somalia for centuries. And the Ethiopians came in on their tanks with their guns, destroying the peace the Courts had worked so carefully to build. They raped, murdered, looted. I saw it with my own eyes. I was a doctor then, and I tell you we did not have enough beds in the hospitals for the wounded. The patients lay dying side by side on the floor, and their blood ran down the hallways in rivers." His eyes shine with pain and rage. "That was when I knew I could not stand by. That was when I left to fight the invaders with my Shabaab brothers on the streets of Mogadishu. We were the army of the Islamic Courts."

Sparks from the fire shoot out and up, lost in the stars. "We took the city back from the Ethiopians, and there was peace again. But . . ." He sighs. "It was short lived. The same thing has happened again. The Western powers found another foreign army, AMISOM this time, and they hit us when we were still recovering. The Courts were destroyed and we few Shabaab are all that is left.

"The Westerners propped up new politicians—the same tribal warlords we fought so hard to depose! And now those Westerners turn a blind eye when these politicians rob from the mouths of children just to buy villas and Land Cruisers and take shopping trips to Dubai.

"*That* is who is running our country, brothers." He looks around the silent circle. "And their mentality is spreading. Now I ask you, when a plant is diseased, do you go through and try to cut off all the small leaves that are infected?" He surveys the rapt faces staring up at him. "No, you have to pull it out by the roots. You have to burn it so the disease cannot spread and kill the whole crop. That is what we are doing, my brothers. We must fight differently. We must fight smarter to rid our country of all that is twisted and corrupt. But we will win, brothers. We will destroy all that threatens the good of our nation, and use the ashes to fertilize new shoots."

The fire reflecting in his eyes tingles to my bones.

I know there's more to the fighting than what he's saying. I remember how it was when Al Shabaab controlled the city.

I remember how they stoned a man who was drunk, killed him right there on the street where he lay. I remember how they took Dahir and all those other kids, forced them to fight. But still, when I listen to the Doctor, all of that starts to blur, and the future he paints begins to take shape and become the more real-seeming thing. I mean, he's right about the politicians. It's true that they're rich and the rest of us are poor. The government doesn't seem interested in fixing things. Dads have to leave to work in Saudi Arabia because they can't be history professors or even fishermen. The Doctor says we can change things, make them better. That once we've taken back Mogadishu, we'll share the wealth and all the mothers and fathers who left will come home.

Is this how it happened to Dahir? Maybe it was impossible to listen to the Doctor for three years without either going crazy or letting himself start to believe that maybe things could be better if Al Shabaab was given a chance again. It's not like anyone around here is dumb enough to question what the Doctor says. No one's going to raise their hand and ask him how, back when Al Shabaab actually was in charge, shooting people in the street for playing soccer or wearing lipstick was any way to show God's mercy.

I try to remember all the stuff I learned in *duqsi*, like *God loves not the aggressor,* and how jihad isn't supposed to be about killing. That it's about becoming a better person first, and then fighting oppression and injustice peacefully. But all we hear is how great things are going to be when we drive the invaders and the warlords back out. We're told again and again that what we're doing is noble, that we're fighting just like Mohammed and his men did, and we're only trying to take back our country from the oppressors who took it first. And doesn't that make it a righteous war?

I tell myself I won't end up brainwashed. Of course I won't.

But what if Dahir told himself the exact same thing?

The only time I don't feel totally confused, anxious, or exhausted is when we swim. In the water, for a little while, nothing bad can touch me, and sometimes it feels like maybe I really could just float away. Even if it's one of the days when the General comes down to observe, his psycho I-might-kill-you-I-might-not stare doesn't bother me so much. It's like being in the ocean is a shield. Could be it's because I know he actually *can't* reach me once I'm in the water. The General watches us, but he never gets in.

"He doesn't know how to swim," Bashir told me one day while we were treading water. He kept his voice low. "I overheard him telling Yusuf. Yusuf offered to teach him, but the General said no. I think he was embarrassed."

"That's dumb. Everyone who knows how to swim had to learn at some point."

Bashir shrugged. "How would that look, though? You're the Butcher and your men see you flailing around all helpless and shit in the water?" He shook his head. "Can't show any weakness if you're the General."

I watched General Idris, the Butcher, from the corner of my eye. I watched him watching us.

We finished swimming, went back for prayers.

One day turns into another, all so similar that it hardly seems possible to keep track of how many have passed.

I get no closer to figuring out how to rescue my family.

We drill. Shoot the figures painted on the walls.

We eat.

Sleep.

Pray.

Repeat.

Repeat, repeat, repeat.

TWENTY-FIVE

We're headed into the rising sun, toward Mogadishu.

Only the best and brightest of the 106s for this, our first mission: fat Ahmed, scrawny Gari, one-eyed Bashir, snaggly Toothless, half-brained Weli of the short pants, and me.

Gari won't stop picking his nose—it's some sort of disgusting nervous twitch. Weli keeps exclaiming, "God is wonderful!" with every tree, rock, or hole in the ground we pass on our drive. I'm not sure why. Ahmed is carsick. Hell, we're not even dressed in our military *khameez*. We've been given a mismatched assortment of clothes and flip-flops. We look like remedial students on holiday, not battle-hard militia.

All of our weaponry has been taken away, which is probably a good thing. While we were still on guard riding through the bush, Toothless kept dropping his gun on the truck bed, making us all scream and swat at him while he lisped, "Thorry, thorry!"

Honestly. My half-blind eighty-year-old *ayeyo* is more in-timidating than this crew.

Which Bashir says is exactly what General Idris wants. To-day we need to blend in.

The General is sitting with us in the back of the truck. Commander Yusuf got sick at the last minute, so the General stepped in to lead us, which has pretty much quadrupled everyone's anxiety. He's walking us through the plan. As far as secret missions go it seems pretty lame, but since none of us except Bashir have actually been on a mission yet, I get why the General doesn't trust us with anything harder.

"You, Ahmed, tell me your route," the General says.

Ahmed, sweating and stammering under the General's eye, says, "I—I go first to Sheikh Muhumed's shop."

"And what's the code phrase?"

"I ask to buy toothpicks. And, uh, a bus ticket."

"To?"

Ahmed closes his eyes, thinking hard.

General Idris swears colorfully about the merits of Ahmed ever being brought forth from his mother's anatomy. "To Liboi, son!"

"Liboi! Yes, sir!" Ahmed shouts.

"And then?"

"He takes me down into the tunnel under his shop and shows me the supplies. And I carry them, sir."

"Where?" the General demands, squinting.

Bashir mouths the answer to him behind the General's back.

"To tunnel 50," Ahmed says, glancing between Bashir and the General. "I follow tunnel 15, go left at tunnel 48, then right into tunnel 50." He picks at his sweaty shirt, trying to discreetly air his armpits.

"Good," the General grunts, and Ahmed practically melts with relief onto the truck bed.

"General Idris, sir? What if someone else comes in wanting toothpicks and a bus ticket to Liboi?"

"Idiot," the General replies to Gari. "Sheikh Muhumed doesn't sell bus tickets. He's a grocer. Only a *doqon* like you would go in there asking for them. Now, tell me *your* route . . ."

We've all got our different pickup locations and delivery points, each somewhere along the intricate web of would-be sewers that Al Shabaab commandeered and added onto. I'd always heard the rumors about Al Shabaab being in the sewers-turned-tunnels (after the government fell in the nineties with them only half built), but I thought it was something parents told kids to keep them from playing down there. Apparently not.

"What are the supplies for?" I ask, trying to sound casual.

The General turns on me, his face a twist of suspicion. "Not your concern."

"My cousin in Unit 102 said they are for a special event," Weli says brightly.

"Shut your mouth!" the General snaps, and Weli does,

burying his head between his shoulders like a turtle. The General rounds slowly on the rest of us. "No one is to talk about this mission, or any mission, got that?"

"Yes, sir!" We all lower our eyes and cower appropriately, but my brain is ticking. A special event. Is that the "something big" Mr. Jones wanted me to find out about? My stomach does a somersault at the thought. Is one of Mr. Jones's henchmen going to find me in town and demand to know what I've found out? I was supposed to get myself on a mission into Mog when I knew something, but I've got nothing. Less than nothing. What will Jones do when I tell him I've got no answers? But maybe they don't know that Al Shabaab is stocking the tunnels. Maybe telling him about this mission will be enough information to free my family.

I run over my own plan for pickup and delivery in my mind—*left into 78, right at 61, left at 57, drop off in tunnel 55*—until it takes on the feeling and cant of a prayer. Until there's no room in my head for anything else.

We're dropped off in pairs, Weli and me on a sleepy street corner about a kilometer from where we need to be. It's as far into the city as the General will go. Any closer and Bashir says there will be AMISOM checkpoints, and the General's face is on too many "Wanted" posters. And besides, a bunch of boys in the back of a pickup doesn't look real great, especially if a soldier gets curious and finds our gun cache behind the driver's seat.

"Be back here by *Asr* prayers," the General warns us. "Don't make me wait. If you're late, you'll be considered a deserter. What happens to deserters and traitors, boys?"

"They die like dogs, sir!" we chorus.

The truck pulls away in a cloud of dust. Rubbing grit from our eyes, we start walking toward the city center. For the first time ever, the traffic and noise and people feel chaotic, hectic. The solitude of the Fort has hardly been relaxing, but you get used to the order and routine.

It's funny what you notice when you've been away from a place for a while. This isn't my neighborhood, but I know it. Like a lot of town, there are bombed-out buildings everywhere, and lean-to shelters covered in plastic, streets rutted and clogged with old trash. Women sell vegetables in front of their houses. Kids play. Old men in *koofis* sit on front stoops and yell at the kids. But today what I notice most is all the construction. Wooden scaffolding clings to new buildings, and men cling to the scaffolding. They hammer and hoist and saw and plaster with an urgency that seems impossible in the pounding heat.

Was there this much new stuff going up in my neighborhood? It feels like those times when a drenching rain follows a long drought and the whole desert explodes in fuzzy new growth. People are actually trying to make something of the city, not just huddle inside and survive. Al Shabaab is gone, so there are no gun battles on the street, no rockets whistling through the air, and people are rebuilding with a sort of energy that's almost frightening.

And then I realize, actually, they *are* here. *I'm* Al Shabaab. *I'm* here. And suddenly, even though I'm dressed in normal clothes, and even though I know I'm not actually one of Al Shabaab's true soldiers, it doesn't matter. I feel like I've got the word *terrorist* stamped on my forehead, like everyone we pass surely knows where Weli and I have come from.

We part ways at Sodonka Road. Weli heads for his rendezvous point, and I make my way toward a photographer's studio on Howlwadag Street, where I'm supposed to ask for washing powder and a Fanta. As I hurry through the side streets, I wonder if maybe Mr. Jones won't even try to find me today. Do I want him to, or not? On the one hand, thinking about him makes me desperate for news of my family. But I want to see Mr. Jones about as much as I want to stick my hand down a cobra's hole.

I jump over an algae-green puddle that smells of sewage and make a wrong turn down a dead-end alley. I circle back, deciding to keep closer to the main street I'm following east. I have a couple of hours to accomplish my mission, which should be plenty, but I'd rather not risk being late and dying like a dog.

The closer I get to my destination, the more tingly my neck gets, as if the chip is being activated or something, like in a sci-fi movie. If Mr. Jones doesn't make contact before I go in, it'll be too late. Maybe I—

"Hey, boy."

The voice sends me leaping sideways, nearly getting caught in a sheet hanging on a laundry line.

"Hello!" I shout at the man standing in a doorway, managing to sound both cheerful and terrified.

His posture is relaxed and he's idly chewing a *miswak* twig, but his eyes are alert, locked on me. "What's your name, kid?"

I look around, but the alleyway is empty except for a hobbled white goat nibbling at trash. "Who are you?" I ask.

The man's mouth lifts into a half grin. "Our friend sent me. He wants to talk to you."

"Friend?" I ask. It can only be Mr. Jones. But what if this is a trap? What if the General planted this guy here to test me?

"I'm supposed to take you to him." He pushes himself out of the doorway, and for the first time I notice he's wearing good shoes, nicer shoes than anyone who lives in this neighborhood should have. Not shoes, actually—boots. He's dressed casually, but his biceps strain at his sleeves. With a build and boots like that, he's got to be Somali army. Maybe even secret police. "Let's go," he says.

I retreat a pace. "What does he want to talk about?"

The man deftly spits fibers from the stick onto the ground. "Price of lightbulbs."

NICE BOOTS leads me to a door in the alley behind a welding shop. He gives a fancy knock, and a guard with a gun lets us into the compound. There's little space to maneuver through the jumbles of metal that rise up like skeletons, and we twist our way to a concrete-block outbuilding. When he opens the door, I find Mr. Jones already there, sitting in the only chair in the room. The building has no windows. Only a small LED lantern sheds a dull light.

Jones motions for me to sit on a mat on the floor before him. In English and without preamble he asks, "What have you got for me?"

"Hello. *As-salamu alaykum,*" I say, feeling, as I sit, like I'm a servant addressing a king. It all seems staged, like that's exactly how Jones wants me to feel.

He looks down at me. "I know you haven't got much time, Abdiweli, and I've been waiting. Let's just get to it. What have you found out?"

I shift, thinking about what I've decided on the walk with Nice Boots. "I—I want to see my family first."

"That depends on what you've found out."

I shake my head. "Let me talk to them, at least. How do I know they're not dead?"

Mr. Jones's face finally changes. He smiles slowly and shrugs, as if it makes no difference to him. He nods at Nice Boots. "Call them," he says in Somali.

Nice Boots takes a phone out of his pocket. Jones lights a cigarette, the spark from the match throwing his shadow onto the wall behind him. For a second it looks like a monster hovering over his shoulder.

"Hello?" Nice Boots yells into the phone. "Yah! Hello! Put the mother on."

My heart goes to my throat, watching as Nice Boots pushes a button so the phone is on speaker. There's a rustling and a long silence, but finally I hear a cracked voice. It's soft but unmistakable. "Hello?"

My mouth falls open at the same time tears shoot without warning from my eyes. "Hooyo?" I say, scrambling toward Nice Boots. The other soldier grabs my arm to keep me back.

"Abdi? Abdi?"

It takes all I've got to keep the sob from my voice. "Hooyo, are you okay? Did they hurt you?"

"Abdi! *Alhumdulillah!* I thought you were—"

Nice Boots punches a button and the line goes dead.

I blink, uncomprehending.

Then, before I know what I'm doing, I scream, "You asshole!" and lunge for Nice Boots while the guy with the gun wrestles my arms behind my back. "Get her back on the line! Get her back on!"

Nice Boots sneers at me and tucks the phone back in his pocket.

"Tell him to call her back! Now!" I yell at Mr. Jones.

"Sit down, Abdiweli," Mr. Jones says.

I am shaking all over, and I can feel that my cheeks are wet, but all my fear has burned away in rage. I writhe in the gunman's arms.

"Sit," Mr. Jones says, his voice still soft, but with an edge now. "I don't have time for theatrics, and neither do you. Your family is alive; there's your proof. I'm not the enemy here. Al Shabaab is. Let's remember that and stay focused on what we need to do. Now. *Sit. Down.*"

It takes me another few seconds, but finally I stop resisting and let the gunman push me back to the ground in front of Mr. Jones. I am shaking from head to toe.

It dawns on me suddenly that over the last few days I've basically stopped trying to think of new ways to rescue my family. Guilt and shame flame in my gut. I've been sleepwalking, letting the exhaustion of the exercises and everything else distract me. Hooyo's life, Ayeyo's, Hafsa's, the twins'—they all hang by a thread over an abyss.

I am that thread. The only thing between them and death.

And I'm failing them. I'm letting them slip away.

"Tell me what you've found and they'll be fine, Abdiweli."

I try to pull my thoughts together, to push words past the echo of my mother's voice: *Abdi?* "I—I'm here on a mission," I finally choke out.

"Yes, we know that," Mr. Jones snaps. "Have you found out anything about the attack Al Shabaab is planning?"

I breathe through my nose. *Steady, Abdi.* "I'm supposed to pick up supplies and move them into position."

Mr. Jones pushes his glasses up on his nose and waves at Nice Boots to take notes. "What supplies, what position?"

"I haven't gotten them yet, I don't know," I say, trying not to show my relief that this information seems to be going over well. "But I'm supposed to take them into the sewer tunnels under the city."

Mr. Jones doesn't seem surprised that the Boys have tunnels. So much for using that as leverage.

"Where?" he asks.

"Tunnel 55."

"Where is that?"

I look at him, wary. "I don't know. The tunnels are numbered. I start at a shop on Howlwadag Street, and when I get down there, I make my way to tunnel 55." I trace a line on the mat between us like a map. "Follow tunnel 78, go right at 61, left at—"

"But where is it?" Mr. Jones interrupts me. "In terms of the city? What is tunnel 55 under?"

"I don't know."

He waits. "What else have you got?"

"I—I— What do you mean?"

He steeples his fingers together and presses them against his lips. "I mean, the things you were supposed to find out. The things that will keep your family alive. I mean . . ." he says, ticking them off, "*what* is going to happen? *Where* is it going to happen? And *when*?"

My throat goes dry. "The 'where' is tunnel 55—"

I hear Nice Boots sucking his teeth in disgust. "This boy don't know nothing," he mutters in English.

"You don't even know what you're going to transport when you get there," Mr. Jones says. "It could be food, blankets, porn mags. I need to know where the attack will happen. You're talking about resupply caches." He leans back. "I'm disappointed, Abdiweli. Don't you even care what happens to your family?"

This is not going well. Jones seems to know more about my mission than even I do. "Mr. Jones," I try, "I'm just a soldier. I'm not somebody special. They don't tell soldiers anything."

The reflection in Jones's glasses flickers. "But I didn't send you in there to just be a soldier. Your brother *is* there, and he *is* someone special, am I right?"

"Yes. He's a commander."

"So I need for you to talk to Commander Dahir," Mr. Jones says.

"But he won't—"

"I don't care how you do it, Abdiweli. But your family is counting on you. Next time we talk, you have to give me something. What you've brought today . . ." He sighs. "It's nothing we don't already know. Honestly, I'm not sure it's even worth sending you back in. You don't seem motivated."

My mother's voice wavers in my ears. She sounded so small. Is she sick? In pain? What have they done to her? "No," I say, "I am. I'll try harder. Please."

Jones extinguishes his cigarette on the floor, rubbing the butt to nothing with his toe. "Look, I wasn't going to tell you this today because it will just make you nervous, but I think you deserve to know."

I go still. "Know what?"

He folds his hands in his lap. "I've gotten word from my

superiors that they want to cut this operation short. They tell me I'm wrong to think you'll deliver. Looks like they might be right."

"Cut it short?" I frown. "Does that mean you wouldn't need me anymore?" As soon as the words are out of my mouth, I get a bad feeling. It can't possibly be that simple.

"Well, no. I suppose I wouldn't."

I wait.

He shrugs lightly. "They wouldn't even need me. Drones are all piloted remotely." He mimes pointing a gun, pulling the trigger. "It's actually a lot like a video game."

My vision tunnels as what he's saying sinks in. "I thought you didn't want to resort to bombing. That's what you said."

"What I said was that I want to stop an attack on civilians. We'd like to bring the Doctor and the General in, but if we can't, we'll do the next best thing. Believe me, no one is going to cry over dead enemy combatants."

My brain pushes through the military-speak. "You mean you'll bomb the Fort, and it's okay if everyone inside dies."

"We'd kill every last one of them, Abdiweli, if that's what it takes."

I stare at the ground in front of me, feeling my body start to sway. Enemy combatants. Yeah, right. He means Toothless and Gari, Weli and Bashir. Me, if I'm still there. I feel my lungs start to ache, like I can't get enough air into them. I have to stop myself from clawing at my throat. *Keep it together, Abdi. Tell him what he needs to hear.* I force the words out. "How long do I have? To get you the information?"

Jones lights another cigarette. He takes a long drag, making a show of considering the question. "I'd say I need something solid within the next week. After that . . . no promises."

I manage to nod. Stand up on shaky legs. "I'll do it."

He smiles, smoke running out through his teeth. "Good boy."

TWENTY-SIX

Traffic is especially bad this morning on the way to Maisha. The police stop us at a roadblock as we're headed into the Ring. And then they stop us again when we've barely gone a half kilometer.

"What's going on?" Sam glances at the dashboard clock as we're waved through the second one. She flicks on the car radio, searching until we find a news report.

"... *drove a car packed with explosives to the entrance of the popular bar. It detonated at 11:29 p.m., killing the driver and three civilians and injuring more than a dozen others. Al Shabaab has claimed responsibility for the attack in an online statement. Sangui City police are conducting house-to-house operations to track down those believed linked to the killers, amid growing concern that the government is not doing enough to protect citizens from terrorism ...*"

I can't move. All I can think is *shitshitshitshit*. Nothing beyond that. Nothing articulate. Just a dull, animal-like fear, a paralysis. I manage a few monosyllables when Sam gives me concerned looks and wants to talk, but that's it. When she drops me off, she says, "Abdi, do you want . . . ," but I mumble that I need to go or I'll be late for first period and jump out of the car. I don't look back until I hear the crunch of her retreating car wheels on gravel.

Algebra is buzzing with news of the bombing. I look for Muna, but she's not there. Several of the other Somali girls whisper about getting phone calls from friends and relatives, telling them about police banging on doors in Eastleigh last night, knocking people around and threatening to haul them off to jail if they didn't pay bribes. One girl sits quietly with a deadened expression, and when asked what's wrong, she says she got a phone call from her brother's roommate. Her brother didn't have money to bribe the police and had been taken in. She hasn't had any word from him since.

English is the same. Still no Muna. I wonder if she's sick. I make my way through the morning like a robot, not hearing anything the teachers say.

At tea break I notice that the cook has left her newspaper on the stool outside where she sits to peel vegetables. While she's busy, I quietly pick up the paper and take it behind the gardener's shed where no one can see me. Sunbirds chatter and scold over my head.

In big, bold letters, the paper shouts "TERRORIST AT-TACK: 3 Dead in Brutal Bombing." There's a grainy photo of an Al Shabaab Boy wearing a *keffiyeh* and brandishing a gun, and another picture farther down the page of the outside of the club where the bombing happened: smoke and rubble and bloodied bystanders are lit up with camera flash. Politicians are quoted. They rumble about quick arrests and swift, sure justice. The only other story on the front page carries the headline "Is Refugee Deportation the Answer?"

"Did they catch anyone?"

I spin toward the voice, blinking into the darkness under a fig tree's arms. "Muna?"

She's sitting on a short plastic stool, deep in the foliage like she's trying to be swallowed by it. So far back that I hadn't even seen her. I walk over slowly, my eyes adjusting to the gloom, holding out the paper.

She stiffens, looks away from it like it's something foul. "I don't want to see."

"They haven't named any suspects yet," I say. "Just Al Shabaab generally."

Muna presses her lips together and nods.

I fold the paper and lay it on the ground. I hesitate, remembering Mama Lisa's warning to keep my distance. But I can't just leave her here like this. And besides, I don't feel like going back out and dealing with the world either. I squat down to Muna's eye level. Her hands are clasped in front of her, and she's hunched over her belly.

"Are you okay?" I ask.

"Yeah," she breathes quickly. "I'm fine. I should get back to class."

She doesn't move.

"How long have you been here?"

She stays silent. But after a few seconds she can't hold it back any longer. Her face crumples, and tears join the tracks already on her face. She swipes at them. "I'm sorry. I'm being stupid."

"No. It's okay," I say helplessly. "You're not being stupid. Did you know someone who got killed?"

She shakes her head, her breath catching like she's been holding it. She squeezes and twists her fingers. The tips of her nails are orange with old henna.

"You know, the whole time they had me, in Somalia, I cried only once." Muna holds up a finger. "Once. Day one. The first time . . ." She swallows. "They took me to be a 'wife' for a commander. And after that, I knew there was nothing worse they could do to me, and I stopped. For two months, I said nothing. No words. No tears. I just cooked and cleaned and did what wives are supposed to do." Her body is scrunched up tight and shivery.

I don't know what to say. Nothing I can think of is adequate.

She stares at the folded paper in the grass. "They took me out of my grandmother's house. She begged them to take her instead of me, and they laughed. Thinking about it later made me too mad to cry."

I want to tell her she doesn't have to talk. But the words are stuck in my throat.

"I thought once I escaped, once I came here, I might cry. You know, I might be *normal* again. But I never did. I thought maybe I had some medical problem. Like . . ." She breathes shakily. "Permanent damage. But now, all of a sudden, after all these months, I hear about this bombing that doesn't have anything to do with me, and I can't handle it." She's swaying slightly, forward and back. "This isn't even my city."

I start to reach for her, but catch myself.

"Damn them," she whispers.

The words are a cold knife through my heart. Ice spreads from my chest into my veins.

"Damn them all to hell. They shouldn't be here. They aren't supposed to be here," she says. "I came here to get away from them. They're supposed to stay *there*." A terrible fury is building in her. "You know what I told Ms. Voerster, the counselor? I told her that I had stopped hating the man who forced me to be his slave. That I had moved on. But it was a lie. How can I move on?" She waves at her stomach. "With this?"

I want to dissolve into nothing. I want to disappear, shatter into dust. I want to tell her to stop, not to say anything more. I can't take it.

She looks past me, her eyes glassy. "I am afraid of what's growing in me, Abdi. I'm afraid that I will look at her face and see him for the rest of my life."

Her liquid gaze settles back on me. And I go cold.

She knows.

I can see it written in the geometry of her face.

She knows what I was. She knows I was one of them. I open my mouth, but there is only hollowness inside me. Nothing comes out.

Suddenly she surges toward me, grabs my mangled hand and squeezes it so hard that I wince. "You know what I'm talking about, don't you? They did this to you."

I'm paralyzed. "Yes," I whisper.

Sparks flare in the depths of her irises. "You understand."

"Muna, I . . ."

"It wasn't right, what they did to us! No one deserves what we suffered! God won't forgive them for what they did to us, why should I?" Her teeth chatter and her nose runs, and I am sinking into those eyes like they are tar. I am drowning.

I want to confess. I want to bleed it out right here at her feet.

I saw the General going off to see his "wives." I knew what that meant. I never said a word.

I know I should tell you, Muna.

I am not a good person. I am a coward.

You should know.

I look up. Her eyes demand an answer.

But all I can manage to say is "You're right. You shouldn't. You shouldn't ever forgive them."

TWENTY-SEVEN

THEN: SEPTEMBER 27
THE FORT, SOMALIA

"Khalid."

He turns, raises an eyebrow. "*As-salamu alaykum,* brother."

He's given me no other choice. I've decided to finally corner Dahir in that most glamorous of private locations: the latrine block.

"*Wa-alaykum salam,*" I reply, catching my breath. I had sprinted when I saw my brother go in, followed by laughs from the guys I left behind calling, "Ha! Da'ud, man! When you gotta go, you gotta GO! . . . Hey, Da'ud, you afraid your shit's leaving the station without you?"

I glance around the block. No one's here but us.

"How are you, Da'ud?"

"I'm good, Khalid."

He waits for a second. "What is it, Da'ud? I've got to . . ." He glances at the odorous hole he's making for.

"It will just take a second. I know you are . . . very busy, brother." I take a deep breath, regret it, try to clear my mind of any thoughts that will show on my face.

Ever since my conversation with Mr. Jones, my brain has been on overdrive. I have to do what he says. I have to find out about this attack the Doctor and the General are planning. I have to save my family. And I don't want Jones to kill these Boys like they're no better than flies. The idea that Weli and Toothless and all the rest of the guys in my unit are anything as dangerous as "enemy combatants" is just crazy.

But how do I get the information Jones wants? I turned the question over and over in my head, like a wave worries a stone. It didn't take long to realize that as much as I hate to admit it, Jones is right. It has to be through Dahir; he's my best chance.

While I carried medical supplies, rounds of ammo, water, and tins of sardines through the tunnels and deposited them in tunnel 55, I thought about how to approach him. All the way back to the base, I thought. All night, awake, listening to the other boys snore and fart, I thought. All day, through exercises and prayers and meals, watching Dahir from the corners of my eyes. Thinking, playing out scenarios. How do I get him to talk to me when he barely even acknowledges my presence? I can't tell him outright that I'm a spy. He's one of them. I'm too afraid that he'll go and tell on me to the General, flesh and blood or not. He'll think it's his duty. Commander Khalid, soldier on the straight and narrow. That's all I've seen of him since I got here. No, I realized there's really only one way to play this. My brother is a totally different person. So to get him to listen to me and, more importantly, *talk* to me, I have to be different too.

If he's going to be Khalid, I have to be Da'ud.

I lick my lips, hoping the heat is a good enough cover for why I'm sweating bullets. *Be cool,* I tell myself. "I—I want to help . . . do the, um, things . . . more."

Real cool, Abdi.

I clear my throat, try again. "I mean, I want to start fighting jihad. With you. For real. I want to help."

Dahir/Khalid's eyes soften slightly. "You *are* helping, brother. You're being a good soldier. You're doing well in your training."

I tense. Has Dahir been watching me? How does he know how I'm doing? I thought he was ignoring me.

"Keep it up," he says. "Your time will come."

He starts to turn away, and I reach for his arm. "But, wait! I'm ready now. Khalid, you were right." His eyes flick back to me, and I barrel on. "I know now what you meant about the Doctor, about his wisdom. I've been listening to him, thinking about what he says. And I think I understand now. I understand that I have to choose sides and fight—otherwise I'm just letting them win." I quote Khalid back to Khalid.

Don't lay it on too thick.

"I—I mean, I'm learning," I correct, dropping my gaze. "And I have a lot to learn still, but I'm committed. I want to do whatever I can. I want to help the Doctor."

Khalid's face softens even more, and I feel sick to my stomach. He's buying it. "I'm glad for you, brother."

". . . So? Can I do something? Help with whatever you're planning . . ."

He frowns, and alarm bells go off in my head. *Too much, Abdi! You're too transparent!* I try to cover. "I mean, there will be more missions, right? Fighting missions? Some of the other boys are training to be bombers." I hesitate. *That's not what I want. Better be careful what I volunteer for.* "Khalid, I can help. I'm good with my gun. I'll do whatever you need. I want to be useful."

Khalid's frown smooths. "Not yet, Da'ud," he says. "But your eagerness is admirable."

That tone. I'm just a dumb, exuberant kid brother. For a moment, the urge to hit him comes back. I look at his clear eyes, his untroubled face. Does he even think about Hooyo and the others? I shouldn't feel bad about lying. Me lying to him is his fault, not mine. I don't want to be here! It's because of him and his Boys that Hooyo and the others are prisoners. If he'd just left Al Shabaab when he'd had the chance, Jones wouldn't have ever kidnapped our family.

"Khalid," I say, forcing my anger down, "I can help. You know me. You can trust me."

I say the words and realize it's almost like Da'ud isn't even me. Like he's this completely different person who is loyal to his brother and Al Shabaab. I've just slipped into his skin.

A boy walks into the latrine, giving us a puzzled glance.

"I'll talk to General Idris," Khalid says. "But I can't promise anything."

It's clear that he's telling me it's time for me to go. I back out of the block.

It's a start.

THE NEXT three days pass in a blur of nerves and exhaustion. Khalid goes out of his way to avoid me. I learn absolutely nothing that I think will be of interest to Jones. With only a few days to get Jones his information and no sign that Khalid/Dahir's going to come through for me, I'm getting desperate.

I'm in line for dinner on the third night when I overhear some of the guys say the Doctor's back. No one's seen him, though; he's been holed up in A-block with the General. Word's going around that he's called for a meeting with all the commanders over dinner. My heart leaps into my throat. Somehow, I need to hear what they're talking about. I've got to get something, anything to bring to Jones.

Unfortunately, grunts like me don't merit invitations to commanders' dinners. I slip out of the line and duck behind the kitchen, where there's a good view of A-block. Maybe there's some way to listen in through a window? But the General's office, where they'll meet, is on the third floor. There's only one entrance to the building, and it'll be guarded. So how to get in? I'm so focused, staring up at the building, that I never hear the footsteps behind me. When I feel a tap on my shoulder, I jump, cursing.

I turn to find Bashir. "Dude! What?"

"What are you doing out here? Spying on Safiya?" He winks. "I wouldn't blame you."

"No. I'm not doing anything," I say, trying to think of a good excuse. "I was taking a walk."

Bashir snorts. "A walk? Here? Next to the dirty dishwater?" He goes to the back door of the kitchen and yells, "Oh, angel of dawn! Light of my darkness! It is I, a poor servant, come to beg a taste of your delicacies. Give me your bounty, oh, morning star!"

"Eat shit, Bashir," I hear Safiya reply over the banging of pots. "I'm busy."

"Come on, beautiful! It's not for me—I've been sent to fetch dinner for the big boys."

My ears prick. He's taking food to the meeting?

"Fine, fine," I hear her grumble. "Give me a minute."

Bashir leans against the wall. "I'll be here, dreaming of your eyes." He fishes in his pockets, eventually pulls out a cigarette butt. He lights the end in a snap of flame.

"What are you *doing*?" I try to knock the butt out of his hand.

He shifts out of my reach, finishes a deep drag and exhales with a moan of pleasure.

"Are you crazy?" I dart a glance over my shoulder.

Smoking is *so* not allowed. It's even worse than chewing *khaat*. If someone sees him, Bashir will get whipped for it, and he knows it.

He doesn't seem worried. "Probably. Probably going to get struck down by lightning as I'm walking across the compound."

He takes another deep drag, the light illuminating his face in the dusk. "Maybe I can add it to tomorrow's confession of my sins." He examines the butt, drops it, and buries it in the sand with his toe. "Or are you going to tell on me?"

"No," I say, stepping back. "Of course not."

Safiya pops her head out the door. "Plates are ready." Her eyes narrow. "I smell cigarettes. Are you smoking?"

"Da'ud was. Don't tell on him."

I splutter. "I was not!"

"I told you not to smoke out here, Bashir. You're going to get me in trouble!"

"Don't be mad." He lowers his voice and pulls a blocky package out of his pocket. "Here, look what I got for you."

She's bringing out a big plate, but when she sees what Bashir's offering, her eyes light up. She shoves the plate at him and grabs it. She examines the paper-wrapped package greedily, then, with a nervous glance at me, tucks it into her dress. "I have to get my *niqab* and gloves on, and I'll carry the other plate."

"I'll take it," I say, jumping forward. "I'll go with Bashir."

"Are you sure?"

"Yeah." I shrug, trying to cover for my eagerness. "You look busy. It's no problem."

Bashir cocks an eyebrow.

"Okay, thanks," Safiya says with obvious relief, and ducks back into the kitchen to get the other plate of food. "Just don't spill it!" she warns me.

I take the full plate from her, careful not to slosh.

"Thank you, my moon over the desert," Bashir calls.

"Enough with the stars and moon bullshit, Bashir!" she shouts from inside. Her head pops out again, though, and she holds her hand to her chest, where I guess the package is. "But thank you," she adds in a whisper.

"What was that you gave her?" I ask as I follow Bashir across the compound, the metal plate piled with food before me.

"Just a little present," he says. "Perfume. Don't mention it; I don't want her to get in trouble."

"Sure," I say. "That's a big box of perfume. Are you sending her the wrong message? Like, you stink?"

Bashir just grunts.

The plates are heavy, so full they threaten to spill over. And there are real chunks of meat in the stew, even a little bowl of dates. Bashir pops one in his mouth before we're out in the open.

"Very considerate of you to help," he says.

Like always, I can't tell if he's trying to goad me into saying something that's going to expose me or get me in trouble, or if he really does think I'm being nice. Or if he just enjoys messing with my head. "No big deal."

The guards in front of A-block only have eyes for the plates we're bringing, waving us through lazily. They know Bashir. *It's almost too easy,* I think. It occurs to me that with Bashir doing this kind of thing day in and day out, he's probably seen and heard more than anyone here. I wonder what he knows.

I follow him up the stairs, toward the sound of voices. I assume we're going to the room where I met the Doctor that first day, but instead Bashir leads me farther down the hall. It's almost dark now, and the hallway is black, other than the light coming from under the door we're headed toward.

I strain to hear, catching the deep voice of the General saying, "Yes, of course, Hakim Doctor, but it still won't be easy getting a team into position . . ."

I slow my steps and hold my breath, willing Bashir to do the same.

". . . and we should consider the currents in terms of timing, sir."

With a jolt, I realize the voice belongs to my brother.

"Hurry up," Bashir whispers to me, pausing in front of the door. He knocks softly. "General Idris, sir. Your dinner."

The conversation stops immediately.

"Come in," the General booms.

Bashir pushes the door open, and I trail behind. Khalid's eyes jump to my face when he sees me, but I try to keep my expression blank. I set my plate down in the middle of the circle of men.

"Bring us water to wash," one of the commanders says. Bashir and I both nod and scurry out the door.

My heart hammering, I listen hard for the voices to resume, but can't hear anything. I have to make an effort to keep a growl of frustration from escaping.

"I'll take the water back up," I say as we walk across the sand toward the tap.

Bashir gives me a look, but says, "Okay."

I try not to make eye contact as we fill the jugs, and he hands me a washbasin and a slice of soap. I can feel his gaze on the back of my head as I walk back to A-block. My legs want to run, afraid of what I'll miss, but I force myself to go slowly and to not look back. The guards wave me through again, and I try to make my steps as quiet as possible. Murmurs turn to words as I creep closer.

". . . They should all be chosen carefully."

"Of course, Doctor, only the best."

"I don't just mean the strongest in body."

"No, of course, Hakim Doctor." My breath quickens. That's Khalid. "They must be strong of heart."

"Unwavering," another boy adds.

"And smart. This sort of operation can change in the blink of an eye, and we all must be ready to react and adapt."

There are noises of agreement.

"It would help if they didn't get seasick," the Doctor says, and laughter fills the room.

Thoughts zing through my brain. They're talking about getting a team together, maybe. Something about the ocean currents. An attack from boats? Piracy?

"Where is that boy?" I hear the General grumble. "The food will be cold."

I suck in a breath. I wait a second, knock, then push the door open. Head bowed, I take the basin to the Doctor first. I set it on the floor behind him, and he twists so I can pour water from my jerry can slowly over his outstretched hands.

"*As-salamu alaykum*, Da'ud," the Doctor says to me. The

direct address almost paralyzes me. For a second I'm convinced he knows what I'm up to.

I force myself to reply, "*Wa-alaykum salam* . . . sir."

The Doctor watches my face as he soaps his hands. "How are you, Da'ud?"

I feel all the eyes in the room on me. "Very well, sir. *Alhumdulillah.*"

"Praise God," the Doctor repeats.

He finishes washing his hands and flicks the excess water onto the floor. I move around the outside of the circle to the General, who's seated next to the Doctor. The room is unnervingly quiet. I can almost feel the suspicion in the General's gaze, and pray he doesn't notice the tremble in my hands as I pour the water.

"So, Khalid," the Doctor says, finally breaking the silence, "you are familiar with the currents?"

"My father was a fisherman, sir. He taught me."

I glance at Khalid. His back is rigid with the pride of being consulted by the Doctor. He doesn't look at me. It's as if I'm a stranger.

"When do you suggest timing the event?"

"It depends on whether the entrance or the escape should be swifter, Hakim Doctor," Khalid says, finally glancing at me.

I try to remember what Aabo said about the currents. They're strong. And they change, going south half the year, and north the other half, but I can't remember which is when.

"The time of day will be important too," Khalid says, "not just the time of year. Because of the tides."

The General clears his throat at me, and I jerk my head up. I've kept pouring water, even though the General has already shaken his hands dry. I swiftly move to the commander seated next to him, nearly sloshing the gray water in the bottom of the basin onto the floor.

"Careful, you," Commander Rashid growls softly, taking the soap.

"We should be in position several days before," the General says. "And once we have achieved our objective, we will need to move out quickly. I think then the timing should be such that the currents favor our exit."

The Doctor nods, considering. "You will look into the timing, Khalid? We want to be exact."

"Yes, Hakim Doctor."

I keep making my way around the circle. I'm trying to stretch things out as long as I can, but there's only so much delaying I can manage when the men are hungry and eager to wash so everyone can pray and eat.

"I will speak with the men in Hamar Weyne about securing the boats."

My heart pounds. Answers to two of my questions are coming into focus. *Where:* Hamar Weyne, a neighborhood in Mogadishu. Is that where the attack will happen? *When:* Dahir will figure it out according to currents. But *what?* What are they going to do?

Last to wash is Khalid, who does so quickly, still ignoring

me. *Look at me!* I want to shout, but I bite the inside of my mouth. When Khalid turns back to the center, I hesitate, trying to think of some reason to linger.

But the General looks at me pointedly and says, "That will be all, Da'ud." I nod and pick up the washbasin to go. As I'm pulling the door closed behind me, I hear the Doctor begin a prayer. I leave it open a tiny bit, as if I don't want the noise to interrupt.

What I've heard fills me with adrenaline. But then I think about it. What have I actually learned? I know where, maybe. And that when depends on currents, but that's it. That's not an actual date. It's not enough. It won't satisfy Mr. Jones.

I walk to the end of the dark hall and gently set the basin on the floor. I peer around the corner, down the stairs, where the guards still sit in the doorway, talking quietly. They'll be expecting me back down soon, but they won't be suspicious yet. I hear the men's voices rise again as they begin to eat.

Slowly, painfully slowly, I tiptoe back, aiming for the band of light spilling from the small crack I left in the door. I come close enough to catch ". . . will be a good test."

"You don't think it will tip anyone off, General, sir? The plans are so similar," Khalid says.

I try to still my breath, stationing myself outside the sliver of light. I hesitate, then move so I can see inside the room.

"It's a good point, Khalid," I hear the Doctor say. "But we need to know what to expect. If there are any problems, we want to take care of them now."

There's a pause, where maybe Khalid is thinking about arguing. But in the end, he just says, "Yes, Hakim Doctor."

"I'm sure you are not questioning the Doctor's directive, Khalid," I hear the General say, an edge to his voice.

I lean forward, straining to hear.

And at that exact moment a hand comes out of the dark and clamps over my mouth.

TWENTY-EIGHT

THEN: SEPTEMBER 30
THE FORT, SOMALIA

"Shh!" a voice whispers close to my ear.

The hand stays pressed over my mouth as I'm yanked back, away from the door. My body floods with panic. I flail to keep my balance while trying to not make any noise.

Not that it matters.

I'm as good as dead.

The arm keeps dragging me backward, and I wait for a knife to slide across my throat, or a gun to be shoved into my ribs. I wait for the shouted warning to the Doctor and the others that they're being spied on.

"Be still; they'll hear you!" The voice is quiet but harsh in my ear. It smells like cigarettes.

I twist around and my captor releases me. I look at him, agog. Bashir glowers, his misshapen face looking even more menacing in the half-light. He puts a firm finger to his lips.

What's happening? Why doesn't he want them to hear me? Why isn't he raising the alarm?

But Bashir just jerks his head toward the stairwell, and for good measure gives me a push.

I turn and walk, every nerve on edge. Maybe he doesn't want me to get into trouble. Maybe he thinks I'm just dumb and curious. But Bashir is a personal servant to the General. He's the Doctor's cousin. He may bend the rules a little, but surely he can't let me walk away after catching me spying.

Bashir picks up my abandoned jerry can and washbasin and thrusts them at me, sloshing dirty water down my *khameez*. He follows me mutely down the stairs.

The guards at the bottom let us pass, but their faces are suspicious.

"I found him," Bashir says to them, rolling his eye. "Country boy. Who gets lost in a three-story building?" We walk in silence toward the kitchen and the barracks.

Should I try to run? My eyes dart around the compound. The walls are high, and I'd never make it over and through the razor wire without getting shot by one of the guards on the wall. Is Bashir taking me back to the cells? Will the General have me tortured? Make me tell him all about Mr. Jones? Or just kill me?

"You're a fucking idiot," Bashir growls once we're out of earshot of the guards. He shoves me toward the water tap near the kitchen. "Put that down," he says, nodding at the washbasin I'm still carrying.

As I do, my mind races. If I'm going to run, it has to be now. Maybe I can climb up to the roof of the 104's barracks and try to jump onto the wall. But before I can make a move, Bashir clamps his hand back down on my arm and comes in close. "Are you spying on them?"

"I— No!"

His eye bores into me.

"I was just, you know, curious!" I pray he can't see my terror or smell the sweat pooling in my armpits.

Bashir's lip curls even more. That's it. I'm screwed. There's nothing for it. I'm going to have to run. Before I can lose my nerve, I leap up out of his grip. I swivel, sand grinding under my feet. I feel Bashir fumble to grab my sleeve, but I slip out of his grasp. I'm three meters away before I hear him hiss, "Lightbulbs!"

The code word catches me up as surely as if I'd tripped.

What the hell?

I turn slowly back. Chest heaving, I stare at him.

Bashir cranes his neck, checking to see if we're being watched. When he looks back at me, his face is twisted into a grimace. "Are you serious? It's you? *You're* who Jones sent in? You're our goddamned savior?"

Dumbstruck, I can't answer.

Bashir sucks his teeth. "What, you thought he entrusted this whole mission solely to you? Come on, you idiot. Follow me. We need to talk."

IT'S FULL dark and we've missed praying *Isha* by the time Bashir gets the whole story out of me—my family being held hostage, what I'm supposed to find out, Jones's threat to bomb the Fort if I don't get him something in the next four days, and what I overheard tonight. We're sitting in what Bashir calls his perch, a little outcrop on the side of the Fort wall, above the sea. Stars are smeared across the sky.

To get here, Bashir led me through a winding jumble of rocks at the far edge of the Fort's parade yard and into a dark, wet, sea-carved tunnel. I don't know how he even found this place. We had to squirm through the tunnel on our stomachs. Water laps below, and we're out of sight of the guards posted on the walls. This is how Bashir gets in and out of the Fort without being seen, he explains, and sometimes he just comes here to think.

Right now, he's thinking about Jones's ultimatum, and how Jones never said anything to him about a deadline.

"Maybe he's bluffing," I say.

"Not sure I want to risk it. Don't forget what they did to that base in Jilib last year. Drones bombed it, and a hundred and twelve Boys went up in smoke."

I sigh. "When's the last time you talked to him?"

"A week or so before you got here. I told him about the raid on the AMISOM checkpoint where we picked you up." He rubs his neck, where his chip is.

"And Jones told you there was another spy, but not who?"

"Yeah."

"But why wouldn't he?"

"Good question," Bashir says darkly. "You'd think he'd want me to help you. I mean, I've always suspected you—you've got that look like you're thinking too hard about everything. You know, like you're constipated?"

"Thanks."

"But I wasn't sure." He bites at his thumbnail. "He thinks I'm taking too long."

I almost smile. "Don't tell me you're jealous."

Bashir snorts. "Please. I just don't want to miss out on my reward."

"What's that?" I ask, suddenly sober, thinking of my own reward: Hooyo, Ayeyo, Hafsa, the twins.

Bashir stretches. "Money."

"That's it?" I ask. I can't keep the disappointment out of my voice. "You just want a payout?"

Bashir gives me a look. "It's not like I'm going to buy a fancy wardrobe or something. Money is a means to an end, my friend. It's what's getting me out of here. I'm going to start a new life. Somewhere else." He pauses, and when he speaks again, his voice is low and tough, like he's expecting me to laugh. "Me and Safiya. I'm taking her out of here too." He keeps his eye focused on the horizon.

"Safiya?" I ask, blinking. "For real? I thought all that flirting was just you messing around."

Bashir just keeps looking out. "She can't stay here."

I stare at the water too. I can see the distant lights of fishing boats bobbing in the dark. I try to imagine Bashir and Safiya running away together, hand in hand. I can't quite see it, but it seems there's a lot I didn't see about Bashir. "So what now?"

"What do you mean?"

"What's our next step?"

"You mean you want to work together?"

"Well, yeah," I say, surprised. "What else would we do?"

Bashir is quiet for a little while. "It's more dangerous that way," he says. "I bet Jones didn't tell us about each other because that way we can't tell *on* each other if we get caught. What if the General gets wise to me? Aren't you worried I'll rat you out to save my neck?"

I let what he's saying sink in. It's a question, but not the one he's asked. Somehow I know he wouldn't do that to me. He's asking if *I* can be trusted. "I won't rat you out, Bashir. What good would it do me? I have to get this information to Jones. It's the only way my family goes free. And besides, what choice do you and I have? We know about each other now."

He mulls this over. "What if Jones thinks he doesn't have to keep his promises to both of us?"

"Like if we get the info for him as a team but one of us takes credit for it?"

"Exactly."

I don't respond immediately. "I don't know. I don't think there's any good way to prove to each other we won't. We just

206

have to be willing to take that chance. I guess if you don't feel like you can trust me, then, well, I understand."

He doesn't say anything for a while. Then, "Have you thought about after? I mean, years from now."

"After?" I ask, not sure what that has to do with anything.

"I have," he says. "A lot. And I realized at some point that for me, at least, there's no going home. Being a spy now means putting a target on my back forever. If the Doctor and the General go down, eventually someone will put it together that I was involved. I'm just too close to the General. So getting out of here, getting Safiya out of here, it's all I've got."

He picks up a rock, chucks it out at the waves.

"Bashir, I . . ."

"I'm not telling you that so you'll feel sorry for me. It's just how things are. And the thing is, you're right. There's no way either of us can be sure of the other." He pauses. Looks at his hands. "But I also know this: I'm tired of it. I'm tired of being alone in my head with all of this. I haven't told Safiya because I don't want to get her involved, you know? The less she knows, the better." He wipes a hand over his face. "Back in Mogadishu, being related to the Doctor meant living in a sort of . . . no-man's-land. No one trusted my parents. They wouldn't trade with my mother. Didn't want to stand beside my dad at the mosque. And it sucked. My parents are good people; they don't have anything to do with the Doctor and all this. But how do you tell people that? How do you prove it? You can't prove you're not secretly a terrorist."

I'd never really thought about that sort of thing before. My father had told me that the best way to survive was to not trust guys with guns. Would he have told me to stay away from Bashir, if he thought he came from a family of men with guns? The idea jolts me.

"So," Bashir says. "I'm going to trust you, even if you can't prove you won't screw me over."

I swallow, feeling like he's just opened up his chest and shown me his beating heart, and said, *Look, I know you could stab it if you wanted to, but I choose to believe you won't.*

I'm tired of it too, I realize. I don't want to be so afraid all the time. I don't want to be alone in my head anymore.

For a long while we're silent. Finally Bashir sticks his hand out. "But you gotta get your shit together. I snuck up on you way too easily tonight."

I shake it and say, very seriously, "That's because you walk like a little girl."

He grins. "Takes one to know one."

The chuckle that rattles up from my throat takes me by surprise. Laughter feels weird and hurts my mouth. My eyes water.

"Jones has got the right idea," Bashir says, his smile slipping away. "Getting intel from your brother is the best shot we've got. Jones didn't choose you randomly, or because you wanted to defect, like me."

My brief feeling of lightness fades. I take a deep breath of ocean air. "It *would* be a good idea. If my brother actually talked to me."

Bashir has to turn his whole head to get a solid look at me. He rests his skinny wrists on his knees and waits for me to go on.

"He's just . . . so different. It's like I'm nobody to him anymore." My throat starts to tighten. Great. I'm about to start crying. I pretend to cough, turn my head so Bashir can't see my face.

He tilts his head to the sky, suddenly very interested in the stars.

I rub my nose on my sleeve and ask in a gruff voice, "So this attack—what do you know about it?"

"I know the General has been more interested in my projects lately."

"The bomb-making stuff?"

"Yeah. Maybe he's planning to bomb something."

"Okay, that's useful. So we've got that and the boat stuff. Have you heard anything else? I mean, you're practically the General's personal servant. What do he and the Doctor talk about?"

"They're not dumb—they don't just blab away when I'm around. I try to listen in every chance I get, but I can't make them suspicious of me."

"You must have heard *something*."

He frowns. "I know the General has been siphoning off money and putting it into an account in Jeddah."

"What? Really?"

"Yeah, I overheard him talking on the phone to his banker. I'm pretty sure that at least half of what we take in taxes goes into his pockets."

"Taxes?"

"The money the businesses in the towns we control have to fork over for our 'protection.'"

"Does the Doctor know he's taking money?" I ask.

"Hell no, are you kidding? The General would be out on his ass."

"Does Jones?"

Bashir shrugs. "I told him. He didn't seem to care that much. As far as he's concerned, the more corruption on the inside, the better. We have fewer resources that way. It makes us weaker."

I try to think of how we could use this information, but it sounds like the Doctor is the only one who'd be interested.

"I also heard the Doctor and the General talking about maybe having to leave the Fort after this attack. That could be why we're stocking up the tunnels. Sounds like it's going to be big enough that we won't be safe here anymore when they come looking for us."

We're both quiet, thinking.

At last I say, "I've just got to get Dah—*Khalid*—to bring me in on the plans. That's all there is to it. What, where and when." I hope my tone is at least convincing to Bashir.

"Yeah," he says. He sighs deeply, stands, extends a hand to help me up. "That's all."

TWENTY-NINE

I wait for Sam to bring up last night's attack as we drive home from Maisha. I can tell she wants to. She keeps sneaking glances at me and clearing her throat like she's about to start a conversation. Talking is the last thing I want to do, though, so I pretend to fall asleep. When we get back to her apartment, I go to my room and try to do my homework. But I can't concentrate. I take my books out to the living room and start an episode of *CSI: Miami*.

Sam bought seasons one through five off a guy selling pirated DVDs on the street a couple of days ago. She was so excited to show them to me, I didn't have the heart to tell her she could have downloaded them off the Internet. Sam's technology game could use some work. The fact that she even has a DVD player is sort of a miracle. It's only when the episode is fifteen minutes in that I realize it's the one about Horatio "H" Caine's mentor getting blown up as he's trying to defuse a bomb. Great. Of course it is. My brain immediately jumps back to exactly the subject I was trying to avoid thinking about: the Boys and their bombs.

"You okay?" Sam asks from her end of the couch.

"I'm fine," I say, forcing myself to refocus on the television. Alexx Woods, the medical examiner, is opening up the dead guy's chest, revealing all his chewed-up guts and explaining about the "white butterfly effect." Basically, the body looks fine on the outside, but because of the extreme pressure of the explosion, his guts are mush. His lungs have collapsed into something that now looks like the open wings of the insect the effect is named for.

"The blast pressure's even worse underwater," I say, without thinking. *Stupid, Abdi.* Now is no time to be flaunting my intimate knowledge of explosives. Not when Somali boys like me are blowing up buildings just a few miles away. "I-it's in another episode," I say.

"Gross, yet strangely fascinating." Sam gives me a worried look. "And maybe not the best choice of topics to dwell on today." She picks up the remote and starts to scan for a new episode. "About the attack last night . . ."

I tense.

"I know it must be hard hearing about stuff like that. I mean, I can only imagine what living through the wars in Mogadishu was like, and now to see the same sort of thing happening here . . ."

I let out a breath I didn't realize I'd been holding. What had I expected her to say? Did I think she was going to accuse me right here and now of being an Al Shabaab Boy? And then what? We go back to our TV show? "Yeah," I say. "There was a lot of that back home."

She tries to catch my eye. "Maybe we could look into that counseling I was talking about? If you want."

I pick at a spot on my finger nub. "Maybe later."

She lets it go, but for a long time keeps watching me, like she's forcing herself to keep quiet. Finally she stands up. "Kuku Express for dinner?"

"Sounds good," I say, pretending to be absorbed in the new episode she's chosen.

This one is better, just something about dead drug dealers. I watch techs carefully examine evidence over a snappy music track. They handle a splinter of wood, a strand of hair, a wool fiber with the sort of reverence usually reserved for the bones of saints. Like they are priceless artifacts. And maybe they are. Those little pieces are the proof that even in the middle of blood and chaos there is a sacred sort of order that always points to the truth.

I watch, and try to believe.

THIRTY

"You take it," Gari says, already starting to pull his shirt over his head.

"No way, man!" Samir chokes, barely able to talk, he's laughing so hard.

"Aw, come on!" Gari says, swiveling between all of us, looking for someone among the 106s dumb enough to trade T-shirts. We're hanging around the back of a technical, waiting to go into Mogadishu for another tunnel supply mission. Our mismatched civilian clothes are awful, as usual, but Gari's gotten the worst of them: one of those NGO handouts that just says "I breastfeed!" He can't give it away, not even to the guys who don't know English, not after Toothless saw it and fell over laughing.

Gari fumes and pulls the T-shirt back on, turned inside out now. He crosses his arms over his chest. "*Wallahi,* you're all so immature."

Bashir is a little outside the circle, not paying attention to us. I wonder if he's thinking about the same thing I am. My week is up tomorrow, so Jones will probably get in touch with me today. Maybe Bashir too. We've decided to tell him we know about each other, that we're working together, and that we expect him to honor his promises to both of us. As far as what information we'll give him, we know it has to be enough to keep him happy, but not everything. Not until we're sure he's going to deliver on our rewards.

We figure what we know boils down to four key points: (1) the attack will most likely happen in Mogadishu, (2) it will probably involve a bomb, (3) boats are needed and (4) timing will depend on the currents. We've decided to tell him only 3 and 4 for now. I just hope it's enough to keep the drones away.

"Brothers!" the General shouts, and we all snap to attention. We've been waiting on the order to load up for a while now, but the commanders have been huddled up talking to him. "Change of plans! Everyone into uniform and back here immediately! Go!"

In the stampede to the barracks I hear Gari mutter, *"Alhamdulillah."*

Within five minutes we're back and assembled, watching General Idris pace before us. "The time has come to fight."

We're quiet, but a perceptible shiver runs through our lines.

"At this very moment, twenty kilometers south of here, the town of Merka is under siege. AMISOM forces have attacked and are trying to take the city from us. Your job today is simple:

Drive the bastards out. Show them that this is our land, and that they have no place in it!"

"Yes, sir!" The response is quick and eager, all of our nervous excitement squeezed into it.

"Holding Merka is vital, and we're counting on all of you to fight like warriors to keep it." He pauses, glaring out at us. "Brothers of the 106, you'll be split up among the 102s and 104s, taking orders from Commander Khalid and Commander Rashid. You have trained for this, soldiers, and you are ready. Don't let us down. God is great!"

"*Allahu Akbar!*" we echo.

The words vibrate in my chest, all the way down my spine.

The General salutes us and leaves, and the commanders take over their units, rapidly dispersing the 106s between technicals. I'm hoping to get assigned with Khalid and the 102s, but Commander Rashid points Bashir and me to a truck full of 104s.

"Why is holding Merka vital?" I ask Bashir under my breath.

"The Black and White," he says, and climbs up.

When I give him a confused look, he explains, "Charcoal and sugar. Merka's got a new port. Charcoal goes out, sugar comes in. We tax both. Big money."

Taxes. That's what he was talking about the other night: money for Al Shabaab "protection."

Bashir eyes his normal spot in the truck, which all the guys in our unit know not to take. Usually he makes sure he's sitting so his vision is needed only on his right side, his left flank next to the cab of the truck. But a 104 has already claimed it.

"Charcoal production is big in the interior," Bashir says, giving up and finding a different place to sit. "Businessmen sell it to the Persian Gulf states. And a lot of that charcoal money goes toward importing sugar, which is sold down in Kenya on the cheap."

The truck's engine revs. I grab the edge of the cab, and we hunker down as the technical pulls out. Weli, Toothless and Samir are with us too, all clutching their guns and trying desperately not to appear scared in front of the 104s. We roar through the gates, and the guards salute and lock the big metal doors behind us.

"The General knows it's important to keep Merka because that's where we get a lot of our cash," Bashir goes on, and I can tell that the 104 guys are listening, even if they're pretending we 106s don't exist. We peel off down a dirt track through the bush. "Kismayo is the largest port for the Black and White, but there are a lot of tribal militias fighting over it down there. It's hard to break in, even for us. In Merka, we've got a better hold, and the General wants to make sure we keep it."

It's only then that it hits me. Really hits me. We're being sent into battle. Forget tunnels and supply runs. This is for real. I try to shake off the beginnings of a mind-numbing fear. Come on, Abdi, haven't you noticed that you've all been training your asses off? Learning the wedge and the echelon formations for following the leader into battle? Did you think this was all a game? That it was going to stop with shooting at human shapes on the wall? I grip the stock of my gun more tightly, the wood slick under my sweaty palms. I wonder if I look as terrified as the other guys.

"Big boys now, huh?" a 104 asks. He peers down his nose at us, clearly enjoying our squeamishness.

We don't answer.

"You ladies gonna be okay in there? I don't need to be baby-sitting some pants-pissing toddlers while we're getting shot at."

"No, we're good," Bashir says quickly. "You don't have to worry about us."

"Don't listen to Nur," another 104 tells us. The Boy is pudgy with deep acne pockmarks covering his cheeks. I think he's called Scarface, in fact, because as a rule, guys here are assholes about nicknames. "Half of us puked on the way to our first battle."

"I'm not sure that's comforting," Samir from our unit mutters.

"How far is it?" I ask.

"Not far," Scarface answers. "Thirty minutes." He tugs his *keffiyeh* over his eyes to block the sun. "Going to have to be on point there. Get some rest while you can."

WE DRIVE through low, sandy hills covered in scrub. The earth turns from gold to red under a washed-out sky. Soon Commander Rashid, who's sitting up front, yells, "Weapons ready!" We all raise our guns, bristling outward. Then we're roaring out from the bush onto a broader road. I can feel the guys tense around me. The road's still just an empty track, but it's well used.

"Don't forget to take the safety off, kids," Nur says.

The 104s within earshot laugh.

"We're not idiots," I say. But I discreetly double-check my gun to make sure.

I've never been to Merka, but I've heard about it. It's supposed to be really pretty, all old white coral-block buildings hugging the coast, and not so bombed out as Mogadishu. We come in from the east with the sun at our backs, passing abruptly from dunes and brush to neat clusters of houses ringed in fences made from thick bundles of acacia thorn. Soon buildings rise up, shining pearly white against the red sands. I hear faint pops of gunfire and see smoke coming from the center of town.

The 104 Boys wrap their *keffiyehs* around their heads, covering their faces. We 106s glance at each other, not sure what to do. Then Bashir puts his scarf around his face too and we all follow suit. I'd always thought the Boys wore their scarves like this because they didn't want to be recognized, but looking around, I realize the scarf is more like a battle-mask. It's supposed to make us look ferocious. And it works. We look a thousand times more terrifying and untouchable than we did when we went on tunnel supply missions in civilian clothes.

Our truck is first in the convoy of technicals, and the driver speeds up as soon as we hit the main street. I see figures ahead in the dust, scurrying to get themselves, their children, their goats out of the way.

"Flags!"

We hoist our black flags in the back, and the wind makes them snap. Any time we pass people, we shout, "God is great!"

and "Al Shabaab victorious!" but hardly anyone shouts back. I see women cover their faces with scarves and disappear into houses. A little boy pulls his trousers down and shows us his butt, and Nur snarls and lurches up like he's going to come after him, but the boy's gone in a flash, trousers up and running.

"Relax," Scarface tells him. "It's just a stupid kid."

"Relax? That's the kind of shit that turns into insurrection over time!" Nur thumps his chest. "This is our town. These people are going to have to learn. Al Shabaab *guul!*" he shouts again, and shakes a flag at four old men who sit outside a tearoom. They blink at us silently.

"Stupid fuckers."

Bashir and I exchange a glance. You've got to be either stupid or crazy to talk that way about your elders. From the looks of Nur, maybe both.

Other than the posters advertising mobile phone credit, or the occasional motorcycle, the town looks timeless. The ocean swells up royal blue behind the plastered-white buildings. It's so beautiful that for a moment it takes my breath away.

We pull up on the east side of town, near the port. The driver kills the truck engine near a walled-in yard the size of a soccer field. Here the clean beauty of town abruptly stops. The yard is filled with towers of charcoal in plastic sacks. The sand all around is stained greasy black. So are the workers who unload sacks from trucks.

I can hear the gunfire better now. It's still just coming in short bursts, but it's enough to make me start to sweat.

I watch Khalid's guys jump out of their truck and assemble under his eye.

A handful of traders emerge from a small office attached to the charcoal yard. They mutter together and rub their palms on their *macawis* sarongs, watching our approach nervously.

We get out and assemble next to Khalid's unit. I try to catch his eye, but he looks straight ahead.

Commander Rashid pulls his scarf from his mouth. "Okay, listen up," he yells at us. "AMISOM troops have taken control of the west side of the city. They're trying to take more, street by street, but our guys are repelling them. We have the better positions. But our brothers need more cover, and more of us on the ground, engaging them directly."

I swallow. Direct engagement. That means pointing a gun at someone and pulling the trigger.

"You four," Rashid says, pointing at Scarface and three 102s who came in on a different truck. "Get into position on the top floor of that building. You'll be sitting sniper, on watch for approaching enemies. If you see them coming, call." He tosses one of the Boys a phone. "If they get close enough, take them out. Got plenty of ammo? Good. Go."

The four salute and take off.

Rashid hesitates. He and Khalid exchange a look. "You too, Da'ud, go with them."

My mouth falls open. "M-me?" I stutter.

His brow pinches, like he's already regretting the order. "Now, soldier!"

Khalid's face under his scarf is unreadable.

I salute and take off after the other Boys, my stomach in knots. Sitting sniper is an important position and supposedly something only the best shots get chosen for. I'm decent, but nothing special. Why would Rashid want me up there?

Behind me, I hear Khalid say, "You six stay in the trucks and man the RPGs. All the rest of you, fall in after me."

I glance back, hoping Bashir is one of the six, but no luck. He hefts his gun and follows Khalid.

Scarface and the others have already disappeared into the city streets ahead of me. I hurry to catch up, rounding the first corner in the maze of alleys just as a man emerges from the shadows to block my way.

"What are you—"

He shoves something into my hand and backs off without a word.

I look down to find a phone, a call already in progress. I raise it slowly to my ear, dread filling my stomach. "Hello?"

"Abdiweli." The voice is smooth and familiar.

I duck my head and then peer over my shoulder, half expecting one of the Boys to be right behind me. The street is dead, though. I slip into an alley. "Are you trying to get me caught?" I ask in a frantic whisper. "I'm with my unit! Are you here?"

"Don't worry about me, Abdiweli," Mr. Jones says. "I'm far away. We were lucky to catch you on your own, but I assume you don't have long. Better get talking."

Sweat runs down my back. *Only what Bashir and I agreed on,*

I remind myself. "Why didn't you tell me you already had a spy at the Fort?"

A gravelly chuckle comes over the line. "You've met Bashir."

"We're working together," I say.

"Oh, you are, are you?"

"Yeah, and we both expect you to keep your promises."

"Sure, Abdiweli, of course," Jones says easily. "Provided you give me what I need."

"My family, his money."

"I haven't forgotten. It sounds like you have something for me?"

I glance over my shoulder again. "I overheard the Doctor and the General speaking with the commanders."

I can almost feel Mr. Jones straighten and focus. "Oh?"

"Boats will be involved in the attack."

"Good, very good, Abdiweli. What did they say, exactly?"

"They were talking about the ocean currents and timing their getaway with them."

"How so?"

"The currents here change with the seasons. Half of the year they go north, and half south."

"So? When will they attack?"

I grit my teeth. He's like a hungry dog, wolfing down information faster than I expected. "I don't think it will be for a while still. They were talking about doing practice runs and making sure they have the right team."

"Practice runs. Interesting. But when, Abdiweli? I need a date."

"It shouldn't be hard to figure out. Like I said, they want to time it with the currents so their escape is swift."

Jones thinks about this. "But where is the attack? Where are they launching from? Which direction will they travel? We'll need to intercept them."

I am momentarily tongue-tied. *Stupid, Abdi.* I hadn't thought about the fact that I would have to tell Mr. Jones that the attack would be on Mogadishu for any of the other info to have much value. Going with the currents matters only if you know where you're coming and going from. I don't know whether the attack will come from the north or the south of Mogadishu, or where the team will escape to. Will they come back to the same place they launch from, or ride the currents to a different rendezvous? All I can tell Mr. Jones is the truth, which sounds lame as hell: "I—I don't know."

He sighs lightly.

"It's something!" I protest. "You know that the attack will be on a coastal city now."

"In Kenya?"

"N-no," I say, surprised. "In Somalia."

"Are you sure?"

"Positive."

Jones is silent. Finally I blurt out, "What about my family?"

"What about them? You haven't given me anything, Abdiweli. Almost where, almost when, but nothing of what. It's not enough. I need exactly where, when and what. And what about the Doctor and the General? Where will they be in all this?"

I rake my fingernails over my scalp, trying to figure out what to tell him.

"Remember what's riding on this, Abdiweli. Either we stop the attack the surgical way, or we send out the drones to your Fort and all your buddies fry. And let's not even talk about your family."

A red-hot flush of anger fills me. My throat clenches. But his words have hit their mark, and he knows it. Jones waits. Finally I say, "Bashir thinks there's probably going to be a bomb involved. He's the one who'll make it, most likely."

I can almost see the yellow-toothed smile through the phone. "Good. Very interesting."

I pound the nearest wall with my fist until my knuckles sting. We weren't supposed to share that bit with Jones. But what choice did I have? In the silence I can't stop myself from asking, "Is my family okay?"

"They're fine," Jones says without elaboration, then, "What else?"

"That's it!" I say, throwing my now-bleeding hand up. "That's all I've got."

There's silence on the other end of the line. The longer it gets, the more panic rises in me. "Hello? Jones?" More silence. I know he's still there, but his silence is worse than anything he's said so far. I lick my lips. "I'm working on getting more. Khal—I mean, Dahir—he's starting to trust me. I can find out what you want. I swear it!"

I hear the flick of a lighter, an eventual exhale of smoke. "Listen, Abdiweli. I'm not the only one here who needs this

225

information. We have a lot riding on stopping this attack and bringing those men in. What you've given me so far isn't going to satisfy my bosses."

Part of my brain wanders. Why do his bosses care so much about an attack in Somalia? There are suicide bombs and battles here that kill dozens every week. What would be so different about *this* time?

"I'm almost there with Khalid," I say. "Give me another week."

I wait, listening to Jones smoke.

"One more week," he finally says.

Then the line clicks and he's gone.

THIRTY-ONE

THEN: OCTOBER 2
MERKA, SOMALIA

Up on the highest floor of the building I try to concentrate on scanning Merka's streets for approaching AMISOM soldiers. But I can't stop hearing Jones's voice in my head: *one more week.*

Behind me, Scarface and another Boy sit sniper in the north- and west-facing windows. The other two guys are on the roof above us.

They all looked surprised to see me show up, but no one questioned my being there. I wonder how many times they've done this sort of thing. They gave me the easiest position: the window on the southeast-facing side, overlooking the charcoal yard and our territory. No attack should come from this direction.

Nobody speaks. The only noise is the wind rustling through the empty rooms of the building and the occasional chatter of gunfire. The town is quiet otherwise. Beyond the rooftops I can see the ocean glinting. Far enough away that it's just a black speck against the brightness, a little boat. It's still an hour or so before *Dhur* prayers. I wonder if we'll stop to pray. I change positions again; my arms keep falling asleep holding my gun steady on the edge of the windowsill. No one's ever mentioned the fact that sitting sniper is sort of . . . boring. Too much time to think.

I force myself to pay attention, to watch the zigzagging streets. There are people out, a woman selling green mangoes on a mat in the dirt and an old brick mason a street over. The mason is stubbornly repairing a wall that looks like it got hit by a mortar, a wall that will probably get hit again before the year's out. A donkey dozes while standing beside him. None of them seem impressed that a battle is in progress. I know people like this in Mogadishu who are just fed up with constantly running and hiding. My neighbor, Mr. Omar, goes to his little shop every day regardless, saying, "If this is the day of my death, so be it; it's God who decides."

I glance over my shoulder at Scarface, but he doesn't look like he's watching anything more interesting than I am. The gunfire hasn't gotten any louder or more frequent, but we have no idea what's going on out there. I hope Bashir's far enough back, and in a good position. He can shoot just fine, but with his eye, he's definitely at a disadvantage. We all give him shit about it at target practice, acting like he's going to accidentally shoot one of us, but now it's not funny. Not at all.

A little girl comes out to talk to the woman selling mangoes. For a second, my breath catches. She's wearing a dull yellow headscarf, just like one my sister Hafsa has. She's about the same age too. Her back is to me as she talks to the woman. I know it's not Hafsa, but some part of me has this crazy spark of hope, like maybe my sister got away. Maybe she's here, of all places, in Merka. Right below me.

The little girl turns in my direction, and I pull back into the shadows. Of course it's not Hafsa. It's some other little kid. She sways back and forth, half dancing to some unheard song. It's like she was put there to remind me of what Jones is dangling in front of me. The girl's mother, I guess more aware of the danger, pushes her toward the door of their house. The little girl reluctantly steps back inside.

Dhur comes, and when we hear the call over the minaret, we look at each other, then slowly begin prayers. There's no water to wash with, but none of us seems to want to be the one who decides we shouldn't pray. There's no telling which of us are snitches. We finish quickly and get back to our positions.

Toothless makes an appearance around noon, bringing us food for lunch. Just some *canjeero* and bananas, but we're hungry by now, and devour everything.

I settle back into position. The sun is baking, and with the food in my belly I can tell it's going to be a struggle to stay awake. I look out at the horizon over the water, the same useless questions about the attack slugging through my brain: what, when, where. How do I get Khalid to let me in on the plan? As always, there are no answers.

The first shot makes me jump.

I slowly raise my head to peer out the window. The gunfire

was close, only a block or two away, coming from Scarface's side of the building. We glance at each other. If the fighting is this close, it can't be good. That means AMISOM is in our territory.

The next shots are even closer, more rapid. Scarface and the other guy crane their necks to see what's going on, but the view is blocked. The other guy checks the phone, but there are no messages. He goes up to the roof with the others who might have a better view. Scarface and I sit alone in tense silence.

All of my attention is focused in the direction the shots came from, but some little twitching in the corner of my eye pulls my gaze back to the street with the gray-haired brick mason. He's standing motionless, trowel in hand, like he's listening. At first I think his attention is on the gunfire too, but then I see that he's looking in the opposite direction, into a courtyard. He makes a little motion with his hand, like he's telling someone to come. I look back at Scarface, but he's watching his streets.

"Hey, there's a—"

"Shh," Scarface says, and brings his eye down to the sights on his gun. "Movement over here. Troops are coming."

"Us or them?"

"Us, I think. Get ready. If our guys send the *kafirs* this way, take them out."

I swallow. "Take them out. Right."

Scarface must hear the hesitation in my voice; he looks up at me. "It's them or us, man. Don't forget that." He doesn't wait for an answer, puts his head back down. "Get over here and cover this window until Jebril gets back."

Jebril must be the guy who went upstairs. I look for the mason again, but he and his donkey are gone. His tools and mortar lie abandoned. I stand to go to Jebril's window, but as I do, something moves where the mason was, dragging my eye back. Hovering where I can't be seen, I look again.

"Hurry!" Scarface growls. "They're almost here."

But something is off. I can feel it. I scan the area around the half-plastered wall, taking in every inch of rock and dirt until—there.

The slender barrel of a rifle pokes out from around the edge of the courtyard wall, pointing toward the gunfire.

"I've got something over here," I say.

I lift my gun to my cheek. My finger settles on the trigger. Is the person behind that gun one of us or one of them? Most likely it's our guy; it's our territory on this side, but there was something weird about the way the mason was acting. I remember the hard, silent stares from the civilians we passed on the road in. Merka is our territory, but not exactly friendly.

I can hear soldiers now, at least ten of them running fast from the other direction, taking shots as they go. Are they Boys or AMISOM? They're going to come right into the line of whoever is holding that gun. If the person behind the wall isn't one of us, they'll be picked off, one by one. I wait, sweating, trying to figure out what to do.

"Da'ud!" Scarface says, louder than he should. "Get over here now!" He turns to motion at me, his white-and-black *keffiyeh* shining in the sun, and at that exact moment I see his shoulder explode in a spray of blood. The crack of the gun barely registers as I watch Scarface spin with the force of the bullet. He yelps and falls back, grabbing the wound.

I curse and run to him at a crouch. The bullet must have come from up high—one of the nearby buildings probably. Maybe it was one of our guys, an accident, but I doubt it. Someone fired when they saw his *keffiyeh*. "I think we're in the middle of an ambush!"

"Get back into position," Scarface grunts.

I hesitate, watching blood stain the white in his scarf.

"Go!"

I crab walk back to my window and check the hidden gunman. He's still there, and the soldiers are still heading in our direction. I can see them now—it's our guys, running backward, hopping between doorways as they fire back at whoever is chasing them. With a jolt, I recognize Khalid. Then Bashir and Samir.

They're headed straight for the gunman.

"What do I do? What do I do?" I groan. Should I yell and warn them? Will it be enough time, or will the hidden guy hear me too and just come out and spray them all in the back? And are there more soldiers where he came from? There must be. There's at least the other one who shot Scarface. As our guys edge closer, I see the gunman's rifle nose out farther. He's getting ready. I squint into my sights. I can see his boot toe. Definitely not one of us—our guys are all in sandals. I can see his hand now too.

I take a deep breath and squeeze the trigger, spraying the wall and hopefully the hand holding the gun. When the dust clears, the muzzle is gone. Every nerve is on fire as I freeze, waiting.

"Did you get him?" Scarface asks through gritted teeth.

"I think so!"

Khalid and the others are still approaching. There's too much going on for them to notice my shots and realize they might be walking into a trap. I start to poke my head out of the window to yell, but a bullet zings by my head, barely missing me.

Shots come from our guys on the roof. Are they shooting up at the sniper who was trying to hit me, or down at the enemies chasing Khalid and the others through the streets? Everything is chaos; I have no idea what's going on. This is nothing like it is in the movies. Someone should be giving us orders. I don't know what to do. I roll back to the window to check on the gunman, and to my horror see that the gun muzzle is back, and my brother is only steps away. I raise my gun again and hear pops against the building as bullets bite the wall near my head.

Khalid's almost directly below me now. I see the gunman peek quickly around the corner, but don't have time to fire before he's hidden again. Khalid shouts for the other guys to follow him. He's eyeing a wall they can take cover behind. But that wall won't protect them from the hidden gunman. Khalid is basically leading our guys into slaughter.

Bashir comes into view again, shouldering a limping 104.

"Come out, come out, you son of a . . ." I mutter at the gunman, trying to keep my sights focused even as sweat runs into my eyes.

And then the gunman turns the corner, just enough that I can see his torso, his AMISOM patch the only spot of color on his crisp fatigues. I don't have time to think. I just pull the trigger and the soldier falls away, staggering backward where I can't see him. Red splatters the white wall. Immediately two other guys replace him. Cover blown, they're done hiding. The Boys are about to back into them.

I'm cursing and firing as fast as I can, peppering the soldiers with bullets, hearing bullets sing past my ears. The AMISOM soldiers get rounds off, and the Boys scatter and duck. Samir is left without cover and creeps along a wall, attempting to stay flat, trying doors. The soldiers keep coming around the corner. God, how many of them are back there? I'm going to run out of ammo! I fire until my clip is empty. The AMISOM soldiers take cover in doorways, firing at our squad, firing up at me. I watch Samir from my unit go down. He isn't the only one. Bodies of Boys and AMISOM soldiers lie in black smears of blood in the dust. Gunfire explodes all around, coming from below, from above, from us, from them, echoing off the walls until it sounds like we're all rattling around in a giant tin can full of rocks.

I fumble to get another clip out of my pocket and rammed into my gun. We're pushing them back. The AMISOM troops are retreating into the courtyard they came from, firing on anyone who tries to follow them. They must have an escape route back there.

I keep shooting until long after they're gone. Until my clip is empty again. Until our guys have scattered too. Until I can hear my name being shouted through the ringing in my ears. I look back. Scarface is yelling at me. I'd nearly forgotten he was there. He's wrapped his *keffiyeh* around his shoulder wound.

"It's over," he says, panting.

It's true. Everything is quiet. I look back down.

"We got them?"

"We got the fuckers." He laughs with relief, winces. "Are you okay?"

Am I okay? I nod. I taste blood in my mouth. At some point I've bitten my tongue.

"Let's go. Jebril says we need to get back to command. Help me with this."

I grab Scarface's pack and gun. They feel like they weigh nothing. All the colors seem too bright.

"You did well, brother," he says, holding his arm to his chest and slowly starting down the stairs. "You're a real soldier. A killer."

A real soldier.

My head pulses. I see soldiers falling under my rain of bullets.

I put my hand out to steady myself on the wall.

I feel drugged. I feel huge. I feel terrified and ecstatic and numb all at the same time.

A real soldier.

A killer.

THIRTY-TWO

NOW: DECEMBER 13
SANGUI CITY, KENYA

Today makes ten swimming lessons. Both Alice and Muna are able to tread water and do a basic dog paddle. They've stopped being afraid of getting their faces wet, or their noses full of water. Muna goes deep enough now that she can float, a look of sleepy bliss on her face. She says it's the only time she's really comfortable, when the weight of her baby doesn't make her back ache and her feet sore. Her time is near, I think. Or at least, it seems impossible that her stomach could grow any bigger.

I had sort of expected that Muna wouldn't want to go swimming after the attack on the bar. "We don't have to do lessons today if you're not up for it," I'd said.

She hadn't come back to class after I found her behind the gardener's shed, but she was there the next day, quiet, with circles under her eyes.

"Why would I not be up for it?" she'd asked as we filed out of class.

"Well, because, I mean, the attack . . ."

Her chin had lifted, eyes flashing. "What about it? Just because some *ciyaalsuuq* fools want to cause chaos doesn't mean I have to stop living my life. They don't own me. If I want to go swimming, I'm going swimming."

As she strode away, I hid a smile. For a second she had sounded just like my mother.

Looking around the shallows today, I can't help but feel proud. Three other girls have joined the lessons by now, and they've all become pretty fair swimmers. Honestly, they're way better than most of the Boys I tried to teach at the Fort. They actually listen to me, and don't spend most of their time jumping around and trying to drown one another.

"Time to go!" Mama Lisa calls from the shore.

I follow the girls, watching Muna holding her skirt out at her sides so it doesn't tangle around her ankles in the water. Everyone is in a good mood, excited by their progress. Even Adut, the South Sudanese girl who barely spoke a word the first time she came to lessons, is now animatedly discussing with a Congolese girl whether they should do the Twist-and-Shout Slide first or the Wild Wave Pool at Splash Land this weekend. They're all excited about the field trip, if still a little nervous about passing the swim test.

"Bravo, ladies!" Mama Lisa says as we towel off. She beams, even at me.

"Ask her now," Muna says under her breath.

"Okay, okay," I say. I stall, fiddling with my shoes while the girls all go ahead. When Mama Lisa and I are the last ones left, I clear my throat.

She turns around. "Abdi! Well done. You are an excellent teacher. Where did you learn to swim?"

"My father taught me when I was little. He was a fisherman. Mama Lisa?"

"Yes?"

"The, um, the field trip to Splash Land— Um . . . I mean, is it possible . . ."

She slows her pace so the girls ahead can't hear us. "You would like to go."

"Yes, madam." I sneak a glance at her.

"I've been thinking about that." She stops and turns to give me the full measure of her stern gaze. "I have been watching you, making sure you keep your promise to be a gentleman." She looks at Muna.

I see the look and feel my face burn. I'm still not sure what to say or even what to think about all that. What is it Mama Lisa sees to make her worry that I'll make a move on Muna? I've been careful not to do anything I thought would be considered flirting.

Mama Lisa interrupts my confused thoughts. "You care for her."

"Just as a friend, madam," I say quickly.

She doesn't say anything for a little while, and my hopes start to sink.

"Maybe that's not such a bad thing," she says softly, almost as if she's talking to herself.

I cut my glance sideways, and she catches my eye. "You can come with us, Abdi."

"I can?" A grin splits my face. "Thank you, Mama Lisa!"

"I'll even talk to Sam about it. Maybe she'll come too, as a chaperone."

I feel like I could bounce off the sandy path and touch the treetops stretching above. Something about Sam tickles the back of my brain, but before I can figure out what it is, Mama Lisa is saying, "I really am proud of you for taking the initiative to help these girls learn how to swim. It's not just a skill they're learning. I see their confidence improving. Many of them were afraid of the water, and now they look forward to these lessons. It is a rare thing to be able to turn a fear into a source of strength. You've done well."

Heat creeps up around my ears again, but this time it's a pleasant feeling. Mama Lisa doesn't dish out compliments lightly. "Thank you, madam."

All at once the sun sparkling through the leaves and dancing across the dirt road seems extraordinarily beautiful. Birdsong fills the early evening air.

"We will be sad to see you go."

My happiness pops like a balloon. "Go?"

"Abdi," Mama Lisa says gently. "Soon you'll have to go to a public school. You know that."

"Yes, I guess so." Of course I do. It's just that after more than a month here I'd sort of put leaving Maisha out of my head.

"This is a center for girls. For a particular kind of girl."

"Yes, madam."

"You'll like public school. You'll meet boys your own age and make friends." She smiles, the lines around her eyes crinkling. "But we will miss you just the same."

THIRTY-THREE

NOW: DECEMBER 15
SANGUI CITY, KENYA

I wake up feeling fine. Better than fine. Great, maybe. The sun is shining. I get to go to Splash Land tomorrow. Sam is going to go too. I'm pretty sure I aced my math test yesterday. In fact, the last few days at school have been almost boring. In a good way, like I'm a normal kid with a normal life going to normal boring school.

And then, in the car on the way to Maisha, Sam drops her bombshell:

"I found a family for you to stay with."

"Wh-what?" I ask. I turn my good ear toward her, like maybe I've heard wrong.

Her face is plastered with a too-big, isn't-that-awesome smile. "It's going to be great! They're a really nice Kenyan-Somali family with a bunch of kids. There's even a boy your age.

They live in Eastleigh, where there are lots of other Somalis, and you'll be going to one of the best public schools in Sangui."

"But I— Already?"

Sam's smile falters. "Abdi, finding a family to take you in was the plan the whole time, remember? Staying with me was only supposed to be temporary. We're really lucky we found such a good placement."

I don't reply, afraid of how my voice will sound. The world passes by my window. "When?"

"Sunday."

I swallow once, twice, trying to work the sandpaper feeling down my throat.

Sam's still watching me. "I like having you stay with me, Abdi. You're a great kid. It's just that the whole arrangement is unprofessional. You're my client. Living with a family makes a whole lot more sense."

She starts to list all the ways it's going to be fantastic—new school, stable family with a mom and dad and siblings, my own community—but the more she talks, the worse I feel. I turn away, so her words grow faint in my bad ear. I don't want a new family. I've got a family. Even if they're, well . . . What's so wrong with staying with Sam? Why is it that now, just when I start to feel comfortable, just when everything settles down, it all gets snatched away? Things are fine how they are. Maybe it's unprofessional, but so what?

"Abdi? Are you okay?"

"I'm fine," I say, facing the window.

I feel like my seat belt is the only thing keeping me stuck to the earth. Like if I unbuckled it, I'd float up and out the cracked window, disappearing like a wisp of smoke.

"SOMETHING'S UP with your boyfriend, Muna," Alice says.

My voice is a growl. "I'm not her boyfriend." I flick through the pages of my book, seeing nothing. I'm supposed to be working on my report on *Things Fall Apart*. But the sun glaring off the white pages is giving me a headache.

"Shh," Muna says to both of us. "Is everything okay, Abdi?"

"I'm *fine*," I say. "Why does everyone keep asking me that?" I glower at what I've written so far:

Things Fall Apart is a book about

From the corner of my eye, I see the two girls glance at each other. A flush creeps up my neck. Half of me wants to spit out that this is my last day at Maisha, but the rest of me worries that then I'll do something horrifying like cry. I slap my book closed, startling Muna.

"This is pointless," I say.

"No it's not," she says, frowning. "It's a good book, and you'll get in trouble if you don't finish your essay. You won't have time to do it after school. We've got swim lessons and—"

"Swim lessons are over," I interrupt. Immediately I want to take it back. Where did that come from?

Alice blinks. "What? Why?"

243

"Because I'm tired of giving them," I say, feeling an ugly twinge of satisfaction at the expression on Muna's face.

"Since when?"

I curl my lip. "Since always. Since I realized you're both lost causes. It's pathetic, actually, watching you try."

Both of the girls are staring at me like I've just slapped them across their faces. Part of *me* is staring at myself, astonished at what an asshole I'm being. But that part of me can't seem to make the rest stop. I'm full of something red hot and boiling. I mime splashing around like I'm drowning. "Watch me, I'm so graceful! I'm practically a mermaid!"

Muna's shock turns to anger. "What's wrong with you? You're being a jerk."

I expect Alice to be twice as furious as Muna, but she simply looks surprised, hurt even. "You know the field trip to Paradise Island is tomorrow. We still need to practice, or we won't pass the swim test."

I swipe up my book and papers, shoving them into my backpack, relishing the sound of things crumpling. I have the sudden urge to pull them back out and rip every single page from the books' spines. "Who says I give a shit about your field trip? I wish you'd shut up about it already." I stand, sling the pack around my shoulders. "I'm out of here."

As soon as I'm upright, I find myself desperate for one of them to tell me to stop, sit down, I'm being stupid. But neither speaks. And that makes me angrier still. But so what? What does it matter if they think I'm a jerk? I don't need this. I don't need them, or Sam. I was just fine before Sam and Maisha and algebra class and goddamned swimming lessons.

I'll decide when I leave. Me.

I see something in the grass where I was sitting. The yo-yo Sam gave me has fallen out of my pocket. I pick it up. Stupid kids' toy. I cock back and throw it as hard as I can toward the end of the garden. It's a streak of neon yellow and then it disappears over the wall.

A vicious sort of exhilaration, blinding and burning, rich and ripe, sweeps over me. It carries me across the yard, down the driveway, and right out the front gate.

THIRTY-FOUR

THEN: OCTOBER 2
MERKA, SOMALIA

When we get down to the street, a Boy comes to help Scarface, taking his pack and gun from me. I follow them toward the charcoal lot, keeping an eye out for Khalid and Bashir. Boys mill through the alleys, checking the dead and wounded.

"Hey you, 106, Come here!" I turn to see Nur yelling at me. "Get that side," he says, a dead AMISOM soldier's wrist in his hand. He wants me to help drag him.

All my adrenaline flushes from my system, just like that.

"Wait," Nur says, and his knife flashes. He cuts off the guy's name badge, "MAINA," and stuffs it into his pocket. He grins at me. "Souvenir." Then he grabs the soldier's wrist again. "Come on!" he says, when I don't move. "Don't be a pussy. We've got to get all the AMISOM bodies back to the trucks. Commander Rashid's orders."

So I take the dead man's hand in mine, and I start to pull.

I think of nothing, I see nothing but the street ahead of me. The hand is cool, squishy. My brain flickers a question: *Did I kill this man?* But I stamp it out as quickly as I can. *No no no no no no no no no no.* I will think of nothing. Not this man, not his fingers brushing my skin. My eye finds a single sandal, abandoned in the dust ahead, and I focus on that. I think of nothing. Nothing. Nothing. Nothing.

We deposit the body by our technicals, next to four others. They are covered in dust, none of them looking quite dead, just as if they are taking very dirty naps on the ground.

"*Kaalay*, kid. Come on," Nur says.

I force myself into motion and follow. It's only then that I notice the crowd.

Hundreds of civilians are gathered around our trucks in the charcoal yard. The bright scarves of the women and white *koofi* caps of the men stand out starkly against the Al Shabaab soldiers in drab green who surround them, guns at the ready. The black charcoal mountain looms overhead.

With a wash of relief I see Khalid, Bashir, Toothless and a couple of the other guys from my unit. Their scarves cover their noses and mouths, but I recognize them. Nur nudges me again, and I pull my *keffiyeh* over my face too, fumbling at it like my hands aren't working right. It doesn't matter; no one is looking at me. The civilians' eyes are all fixed on the man standing above the crowd in the back of a truck bed.

It's the General. When did he get here?

His voice thunders, "Shame! Shame on you, people of Merka! You have let the infidels and traitors walk in your midst! They have plotted and schemed while you turned your heads! Don't tell me you were frightened of them. Why would you ever be frightened of them? Look! Look at how pathetic they are now!"

The crowd jostles to peer at what the General, the Butcher, gestures to at his feet. I can't see anything; the crowd is too thick. Just then Commander Rashid's voice rumbles low in my ear, "Go line up on that side, soldiers. Keep this crowd in order."

As I move around the civilians, I feel eyes swivel to me. I get too close to a little boy and he bursts into tears, stuffing his face into the folds of his mother's skirt. She quickly shushes him, looks at me like I'm about to snatch him away from her. I've never seen anyone look at me like that.

We frighten them.

I frighten them.

I stumble away. General Idris's voice rings clear, seeming to come from everywhere at once. "Take heed!" he shouts. "Look at what happens to you when you choose the wrong path, the path of death and evil!" He nudges a bundle of rags on the back of the truck with his toe.

And now I can see better. It's not rags. The bundle has a face.

"There is no hiding from God!" the Butcher says, shaking a finger at the crowd. "God sees everything! *'And they thought that their fortresses would defend them from God! But God's torment reached them from a place whereof they expected it not, and He cast terror into their hearts!'"*

I haven't heard the General talk like this before. Usually he leaves the preaching to the Doctor. I see a few in the front of the crowd nod their heads and mutter their agreement. Most of the faces stay carefully still.

"We are *Harakadka Mujahidinta Al Shabaab!*" the General shouts.

The Boys around me cheer. I force myself to shake my gun in the air with them, but can't find my voice.

"And we fight for freedom from tyranny!" he goes on. "Freedom from the likes of these men! Today we held Merka and did not let it fall into their hands, because God is on our side! God is great!"

Murmurs echo again from the crowd, but apparently they are not enough.

"God is great!" the General shouts at the people before him, demanding a response.

"*Allahu Akbar!*" the crowd echoes, with as much gusto as it can manage. I see a woman pull her scarf over her face, her shoulders trembling.

"Many of the AMISOM dogs are already burning in hell." He turns to a cluster of civilian men being corralled at gunpoint to one side. "But these collaborators will have time to think about their sins before they join them. Take them to the vehicles!"

As the Boys prod the men, I realize one of them is the old

man who was repairing the wall under my sniper post. A black line of dried blood runs from one nostril. My pulse quickens. I know he was helping the AMISOM soldiers, but . . . this is all wrong. He's just an old man. Can't the General see that? His arms in their shackles look like dried-out old twigs.

My *keffiyeh* suddenly feels like it's strangling me. I claw at it, tear it from my mouth so I can breathe. I'm exposing my face, but I don't care anymore.

The General shouts, "Today you will thank God for the freedom—"

He's interrupted by a shout and a swelling of movement in the mass of people just in front of me.

He tries again. ". . . The freedom we have bled and died for—"

But a woman's voice pierces the air. *"Nooo!"*

General Idris, having lost the crowd's attention, squints at the commotion. Two men are trying to calm a woman who is straining on her toes, trying to pull herself from their grasp. I hear the men's furtive, pleading voices. They glance back at us nervously.

"No! Let me go!" The woman jerks free. She is well dressed, and has the furious look of someone rich and important who isn't used to being kept quiet. "Where are you taking my father? He is an *oday* here! How dare you? You cannot have him, you devil! He is an old, sick man!"

I feel my knees go weak. All of the prisoners are looking at her except one. The old mason has turned away, his clenched jaw quivering.

"This is not God's will!" she spits at the General. "God is merciful! *You* are the evil one! *You* are the Butcher! Slaughtering children! Beating old men! Making endless war. You have ruined our country!"

The General's face darkens. "Take her out of here."

"No!" she screams. "Leave my father! Have pity! Take me!"

The men are still pleading with her. They take hold of her arms again. They want to get her out of here. They know what can happen to her. But she isn't making it easy. She squirms free.

"Take me!" She turns on the Boys guarding the crowd. For a second she locks eyes with me, maybe because I'm the only one whose face is exposed. "You and your devils can rape me until I'm a bloody corpse, you filthy—"

The gun butt comes out of nowhere. A soldier has come up quietly and smashed the side of her face.

For a moment all is still. The woman's body slumps sideways like a doll.

"Fadumo!" her father shouts, suddenly alive and struggling against his guards. It's a wonder his wrists don't snap with the effort.

I'm frozen to the spot as the people around the woman roar at the soldier. The woman's limp form is lifted and carried away, rushed to safety through a break in the line of Boys. I feel myself being jolted from side to side. I watch Boys wade in to pull the soldier back out of the hands of snarling civilians. His *keffiyeh* falls away from his face.

It's Nur.

My vision is tunneling to black. I grind my teeth, trying to keep from losing control. This is crazy. Someone stop it. Where is Khalid? Does he see this? Nur is pulled out of harm's way. His face is scratched, his frightened eyes big as coins. Boys next to me point their guns at the crowd, screaming for order. I shake myself, turn to face the sea of faces. I grip my gun, and with a jolt find that I am relieved to have it.

The eyes turned to meet me blaze with hate. Blaze at *me*. Accuse me of bloodying their elders and beating their daughters.

No, I want to tell them, *I'm not one of them! This isn't me! I'm not like them!*

But I don't. My feet don't move me to their side. My hands don't drop my gun in disgust. I stand beside my brothers. I help shield Nur from their wrath. The crowd surges like an angry sea, and for a second I think they're going to rush us, guns or no guns.

But then the Butcher raises his gun in the air and fires it off in an ear-shattering volley. The people, almost as one, crouch, cover their heads. I hear dampened screams.

In the silence that follows, the General yells, "Everyone back to work, back to your homes!"

The air is deafeningly quiet. The spark of rebellion is gone, a silly dream. Already the crowd has broken from one angry, powerful mass into little clusters that quickly melt away, disappearing into a warren of streets between bone-white buildings. They only glance back to make sure they're not being pursued.

And then we're alone. And that's it. It's over.

We wrap the bodies of Samir and the other Boys in cloth and put them in the technicals. The prisoners are loaded into another truck. The old man fumbles—it's too hard to climb in, and he has to be lifted. I stare at the tufts of white hair on the back of his head.

"Get in the truck, kid," Scarface says softly. "Before anyone sees you standing around."

And somehow I do. I get in the truck. And we drive away.

Everything is over.

And nothing is the same.

THIRTY-FIVE

THEN: OCTOBER 2
THE FORT, SOMALIA

The truck shudders to a stop inside the gates of the Fort. I drag myself out and help to shoulder the shrouded body of Samir. At Commander Rashid's instruction, we take him to C-block, where he'll be washed and made ready for burial first thing in the morning. We were lucky. Only one 106 was killed. The 104s follow us, carrying two of their own dead.

We lay the Boys on tables and wordlessly turn toward the barracks, ready to collapse onto our mats. I barely knew Samir, but I can't stop seeing him fall on the street below my sniper perch. I have a feeling I'll be seeing his face in my dreams. If I ever sleep again. My body is exhausted, but my brain spins endlessly through blood and dust and bullets.

The Fort is on the edge of dark. The stars have just begun to emerge, and bats swoop through the half-light. I'm pretty sure we've missed dinner, but it doesn't matter. I'm not hungry.

"Hey," Bashir says as we fall into step together. "You okay?"

It seems like too hard of a question to answer, so I just say, "Yeah."

We walk in silence, and before we get to the barracks, he turns for the kitchens.

"You're not going to bed?" I ask.

"I'm going to go see Safiya first," he says.

"Oh. Okay."

I watch him lope away, wondering how weird it would be if I ran after him and asked if I could hang out too. Being with the other guys and pretending to be okay right now just seems like too much. I've opened my mouth to yell after him when I hear my name.

I turn to find Khalid standing with the Doctor near the entrance to his quarters. A jolt goes through me. I barely saw Khalid at all in Merka. Does the Doctor know what happened there? Has anyone told him about taking that old man prisoner? Is that what they're talking about? I lost track of our captives when we left the city, and now I don't see them. Maybe they were taken to some other place entirely. Khalid would know. I hurry over and salute.

"Da'ud," the Doctor says. He looks me up and down like he's trying to figure something out before he goes on. "I heard you did well in Merka."

Despite everything, I feel pride swelling in my chest—even though I know what he's saying is that I did a good job killing people. I feel proud and I feel sick, all at once. "Thank you, sir," I manage to say.

"Commander Khalid has a job for you."

A job? I stand up straighter. Something to do with the attack?

The Doctor tells Khalid, "See that it's done properly. I will ask the General to assemble the others."

Once he's gone, I turn back to my brother, wanting to ask him about the old man, but stop when I see his face. He looks worn out, even more than me.

"Come on." He starts around the back of A-block, under a grove of acacia trees. I've never been back here before. I didn't think there was anything behind the Doctor's quarters but trees and rubble. Maybe he's taking me to a planning meeting in a secret room where no one will see us. But Khalid stops under the trees and looks up. I follow his gaze. The brightest stars are caught in the branches.

"You proved yourself a warrior out there."

The same queasy feeling of pride swells in me again. *You killed to save your brothers,* I tell myself angrily. What was I supposed to do? Let Khalid and Bashir die? I force myself to focus.

"I've been thinking about what you said," Khalid goes on.

"What I said?"

"About wanting to help. About how I would need someone on the mission I can trust. I think you were right."

I hold my breath, not daring to move. This is it. He's talking about *the* mission.

"I've spoken with the Doctor, and when he heard how you performed out there, he agreed that you could be an asset to the team. But he's not one hundred percent ready to bring you in yet."

"Yet?"

"He wants you to do this . . . job . . . first. He fears that your faith is not strong enough. That you may not be willing to carry out difficult tasks set before you."

I frown. "What? Why? I fought for us. I did difficult things." *I killed people.* Bile fills my throat and I have to force it back down. *Don't go there now, Abdi.* "I'm ready," I say. "Is it another mission? I can go, I can be ready. Where is it?"

For a second, something like pain flashes across Khalid's face. "It's here."

"I don't underst—"

Khalid pulls something from his pocket, stopping me. In the low light I can barely make out that it's a book. He hands it to me.

"What is this?" I say, squinting at it. The cover is a painting of a half-naked white woman, swooning into the arms of a beefy man with long hair. I give Khalid a confused half smile.

"It's *haram*, is what it is," Khalid says, his face still. He doesn't find it funny.

My smile fades. The book sits between us like something smelly. I don't know what to do with it. I try to give it back to him, but Khalid's hands are clenched at his sides.

"We found it in the kitchen girl's things," he says.

It takes me a second to put two and two together. The wrapped package I saw Bashir give Safiya. It wasn't perfume. It was a book. A romance novel in English, not something to flash around in a place like this. But still, why does Khalid look so mad? I shake my head. "I really don't understand."

257

"That book is filthy. Fornication outside of wedlock, adultery, blasphemy . . ."

I wait, confused about what this has to do with me. Or . . . does Khalid know I was there when Bashir gave it to her?

But instead of getting mad at me too, Khalid says, "You will punish her. That's the job."

"Punish her?"

"Da'ud," my brother says, "this sort of Western imperialist trash is what we're trying to wipe clean from our country. And she flaunts it right under our noses. She might as well have defecated in the middle of the mosque. She has to be taught a lesson. The General is assembling the Boys in the yard right now. Come, she's here in the cell. You'll bring her out." He turns away.

With what feels like a punch in the face, I realize I *have* been back here before. The corner Khalid is heading for is the cell where I was held the first two days I was here. I grab my brother's arm. "Wait, what is it you want me to do to her?"

He stops, straightens his back. "She will receive the standard punishment: a whipping. Twenty lashes. You will lead it, landing the first blows, and then the rest of the men in your unit will follow."

I stare at him. "Twenty lashes? For reading a book?"

"It's not just a book, Da'ud. It's what it represents. We have to show the Boys that this sort of thing is not tolerated. If we let her get away with it—a servant girl—they'll think they can get away with worse."

"But . . . the Doctor wants me to do this?"

Khalid narrows his eyes. "If you can't go through with it, tell me now, brother, because the justice we will soon deliver—this mission you are being tested for—will be a thousand times more terrible and glorious than what you will do tonight. This girl is nothing. But by punishing her, you prove yourself true to the faith and worthy of the cause." He stops, searches my face. "Can you do it?"

I stare at him, trembling, wanting to scream, *No! No, no, no! This girl is not nothing! And whipping her for reading is wrong! Don't you remember watching American movies at Salama Cinema? You loved them! They were fun. They let us forget about all the bad stuff around us. They made us happy.* But looking at Khalid now, I realize that if I were in Safiya's shoes, caught watching a Hollywood action movie, he'd feel like he had to punish me too.

My mind spins. Where is Bashir? What will he do when he finds out about this? I can't hurt and humiliate the girl he loves. I can't. It isn't like my hands are clean; I killed people today. But what Khalid is asking me to do feels wrong in some whole other way. I killed to save him and Bashir and the others. This? It's different. He wants me to cause pain where none needs to be. Because of some stupid book. I start to tell Khalid all of this, but as I open my mouth, I find my mother's face floating before me, my *ayeyo*'s, Hafsa's and the twins', and I'm frozen. What happens to them when I say no?

I look at my brother. He's barely recognizable anymore.

It's them or us, I hear Scarface say. *Don't forget that.*

I hear Jones ask, *Do you want your family to be safe? What are you willing to do?*

I swallow the choking feeling in my throat, and realize this was never a choice. I've started down a dark road, and now I can't turn back. It's too late for that.

"Yes," I finally tell him. "I'll do it."

THIRTY-SIX

THEN: OCTOBER 2
THE FORT, SOMALIA
SAFIYA

By the time they are ready, her panic has dulled. At first it was sharp, like the knives she uses every day to chop and cook their food. But like the knives, the fear cannot stay sharp for long, and soon the blunt blade is sloppy, hitting places it shouldn't. Opening up memories.

Safiya thinks of her littlest brother, only just starting to walk when she left, running into everything, lumps on his forehead like eggs. He would be three by now. Where is he?

She remembers a secret boyfriend she had once. He was recruited into the ranks of Boys long before she was. Dead before he turned seventeen. She can't remember exactly what his face looked like. Just that he was sweet. Once he brought her cold soda from a store with a generator. The curvy bottle had beaded with moisture, and something about the way it felt in her hand made her blush for reasons she couldn't quite understand.

It is dark. But that isn't why she can't see the Boys. It's because she has been tied to a pole, her back to them. All she can see is wood grain and the flickering orange light from the Boys' torches. The flames make the grass shadows dance under the trees.

And for a long time, long enough to hear the Boys grow restless and start to whisper, nothing happens. She's on her knees. Her arms go prickly where they are tied above her head, then numb. She stares at the wood grain, getting lost in it, finding worlds in the places between the lines.

Finally she hears the Boys stirring. Their anticipation swells. Shadows jerk and waver.

Two Boys come and stand close to her.

They say something, a proclamation of her guilt. A sentence: twenty lashes. She tries not to listen. She tries to stay in between the wood grain.

But then a hand grabs her dress from behind, and there is a little *snick* of fabric under a knife, and the cloth is ripped along the line of her spine, her whole back undressed, peeled like an overripe mango. Her breasts hang free. She cannot move her arms to cover them.

Her headscarf is pulled off.

The undresser moves away, but the other Boy stays.

They are not finished.

The night breeze is cool on her skin; she feels goose bumps rising. Her flesh is aware of everything.

The first lick is fire, cold and then hot.

She screams, awake, alive, nakedness forgotten.

The second lash is worse than the first. She had no idea something could have so many dimensions of pain. Brilliant like starlight, deep and dull like a hammer.

By the fifth, she is out of air for screaming.

She is aware of the whip changing hands, but it isn't until the eighth stripe across her back that she fully understands that twenty of the Boys will have a turn.

These Boys she cooks for, morning, noon, night.

Whose shit she buries in the latrine.

Whose clothes she washes in salty and then fresh water, and hangs out to dry.

Whose oily bodies she endures when they come in the middle of the night and she is too tired to fight.

These Boys who go out of the gates alive, and who come back full of holes, empty of life.

Who have piled up in graves beyond the wall, too many to remember.

Who are always replaced, a never-ending spring of young men.

Twenty Boys will have the whip handed to them. Each will look at her back. Each will get to make a decision. Twenty chances for the pain to stop.

It doesn't stop.

After thirteen she loses track.

These Boys.

Each of them a band of fire on her body.

Each one a mark.

THIRTY-SEVEN

THEN: OCTOBER 2
THE FORT, SOMALIA

When it is over, the General dismisses the Boys to the barracks for bed. I look for Bashir among the faces that slowly fade from the torchlight, but can't find him.

Safiya barely moves, her back a mess of red ribbons. General Idris tells me to take her to her cell. I untie her hands from above her head and have to catch her because her legs won't hold her up. I hear her moan softly as my fingers close around torn flesh. Her blood is sticky and warm, and little insects, attracted by the light and the smell, are starting fly around her.

I whisper, "Put your arms around my neck." She manages to, and I brace her against my back, half carrying, half helping her stumble to the dark cells. She is lighter than I expect her to be. She had always seemed larger under all her dresses and layers and bluster.

When we are out of earshot, I begin to say softly, "I am so sorry. I am so, so, so sorry."

She doesn't answer. I'm not sure she's fully conscious, though her feet continue to plod forward. Her breath is a wet rasp deep in her chest.

I don't press. Forgiving me is probably the last thing on her mind right now.

When we're almost to the cells, I see a figure before us and tense. *Please, no more,* I think, expecting someone like Nur. But instead of his jackal leer, I find only the stony face of Bashir.

He puts down a basin of water and rags as we approach. "I've got her from here," he says, the fury in his voice barely contained. He lifts Safiya off my shoulder and helps her toward a clean mat he's placed on top of the filth in the cell.

"Can I help? Can I do something?"

"No." He eases Safiya down. I hear her whimper, and him say something soft and reassuring.

"I can get medicine, or—"

Bashir spins toward me, all gentleness gone. His eye flashes with rage. "I think you've done enough. Get out of here."

I stumble back, feeling each word like a spike through my chest. "I didn't want to do it, Bashir. You know I didn't. Khalid said it was the only way they would trust me."

The excuses sound so pathetic.

Bashir doesn't answer. He doesn't look at me, but I can see him breathing hard, trying to keep calm. He brings the water and rags and sets them on the mat next to Safiya. He pulls a candle out of his pocket and lights it, placing it back in the recesses of the cell where it won't be so visible. Someone may still see it, but I hope they just let it go. Her wounds will become infected if they don't get cleaned. I keep backing away slowly. Bashir drips the first rag full of water onto her skin. She keens softly.

"Go, Da'ud," Bashir says.

And there's nothing I can say to make things better. So I go.

THIRTY-EIGHT

NOW: DECEMBER 15
SANGUI CITY, KENYA

I'm far, far away from Maisha by the time my anger is through with me. After storming out of the gate, I'd started running, blindly tearing down the winding streets of the Ring. It's only now that I'm completely spent that I find myself gasping for breath on the side of the road, with no idea where I am. How much time has passed? It's got to be two or three o'clock. What do I do now? Where do I go? Back to Maisha? An image of the yo-yo disappearing over Maisha's wall darts through my head, and a swell of shame fills me. I can't go back there. Not after what I said to Muna and Alice.

As the last of my fury drains, it's replaced with a sick feeling. Muna's right. I am a jerk.

Why did I snap at her and Alice like that? Why did I say I don't want to do swim lessons anymore? That wasn't true at all. Why did I have to be such an asshole? All I know is that it felt good to snatch something away from them. And that I feel horrible now. *Nice job, Abdi. The only two people who were even remotely close to being your friends are probably now discussing how much they hate you.*

I'm so lost in my thoughts that I almost plow into an old woman who's stopped ahead of me. I catch her elbow to keep her from falling, and she scolds me with a *"Pole pole, kijana!" Slow down, kid!* The cars and people ahead of us have come to a complete stop.

"What is it?" I ask the old woman. It's too early for a traffic jam this bad.

"Polisi," she grumbles.

My heart takes off like a startled bird. I crane my neck. She's right. They've put sawhorses across the road to narrow it to two lanes of traffic. A couple of cars have been pulled to the side for searches. There's even a sniffer dog. It's just like the roadblocks that Sam and I went through on the way to Maisha on the morning after the bombing.

I feel a push and step forward. People are piling up behind me. I look around for side streets I might be able to casually turn down, but there are none. The police must have put their roadblock in this spot because there are no escape routes.

You haven't done anything wrong, Abdi, just keep walking. You can't turn around and go back without being completely obvious. Already I notice that one of the officers is eyeing me, his lips pouted in suspicion.

I try to walk behind a tall man. Maybe they won't even

notice me. When I get closer, I see that some people on foot are being let past with just a nod, but others are being stopped to have their bags checked, their pockets turned out. As I watch, a man raises his arms and a cop begins patting him down.

I feel myself tensing to run. *No, idiot, that's what got you taken to the station and locked up the last time. Why would you run? You're not guilty of anything except being Somali. Just keep walking.*

I'm almost there. Sweat beads and rolls down my back. I try not to make eye contact with anyone. The dog tips his nose up at me as I approach, but the officers are busy with other people. With my heart in my throat I realize I'm going to pass right through.

And then, "Hey! You, boy! Stop!"

I freeze, electrified with fear. Then I'm being yanked to the side by my collar, nearly falling over.

The officer's fingers dig into my arm. "Didn't you hear me? I said stop!"

"I'm stopping," I say, raising my hands.

"Don't talk back like you're somebody!" he yells, eyes wide. "Get your hands on your head!" He jabs me in the ribs with a baton, toward a wall where several other guys sit in a row, hands in zip ties, eyes blank. Most of them look Somali. I hadn't noticed them before. One of them has a blossoming black eye. Another boy in a red shirt looks up at me.

For a second I'm rooted to the spot.

It can't be.

It's not possible.

Bashir.

Whole, with both eyes, his bones and skin intact.

The whole world stills, starts to kaleidoscope into Bashir's face, and all I can think is, they've captured him. They're going to send him back. They're going to send *me* back.

Some rational part of my brain is probably trying to tell me that I'm not making any sense, that the police and the Boys aren't on the same team, but most of my mind is a black hole, as deep and senseless as the one Jones tossed me in. Suddenly I'm an animal, I'm fighting like a wounded lion, snarling, lashing out, trying to run.

I get one meter before I'm slammed against the ground, hard enough that I feel my teeth clack and shift, and then the officer's knee is jammed between my shoulders, making me gasp for breath. "Runner!" he shouts, and then feet pound, and from all directions curses are screamed in my face, descriptions of what's going to happen to me if I don't be still. I try to do what they say, but they hit me anyway, blows around my ears and face, kicks to my kidneys. My legs are spread; hands grope up my thighs and around my waist looking for weapons.

It's all one vortex of sound: "Fucking Somali trash! Desert rat! We've got one! Is he one of them? Get his hands secure! Bring the ID photos! Get his legs! Stay down, you son of a whore, stay down!"

My body screams, but I force myself to be still, to not let the beating make me twist and writhe. Finally, they stop and I can suck down a breath. I turn my head back toward the line of guys against the wall. Most of them are watching, wide eyed, silent. I look for Bashir, call out his name, but he's not there. The boy in the red shirt is watching me. I stare at him.

It isn't Bashir. Not even close.

My face is pushed into the asphalt. I can't catch my breath. My ear fills with ringing again.

I hear the noises change, the tenor of the voices shift, and suddenly a white face is swimming in front of mine.

It takes me a second to hear her. "Abdi!" Sam is shouting. "Get him up! What did you do to him? He's not done anything!"

"Sam?" I try to say. I can only see her out of one eye.

An officer tries to take her by the arm and pull her back, but she shakes him off. "Don't touch me! I'm with the UN and he's with me! Let him go! I've got his papers right here! He's not one of them!"

I feel hands pulling me up, Sam dragging me off the ground. The officers argue with her. "Why did he run? Doesn't he see this is a police stop?"

Sam's chest heaves. Her hair has halfway come out of its clip and it's a wild mess around her red face. She's trying to look authoritative, but I can feel her hands trembling, even as she grasps me tightly. "He's not done anything wrong!"

I want to tell her to stop. I've seen the expression on these officers' faces before. It's familiar, the look of men who don't like being bossed around by women. They'll hurt her without thinking twice.

No one moves. It's a standoff between Sam and the police. And then out of nowhere, there's honking and a roar behind us, and we turn to see a black Mercedes chewing up the side of the road. It shoves its way around the line of cars. It hasn't seen the roadblock yet. By the time it does, it's too late. In a screech of brakes and metal it slams into a police truck.

The officers all swivel, and as quickly as they were on me, they pounce in the other direction.

"Get him out of here!" one of the officers snarls at Sam, and shoves me at her.

Sam doesn't speak; we go. As we scurry, I see officers hauling out the driver, who is as limp as a piece of spaghetti. One officer grabs him and shakes him by the shirtfront. The drunk man throws up all over the officer's chest.

Sam pulls me by the arm to her car. "Get in." She doesn't look at me as she's throwing the car into reverse, jamming her foot on the gas. I sink in my seat, the stopped cars in the other lane flying by, feeling my heart continue to thrum.

It's only once the roadblock disappears from view that she speaks. "What the hell are you doing out here? Why am I getting calls from Mama Lisa that you've run away?"

"I don't know," I mumble.

"You don't know?" she asks, her voice rising, starting to crack. "What do you mean you don't know?"

And without warning it's back, all that hot anger. "Why do you care?" I shout. "You're not responsible for me anymore, remember?"

"Of course I'm responsible! I don't want to see you in jail again! Or worse! Don't you know what they do to terror suspects?"

"So I'm a terrorist?"

"No, Abdi, no!" She rakes her fingers through her hair. "Of course not—that's not what I'm—"

"Well, what if I was?" I ask. "What if I deserve whatever it is they do to terror suspects?"

She's barely looking at the road; her wide blue eyes are on me. "What are you— *Shit.*" She slams on the brakes, almost hitting a car in front of us. "What are you talking about?"

My fury turns to dust in my throat. I feel like I'm on a ship in a storm. One second I'm wild with anger, and the next I'm paralyzed with sadness. Up and down, over and over until I just want to throw myself overboard and be done with it. "You should've just left me there," I find myself saying. "That's what I deserved."

She gives me a sharp look. "Okay, that's it," she mutters. She swings the wheel and shoves us through traffic. Drivers lay on their horns but she ignores them. I start to ask where we're going, but can't seem to make myself move.

She turns off the main road and down a side street, and then we're in Sangui's Old Town. The tumble of ancient white buildings reminds me of Mogadishu, and suddenly I'm achy with homesickness on top of everything else.

We're silent as she winds down the ever-narrowing streets. From within my haze I think dully that it's like driving back in time; the buildings get older and the streets smaller, more full of fruit and fish vendors than mobile phone and sneaker sellers. It's quieter too. She drives until we can't drive anymore, until we hit the seawall. She parks the car and turns the engine off.

"Abdi, look at me."

I face her, but can't quite make myself meet her eye.

She takes a deep breath. "I don't know what you've been through, Abdi. I can only imagine."

You don't want to imagine, I think to myself.

"But . . . Please look at me?" I force myself to, and she goes on, "I know that sometimes you probably feel like everything has gone wrong and there's no way to ever make it better."

I stay quiet.

"But to think you deserve to be hurt . . ." She presses her lips together. "You're a good kid, Abdi. No, listen." She reaches out and grabs my hand to keep me from turning away again. "Maybe you've done things. Maybe you . . ." She looks away, doesn't finish. And I know, dully, that she knows, or at least suspects who I was.

Maybe I killed people, I almost say. But as I do, I realize that's not even the worst of it. "I let people die," I say, and feel my face go hot with tears I can't seem to shed. "I left them. I abandoned them."

Bashir.

My brother.

How many others?

They were willing to give up everything, even to die for me. There were a million things I could have done to save them. But I didn't do any of them. And now it's too late.

Sam is quiet. Then she asks, "Do you want to tell me about it?"

And suddenly I feel it all bubbling up, and *yes,* I want to tell her. I want it all to spill out. It's like that moment when you're sick and you know you just can't keep the bad stuff down anymore, and no matter what you do, no matter if it's embarrassing and painful, it's all going to come out in one nasty, messy rush.

So I open my mouth. And I tell her.

THIRTY-NINE

THEN: OCTOBER 3
THE FORT, SOMALIA

Guide us to the straight path, the path of those upon whom you have bestowed favor . . . The words of my prayer are the same as always, but this morning they don't echo in my heart. They sound dull and flat, like rocks dropped onto the sand.

I barely slept last night, and when I did, I dreamed of being chased over the desert by something dark and shapeless. I spent most of the night staring at the ceiling, watching my whip open the first cut across Safiya's back, over and over again. Bashir never came in to sleep. I haven't seen him since he sent me away.

I stumble through exercises and breakfast and am on my way to tactical when Khalid pulls me aside.

"We're wanted for a meeting," he says, "about the mission." He waits for my reaction, but I can't manage anything more than a nod. A tiny worry line appears between his eyebrows. "Come with me."

I follow my brother silently to the General's quarters. I know I should be excited that I'm finally being brought into the plan, but I just feel empty. I force myself to pull it together and at least look alert. *This is it, Abdi, you're here. This is what you've been waiting for,* I remind myself. If whipping Safiya was the price, the least I can do is not waste her suffering. I risk the Doctor and the General changing their minds about including me if I look like I regret what I did.

The Doctor and the General are already in the room when we get there, talking together softly. I'm surprised but happy to see Scarface. He jerks his chin up at me in acknowledgment, his arm in a white sling. There's also a boy from Khalid's unit whose name is Muhumed, I think, and Commander Rashid.

I sit next to Khalid, all of us in a circle turned toward the Doctor. Just as it looks like he's about to start talking, Bashir steps in.

"You wanted to see me, sir?" he asks the General.

"Yes, come in. Sit."

Bashir looks around the room, his eyes widening in surprise, then narrowing when he sees me. He sits on the opposite side of the circle, pointedly not looking in my direction.

I swallow. Did Bashir know he was being invited to this? If so, why didn't he tell me last night? Then I drop my gaze to my feet, knowing why.

"Brothers," the Doctor says, pulling my attention back. "Some of you understand why you are here today; some of you do not."

He looks around the room and I see Muhumed's back straighten. He must be new, like me. I don't know anything about him, other than he seems to be one of those natural athlete types—the kind of guy who's good at every sport he tries. I can see why he'd be a good soldier.

"The mission you will soon undertake is of utmost importance," the Doctor says. "You have been called together because you have been found worthy. You have the skills and the heart for this job, and you are essential to its success. You honor your country and God by being here." He looks at each of us, one by one. "As most of you know, I will not be leading the mission. But I will be watching from close by, and praying for your success.

"This is the moment in which you become the sparks that light God's fire. Each of you is a match. This mission will not be easy. It will likely be the hardest thing you have ever done. It will not bring you glory. It is a mission solely for the glory of God. And so you must, from this point on, think of the mission first, above all else. You must keep an oath of silence about all that you will learn today. Always remember that the devils are hard at work too, and have most likely placed spies among us."

I pray to keep my face from twitching.

"These spies would tell our enemies our plan, and who is involved. Can you swear to silence, my brothers?"

Echoes of "Yes, Hakim Doctor" swell in the room, and the other Boys raise their hands, making an oath. I follow their lead, hoping the trembling in my hand isn't as obvious as it feels.

The Doctor settles back, turning things over to the General.

"The Doctor is a kind man," the General says, "but do not mistake his kindness for weakness. I will say what he said again, and mark my words: if you so much as breathe a whisper of what you hear in this room to *anyone*—and I don't just mean the men in your units; I mean the stars in the sky, the trees, the air, anyone, any*thing*—you will be slaughtered like animals and cursed to the hottest pit of hell. And that will be just the beginning. Am I understood?"

"Yes, sir," we say.

The General unfolds a map of Mogadishu onto the floor in the middle of the circle. "We'll go over the whole thing again, for the benefit of our new team members." He looks at Muhumed, Bashir, and me. "Pay attention, boys."

The General touches the center of the map, where yellow earth meets blue water. "Mogadishu," he says. He slides his finger north. "Lido Beach. You've heard of it?"

I glance at Khalid. Everyone knows Lido. It's the most popular place in Mogadishu. A stretch of gold sand and turquoise water, it's always crowded with families.

"Here," the General says, "is the Ocean View Resort, where Mogadishu's finest citizens—businessmen, politicians, the rich and famous—all rub elbows. It is where army generals meet and plot our deaths. It is also our target."

I try to keep perfectly still so my mounting fear won't show.

"In two weeks' time you will deploy to the city. On the eighteenth, which will be the third or fourth night of Ramadan, a feast is planned. All the most prominent politicians and religious leaders loyal to the government will break their fast together in a show of solidarity. It will be a huge affair, with hundreds of invited guests, and security will be extremely tight. The entire area will be cordoned off days in advance, and everyone coming and going will be searched."

The General brings out another map, a satellite image of Lido Beach and the Ocean View Resort magnified. "This is as close as our tunnels come," he says, pointing to a side street about two hundred meters away from the resort. "Our men have been working on digging to reach a dry well below the resort laundry facilities for the past week. They'll complete the tunnel on the morning of the eighteenth, after the resort has been swept by security for a final time. That will be our entry point." He looks to Bashir. "You and I will talk separately about the vest you will design and make."

"Y-yes, sir," Bashir says, eyes wide.

I feel Khalid shift next to me. Vest? A suicide vest?

"Bashir will go with Soldier Zero to help him get ready. They'll enter here and end up here, in the basement. Bashir will exit the same way, and Soldier Zero will be on his own from that point. This veranda overlooking the ocean will be where all the politicians and their families will be seated and served. Soldier Zero will complete his mission at sundown, after prayers, when all are assembled for the meal.

"We will show our nation that these so-called leaders cannot rape and pillage without consequence," the Doctor says. "The price of their greed will be taken in flesh. No one will be spared."

Slowly, what he's saying comes into focus. A suicide vest, made by Bashir, delivered to a room full of people. So that's the plan? Soldier Zero will go in and blow himself up, killing everyone as they eat? Families? Kids? While they break fast during what should be the most peaceful time of the year? How many people did the General say will be there? Hundreds?

It's hard to concentrate on the rest of the plan. My head swims. Sure, there are suicide bombings every few months in Mogadishu, but I can't remember the last time more than a dozen died. This is going to be on a whole other scale.

We're sitting here planning mass murder.

"And you, Soldier Zero, you'll be ready when the time comes?"

I almost miss who the General is directing the question to.

But then I hear my brother answer in a clear, steady voice, "Yes, sir. I will be ready."

FORTY

THEN: OCTOBER 3
THE FORT, SOMALIA

When I leave the General's room, I can't speak. I move like I'm sleepwalking. All I want to do is get out of A-block. I pass Bashir, who is finally looking at me, but I don't stop. I stumble down the stairs as fast as I can without running and, once I'm out of view, throw myself around the corner of the building.

Alone, next to the garbage pile, I collapse against the wall.

Khalid . . .

Dahir . . . is going to . . .

I can't even think the rest. All I can do is stare at the sand between my feet, his name running over and over in my head. *Dahir Mohamed Abdullahi Kulane* . . . Like I can change what I just heard by saying his old name enough times.

I feel a touch on my shoulder and jerk my head up. I suck down a gasp when I find the Doctor standing over me. I start to scramble to my feet, wiping my nose, but he puts a hand on my arm.

"No, no, it's okay, sit." He lowers himself to the ground too, like he's just another one of the Boys, not the leader of this entire movement.

"But it's dirty, and . . ."

"Never mind." He looks directly at me, until I have no choice but to meet his eye. "Are you all right, Da'ud? It's a lot to take in."

I have no idea how to respond. What do you say when you find out your brother wants to die? To die in order to kill people? Hundreds of people. And that this man sitting next to you is the person he's doing it for? Finally I choke, *"Whoever kills one man, it is as if—"*

"—He has killed all of humanity. Yes, I know, Da'ud," the Doctor says, finishing the *ayah* with a sigh. "I know. I wish there were some other way to do this. I wish the men in power now were godly men. I wish they cared that they were leading us all down a long path of servitude and poverty. But they're lost, Da'ud, and they don't want to be found." He looks out at the shadows created by the branches of the acacia trees. "I have tried the way of talking. I've tried reasoning with these sorts of men, and I've realized, after years of frustration, that there are simply those who will never change their minds and hearts, no matter what truth you tell them."

I know I'm risking everything by arguing, but I can't seem

to stop myself. "But killing all those people . . . and there will be children there too."

The lines across his brow grow deep. "That is my heart's burden to bear," he says. "Not yours. Yes, there will be bloodshed, but the innocent who die will be martyrs to a larger cause. I know in my heart that this is what must happen to bring God's kingdom to earth. Remember what I said about the diseased plant in your field? There's no cure for it in these men. And we can't allow the disease to spread, Da'ud. This is the only way."

I do remember. The plant has to be pulled out by the roots, burned. And its ashes will fertilize new crops.

"Do you understand?" he asks.

I press my nails into the inside of my palm. I press so hard that later I find four little crescents of blood there.

"Yes, Doctor," I say.

And inside I am screaming.

Screaming as loud as a hurricane. And what I'm screaming is this:

My brother is not a match.

He isn't a piece of cardboard and sulfur to scratch into brilliant flame, use and toss to the ground. He isn't disposable, replaceable, twenty to a pack.

And people aren't plants.

Pulling them up and burning them doesn't make all the rest of the people better.

I want to scream it so hard that my throat shreds.

The Doctor stands, his kind face searching for my under-standing. "Are you ready to get back to work?"

I don't scream. And I don't scream. And I don't scream.

I stand up. "Yes, sir."

I can feel his eyes on me as I walk back toward my unit. My legs are stiff, and they are jelly all at once. The Boys I pass are busy with a drill. They thrust the muzzles of their guns up over their heads, over and over, like they're trying to slice holes in the sky.

FORTY-ONE

"You have to eat something," I say. Through the flap on the door I push the bowl of stew closer to Safiya's curled form. Her bloody back is to me, as good as an accusation. Bashir has covered it in a sticky mix of iodine and aloe, but it doesn't stop the flies from crawling and buzzing all over the stripes of puckered and oozing flesh. I shudder, peering through the slot into the dim cave of a cell, remembering my time here. It's as filthy as ever. There's no way she won't get an infection.

"It's not as good as what you'd make, but it will give you some strength," I say. "The other girl made it, Lul. She's taken over while you're . . . sick."

No answer.

"Or at least eat some *canjeero*," I plead. "You don't have to talk to me, just eat."

The only thing that moves are the flies and her side rising and falling with her breath.

I lean back and put my hand over my eyes. The sun feels like a serrated knife, clawing into my skull. I am so tired. I didn't sleep again last night. Whenever I closed my eyes, I could only see my lash coming down on Safiya's back, or the woman in Merka's head snapping sideways, or my brother, arms outstretched like a saint, disappearing in a cloud of fire. I tried to think about my family instead, but that was even worse.

"What are you doing here?"

The voice makes my spine stiffen, and I turn slowly.

Bashir is walking toward me, carrying a gourd. It's the traditional kind used to hold camel milk. I wonder where he got it; they don't serve camel milk here at the Fort. Then I remember that Bashir is resourceful. If he can find romance novels in Somalia, he can find camel milk.

"I brought her something to eat," I say, feeling useless.

"Did she eat?"

"No."

Bashir brushes past me. "She hasn't been able to keep much down."

He unlocks the door and kneels next to Safiya. He murmurs something to her, but I can't hear if she responds. He lifts her head, his hands suddenly soft like he's handling something as delicate as a butterfly wing. She pushes herself up onto one elbow, sending the flies into a tizzy. Bashir puts the gourd to her lips.

I feel like I'm watching something private, so I step away, lowering my eyes. I should leave, but I can't. My feet are stuck. And I don't know where to go. I've skipped out of tactical, and I can't very well show up midway through. I'll go as soon as Bashir tells me to get out of here, I decide, which should be any second now.

But he doesn't. Safiya takes a few weak sips, then lies back down again.

"How is she?" I ask.

"Not great, thanks," Bashir says, still not looking at me.

I cringe. "Can I help?"

His shoulders go slack and he sighs. "She'll be okay, as long as nothing gets infected. I've been putting ointment on her, and now she just needs to rest." He waves his hand viciously, sending flies off in other directions.

"How long will she be in here?" I ask.

He shrugs. But I can see the fear in his face. Once she gets better, will they put her back to work, or send her away? They can't send her away, I tell myself; she knows too much about the Fort. But what if she doesn't get better fast enough? What if she can't work? How long will they let her lie here? I shudder, trying not to think about the alternative. They won't just let her sit around uselessly, one more mouth to feed.

Watching Safiya's back, something the Doctor said yesterday comes to mind, clearly in focus now. He said that the people he wants Khalid to kill are beyond talking to, beyond redemption. It was the same with Safiya. This is what he meant. He didn't want to talk to her, to explain why he thought the book was wrong. He's given up trying. The whip was easier.

"I'm so sorry, Bashir," I say, my voice barely a breath.

He lets out a long hiss of air. "I know you are, *doqon*," he finally says. "Don't forget I had to whip her too."

We don't say anything for a while.

Then, "I'm sorry about your brother."

"Yeah. Me too," I say.

He looks around. "The guards will pass by here on patrol in a few minutes. We need to go. Where are you supposed to be?"

"Tactical. You?"

"Weapons."

Neither of us moves.

Finally I open my mouth. "Bashir, I—"

"Shut up," he says tiredly. "Just . . ." He raises his hand, like he can't bear to hear anymore. ". . . don't."

We sit in silence for a minute longer, and then Bashir goes into the cell to whisper to Safiya that he'll be back again soon. When he comes out, his face is set in hard lines. He locks the door again, then says, "Come on. Let's get to the perch before anyone sees us. We've got a lot to figure out."

FORTY-TWO

THEN: OCTOBER 4
THE FORT, SOMALIA

"No," Bashir says. "We can't tell Mr. Jones."

I gape at him. "What? What do you mean? This is it! This is what we've been waiting to hear!"

Seagulls mew and dip on the breeze coming off the water below us. They dive for fish in the chop of the waves hitting the rocks, fight over what they pull out.

"Don't you see? He'll just bomb us all to hell."

"But he said he wouldn't, if we can get him what he wants!"

Bashir shakes his head. "I've been thinking about it, and here's the thing: Why would he keep a promise to *us*? Why would he *not* bomb the Fort, if he knows for sure the attack will be staged from here?"

"Because . . ." I trail off.

He's right. Jones has no loyalty to us. He says he wants to stop the attack with as little killing as possible, but like Bashir's already reminded me, it wouldn't be the first time the Americans bombed Al Shabaab bases. Just look at Jilib and the 112 dead Boys. Jones has made it clear he's got no qualms about snuffing us out.

"At the very least he'll kill your brother before he has a chance to blow anything up."

"So what do we do?" I say, trying to fight off a choking sense of desperation. "We have to tell Jones *something*."

"We'll tell him just enough so he knows the attack is happening, and when, and that we're going to stop it. But not so much that he can take things into his own hands."

I almost laugh. "*We're* going to stop it? How?"

"I'm not sure." Bashir sighs. "I mean, not without getting killed."

A gull swoops past us, pursued by two others. It holds a shimmering, squirming thing tightly in his beak. I frown. "Not without getting killed . . ."

A rueful smile passes over my friend's face. "Look, I like you, man, but I'm not sure I'm ready to die for you. I need to be alive to spend my money and take care of my lady. No hard feelings."

But as the surf breaks below, an idea begins to take shape in my head. I think about that day in the schoolyard three years ago. I think of Khalid hanging halfway over the wall. He must have known even then that what he was about to do would one day cost him his life. One way or another. He did it anyway.

He did it for me.

"No, not you," I say. "It has to be me. *I* have to die."

I'M WORRIED that Jones isn't going to play along when we explain my idea to him. Or part of my idea, anyway. We tell him only that we found out that the attack will happen on the eighteenth in Mogadishu, and that it will be coordinated among a bunch of different Al Shabaab bases. We don't know which ones. That way even if Jones does decide to bomb all the bases he knows about, there's no guarantee he'll stop the attack.

Jones was pissed, which we expected, but in the end he promised he wouldn't bomb the Fort, for what that's worth. And he agreed to help us with a few key parts of the plan. But he left us with a warning. "I'm taking a real risk on you kids, so here's what I expect in return: The attack gets stopped. That goes without saying. But I want the Doctor or the General, preferably both, alive, in my custody, by the end of the night of the eighteenth. Otherwise no families go free, no payouts happen. And you might as well start considering yourselves dead martyrs."

Two weeks seemed like plenty of time to get our plan in place and make sure we're ready, but it's not like the General's letting us slack off. All our time is still scheduled. Until we leave for Mogadishu, I'm still expected to crawl around in the dirt and do target practice and make sure no one drowns during swim lessons. When I'm able, I go early or stay late at the beach, timing myself to see how long I can swim underwater, picking up rocks off the ocean floor and testing how much weight I can carry before I sink. At night, before I fall asleep, I practice holding my breath. At first I can only go a minute, but soon I'm able to count to 115.

Bashir's got even less time because he's supposed to be working on the bomb and also still catering to the General. We don't get called in for any more strategy discussions, and when I ask Khalid why, he only says that we'll get more info once we get to Mogadishu. Basically, no one's telling us any more than they need to. Bashir and I meet to discuss things when we can, but sneaking away to the perch is even harder now. I get the sense that the General is keeping an extra-close watch on all of us who are on the team. Bashir does manage to let me know that the vest the General wants him to make is supposed to have a blast radius big enough to take out everyone in the restaurant. Maximum destruction.

On the fourteenth the new moon is sighted, which is the official start of Ramadan. Normally, Ramadan is the best time of the year. The fasting is tough, but back home everyone moves a little more slowly, takes it easier. Hooyo and Aabo always invited all our relatives and neighbors and shared food as if the supply were endless, because, as Hooyo would remind us fiercely, wasn't that our duty? After all, there were others even poorer, and Ramadan was a time for charity. But here, nothing changes. Not for the better, anyway. Instead of dates and fat *sambusas* and fried *kac kac*, we break fast with the same old beans and bread, plus extra helpings of prayer. We still have to do all the same exercises. The hard-core religious guys get right into their holy deprivation, but it makes the rest of us irritable and homesick, even if no one dares say anything.

This year there's also the possibility that my brother will blow up a resort and kill a few hundred people, so, like, yeah, *Ramadan Kareem,* everybody.

"But what if Jones decides not to put up the posters?" I ask Bashir for maybe the thousandth time as we walk to the technicals in the early morning haze. The seventeenth has finally arrived and we're headed to Mogadishu before exercises start, when our departure won't be noticed by too many of the Boys.

"Don't doubt the plan, Da'ud," he tells me. "Do you think James Bond gets his shorts all in a twist right before he's about to go on a mission?"

"You've never even seen the movies."

"But I know James Bond is a steel-jawed, no-second-guessing sort of dude. We gotta be like that. Jones'll have the posters up by the time we get there. He'll do it, don't worry. I could hear it in his voice."

The first part of our plan involves Jones getting Khalid's face plastered on "Wanted" posters all over Mogadishu so there's no way my brother can just waltz into the Ocean View Resort. But Jones has to do it today, after all of our team is already there in Mogadishu and there's not enough time for the Doctor or the General to think too hard about a replacement. They'll have to either scrap the whole plan, or . . . we move on to part two.

Bashir looks toward the kitchen, maybe hoping to catch

a glimpse of Safiya before we leave. I do too, but we can't see much through the mist. Safiya's been put back on duty. She's doing okay, but you can tell she's still in some pain. There's a stiffness to her movements. She won't talk to me. She's not talking to anyone but Bashir, actually. Not that I blame her. Hopefully, after all this, she won't have to think about me or any Boy ever again. She and Bashir can take their money and . . . but that's getting too far ahead of myself. One step at a time.

First, we've got to get to Mog with the Boys without getting stopped by AMISOM at checkpoints. We're being extra careful today, and instead of one of our trucks dropping us off on the outskirts of town like we do on tunnel supply missions, we'll only go as far as Afgoye. From there we'll split up and take minibuses into Mogadishu. All of our gear has been smuggled into town already in the back of a charcoal truck, and will be waiting for us in the new tunnel below the hotel.

Khalid is standing by the technical when Bashir and I get there. Like us, he's in civilian clothes, a soccer jersey like one he would have worn back before he was kidnapped, and the sight of it sends a sudden pang of homesickness through me. I swallow it down, making sure my face is smooth by the time I'm close. Soon, I'll see Hooyo and the others, *Inshallah*.

The General, Commander Rashid, and Muhumed are with Khalid, but where's Scarface? And why is Nur here?

General Idris looks us over. "We have a change to the mission team. Scarface's arm isn't healed enough, and he's being replaced by Nur."

Bashir and I exchange a tense look. Doesn't the General remember what a loose cannon Nur is? Or maybe he was chosen precisely because he's so zealous and isn't afraid to bash women's heads in. The change won't affect our plan, but I wish the General would have chosen someone—anyone—else to replace Scarface.

"I will be in close contact with Commander Rashid. He's in charge, and I expect you to follow his every order with speed and to your utmost ability."

"Yes, sir," we say.

"Then there's nothing else to say except God go with you." The General gives us one final salute.

We all salute back. Then we load up, and pretty soon we're through the gates.

I take a last look at the Fort as we're leaving, and hope I never see it again as long as I live.

THE MINIBUS I pack into with Muhumed is cramped and noisy. It's made for fifteen people, but like always it's packed with closer to twenty, and that's not counting babies. It always seems like there are more people coming into Mogadishu than leaving. It's where the markets wait with open arms, where young people come to try to make their fortunes, where the quiet desert countryside abruptly becomes a teeming, pulsing city.

A plastic replica of an open Quran and a fuzzy purple monkey sway from the minibus's rearview mirror. Every time I catch myself in the reflection, it's a shock. I look so different now.

Hollow, bug-eyed, like someone I wouldn't want to meet on a dark street.

We pass endless shops covered in hand-painted advertisements: an array of possible hairstyles on a barber's; sides of meat on a butcher's; mobile phones, wedding dresses, breakfast food. Tuk-tuk taxis buzz around the minibus, searching for passengers like bumblebees search for flowers. We go through three AMISOM checkpoints, but each time the soldiers just open the door and take a good look at us, as if someone's going to pop up and confess to being a terrorist. Sometimes they poke inside people's bags, or ask for ID, but nearly everyone on the bus is from the countryside and most don't have ID, so at least we're not alone when we shrug helplessly. It's almost too easy, but that doesn't mean I'm not sweating bullets the entire ride.

At the last stop before we're in the city, the soldiers pull one guy off that they must not like the look of. He goes with them, hands raised, a plastic sack of bananas dangling from his thumb. He doesn't seem angry or confused at being pulled aside, just tired, like maybe this has all happened before, and as long as he doesn't make any sudden moves, everything will be fine. I watch him as we pull away until he disappears in the dust, feeling oddly guilty for leaving him behind.

The bus drops us off near the roundabout under the Daljirka Dahsoon monument. The ring of blue-and-white flags flutter around the obelisk like little slices of sky. We're all supposed to make our way to a half-defunct hotel by noon, staggering our entrances. As we walk, I scan building walls.

"Where are they?" I mutter to myself.

"What?" Muhumed asks.

"Nothing," I say. But I keep my eyes peeled. Jones is supposed to have put up the "Wanted" posters by now, but my brother's face doesn't look back from any of the walls. Maybe this isn't the right sort of street? Maybe he hasn't gotten to this area yet? Maybe Bashir was wrong, and Jones is laughing at us, planning his drone strike at this very moment. We pass some sort of municipal building and I see "Reward" posters. My eyes skitter over the faces, stark black and white. I recognize the General and the Doctor, but all the posters are wrinkled and old; there are no fresh faces here. Definitely not my brother's.

My chest tightens. Maybe Jones hasn't had enough time yet. After all, this isn't even where Bashir asked him to concentrate them. He's supposed to get fliers distributed to the police and AMISOM, and plaster them around the markets and the Ocean View Resort.

He'll do it. Bashir seemed sure of it. I just need to give him a little more time. We told him not to be too early, after all.

When we make it to the hotel, Muhumed checks the phone he's been given. We're supposed to wait at the cafe across the street until 11:47. Nur is already sitting at a table when we get there. The Doctor has told us we're exempt from fasting while on the mission—he wants us sharp and ready—but no one orders anything. We don't want to attract attention. I check out the hotel. It's nothing fancy. There are scads of them just like it all over Mog. Six stories high, but finished only through the first three. The roof is a skeleton of concrete and rebar, waiting for the next time someone scrapes together enough money to give it another floor. It looks like it's been a while; one whole corner of the third floor has been blasted away in the meantime, like some giant has been gnawing on it. It's hard to find a building in Mogadishu that doesn't have scars. Plaster on top of bullet holes on top of mortar holes. For a second I'm reminded of the old mason from Merka who was taken prisoner. I never found out what happened to him.

I crack my knuckles and force myself not to jiggle my knee. From the hotel it's about a ten-minute walk to the Ocean View Resort. Close enough to get there fast if we need to, far enough away that we can fall back here if something goes wrong. Could I sneak away somehow and go look for the posters? If Jones doesn't put them up, alerting anyone and everyone that Khalid's with Al Shabaab, how am I supposed to convince him he can't show his face in the Ocean View Resort tomorrow?

Nur jabs me in the arm. "What's up with you? You look like someone shit in your porridge." He brays a donkey laugh. Muhumed gives him a disapproving look.

My first instinct is to tell Nur exactly where he can stick his questions, but I don't need to piss him off right now. "Nothing—just thinking about the job."

Nur gets serious. "Yeah, man. Me too. I can't wait to see the look on the faces of all those—"

"It's time," Muhumed interrupts.

We stand up, leave a sprinkling of coins on the table to pay for loitering and make our way to the hotel. Inside, it's musty and dark. The walls might once have been painted to match the bright blue of the national flag, but now they're faded and peeling. The front desk is empty, and the only guests in the lobby are a couple of sleeping cats. It looks like it's been years since anyone actually stayed here.

We take the stairs to the fifth floor, like we've been told to do. The other landings open onto dim corridors, but on the unfinished fifth there's a new-looking metal door blocking us from seeing down the hall. Muhumed knocks quietly, and a panel slides back. A single eye peers out at us as we repeat the passwords, giving the signal that everything is fine. Finally, the door creaks open and Bashir lets us into an even darker room. There are few interior walls, mostly just columns sketching the idea of where walls might one day be. All the windows have been shuttered or covered in heavy, dark fabric. It's stiflingly hot. The only light comes from a computer in an adjoining room.

Commander Rashid and my brother come out to greet us.

"Welcome to the operation," Rashid says. "Make yourselves comfortable. Get a little sleep if you can. It might be your last opportunity for a long time."

FORTY-THREE

Rashid comes to the doorway and looks at the five of us sitting in the dark. "We need supplies." He holds up a list on a crumpled piece of paper.

"I'll go," Khalid says quickly before anyone else can stir.

After hours without anything to do but check and recheck our weapons, everyone is both drowsy and on edge. Bad combo. Sleeping, like Rashid instructed, would be smart, but it's impossible. Bashir is busy doing something with the vest, and Muhumed's on lookout at one of the windows, but Nur, Khalid and I have been sitting around with our fingers in our ears for too long. We've been warned to keep the talk to a minimum. I've had way too much time to stare at the walls and think of all the many ways all of this could go horribly wrong.

Rashid looks past Khalid at the rest of us. "You should stay here, brother, out of sight."

"I'll be fine," Khalid says, standing up. "Besides, I need to stretch my legs; I'm getting stiff." He reaches for the list. "I'll go the opposite direction from the resort, north to Bakara Market."

I spring up too. "Can I go with him, Commander? Sir?"

This is almost too perfect. I had figured someone would have to go out eventually and whoever it was would discover the posters, but didn't think it would be Khalid volunteering. By now, surely Mr. Jones has had enough time to put them up. If Khalid sees them himself, he'll understand that he won't be able to get into the resort unnoticed. It's risky, Khalid going out at all if posters of him are up, but I'll be there to make sure he sees them, gets out of sight, and gets back to the hotel as soon as possible. I'm already practicing the way I'll amp up the drama, what I'll say to really drive it home that his cover's been blown. The police will have the posters, I'll tell him. And all the security guards at the resort.

Rashid narrows his eyes at the two of us. I wonder what he's worried about. I'm sure he trusts Khalid, but maybe he thinks I'll try to talk my brother out of his mission? Or it could just be what he's said, that Khalid should be staying here out of sight. But finally he hands Khalid the list and a wad of cash. "Be back in an hour."

Khalid doesn't look at me as Nur lets us out the metal door and we start down the stairs. My brother probably doesn't want me coming with him either. Maybe *he's* the one worried I'll try talking sense into him.

I follow Khalid through the alleys. It's the first chance I've had to speak to him alone since the day I cornered him in the latrines. I know I shouldn't, that I should wait until all of this is over to talk about that day, but I can't seem to stop the words from spilling out of my mouth. "I'm sorry, Khalid."

He glances back. "For what?"

"You know what."

He's quiet for a minute. I wonder if he's going to tell me again that he's glad he ended up where he is now. But finally he just says, "It doesn't matter now."

"Why didn't you ever come back home?" I blurt, unable to keep it in. "Just to let us know you weren't dead, at least?"

His shoulders tighten. "It wasn't allowed." After a brief silence he adds, "Besides, Hooyo wouldn't have let me leave again."

A ghost of a smile finds its way onto my face. "No, she would have chained you to the wall if you'd tried."

I'm shocked to hear him snort a laugh. Blood pulses in my ears. Maybe there is some small part of the brother I once knew left. The part that misses his mother, his home.

The part that saved my life.

He glances back at me, and something in my face must remind him that he isn't supposed to laugh at stuff like that. He goes stony again. As he turns away, I can feel my chest cracking, like it's some dried-up and brittle shell. My big brother. *Dahir.* He's right there. I could reach out and touch his arm. I force down the urge to grab him and tell him we could run, right now. Be done with all of this.

"You know why I have to do it, right?" he asks, not turning around.

No, I want to say. *Not at all.* There is not one part of his dying that makes any sense to me. How can he think killing all those people is somehow what God wants him to do? Can't he imagine our parents' faces if they knew what he was planning? Doesn't he know that if he blows himself up, he'll shatter all the rest of us too?

But I don't say any of that. Those are the things that Abdi would say, not Da'ud. And I feel like I'd rather eat the sand beneath my shoes than be Da'ud right now, but I manage to find his voice in me, because I have to. I have to keep up the facade. Because I know I can't talk him out of it, and keeping up the lie is the only way to make sure he lives.

So while Abdi is shouting *No!* inside, Da'ud quietly says, "Yes."

We keep walking. *Just a little bit longer,* I tell myself. *Be patient. We'll see the posters. The Doctor won't let him risk being recognized. He'll want to replace him. If you're really lucky, maybe he'll even call the mission off. You'll get your brother out of this. He won't die.* I swallow once, twice, force myself to keep breathing normally. If Khalid sees me getting nervous, he'll suspect something. At the very least, he'll think I'm soft, and that's the last thing I need right now.

We're approaching Howlwadag Street. The noise swells. Traffic, music, the voices of shopkeepers advertising their wares. And then we're there, and it washes over us like a tide.

The famous Bakara Market. Always packed, it's exactly the sort of place to advertise hefty rewards. As we bump shoulders and make our way through, I scan for posters. Ayeyo used to say you could get anything from a camel to a coffeepot here. It's even busier than usual, with Ramadan having just started. The shoppers are a teeming sea of people making their way through aisles stacked high with shiny new goods. Rows of buildings with shops on their ground floors surround the market and keep the crowd packed in tight. Everything is stacked in careful pyramids: suitcases, melons, spices, candies, fabric. Electric wires crisscross above, dipping precariously like a net, adding to the hemmed-in feeling of the place.

People are buying special treats to break fast with: dates and *xalwa* and sweet biscuits, putting their orders in for meat and *canjeero*. Brightly colored paper lanterns are strung up to tempt shoppers. I am momentarily dazzled by the frenzy of color and noise; my eyes and ears almost hurt after so much time at the Fort.

I glance at Khalid. Does he feel anything, looking at the decorations and smelling the familiar Ramadan smells? Does he miss those nights of breaking fast by lamplight? The singing, the laughter, Hooyo and Aabo letting us stay up way too late until we would fall asleep where we sat, our faces sticky with sweets? Where are Hooyo and the others this year? Somewhere locked up, wondering if they'll even be kept alive until Eid? They could be just around the corner, or a million miles away.

Khalid pulls the list out of his pocket and glances at it. "Let's go. We should be quick."

I swallow it all down, all my anger, my heartsickness. I follow him into the throngs. *Focus, Abdi. Look for the posters. We do need to be quick. Those times will come again. But right now, push it all down, lock it up, hide the key.*

Khalid buys food for our team's dinner and breakfast: fruit, bread and dried meat at three different stalls. He buys rope and a utility knife. We're deep in the market by this time. I keep trying to glance at the list to see how long it is, how much longer I have before Khalid tells me it's time to go, but he stays a step ahead of me. Panic is starting to swell in my chest. I haven't seen any "Wanted" posters yet, just advertisements for Coca-Cola, mobile phones, Ramadan specials. What if we don't see them? What if Jones never put them up? We can't go back to the hotel without Khalid seeing himself in black and white, plastered to the city walls.

"Just a couple more things," Khalid says. "Come on." He makes for a table selling electronic parts, twisted gobs of wire like a robot spilled its guts. As he's frowning over the mess, I walk a little farther, still searching. Sweet shop, butchery, bakery . . . Wait. There.

The post office. Of course. Official-looking notices flutter on the side of its wall. In all my trips to the market, I'd never noticed them, but they must have always been here.

I glance over my shoulder. Khalid is haggling with a

shopkeeper. I slouch toward the notice boards, trying to get a better look. And then I see them: Faces drawn in rough pencil. Faces blown up from tiny photos, muddy and ambiguous. So many faces. But there, plastered over all of them, he's unmistakable.

The face of my brother.

A grin escapes me before I can catch myself and swallow it. I can't look ecstatic to see Khalid's scowling face on a half-million-dollar "Reward" advertisement. *Dead or alive.* I hurry over and rip one from the wall. Before I turn back, I rub my hand over my mouth, forcing it into a twist of worry. When I'm sure I've got my expression right, I look back at Khalid. He's walking toward me, brow furrowed. He makes a shrugging, where-the-hell-did-you-go? motion and waves at me to come back.

I widen my eyes, shake my head and gesture furtively for him to come to me. Khalid frowns harder, but keeps walking. My spirits buoy as my brother edges his way past the shoppers. I'll show him the poster, all of them on the post office wall, and we'll get out of here. It'll be the beginning of the end.

There's a break in the crowd, and Khalid pushes forward. "What are you doing? This is no time to go wandering—"

A rapid series of earsplitting cracks shatters the air. Everyone ducks automatically, myself included. We're all well trained. It's a familiar sound. Gunshots. Close range. The dust in the street before me explodes with the impact. That was close. I swivel in a crouch, looking for where the bullets came from. Shoppers shout, start to push and scatter, raising more dust, seeking shelter. The building windows and rooftops are clear. I scan once more. Is that someone behind that curtain? It is. I can see the silhouette of a rifle in his hands, three stories up, across from the post office. I look around, trying to see who the man was firing at. I haven't seen any soldiers, so maybe it's a turf war between rival gangs. That's just as common as anything.

"We need to get out of here," I say. "There's probably about to be some sort of fight."

"Abdi . . ."

I turn to Khalid, startled. He hasn't said my real name since the first day I came to the Boys. His eyes are wide but unseeing. He grips his stomach, like he's got a cramp. Then he pulls his hand away.

It's covered in blood.

FORTY-FOUR

THEN: OCTOBER 17
MOGADISHU, SOMALIA

Not part of the plan.

Not part of the plan.

Not part of the plan.

"Just a little farther," I tell my brother, panic choking me, making it hard to speak. "We're nearly there." I glance down at his stomach to make sure he's still holding tight to the wad of fabric I grabbed from a stall in the chaos. It's soaked through.

Khalid doesn't answer. He's leaning heavily on me, limping as fast as he can. His breathing is rough and wheezy. Shit shit shit. Did the bullet hit a lung? What have I done?

Not part of the plan! No one was supposed to get shot.

He needs a doctor, a hospital. That was my immediate thought, until I remembered the poster still clutched in my hand. I can't take him there; he's good for half a million USD, dead or alive. What if someone at the hospital figures that dead is a much easier way to collect?

Dammit!

Who took that shot?

You know who took it, Abdi.

It could only have been Jones. He didn't want to take any chances. Instead of letting the posters do the work, he decided to take my brother out of the picture entirely. He used my chip to follow me, and I guess having one of his men fire on Khalid was just too much of a temptation. The surge of pure, blinding fury makes me light on my feet, and I shoulder more of Khalid's weight. He groans under his breath.

"Come on," I say. "A few more steps."

Finally we reach the alley across from the hotel, where I pause, looking up and down the street. There are a handful of people around, and we're going to have to make a dash for it to get inside. I glance back the way we came. We're trailing blood too. *It doesn't matter,* I tell myself. *Jones knows exactly where you are. If he's going to try finishing Khalid off, there's not much you can do about it now.*

"Look alive, soldier," I tell my brother, and he lifts his head a fraction. I can tell that even this small movement causes him pain. I hustle him across the street and bolt into the lobby, praying no one looks too closely at us. Inside, behind the front desk, a paunchy bald guy startles from where he was drowsing. It takes him a second to register that all is not well, by which time we're halfway across the lobby headed for the stairs.

"Hey!" he says behind us. "Hey, you! What's wrong with him? You can't bring him in here like that!"

I ignore him. My brother makes it up two stairs and moans. I can feel his legs trembling.

"It's okay, it's okay," I tell him, and basically drag him up the stairs. I can tell it hurts, but I don't have a choice. I have to get him up and seen to. Surely one of the guys on our team will have some idea what to do. I saw medical kits in our supplies. "Help!" I shout up the stairs.

I stagger up and up under my brother's weight. His head lolls back. I can't tell whether he's conscious or not anymore. Oh, God, is he . . . But no, I can see his throat moving.

When I finally reach the door, I pound on it. "Let me in!"

The peephole ricochets open and I hear Nur growl, "What do you think you're—"

"Open up!" I demand, and his eye swivels down to Khalid. He throws the door wide.

All at once everyone is up and around me.

"What the hell happened?"

"Oh, shit, is he . . . ?"

"Get him over here, soldier!"

Hands go under Khalid, the door clangs shut, and then we're lifting him up and laying him on a table. His hand starts to fall away from the wound, and I press it, blood squishing under my fingers. He's not moving; his eyes have rolled back.

"Somebody do something!" I shout.

"Call the Doctor," Rashid yells, ripping a blanket off the window so light spills into the room. Nur darts for the phone. "Get the medical supplies," he tells Bashir. "Muhumed, go tell them to boil water in the kitchen!" He lays his fingers on my brother's neck, checking for a pulse. "He's still with us."

I feel a surge of gratitude for Rashid's leadership.

"How bad is it?" Rashid asks, and lifts the wad of fabric, revealing an almost perfectly round hole in my brother's gut, right under his rib cage. A little trickle of blood pulses out of it, and Rashid quickly replaces the cloth. "Is there an exit wound?"

"I—I don't know," I stammer. All I know is that there's blood. So much blood.

"Keep pressure on that side. We need to roll him over and see."

I do as he says, and he and Bashir check my brother's back. Khalid's eyelids flutter, and he makes a strangled noise. His face is drained of color, his lips pale and crusty.

"It went through," Rashid says, relief in his voice. "That's good, it means the bullet isn't lodged inside of him. Give me gauze."

Bashir hands it to him out of the medical kit, and Rashid packs it onto the exit wound. "Roll him back."

Just then Nur appears with the phone. "The Doctor," he tells Rashid, who, after easing my brother over, wipes his bloody hands on his shirt and takes it. "Make sure the gauze is pressed tight on the wound," he tells Bashir, and he takes the phone a few steps away. "Yes, sir," he says, back stiffening. "Yes, it was Khalid, sir. Bullet to the stomach . . . I don't know, sir, it just happened outside on the street. His brother brought him back in."

Rashid glances at me, and I realize I'm just standing there, staring at my brother with blood smeared all up my arms. I start to shake. Or maybe I've been shaking.

"Sit," Bashir says, and scoots a chair up next to the table. His eyes are full of questions he knows he can't ask. I fall into the chair and watch as Nur pulls the fabric back again from the stomach wound and swabs it with an alcohol pad. The pad is soaked with blood almost immediately and Bashir goes to help him, tearing open packs of gauze and wipes.

Nur swabs until the blood is cleared away. Then he leans in, face inches from the wound. "Get me a light."

Bashir scrambles, and after a few long seconds manages to produce a flashlight.

"What is it?" Rashid asks, putting a hand over the phone's receiver.

"Something inside the wound," Nur replies, his face contorted in concentration. "Give me tweezers."

"What are you doing?" I ask, but my words are lost in the movement of everyone around me.

Bashir holds the light while Nur scrapes the hole. "Part of his shirt, it looks like."

My brother makes a noise and his face twists in pain.

"You're hurting him!" I say, starting to stand.

"Let him work, Da'ud," Bashir says, pushing me back down. "He's got to get whatever it is out, or it's more likely to get infected."

I know what he's saying makes sense, but the look on Khalid's face is killing me.

"He's pulling debris out of the wound right now," Rashid says into the phone, coming to stand behind Nur.

Nur shoves the tweezers in one last time, and with a hiss of triumph, grabs something. He slowly begins pulling. The tweezers pinch what looks like a string, and then he gets a better grip, and pulls again. More string follows, then a wet, bloody lump pops free from my brother's stomach.

"Watch out."

Immediately the bleeding starts again, and Bashir comes in with an alcohol swab. "Was that all of it?" he asks Nur.

Nur frowns, pressing gauze on the wound again. "I think so."

"What was it?"

"I don't know. Piece of his shirt maybe."

For a second no one moves. Bashir holds bloody heaps of gauze, and Nur has his hands pressed on the hole, and Rashid and I just stand there, like if we take our eyes off Dahir, we'll break some spell and he'll be gone. His chest is rising and falling, but it seems too shallow. His eyes are closed again.

"He's gone unconscious," Rashid says to the Doctor.

I don't know if that's good or bad. At least he can't feel the pain. What do we do now? I am still holding the "Wanted" poster in my hand. It's crumpled, covered in blood, and when I try to let go of it, the paper sticks to my hand. Muhumed, who's come back in unnoticed at some point, takes the paper from me and smooths it flat. His eyes go wide when he sees Khalid's face.

Rashid is saying, "Yes, sir . . . yes, sir . . . yes, I will, sir." Then he extends the phone to me over my brother's body. "The Doctor wants to talk to you."

FORTY-FIVE

THEN: OCTOBER 17
MOGADISHU, SOMALIA

I take the phone like it's made of glass. "Hello? Hakim Doctor?"

"Da'ud. Are you all right?"

The concern in the Doctor's voice is too much for me, and I have to turn my head and wipe away tears. The other guys pretend not to notice. "I'm fine, sir. But my brother . . ."

"I know, Rashid told me."

"Can you come to look at him? He needs help."

The Doctor sighs. "No, Da'ud, I'm so sorry; I can't. I can't come into the city at all. It's too much of a risk."

My fists curl. Too much of a risk. A risk to the Doctor. My brother is expendable. My brother was going to die anyway. I swallow. "Oh."

"It sounds like he's lost a lot of blood but that he's stable now. Do you know if you're the same blood type?"

"I—I, no, I don't know."

"Then we can't risk a transfusion. But I'm going to talk Rashid and Nur through everything they need to do to give your brother the best chance at survival, *Inshallah*. Okay? The bullet passed through him, so they don't need to try to go in after it. That's good; going in might have caused more damage. We just have to pray that it didn't hit any major organs."

"But how do we know that it didn't?"

"Even if I were there, I wouldn't be able to tell without doing scans. We don't have access to that sort of equipment."

My throat is starting to close. "Not even at the hospital?"

Muhumed holds the "Wanted" poster up. "Someone will recognize him," he reminds me.

The other guys look at the paper in Muhumed's hand. I hear sharp intakes of breath, and Nur curses loudly.

"Da'ud?" the Doctor asks, hearing the commotion.

"They've put up 'Wanted' posters of Khalid. We were looking at them in Bakara Market when he was shot," I tell him limply. "We can't take him to the hospital."

" 'Wanted' posters?"

"With his photo, and a reward for . . . too much money." I feel sick. This is all my fault. I turn from the others and walk to a corner of the room. I can't handle their eyes on me any longer. "Is there somewhere else we can take him? Another hospital or a clinic? Where people won't ask questions?"

"Only the main hospital has the kind of equipment that would help him, and I'm not even sure what state it might be in these days," the Doctor says. "For now, the best thing we can do is watch him closely and pray. I'll tell Rashid and Nur what to look out for that might be a sign of something bad." He pauses, giving me a little time to digest everything he's said. Then he asks softly, "But, Da'ud, tell me more about what happened?"

I try to rein in my scattered mind. "They—" I lick my lips. *Careful, Abdi.* "It all happened so fast. One second I was looking at the poster, and then there were gunshots."

"Did you see the shooter?"

I think of the figure in the window. "No."

"And no one tried to take Khalid from you?"

Cold sweat springs to the back of my neck. "I—no."

The Doctor is quiet.

"I just grabbed him and ran," I say, the words tumbling out. "Maybe the shooter lost us. There were a lot of people in the market. It was chaos."

"Were you followed?"

I have to stop myself from touching the chip in my neck. "I don't think so."

"It's okay, Da'ud," the Doctor says, his voice gentle again. "You did fine. The best you could under the circumstances."

Or you might have killed your brother after all, a little voice in my head says.

A hot, smothering rage bubbles up, mixing into my guilt. Jones. *He* did this. I want to wrap my hands around his throat and squeeze until his life drains out of him.

But you need Jones, I remind myself. *Think past Khalid. You*

*might still be able to save the rest of them. You still have a plan. You
can still see it through. Don't freak out. Do it now. Ask him.*

"Will the mission be canceled, Hakim Doctor?" I hold my
breath while I wait.

"No," the Doctor says after a long silence.

There was a chance he would say yes, but somehow I knew,
deep down, that it wasn't going to happen that way. That it had
to come to this.

"I will have to think about who will take his place. There
are others who—"

"Please," I say, interrupting. I take a deep breath. "I want
to do it."

For a few seconds the Doctor doesn't answer. I wait, my
body growing more and more stretched with tension, expecting him to say no, that it isn't a good idea. This was always going to be hard, convincing the others that I could do this, be
as brave or as dedicated as Commander Khalid. I wait for the
Doctor to say that I'm not in the right state, that I'm too fragile.
That someone else would be better.

But he only asks, "Are you sure that's what you want?"

"Yes," I say, my voice cracking. It's an honest answer, if not
for the reasons the Doctor thinks. "I want to do this for Khalid.
He wouldn't want us to abandon the mission. He would want
me to do it. I want to become Soldier Zero. For him . . ." I pause.
"And for God." Even in my current state I have to wince. The
God part sounds like a lie. Because it is. The God I know would

never want this. I know the lie is necessary, but it still feels like blasphemy.

You and God can work it out later, I tell myself. I try to imagine the God who Khalid and the Doctor think they know, all wrath and justice. "Please," I say, continuing to listen to the Doctor's silence. "I feel called to it."

"Make sure you aren't speaking rashly, Da'ud. This is not a decision to be taken lightly."

"I'm thinking straight," I tell him. "It has to be me, Hakim Doctor. I am sure of it."

Seconds tick by. Then finally, "I think maybe what you say is true." And then he speaks the words I've been waiting for. They'll be my salvation. And maybe my doom: "Yes, Da'ud. If you know that this is what God is calling you to do, then you may take Khalid's place."

I try to keep my breath steady, even as my heart starts to pound and blood rushes through me.

This is it. It ends with me. With this.

"Put Rashid back on the phone," the Doctor says. "I'll let him know. We'll make sure your brother is taken care of, and then later the three of us will talk."

"Thank you, Doctor."

I think I hear the Doctor sigh. "I'm not sure it's something to thank me for, Da'ud. I recommend that you spend the time until we speak in prayer." He pauses. "For your brother. But also for yourself."

FORTY-SIX

The sun is barely up and the streets are quiet as I make my way back from Lido Beach to the hotel. I'm still dripping.

Today is the day. One last swim so I know I'm ready. Physically, I am. I'm not worried about that. What I'm worried about is the blood that I see—my brother's blood—every time I close my eyes. I'm worried about how distracted I am. It's hard to keep the details of the plan from slipping out of my mind when I can't help wondering if, while I've been away, Dahir has been slipping further and further toward death.

Commander Rashid and Nur—who it turns out were once medics in training under the Doctor before following him to the Boys—did the best they could with the instructions the Doctor gave them, but in the end there wasn't much to do except clean Dahir's bullet holes, stitch him up, and hope his insides could sort themselves out. Dahir woke up while they were closing the wound and started to scream in pain, but Nur clapped a hand over his mouth and Rashid gave him a syringe of something. Dahir's eyes went glassy and his lids closed. He woke up again in the middle of the night while I was keeping watch over him and asked for water. I gave him little sips and he asked what happened. I told him, but I think that even before I was finished he was already falling back into a dream.

While I was sitting up with Dahir overnight, I overhead Rashid talking in low tones with the Doctor. "How did they know he was with Al Shabaab?"

I had gone still, listening hard.

". . . Yes, but we've been careful to keep him off missions in Mogadishu . . . Maybe he was seen and photographed in Merka? . . . Yes, I suppose so. But still . . . the timing seems strange . . ."

For the rest of the night I waited for someone to come and put a bag over my head. I'd been found out. It wasn't going to work. At the very least, I'd be taken off the mission.

But the night had faded to gray dawn without incident.

When I checked on Dahir before I snuck out to the beach this morning, he seemed okay but was very thirsty again. I feel like the Doctor said that was bad. He also smelled awful, like something rotten, but maybe that's just because we're not supposed to move him yet to let him use the toilet.

Everything else is in place. Safiya arrived before dawn and sent Bashir a text. He told me she hadn't had any trouble getting out of the Fort via his perch and walking to the little village nearby. From there she caught a minibus into Mogadishu. Hopefully everyone will just think she's finally taken the opportunity to run away, and that it doesn't have anything to do with what's happening here.

Now there's only Jones to deal with.

"Come on, I haven't got all day," I mutter.

I pass an old woman sweeping her front stoop with a twig broom. I round a corner, only blocks now from the hotel. But just as I'm about to step into the street, a hand grabs me and yanks me sideways.

"Lightbulbs," the man says. I barely get a look at his face before he's got my arm twisted behind me and is pushing me down an alley, but I recognize Nice Boots, the soldier who picked me up off the streets and took me to Jones on my first mission into Mogadishu.

I don't fight him. "It's about time."

Nice Boots hurries me down side streets. Right, left, up a set of stairs, left, down two flights. Winding through unfamiliar territory.

"How much farther?" I finally ask, no longer even attempting to keep the venom out of my voice.

Nice Boots just grunts, but soon we're in front of an unmarked door. He knocks and we're ushered in. I smell him before I see him in the darkness—stale cigarette smoke.

"Abdiweli," Jones says. "Good to see you."

He's sitting in a rusty chair, quiet and calm as ever. His eyes are sunk into deep shadow, obscured in the gloom by his glasses.

"You nearly killed my brother," I spit.

Jones motions for Nice Boots to bring another chair. "Sit." When I don't, he says, "Please, Abdiweli. Take a seat and we'll talk. Would you like some tea?"

"Tea? I'd like to know why one of your people shot Dahir." I don't want to sit, but a hand pushes down on my shoulders. I try to shake it off, but it grips me and finally I let myself be seated next to the man I hate with every cell in my body.

"He's all right, then?" Jones asks.

"He's alive, if that's what you mean. But he's not all right."

Jones tilts his head, studying me. "The order was to shoot him in the knee," he says. "Our sniper was overeager. He's been disciplined."

"Fantastic. I'm sure that will make Dahir feel much better."

Mr. Jones's face twitches, and for a fraction of an instant I think he almost looks guilty, like he might even apologize. But just as quickly, he's stone cold again. "Has the attack been called off?" he asks.

I take a deep breath. I still have to work with this guy. My family's lives depend on it. "No."

"I see. Who will take his place?"

I level my gaze at Jones. "I will."

He doesn't look surprised, simply lights a cigarette and waits for me to explain.

"Don't worry, I'm not going back on the bargain we've made," I tell him. "I haven't decided to become a suicide bomber. As long as you keep up your end, I'll make sure no one dies."

"Not even you?"

"Not if I can help it. But if something goes wrong and I don't make it to the meeting point, Bashir will certainly be there."

"Tell me more about what you're planning," Jones says. "I can help you."

I shake my head. "Maybe I would have, but then you shot my brother, so I can't be sure you won't 'help' and screw things up again."

Jones leans back. "We could just tell the resort to cancel the event."

"And then you'll never catch the Doctor," I counter. "He'll stay hidden if there's no attack."

"Just the Doctor? What about the General?"

I bite the inside of my mouth. He's never satisfied. "You'll have to wait to get him. He's still holed up in the Fort."

Jones's lips press together in a thin line, and for a second I'm worried again.

"The Doctor's the real prize and you know it," I say. "Can you manage to keep yourself from killing a hundred or so teenagers to get the General too?" I keep myself from screaming at him while I watch him think, but only barely. What kind of a monster needs time to debate that question?

Finally he says, "All right. Don't be late."

I feel a small surge of triumph. Very small. "I need to get back. The others will start to get suspicious soon." I hold out my hand.

Jones never takes his eyes off me as he pulls an envelope out of his jacket pocket and hands it over. "I'd better not regret this."

"You won't." I tuck it away.

"We'll pick you up at 2315 hours." he says. "Corner of Via Londra and Uganda Road."

"And everything on your side is in place? It's all ready?"

"We'll be waiting for you."

I stand up, turn to go. The guard opens the door for me, and as I'm walking out, I just catch Jones's final words. "*Fi amman Allah.*"

God protect you.

FORTY-SEVEN

THEN: OCTOBER 18, 1400 HOURS
MOGADISHU, SOMALIA

Four hours before sunset, they take me to see the Doctor.

"Can we bring Khalid?" I ask.

Rashid shakes his head, looking grim. "The Doctor already said not to. He said moving him might reopen his wounds. And that carrying a wounded man around will attract too much attention. We can't have any extra eyes looking toward the Doctor."

Of course not. Can't put the precious Doctor in danger.

I try to keep my face the picture of humble acceptance as I nod. I will be leaving my brother here, in this dirty hotel, with no one but half-trained used-to-be-medics to look after him— used-to-be-medics who will most likely have to abandon him here tomorrow if he can't walk or if he . . . I stop myself from thinking the rest. I will see Dahir again. I *will*.

"Are you sure you're ready?" Rashid asks, putting a hand on my shoulder and searching my face.

"Yes. Just let me say goodbye to my brother."

"Hurry. We have to leave in a few minutes or we won't get you back in time."

I avoid the stares of the other guys as I leave the room and squat beside my brother. He doesn't look or smell any better, but he's still breathing, and the blood on his bandages is old and brown, not fresh. He forces his eyes open and licks his papery lips when I gently take his hand in mine.

"I'm leaving," I say.

He squeezes my hand, even though I can tell that the simple movement costs him. "I am proud of you," he says, his eyes glazed and feverish.

I can't reply around the lump in my throat.

"Maybe we will see each other soon," he says. A smile plays around the corners of his mouth.

It takes me a moment to catch his meaning: *maybe we'll see each other because we'll both be dead.* "Don't say that," I tell him. "You'll be on your feet and ordering new recruits around in no time." I force a smile, but he's already closed his eyes again.

I start to stand up, but he grips my hand. "Abdi," he whispers.

I swallow. He called me Abdi. I lower my voice. "Yes, Dahir?"

Some complicated combination of emotions crisscrosses his face: happiness, apprehension, regret. "I'm sorry."

"Shh," I say. I don't ask him sorry for what. It doesn't matter anymore. "I'm sorry too."

"Da'ud," Rashid says from the doorway behind me.

"I love you, brother," I say softly. Maybe he hears, maybe he doesn't. His eyes are closed again.

I follow Rashid out the door.

THE BOAT skims across the water, bouncing on the chop. I squint into the brightness reflecting off of everything. There isn't a cloud in the sky. The wind is soft. It's one of those crisp, gorgeous days when the world is almost too beautiful to bear.

I suddenly feel myself choking up. I don't want to die.

Stop being dramatic, I tell myself. It's what Bashir would say if I'd spoken out loud. He's next to me in the boat, but Commander Rashid is driving, so it's not like we can talk. If I do this right, no one dies and my family will be free and on their way to America before the sun rises again. Bashir and Safiya will be together at last, finally safely away from the Boys. I allow myself a few seconds of dreaming to settle my nerves and then I banish all thoughts of success. I don't want to jinx anything.

Most of your family will be free, anyway, says a small but persistent voice in my head. I can't stop seeing Khalid's blood-drained face.

Dahir. He is Dahir. I won't call him Khalid ever again after today.

We aim for a cluster of black rocks poking out from the sandy shore into the water, a nondescript scab on the beach's otherwise pale, deserted surface. So this is where the Doctor is

330

hiding until it's time for him to come and watch the fireworks. We're about twenty minutes north of Mogadishu by boat.

Rashid throttles down the motor and aims for a gap between boulders, where I can just make out the shape of another boat carrying three figures. One of them stands sentry, gun at the ready. He waits until he's sure it's us, and then slings it back over his shoulder and steps onto the bow, ready to guide us in. The rocks are at an angle that breaks up the waves that would otherwise swamp us or send us crashing into the other boat, but the space between them is just barely big enough for the two boats' hulls. We squeeze in, out of sight of anyone who might be wandering down the beach.

I throw a rope to the guy in the other boat so he can tie us together. I don't recognize him or the second guard. Both look older, sun weathered and rough. Not your typical Boy. They must have been handpicked by the Doctor to guard him tonight.

The Doctor himself sits in the back of the boat. His eyes are on me. Once the boats are linked, he says to the guards, "I'll talk to Da'ud alone."

I board the Doctor's boat. Everyone else gathers at the opposite end of the other one.

"*Ramadan Kareem,*" the Doctor says. His intense gaze, as always, seems to pierce straight through to my heart, which is beating like a moth trapped under glass. "How is Commander Khalid?"

"No better, no worse."

"No worse is a blessing," the Doctor says.

I don't answer, afraid of what I'll say.

"Don't forget, Da'ud, that he was ready for martyrdom."

I swallow. "Yes, sir."

"Are *you* ready, Da'ud?"

I risk a glance up and my eyes lock on the Doctor's. I can no more look away than a fish can spit out a hook. "I—I think so." As soon as the words have left my mouth, I know it's the wrong thing to say. Sweat prickles under my hair. "I am ready," I amend. "I am."

I am ready to end all of this. I am ready to give you to Jones.

A deep tug of guilt follows the thought. Am I really? Am I actually ready for that? What will Jones do to him? Lock him up? Torture him? kill him? As messed up as all of the Doctor's plans are, I can't help but think about how by doing this, I'm one step closer to being like him. I'm sacrificing him for the greater good. *He wants you to go and kill yourself. And hundreds of others at the same time,* I remind myself. *That's his idea of sacrificing for the greater good.* But it still makes me feel ill looking into his face and knowing his blood will soon be on my hands.

The Doctor continues to watch me. I'm reminded of the first day I met him, how looking into his eyes was like looking into the infinity of space, an endlessness where only stars burn.

"It's a brave thing you will do tonight, Da'ud. It will be a selfless act that will live on long after you have gone to meet God and receive your reward."

I feel myself spiraling down into his eyes. I'm not going to be able to do this. "I don't feel brave," I say, truthfully. "I'm scared."

The Doctor nods. "It is all right to be frightened." He studies me. "You are a stranger to yourself, aren't you? Does it feel that way sometimes?"

The words hit straight at my gut. All these weeks of pretending to be someone else. I'm not sure I would even know how to find the person I was before. I don't think I would recognize him. A stranger to myself. "Yes," I admit.

"We all feel that way at some point. Confused, unsure. But even still, *He* knows you. He has shown you your path and He knows you have accepted it. Don't doubt yourself, Da'ud. Don't doubt Him."

And I know it's not what he means, but suddenly I feel like maybe God is talking through the Doctor, telling me that the thing Bashir and I have planned—not what the Doctor thinks I will do—*is* right. I get the overwhelming sense that His eye is on me. Watching me, protecting me.

When I look up, I know the Doctor will find strength and calmness in my face. And sure enough, he nods slowly, a half-sad smile on his lips. "You are ready," he says. "Tonight you will be the match that sets the whole world ablaze."

I open my arms, and he embraces me tightly.

"God's will be done," I whisper.

FORTY-EIGHT

THEN: OCTOBER 18, 1730 HOURS
MOGADISHU, SOMALIA

"You'd think they'd be more careful," Bashir grunts, "to make this passage big enough. Seeing as we're supposed to be carrying ten kilos of explosives."

I pause in my crawling. "We're not, right?"

"Well, five, maybe," he says. "There's got to be some sort of bang, right? Otherwise no one's going to believe you're dead. Just be glad I'm scrawny."

"You sound pretty carefree for a guy who has a bomb strapped to his belly."

"Don't be jealous. Your turn is coming."

"Fantastic," I mutter. "Ow!" My head grazes the ceiling and sand falls into my eyes. I rub them, then keep on going, following Bashir.

After meeting the Doctor, Rashid had dropped Bashir and me off up the beach. We had to backtrack around into the city, which took longer than we planned. Plus, Bashir had a stop to make. By the time we got to the rendezvous, we were running, and just barely on time.

The tunnel entrance was at the back of an electronics store. The clerk took our request for mangoes and a bar of soap, and led us to a dead refrigerator in the back room. With our help he pushed it aside and revealed a tunnel entrance only big enough to enter on our hands and knees.

"Go with God," he'd told us, before pushing the fridge back over the hole and leaving us in the dark.

We've been crawling for long enough that my trouser knees have both ripped. It doesn't matter; I'll have to switch into my disguise soon anyway, which is in the backpack I have strapped to my chest.

"I think I see light," Bashir says.

"*Mashallah.* If I'm going to get blown up, I'd much rather it be outside than down here."

"No one's getting blown up," Bashir says firmly. But then he adds, "*Inshallah.*"

We finally emerge from the tunnel into a stone shaft: the dry well under the laundry room at the resort. I heave a sigh of relief when I can stand again. I dust off and check the phone Rashid gave me.

"On schedule," I whisper.

We shift our packs to our backs and start to climb. I go first. The well looks like it's been here since the Stone Age, but there's a fresh rope to haul ourselves up, just as Rashid said there would be, placed a few weeks ago. The going isn't easy, exactly, but we make it up without falling or detonating.

I push the well lid up to peer into the room. The basement's dark and dusty, filled with stacks of old furniture. The only light comes through a tiny window near the ceiling. "We're good," I say, and push the lid off, careful not to let it bang to the ground. I help Bashir out, then creep across the room to the door that leads upstairs. I put my ear to it and can hear the chugging of laundry machines and people talking. Only after sliding the newly installed dead bolt home do I let go of the breath I've been holding.

I glance at the phone again to make sure I've got service. A couple of bars, enough to get a text. It's 1806 hours, which means the sun should be setting any minute and the call to prayer will start. I'll get a text when it's time to go upstairs in about an hour. Plenty of time to get suited up.

When I get back to him, Bashir is gingerly removing his pack and pulling the vest out. I take my stuff out too, lining it all up: phone, fake ID, uniform. The ID is for *Mohamed Idlib, age 19*. It's Dahir's photo, but we look enough alike that Rashid wasn't worried about it not working. Mohamed Idlib is on the list of extra help hired just for today. Rashid also said that with all the additional staff, no one should be too worried about seeing an unfamiliar face. The tunnel got us past the most intense security—the metal detectors and pat-downs—so I might not even have to use it.

"That is one ugly uniform," Bashir says.

"Yeah." I lift a shoulder tassel and let it fall. It's burgundy, with gold piping and giant shoulder pads. I look at our spread and suddenly feel like I do when I've been underwater my full two minutes. Blind panic hovers around my edges. There are too many ways for all of this to come crashing down around us. Literally. I force myself to think through the plan, one last time, more as a way to keep my brain occupied than anything else.

"You didn't have any trouble getting it to her?" I ask.

"Put the envelope straight into her hands."

"So she's going to leave the stuff . . ."

"Behind the stage in a closet," Bashir says, not looking up from whatever he's fiddling with on the vest.

I watch him. "I really wish she didn't have to be a part of this."

Bashir's jaw clenches. "There wasn't any other way. Safiya's the only person we can trust. She's the only one who can get in there without being recognized."

"Still." I sigh. "Tell her thank you for me."

"Tell her yourself, when this is all over."

I nod. He's right. What else? I'm sure there's something we're forgetting, some detail that will come to bite us all in the ass. "And I'll meet you at ten o'clock at . . ."

". . . the mosque on Via Londra. You know this thing backward and upside down, Abdi. Take some deep breaths or something." He shines a flashlight at the wires, then pulls some tools out of his bag.

I take a shaky breath. "Where will Safiya go?"

"As soon as she's out, she'll get on a bus. I'll meet her on the Kenya border in Mandera."

I feel something spring loose in my chest. "Good. That's good, Bashir. Then what?"

"Uganda. Probably Kampala. Until Jones gets me my money and then who knows. Somewhere cold, maybe. I've always wanted to see snow." He darts a quick glance up from what he's doing. He has a funny expression on his face, almost like he's embarrassed. Very un-Bashir. "You should come with us. After. We can all go together. Start over."

I look at my friend, and it hits me. What if I never see him again after tonight? My eyes smart. "I—I can't. I have to make sure my family is safe," I say.

He looks back down at his hands. "Sure. Of course."

I clear my throat. "Besides, you don't want me around while you're trying to convince Safiya she should take you seriously with this relationship business."

"One impossible task at a time, please," he says, with a crooked grin. He finishes tightening something with a set of pliers and then steps back. "It's ready."

I take off my *khameez*, leaving only my undershirt. Bashir holds up the vest so I can stick my arms through. As he puts it on me, he says, "Now don't forget. This stuff is seriously unstable. People don't call it Mother of Satan for nothing."

"Are you trying to make me feel better or worse?"

"I wish I'd been able to get my hands on something else, but TATP is what comes cheap and easy," he goes on.

I roll my eyes. "You suck at reassurance."

"Just don't knock it around. Or drop it. Or look at it in a funny way."

The vest is extra heavy because it's also packed with little pockets of scrap metal that will spray out everywhere in the explosion. It's a nasty bomb, Bashir had told me earlier, because it doesn't just kill, it maims. That's what the General wanted. Maximum destruction. This is what is currently being Velcroed and cinched to my chest.

Bashir pulls something that looks like a fat pen out of one of the pockets. "Detonator," he says, putting it in my hand. "There are two steps. Switch this on, and it's activated. Then press here."

"Got it," I say shakily, careful not to press anything.

"I've made the cord extra long. Normally, you only need it to be long enough to go from the vest to your arm, but in our case we need length. It's five meters long, which should be plenty." He helps me put it all in the vest pocket again, then steps back to check his work.

"How's it look?" I resist the urge to smooth it so the vest will appear smaller against me.

His brow is still furrowed. "Maybe it'll be better once you put the waiter uniform on."

"Again, not reassuring."

He helps me button the uniform over the vest. When I'm finished, I wait for his verdict.

Bashir purses his lips. "You look like a cheap sofa."

I can't help it, I snort a laugh. "Sorta smell like one too. I don't know who they got this uniform from, but he was foul."

Bashir's smile is fleeting.

I look down at myself again. "This is crazy. There's no way someone's not going to notice. I'm a sixteen-year-old with a fifty-year-old's potbelly."

"No, you look okay."

"Are you sure?"

"Don't be so vain."

We stand there in silence for a little while.

"Well," he says, "I guess that's it. I should get to my post."

"Yeah," I say, barely daring to move.

"I'd give you a hug but . . ."

"Please don't."

He stands before me, his face uncharacteristically serious. He puts a hand on my shoulder. I put a hand on his and squeeze.

"Don't forget," he says. "Make sure you're out of the water."

"I know. Get out of here. I'll see you soon."

He turns to go to the well. "Soon, brother. *Inshallah.*"

FORTY-NINE

The next half hour is the longest of my life. After Bashir is gone, I put the cap on the well and sit carefully in a chair to wait. The light fades and I hear the call to prayer. I check my phone incessantly, worrying that Rashid's text won't come through. At some point I go stand next to the tiny window, trying to get better service, but I feel so exposed that I quickly retreat. Eventually I hear voices above growing louder and louder. Prayers are over and now the staff are busy making sure everything is ready for the banquet. More than once the voices sound so close that I'm sure they're at the door. I can just imagine them rattling the doorknob, wondering loudly why it's locked, and shouting at someone to bring the key.

And what will I do if someone does come? There's the dead bolt that I've locked from the inside, but what if they get suspicious and decide to take the door off its hinges? Climbing back down the well is really my only option, but even then someone could see the rope. Most likely I'd bash into the side of the well and we'd all go sky high.

Finally, my phone buzzes and I nearly jump out of my skin, banging a metal bucket with my foot that makes a noise like a cannon. I freeze, cursing myself, and wait. I don't hear any shouts or the sound of someone running in my direction. But with the noise my heart is making, it's hard to tell. The text from Rashid just says, GO NOW.

Now.

Okay, then.

As I'm leaving the basement, I catch a glimpse of myself in an old mirror. I stop. I turn left and right, trying to see how obvious the vest is, and I'm surprised to find that Bashir is right. It's less noticeable than I thought. I must have lost a lot of weight for it to appear anywhere near normal on me. I don't look all that weird. I check the time again: 1914. I'm supposed to detonate at 1945.

If this were one of my movies, I'd have something snappy to say to myself right now. But this is real life, and I'm just Abdi.

"Abdi. Just Abdi," I tell the mirror.

I go.

THE SECURITY guard at the staff entrance to the dining room scrutinizes my ID, then me, then my ID again. He languidly licks his finger and flips through his list, looking for my name. I have to force myself to stay still. He's going to look more closely and see I'm not the guy in the photo. He'll notice that I'm just a little too bulky under my uniform. I wait with sweat collecting in my underwear for alarms to start ringing, for hands to clamp down on me.

But after finding Mohamed Idlib's name and making a little tick mark beside it on his list, the guard hands my ID back. He waves me through, and then I'm already forgotten. He's moved on to checking the next guy.

I'm swept up in the crowd, ignored by the guests, who are busy talking and mingling. My waiter uniform makes me surprisingly invisible. I have to be aware of not bumping into other people, but that shouldn't make me look odd. It seems like something a lowly waiter would do anyway.

I scan the big banquet hall. It's open to the veranda, with a view of the ocean. A podium has been set up for speeches on the stage later. Platters of glossy dates sit in the centers of each table, picked over. The day's fast has been broken. Now it's time for the real feast. Waiters dart back and forth, bringing food and drink, weaving between large, important-looking men in suits. Most of the women are in brightly colored *diracs*, gold flashing at their hands and wrists. A few wear long, form-covering *jalbabs* with *niqab* veils flipped up, faces only exposed now that their wearers are inside among friends. Plump children chase each other, escaping parents' and nannies' grasps.

I can't help feeling a little repulsed. These are the people I'm risking my neck for? These men and women in their finery

343

with expansive waistlines and drivers and servants and cars and bodyguards? The Doctor is right, they must be siphoning money off from their ministries, taking cuts from the dirty business deals they broker. As if to punctuate my thoughts, a nearby woman in heavy makeup flings her scarf over her shoulder with a jingle of bracelets and snaps at me to come serve her.

I pretend I haven't seen her and head instead for the waiters' stand, where I grab a pitcher of water. I mime the other waiters who are pacing the room, refilling glasses. I don't want to be at the beck and call of these people, but it's not like I can stand around doing nothing. I just have to blend in for a little while, and then I can move on to the next part of the plan.

"Excuse me."

I move out of the way for a woman in a *jalbab*, and have to keep myself from doing a double take. I almost don't recognize her out of her drab kitchen clothes. In the sleek garment, purple headscarf, and with a long gold rope tied loosely around her waist, Safiya is beautiful. I only catch her gaze for a second, but what's in her flashing eyes I won't soon forget.

Her face is as regal as a queen's. It's a face that says, *I'm here, I showed up, but I'm not doing this for you. This isn't about you. It's about something bigger. It's about* my *freedom.*

I give her a little nod that I hope says, *I know.*

And then she turns away and disappears into the crowd, simply one more well-to-do guest.

The noise of the banquet hall washes over me again. I enjoy a few seconds of relief that Safiya's part in this is almost over.

The invitation Jones secured for her, which Bashir delivered on our way to the rendezvous, worked. It shouldn't take her more than another ten minutes to make her drop backstage. And then she'll be gone, off to board a bus to her future.

Several guests give me orders for soda and tea, and I nod mutely with no intention of filling them. As I'm reaching for a glass at a table near the stage, I look up at the woman across from me. The glass slips in my hand, splashing water on a man who jerks back with an angry "Careful, boy!"

"My apologies, sir. So sorry," I say, handing him a napkin. My face burns, but I'm terrified to look up again. I grab the pitcher and swivel, pretending like I don't hear other people at the table asking for their glasses to be refilled. I hurry away, but can't stop myself from looking over my shoulder.

The woman is watching me, a line between her brows. I can't take another step; it's as if she's reached across the room and grabbed me, forcing me to look at her. She gingerly touches her fingertips to the side of her head, where Nur's gun butt smashed her.

It's the rich woman from Merka whose father we hauled off to some unknown fate. She must be a politician, or a politician's wife.

I force myself to look away, to turn and head for the opposite side of the room. Surely she doesn't recognize me. She saw my face for only a second in Merka. But I remember her eyes locking onto me, just like now. She was hit hard enough to be knocked out; the chance of her remembering me is tiny. But I can't shake the feeling that she *does* recognize me, and that she knows this is the last place on earth I should be. My heart hammers forcefully enough that I worry for the explosives strapped to my chest.

Trying to stay out of her line of sight, I circle around behind her table. She's sitting very straight, still frowning, like she's trying to puzzle something out. Is she looking for me?

You're being paranoid, Abdi. She was only looking at you like that because you spilled water on that guy.

But I only spilled the water because she was already staring at me.

What time is it? I pull my phone out. 1936. I need to get moving. Up to now I've been following orders. But from here out, I'll be carefully pivoting the Doctor's plan in a different direction.

I think of Dahir clinging to that wall, halfway over. This is *my* moment on the wall. I'm at the intersection between Before and After.

A hand claps my shoulder and I jump a foot in the air.

"What are you doing? Am I paying you to sightsee? Get back to work!" The annoyed-looking man is some sort of manager, and he pushes me toward the kitchen doors, where waiters keep popping out with trays of food. As I'm hustled away, I sneak a glance over my shoulder to the table where the woman was sitting.

She's gone.

Nearly tripping over my own feet, I scan the room for her. But the manager is still watching me, so I'm forced to duck into the kitchen. A platter is shoved into my hands by a sweat-drenched cook who shouts in my face, "Table twenty-four!"

Woman or no woman, I need to get out of here. I push back into the dining room. The platter gives me a bit of a barrier around my chest so that I don't have to worry about hitting anyone, but where the hell is table twenty-four? Can I just set the tray down at any of these tables? I weave through the guests, scanning the numbers on the tables and eventually winding up all the way back across the room. Twenty-four is only a few steps away from where the Merka woman was sitting. She's still not there, though, and my breathing relaxes a bit. I quickly set down dishes of meat and vegetable stew, *canjeero* and rice.

"Easy there, boy!" a man says, scowling as stew sloshes onto the white tablecloth.

"Sorry, sir." I place the last dish and step back. The manager isn't watching me anymore. But as I'm checking out my escape route, I see the Merka woman standing near the doorway.

Right next to the security guard.

And they're looking straight at me.

FIFTY

I grab the platter like a shield and spin on my heel, nearly bumping into another waiter carrying a tray of drinks. I mumble an apology and slip sideways, making for the stage. Surely Safiya's had enough time to drop off the stuff. No one's raised an alarm. Everything is fine.

"Hey," I hear behind me.

I don't turn around. I'm almost to the stage.

"You, waiter."

I glance back and see the guard coming for me. Forcing myself not to run, I mount the stairs and make for the curtain. My pulse hammers, sweat slicking my hands as I grab the fabric, looking for a way past it. All I can find is cheap velvet and more cheap velvet and no slit to let me through. I look back again. The guard is only a few meters away, closing the distance quickly, but suddenly two men stand up and block his way, old friends hugging and kissing cheeks, ignoring the guard. He looks for a way past, but has to go back around a table, and meanwhile I've finally found the opening in the curtain. I plunge backstage into almost perfect darkness.

My hands out in front of me, I stumble forward and run straight into the corner of something at shoulder level. I hiss in pain, cursing myself for how close the blow came to the vest. *Keep moving,* Abdi. Finally I find a wall, and follow it until I come to a door hidden behind a pile of tables and chairs. I fling it open. Just as I slip inside, light from the dining room shines through the curtains and splashes the walls. God, I hope this is the closet Bashir was talking about. I ease the door shut and wedge a broken chair under the knob.

There's no time to be quiet and wait to hear if the guard's coming. A small window in the corner of the closet lets in enough light to see the shelf. For a second my heart nearly stops. There's nothing there. The shelves are empty. I didn't give Safiya enough time. Or she remembered that she hates me and decided not to help after all. I plunge forward, sweep my hands over the dusty shelves. Finally, in a bottom corner I find a bundle of dark fabric.

"*Alhumdullilah,*" I whisper in relief, and start to carefully peel off my waiter's uniform.

I hear movement outside the closet door, the scrape of something heavy being pushed aside. A flashlight beam waves over the door, slicing in at the cracks. I can't wait any longer. I grab the cloth, the gold rope falling to the floor. It barely makes a sound, but the guard's footsteps go quiet, as if he hears it.

I don't stop. I wrap the rope around my waist and knot it under the vest. Then I put the disguise on over my head, wrestling it as gently into place as I can.

The doorknob rattles. The chair holds, but it probably won't withstand a good kick. Now what? The plan was for me to just walk out the front door incognito, but I can't do that if the guard is right there. I look around for a weapon. Something to knock him out. There's nothing but old tablecloths and fake flowers.

The only useful thing in the room is the tiny window. I wrench it open and start to pray.

FIFTY-ONE

He looks down at his phone for what feels like the thousandth time. 1949. Da'ud is late.

From where he's sitting on an overturned fisherman's boat, Nur looks like any of the dozens of loiterers hanging out on the beach in the cool of the evening. He's just one more guy with nothing to do but sit on the beach and stare at whatever comes his way. But, he thinks with a small, secret smile, most of them probably don't have a super-important mission to handle. Or a handgun and a knife hidden in their waistband. Well, except for Bashir, who is positioned opposite him. And the other guys, waiting just out of sight.

Kids play soccer nearby, the ball a white streak in the dark. Shoes off, a family walks through the soft sand. The father has the littlest boy lifted onto his shoulders. A woman passes him in a long black *jalbab*, heading from the direction of the resort toward the surf. She lifts a hand to her *niqab* to keep the wind from picking it up and revealing her face.

Nur has a perfect view of the interior of the restaurant. There are security guards stationed outside, but he's still close enough to see all those fat-ass government cows shoving food into their faces. His lip curls. They have no idea what's about to happen.

He looks at his phone again. Still 1949. His sneer turns to a scowl. The bomb should have gone off four minutes ago. Maybe Da'ud is having trouble getting into position. Nur still can't believe Commander Rashid entrusted such a pussy little hand job like Da'ud with this mission. He probably wimped out. He's probably still sitting in the basement in a puddle of his own piss, bawling his eyes out.

Nur tries to see if there's any commotion in the dining room, as if maybe someone has been caught by security, but everyone looks happy and relaxed. They haven't gotten any texts from Da'ud saying there's a problem. Nur shifts, scanning the beach. The family has stopped while one of the little girls pokes at something in the sand with a stick. A teenage boy wanders by, his face glowing blue in the light of his phone. Nur can just barely see the woman in black, who is almost to the water now.

They've timed all of this perfectly with the tides. There's still time for Da'ud to detonate before they start to turn, but not much. *Wallahi,* if Da'ud's pussied out on this, Nur's going to personally kick his ass so hard he'll wish he'd been blown into a million pieces.

He watches the woman. There is something strange about her that he can't quite figure out. Not just that she's walking straight toward the water like she's going to stride right in. It's her stiff gait. And her shoulders are broad. *She's probably not even devout,* Nur thinks to himself. *She's probably wearing that face-covering* niqab *because she's ugly. She's hoping her father and uncles can manage to pull off a decent marriage as long as she stays under wraps. If her shoulders are any indication, she probably looks more like a man under there than a woman.*

Nur squints harder at her. He stands up.

Across the sand, Bashir notices and stands up too.

Nur touches the gun at his waist and starts to walk toward the woman. Bashir follows, keeping pace. *Good,* Nur thinks.

The woman stops at the edge of the waves and takes her shoes off. Nur pulls his gun halfway out. The woman starts to walk forward into the waves, ignoring the water soaking her dress. Nur looks at her shoes.

Except they aren't *her* shoes; they are *his* shoes. Men's sandals, exactly like the ones Nur himself is wearing.

No. It can't be . . .

"Hey!" Nur shouts, and the figure in black spins. Nur can't see anything but the person's eyes widening under the *niqab,* but he-she-whoever takes one look at him and starts to run, sloshing into the water. The tide is in, but it's not deep enough here for him to go under. Nur raises the gun at the figure's back. He hesitates. If it is Da'ud, he'll go sky high as soon as the bullet hits him, and Nur isn't sure he's far enough away not to be flash-fried. But if he waits any longer, Da'ud will plunge into the dark water and be gone. Nur lines up his shot.

And suddenly he's flying through the air, hit sideways, sprawling onto the sand.

"Bashir!" Nur bellows, once he has his breath. "What are you doing? He's getting away!"

"I know!" Bashir says, struggling to keep Nur down, pushing him into the sand, hitting him across the jaw with his own gun.

Understanding flashes over Nur's face and he roars, "Traitor!"

Bashir is putting everything he's got into the fight, but Nur is bigger and has had more experience with brawling. He bucks and smashes his knee into Bashir's chest, sending him flying.

Nur's gun is too far away. He grabs for the knife at his waist. Bashir's eye shines white in the dark.

The blade is as thin and sharp as the moon above.

It plunges into the night.

FIFTY-TWO

Any second now the bullet is going to hit my back, and all I'll
see before I die is the world turning to fire. I struggle and heave
through the water, trying to get deep enough to dive in. As I
yank the *jalbab* up around my waist, I hear a shout behind me,
but I don't dare turn around.

"Come on, come on," I'm yelling at myself, and then the
seafloor drops away and I surge forward, plunging underwater.
All at once I'm fighting against the current, the dress, and the
weight of the vest. I pull the *jilbab* and *niqab* over my head and
let the waves suck them away. I feel a hundred times lighter.
But still, the vest is pulling me under. I sink, panic engulfing me
until my feet hit the bottom. I push up, grab a breath of air, try
to look at the shore.

I can't see anything but a dark writhing mass in the sand—
two people fighting? Bashir and Nur? Shit. Bashir's no match

for Nur. I have to help him. I start to push my way back toward land, but then I hear a *crack*. Someone else is running down the beach. I see a spark of light, hear the shots, and then the water sprays up only inches from my face. I'll never make it back out. I fill my lungs and duck under, swimming for my life.

Bashir wasn't supposed to break his cover. But then again, Nur wasn't supposed to recognize me under Safiya's *jalbab*. I try to concentrate on kicking and pulling, not on what's happening to my friend back on the shore. Maybe Bashir didn't break cover. Maybe that wasn't him tussling on the ground with Nur.

But I don't know who else it would be.

My arms and lungs are starting to burn, and I struggle to the surface for air again. I spot my mark, a small fishing boat bobbing on the waves, anchored about ten yards ahead. It would be faster to swim above water, but I can't risk anyone seeing the splashing. So instead I duck back under, like I've practiced, but this time with the vest weighing me down instead of a rock.

I open my eyes, but it's too dark to see anything underwater. I surface again, and the hull of the boat is just a body length away. I'm already loosening the straps on the vest as I reach for the boat's lip. Gasping for breath, I rub my eyes and look back. I can see figures on the beach, but I don't think they see me. No one is shooting in my direction. Is that a lump in the sand the size of a body? Or is one of those figures Bashir?

I circle to the side of the boat farthest from the shore and start to haul myself in, but I'm too heavy. I struggle out of the vest and push it in ahead of me, praying for a soft landing.

The plan is supposed to be simple. I swim the vest out here, sink it, detonate it and disappear. However, at the moment, what's happening is that I'm waterlogged and half choking, my arms are quivering with exhaustion, and I'm trying to heave myself into a boat that keeps tipping and threatening to overturn. I have to get into the boat because, as Bashir explained, the blast pressure from the bomb going off is even worse underwater than above. I'll get pulverized if I'm not in the boat.

Of course, it's not like being in the boat is much better. It's just not *guaranteed* to kill me.

I could keep swimming and try to escape, but Bashir and I discussed it and finally agreed that I have to go out with a bang. "If they don't think you're dead, they'll never stop looking for you," he said.

At last I manage to get myself into the boat, landing in a heap of nets and rigging. I peer over the edge, but all I can see are bodies running around on shore. I pull Safiya's gold rope from my waist and start tying one end onto the vest's armhole. I've just pulled it tight when I hear the roar of an engine starting. I glance back toward the beach, and what I see makes my knees turn to jelly. At least three bodies are pushing a boat into the water. They must be Boys. No one else is going pleasure cruising at this time of night.

Shit. They rallied fast. The boat engine dies, and I hear the choke being pulled again. It turns over once, coughs, but doesn't catch. Frantically, I fumble through the pockets on the vest until I find the detonator. I feed its wire out, grab the rope and heave the vest up and over the side of the boat. The engine cranks again. I can just hear shouts, like someone is yelling at someone else. I let go of the vest and it vanishes under the surface. Not a second too soon. The engine whines like a grumpy beast, then chugs to life.

I'm still squinting at the Boys' boat when I hear a *sssslick*. I turn my head just in time to watch the tail of the gold rope vanish over the side of the boat.

A stream of curses pours out of me. Idiot! I look at what I thought was the rope in my hand, but it's some other line— part of the rigging in the bottom of the boat. As I'm staring at it, the still-attached detonator leaps out of my hand, smacking the side of the boat before following the vest.

I barely know what I'm doing before I'm plunging over the side, kicking with all the fight I have left toward where I think the vest is sinking. As I descend, my ears start ringing, the pressure increasing until it feels like a knife being jammed into the side of my head. But there's no time to move slowly. I finally reach the bottom, my hands grasping. All I feel is sand. Even with my eyes open wide I can't see a thing in the dark. I swipe through the water, over rocks and something metal. I kick, double back, my lungs starting to scream. Suddenly my hand wraps around a loop of rope, and I grab it. Following it down leads me to the vest, and then to the detonator wire. I pull the wire hand over hand until I feel the detonator itself. Then, holding tight to both it and the rope, I push off the bottom, kicking for the surface.

My ears are ringing too hard to hear if the boat motor is close, but as soon as I break the surface, I see it bearing down on me. They're a little to my left. The beam of a flashlight bounces over the boat I was just sitting in. They move on to the other boats nearby, clearly thinking I can't have gotten far. The sound of the engine covers my splashes as I make for the boat. Once I've got a grip on the side, I make sure the rope and detonator are tight in my other hand, and then heave a leg over to start hauling myself back up.

But before I can get all the way in, I'm caught up short. The detonator is still below the surface, its wire pulled tight. I'm left hanging halfway over the side of the boat, holding on to the switch with my arm underwater past my elbow. I tug as hard as I dare. "*Kaalay,* come on!" The vest is stuck on something. I can't risk pulling any harder, or I'll pull out the detonator wire. Maybe it would blow automatically if I did, but I'm not sure.

I need that explosion.

I look over my shoulder. The Boys' boat is circling, their flashlight sweeping over all the boats moored in the bay. They're coming back this way. If I had more time, I might be able to dive back in again and untangle whatever is tangled down there, but I've probably only got seconds before they spot me. If I don't do something now, they'll see me and put a bullet in the back of my head and all of this will have been for nothing. I look down at my submerged hand.

There's nothing else to do.

I climb in the boat, leaving my hand to dangle in the water. My heart pounding, I suck down deep breaths of salty air. I switch the detonator on, activating it like Bashir showed me.

The Boys' boat is almost on top of mine.

At the last second, I flip over onto my back, looking for something to focus on in the darkness. Something that isn't horrible. The stars seem brighter than I've ever seen them. Terrified as I am, I still can't help but notice how beautiful they are. It's almost as if I'm seeing them for the very first time.

Or maybe the last.

As far as last things to see before you die, I guess stars aren't so bad.

I hit the button.

FIFTY-THREE

In the end, maybe it was looking at the stars that kept me alive.

The explosion goes off with a noise like the entire world is ripping apart, and the next thing I know I'm underwater again, shards of wood stuck in my back instead of slicing through my chest.

I don't even notice my fingers until I'm dragging myself through the current, choking down water and air, trying to get away from the burning debris and the Boys who've been knocked out of their boat (but were farther away and probably a lot better off than me). I taste the blood in the water before I feel the pain. I stop swimming long enough to grab my right hand in my left.

Or, grab what's left of it.

Two of my fingers are simply not there.

Weird, I think. Then I realize that if the only thing I can think is *weird*, then I'm in shock. Which means I'm probably not working very hard to keep myself alive. *Kick, Abdi. Move your arms.*

So I do. I kick, I pull.

I let the current carry me away from the lights, until I'm able to turn back in and get to a dark stretch of beach. For a few terrible minutes I think the current is too strong, and I'm too hurt and exhausted to fight it, but finally the shore rises up, and my feet scrape the bottom and I pull myself out, crawling, falling into the shallows so the waves keep crashing over me. I try to breathe and not die.

I feel my hand pulsing like my heart is beating through it. I have to move, I know I do, but I've never been in worse shape in my life.

Get up, Abdi. This isn't over.

Think of Hooyo, Ayeyo, Hafsa, the twins.

I pull my undershirt off and wrap it around my bloody mess of a hand. I'm grateful for the dark. I don't think I could stand to actually look at it right now. Then I get to my feet, take a few weaving steps, discover all sorts of new places where my body has been sliced and mangled, fall down again, get back up, and force myself to stumble toward the lights up the beach. The movement makes me throw up a stomachful of salt water.

The white undershirt is soon black—the color of blood at night. I don't think I'll bleed out, but that's about as optimistic as I can be at the moment. I can feel burns and cuts all the way up my arm. There's a pain in my ear on that side like something inside has gone very wrong. I can't hear anything through it. Did my fingers just blow apart with the pressure and shrapnel? Not pleasant thoughts, but thinking about my wounds and missing appendages keeps my mind from paying attention to my aching legs, which I've forced into a run.

The lights grow brighter, and beachfront buildings loom up from the darkness. I slow, looking for cover. I need to get to the mosque on Via Londra to meet Bashir—*if he's all right, that is,* I think, my insides seizing up. What if he's hurt, or captured, or . . . ? Was that lump on the shore him? Is there any way to know? I can't go back to the Ocean View—the Boys will be long gone by now, and it'll be crawling with police and soldiers. Either Bashir will have snuck away, or they'll have taken him with them. But I have this consuming urge to return to the last place I saw him. Maybe I could sneak into one of the buildings near the resort, just to see.

No. We have a plan. I'm probably already running out of time to get to the mosque as it is. If he's all right, he'll meet me. If he's not . . . But I don't let myself think about it.

I'M NOT the only one scurrying through the streets. People run both toward and away from the blast. Some stand in doorways and mutter together, unsure what's going on. Sirens echo like women wailing at a funeral. I get to the mosque at 2235 hours, according to the cell phone I stole off a distracted man's cafe table as I ran by. I've grabbed dry pants and a shirt off a laundry line, and wrapped my hand in a scarf. It's throbbing with pain. I found a pair of shoes that were left at the entrance of the mosque. They don't fit. It doesn't matter.

I wait until 2251. Five more minutes, I tell myself, sitting in the dark empty hall. Any longer, and I won't make it to the corner of Via Londra and Uganda Road in time to meet Jones. And Jones is the ticket to my family.

I wait.

I wait until 2302.

But Bashir never comes.

FIFTY-FOUR

THEN: OCTOBER 18, 2318 HOURS
MOGADISHU, SOMALIA

The car is already there when I run up to the intersection of Londra and Uganda Roads. It's a dark sedan, nondescript, but I recognize the driver. It's my old pal Nice Boots.

"You're late," he says through the rolled-down window. "Get in." He speaks into a phone. "We're en route."

As soon as I'm in, he comes at me with a bag. I lurch back.

"Hood on or you don't get to see the boss man."

I grit my teeth and let the dark, smelly fabric swallow me for what I hope to God is the last time. Then we're peeling out. We drive in silence. We stop three times at what I guess are checkpoints. After about fifteen minutes we reach an area where I can see lights shining through the fabric. We go through another checkpoint. Then Nice Boots is hustling me into a building, pushing me down echoing hallways. We go up and down a staircase, through doors, until my hood is finally yanked off and we stop. I blink, rub my eyes with my good hand.

We're in a large room lit only with computer screens. A handful of soldiers, Somali and American, are hunched in front of them, talking into headsets. On the far side of the room I see Jones at a desk, phone gripped between his shoulder and ear as he watches a satellite image on a large wall display. Seeing me, he motions us toward him.

"Yes, sir, the asset is here. I'll report back in ten, sir," Jones says before he hangs up the phone. "We thought you were dead, Abdiweli." His eyes skate over my face, my bloody hand. His beard and hair hang shaggy and rumpled, like he's been standing in a high wind. "Your monitor is showing up at the bottom of the ocean."

I turn my good ear toward him. "I'm not dead."

"I can see that. Where's Bashir?"

It takes me a second to reply. "He didn't make it."

"I'm sorry to hear that."

We stare at each other.

"Well, this is your show, kid," Jones finally says. "And the show must go on. Where's the Doctor?"

"My family first."

"I need proof you can lead us to our target before we can move on that."

I don't blink. My best friend is probably dead and I'm down to eight fingers and one ear. I've been through too much tonight

366

to roll over and take this shit from Jones now. "You're just going to have to trust me," I say. "My family first, or no deal."

Jones looks at me, trying to see if I'm bluffing. I force myself to hold his gaze. At last he says, "Come with me."

He takes me into a small office with a wall of windows. The glass is thick, probably one way and bulletproof, and the windows look out onto a long stretch of flat ground, punctuated by red lights that wink into the distance.

"What is this? Where's my family?"

"That's the Aden Adde International Airport," Jones says. He picks up a set of binoculars and flicks a switch on the side before handing them to me. "Watch that building over there."

It's too dark to see anything, but when I raise the binoculars to my face, the outline of a structure rises in eerie green. Night-vision goggles. In front of it sits a small plane. My breath catches in my throat.

"Charlie-One. Load them up," I hear Jones say into his walkie.

For a moment everything is still, but then a door on the building opens. I hold my breath. A line of people file out. At least two of them are soldiers, and then I pick out two taller figures and three shorter ones. My heart starts to pound.

It's them.

They're being herded toward the plane.

Hooyo, Ayeyo, Hafsa, Zahra and Faisal.

My mom, grandma, sisters and brother.

They are alive.

They are right there.

Everything in me wants to break through the window and run to them. I lean closer until the goggles bump the window glass. Hooyo helps Ayeyo, pausing to say something over her shoulder to my sisters and brother, who are close behind. If I know my mother, she's shouting at them to hurry up.

"Where are they going?" I croak.

"Guam," Jones says. "To a base where they'll get the full med-eval and screening. And then Idaho."

"Idaho," I say, the word strange in my mouth. "Where is that? When do they go to America?"

Jones pauses. "That *is* America, son."

I tear my eyes away from my family to look at him. Is he telling the truth? I can't see the lie or the trick in his face.

America. They are going to America.

Ayeyo has disappeared into the plane. Hooyo is standing in the doorway, pulling Faisal, then Zahra, and finally Hafsa in. I can see Hooyo's scarf flapping in the wind around her. A soldier follows them, starts to push my mother inside. She resists, shouting something at him, peering over his shoulder. It's too far to see for sure, but in my mind I can see her cheeks trembling in fury, like they do when she is demanding to get her way. My throat aches with a knot of tears I am trying desperately to hold back.

"Hooyo," I whisper.

She's looking for me.

Her face lifts, and I could almost swear she's heard my voice. She stares straight at me. For a second she is still, but then the soldier is pushing her, and she fights, but he is too strong, he has a gun, and then she's gone, swallowed by the plane.

They were just here, and now they're gone, like they never existed. Like a dream.

The door on the airplane shuts so the side is just one long slick surface. And within seconds the vessel is moving, rolling out onto the runway.

"Abdiweli," Jones says behind me. "They're taxiing. At my word, they'll take off. Tell me where the Doctor is."

I can't look away from the plane.

"Abdiweli," he says again, when I don't speak.

The plane keeps moving, getting smaller, farther away.

I keep my eyes on my reward, which is now slipping into the darkness. "My chip isn't at the bottom of the ocean," I say.

I can feel Jones stiffen behind me, the meaning of my words sinking in.

In my mind I embrace the Doctor as we sit in his boat, and he is telling me not to doubt myself. I whisper, "God's will be done," as I press the chip onto the fabric of his shirt. I made sure to place it on his back, under his collar where it wouldn't be seen. Bashir gave me the glue, and I applied it as we motored toward the Doctor's boat.

"He wanted to watch the explosion," I tell Jones. "From a boat in the harbor. That's why it looked like I was in the water. He'll be gone by now, but he can't have gotten too far. Just follow my chip's signal. You'll find him." But Jones is barely listening anymore. He's already at the doorway, shouting orders to pull my location up on the screen and for someone to radio the team to get ready.

I don't take my eyes off the plane. It's still on the ground. Still connected to me through billions of little molecules of sand and earth. Once they lift into the air, that connection is cut. The shouts and commands filling the other room are a fog of distant noise.

"Tell them to take off," I say, but my voice is lost.

I put the goggles down and follow Jones, who's shouting into his phone, signing a stack of papers with a frantic scrawl. The soldiers around him have doubled in number, running back and forth to monitors and stations.

One of them shouts up from his computer, "Sir, we have eyes on the target. His boat's on the move, about six kilometers north of Lido Beach."

"Tell them to take off," I say again to Jones, in a voice I force to be heard over the din.

Jones looks up, pen poised, phone still to his ear. But for a second I have his entire attention. For that brief moment something passes over his face. It's as if he suddenly sees all of this for what it really is. He sees that he's an old, tired man. A grown-up bully who just moved onto a bigger playground. Maybe he truly believes that he's here to make things better. But for this one moment he understands exactly what that costs. He sees what he's broken in the process of trying to fix us all. *Who* he's broken. He says into the handset, "Charlie-One, you have permission to take off."

IN THE other room the soldiers shout with excitement. It can only mean one thing.

I'd stood forgotten, watching the monitors as the SEAL team closed in. Each of the SEALs was a red beacon on the screen as they swam in under the Doctor's boat. At this point one of Jones's men decided that this wasn't the sort of thing I should be allowed to see, and I got closed back up in the room overlooking the empty airfield. It doesn't matter. I don't need to see this part.

The plane is in the air.

My family, gone.

That's all that really matters.

Isn't it?

Through the door I could still hear the voices over the screen feeds as the SEAL team came out of the water. Gunshots. Shouting, both here and there. The roar of boat engines. Orders barked by Jones. Orders relayed between the SEALs. Mangled chaos, all the noises coming from everywhere and nowhere all at once.

The final triumphant words from afar: "Target is in hand. Alive and neutralized."

The eruption of cheers.

I sink into a chair and stare out the window. I wait to feel sad, or happy, or anything at all.

I feel nothing.

"WHAT WILL you do with him?" I ask Jones. He sits beside me, smoking, looking out the window. The other room is still celebrating. Someone has turned on music and everyone is shouting along. Part of me wonders why he isn't in there celebrating. Most of me doesn't care.

Jones doesn't answer. I knew he wouldn't. It'll be some secret place like the Hole, then. A place where men like the Doctor are tucked away, never to be heard from again.

I can see our blurry reflections in the dark window, like two worn-out ghosts. It seems like it should be daylight already. It feels like an eternity has passed since the sun set, but it's only 0100 hours. My hand is wrapped in white bandages, the best the medic could do until I can get to a proper hospital. He gave me some painkillers, so I don't hurt. But even if I did, with all that's happened, my hand would still be low on a long list of things crowding my brain.

"You did well tonight, Abdiweli," Jones says.

Something in his voice makes me look up at him. He's frowning into the night.

"You don't sound satisfied," I say.

"No, it was a successful mission. It's just . . ."

"What?" *What more could Jones possibly want?* I wonder bitterly.

He shakes his head. "Nothing."

I don't press. I couldn't care less what Jones is worried about now. My family is safe. *Dahir will get better,* I tell myself. I should feel relieved. It's finally over. I never have to go back to the Fort, or carry a gun again. Soon I'll be in America, starting a new life. But somehow all I can think about is Safiya. She'll be waiting for Bashir at the border, and he'll never show. How long will she wait? Will she think he's abandoned her?

"Bashir could have cut his chip out too," I say, mostly to myself. "He could have smashed it. He could be anywhere."

His chip has stopped registering on Jones's system. Jones makes a noncommittal noise. My anger rekindles. Obviously he doesn't care whether Bashir is alive.

Forget Jones, I tell myself. *Think of Hooyo and the others. It's time to wrap this up and get out of here.* "When can I join my family?" I ask.

Jones takes a slug from a paper cup. "You can't go with them, Abdiweli."

"Wh-what?" I snap my head toward him, making sure I'm hearing him right.

He stares into his drink, like he's looking for something in the dregs. "You've been with Al Shabaab too long. My superiors didn't agree to it."

Shock ripples through me. "But—but you're the one who made me join the Boys in the first place!"

Jones finally looks at me, his jaw twitching. "I know. But we're going to set up an apartment for you in Sangui City. Refugee status and everything. You can go to school there and—"

I get to my feet. "Fuck that! Fuck school and an apartment. You think that's what I want? I don't want to go to Kenya! I want my family!" All the fear and exhaustion and fury I've been keeping tightly bound comes roaring to the surface. "My brother might be dead by now because of you, and I'm not losing the rest of them! Whether you help me or not, I'm going there! I'll find them."

"After all this? You'll only get them killed."

I feel like he's punched me in the gut. As I'm standing there speechless, a soldier pokes his head around the door. "Everything okay in here, sir?"

"Fine." Jones waves him away.

I barely register the interruption. "How would *I* get them killed? They're safe now!"

He cocks his head. "Are they? Think about it, Abdiweli. Al Shabaab—and the groups they work with—they have eyes and ears everywhere. In Europe, in America . . . That's the interconnected world we live in. Believe me, I see all the chatter that goes back and forth over the Internet. Hits are ordered from Iraq and carried out in Germany within hours. Maybe Al Shabaab thinks you're dead, but that won't stop them from looking for you and your family. They'll know you're the reason the Doctor's been taken from them. And they'll find your family; there's no doubt. Once they do, don't you think there will be people keeping tabs on them, waiting to see if maybe you're still alive? If maybe you show up in a month or two for a happy reunion?"

I feel my fury go cold, slink up around my throat like a rope being slowly tightened. The ringing in my ear reaches a high, needle-fine pitch.

"They'll wait until you're settled in and comfortable, and then they'll strike," Jones goes on. "I've seen it happen. They'll get their revenge. Maybe they won't even go for you. They'll take out your mother, or your little sister. Something that will make you feel the pain they want you to feel. Something that will remind all their followers what happens to traitors." He stops, waits for what he's saying to finish echoing in my brain. Then he puts a hand on my shoulder. "Alone, they have a chance to blend in, disappear. But with you there, it would be a hundred times harder. Do you really want to take that risk?"

I shake him off. I hate him right now more than I've ever hated him.

Is what he's saying true? Or does he just not want me in his country?

I back away, turn again to the window. If I'm going to cry, I'm not doing it in front of him.

"You did a good job, Abdiweli. Don't forget that. You saved hundreds of people tonight. And your family. They'd be proud."

I don't turn around. I don't shout the things I want to shout at him. That Bashir is dead. That if my brother survives his gunshot wound, he just might die anyway, because the Boys will most likely suspect him of helping me. I want to scream at him that all of this is his fault. That some of my family is safe now, but they were only ever in danger because Jones used them as part of his sick game.

I may never see them again.

"You'll be taken by helicopter to Sangui in about fifteen minutes," Jones says, standing up. "Be ready."

I desperately want him to leave the room. I can feel my legs trembling, and it's only a matter of time before they give out on me. I wait for him to go, but he lingers.

"Here," he says finally, holding a business card out for me to take. It has a phone number on it, nothing else. "I know you'll be fine in Sangui City, but just in case, this is my number. For emergencies only. Use the code word. We're grateful for what you've done, Abdiweli. I want you to know that." He waits. I don't move. He clears his throat, like he wants to say something else.

I keep looking out the window.

He tucks the card in my front shirt pocket anyway. Then he sighs deeply, and walks out without another word.

FIFTY-FIVE

NOW: DECEMBER 15
SANGUI CITY, KENYA

"And so I came here, to Sangui," I say, my voice flat, without a scrap of emotion. "A man took me to a hotel, said he'd be back in an hour to bring me to the apartment. I made sure I was gone by the time he got back."

Sam's car has gotten hot in the time it's taken me to tell my story, even with the windows rolled down. But it's not the heat that makes me feel lifeless.

I've told her everything, left nothing out. It all sounds sort of incredible—clandestine American military missions and microchips under your skin and secret tunnels—and even though I kept expecting her to, Sam never stopped me to ask if I'm full of shit. The whole time I was talking, in fact, she hardly said anything. She just let me talk. In a way, I sort of forgot she was even there. It was almost like after trying so hard to forget it all, I needed to tell *myself* what happened.

"And your family?" she finally asks, when it's clear I'm done.

"Maybe they're in Idaho. I don't know."

"Oh, Abdi . . ." She looks back out at the water. Her eyes are red at the edges. My own are dry. *Permanent damage*, I hear Muna echo in my mind.

I wait for Sam to say something, to tell me that it's all going to be okay, or that what happened is part of God's design, or some other totally useless lie that adults tell kids when bad shit happens. But after a while it's clear that she isn't going to say anything like that. Which is some small relief.

I remember what she said about how talking can help, how it can feel like letting go of a weight. I guess I get that, but instead of feeling lighter, now I just feel constricted, like someone's looped a rope around my chest and pulled it as tight as it will go. I open my car door and walk to the seawall. Sam waits a second, then follows. After the hot car the wind is a mercy. We stand at the wall, casting long shadows out over the water. Waves hurl themselves against the rocks below us, shattering, re-forming. It reminds me of Bashir's perch.

"So I guess I am a terrorist," I say, smiling bitterly.

She turns fully toward me. "*No*," she says, so forcefully that I startle. I can sort of see the word in my mind: N. O. Period. "You're not a . . ." She sighs, as if the word itself frustrates her. She shakes her head. "The world is so messed up, Abdi, but you? You're one of the good things in it."

A sort of strangled noise comes out of my chest. "Sam,

didn't you hear me? I was with them! I did terrible things! I killed people! I was an Al Shabaab Boy."

She shakes her head. "No, Abdi! That man, that horrible Mr. Jones—he made you join them. None of that was your fault!"

"How is killing people not my fault?" I demand. "I pulled the trigger, didn't I?"

Her eyes are wide and for a second she looks desperate and wild, like she wants to reach out and shake me. "You did what you had to do! That was to save your friends, your brother."

"I didn't go back for Bashir! Or Dahir. I should have done something! They're probably dead, and it's my fault. I mean, I'm the reason Dahir joined Al Shabaab in the first place! They never would have kidnapped him if it wasn't for me! All of this comes back to me; it's my fault!"

A wrinkle passes over Sam's face. "What—"

"Oh yeah, that's the best part!" I hear my voice rising to a crazy pitch. I can't make myself stop shaking. I've never talked about that day to anyone, not even my mother.

I can see it all, every second in high definition, like three years ago was yesterday. When the Boys burst into our school, I did what everyone was doing. I ran, without any thought but to get away. I ended up in the schoolyard, crouched behind the latrine with a couple of kids from my class.

The Boys were shouting, firing their guns in the air. Kids were screaming, teachers were begging. From my spot I saw Dahir run past and leap up the wall. I watched him get halfway over and then stop, look around. *Run,* I wanted to shout at him, *Go!* And then I realized he was looking for me and Hafsa. His eyes landed on me and for a second we just stared at each other. That's when I should have yelled, told him to go. How many times have I seen him in my nightmares, just hanging there on the wall, between two worlds? On one side of the wall, freedom. On the other, death. He should have gone. But he didn't. Because he saw what I didn't.

He jumped back down and tackled the Boy who was headed straight for my hiding place.

It took about three seconds for the Boy to smash Dahir's face into the dirt, get his hands behind his back and haul him up, off to the technical.

They took him away.

And I did nothing.

I just sat there and watched. Hidden, frozen.

"It should have been me," I say, barely able to form words. "It should have been me Al Shabaab took in the first place. If they'd taken me, none of the other stuff ever would have happened. He saved me that day. And I—I just left him there in that hotel to die."

"Abdi . . ." She puts a hand on my arm.

My whole body is trembling so hard that I feel like my joints are going to shake loose and I'll just drop into a heap of parts. I pull my arm, but not hard enough to break away. It's like I want her to be the one to let go. Can't she see what I am? A coward who lets his brother and his friends die.

"You can't keep punishing yourself. It was out of your control," Sam says. She doesn't let go.

"But I could have—"

"Listen to me," she says, moving in front of me so I have to look at her. "You did the best you could. And I'm so sorry you had to go through this. I'm so sorry my government does fucked-up things like sending kids into terrorist cells to do their dirty work. I'm just—I'm sorry, Abdi. I . . ." She trails off. She tightens her grip. Her eyes are bright, reflecting the ocean. When she speaks, her voice is almost desperate. "I wish to God I could fix things. I wish there were some way to punish the people who hurt you and your family. But I can't. All I can do is tell you the truth." She waits until I look up at her, then says slowly and clearly, "You are a good person."

"Sam, I—"

"You are good!" she repeats, her voice shaking with anger. "I don't care what happened, what you did. You're human, you did human things. We all do things we're not proud of, but that doesn't make us bad people. Not if we try to fix them. You tried, Abdi. You tried so hard. *That's* what makes you good. We can't always save everyone, as much as we want to, as hard as we try. But you can't carry that guilt around with you forever. You just can't. Your brother and your friend wouldn't want that. They'd want you to live, and be happy. Do you hear what I'm saying?"

All I can hear are waves breaking on the seawall.

Sam is silent.

And then, without warning, all the tears I've been holding back since my brother was shot are pouring out of me, hot and fast. And I can't speak. I can't do anything but sob and hold my head in my hands and feel everything I've lost, feel it fresh all over again.

It's like I've taken all my sadness and wrapped it up in a package inside of me because I don't deserve to grieve. I should get to be sad only if I'm not to blame, right? But I can't keep that package together anymore. The strings that bound it are fraying and snapping, and it's all spilling out. I can't even think about whether I'm good or not. All I know is that I've lost my family, my friend, and my brothers, and I heave great, gut-racking sobs, not caring anymore how I look or sound or who's watching.

The waves hit the stones. Over and over and over.

Sam doesn't say anything. She just lets me cry, and after a while my sobs turn to sniffs. I rub at my swollen eyes. I'm hiccoughing and snot is dripping out of my nose. But I'm empty. I feel like an old rag, wrung out and limp.

We sit silently like that for a long time. I can smell brine and seaweed. I can hear kids somewhere up the beach playing, and the mewling of gulls. Distant traffic drones on the highway, and somewhere a radio is playing an old song.

The sun is directly behind us now, making the light hazy gold and pink, throwing our shadows out onto the water. The tide is going out, and the waves are no longer pounding. They make a slushing noise, rocks being ground down into sand over thousands of years. I find myself thinking that if time had a sound, that would be it.

"Sam?" I finally say.

"Yes?"

"I lost the yo-yo you gave me." I look at my bad hand. "No, that's not true. I threw it away. I'm sorry."

Her face goes soft. "It's fine. We can get a new one."

"Sam?"

"Yeah?"

"You know how you said you could help me trace my family?"

She nods, waits.

"I need to give you different names."

She only looks surprised for a second. Then she says, "Of course. I understand. No problem."

"I'm sorry I didn't trust you before."

She swallows, her eyes going red again. "You have to stop apologizing for everything all the time." It takes a beat, but she gives me a little smile.

I watch the waves. "I'll try."

We get up and walk back to the car. The sound of the water follows us.

It echoes softly, filling all my empty spaces.

FIFTY-SIX

NOW: DECEMBER 15
SANGUI CITY, KENYA

We pick up Kuku Express on the way back to Sam's apartment. While we eat, Sam gets on her laptop and enters my family's information into the tracing registry. Even if we find them, I'm still not sure I can contact them. Jones's warning that I could put them in danger that way rings in my ears. But I have to know where they are, at least. I have to know that they're okay, that they made it, and that maybe they've got a chance at starting over.

Sam's going to look for my dad too. Maybe I could contact him. I wonder if he knows about any of this. Maybe Hooyo's been able to get in touch with him and he's on his way to join them. Maybe he's already there. I try to keep my mind from running away with crazy ideas, but I even wonder if maybe Sam will find Dahir. Maybe he's alive, maybe he left the Boys. Maybe he's in some refugee camp somewhere far away. Or maybe he's even here in Sangui City, looking for me.

It's a lot of maybes. But things don't feel entirely hopeless anymore.

On the way home Sam told me about something called "survivor's guilt." It's a real thing, she told me. A lot of people in situations like mine feel it. They survive something, but can't get better mentally because other people didn't make it. She says she learned about it when she went to therapy after her dad took her out of the doomsday cult when she was a teenager. She'd felt the same way about leaving her mother and brother there. She says she's going to make an appointment with a counselor she knows. I can try talking some more, and see if it helps. I told her I'd give it a shot.

"What time do we meet Mama Lisa and the girls at Paradise Island tomorrow?" Sam asks.

I look up at the puppy calendar and my stomach lurches. How did I not put it together until now? "Tomorrow is . . ."

"Doomsday," Sam says. She keeps her eyes on her computer screen. I wait for her to say more, but she only asks, "How do you spell Zahra?"

I put down my chicken and spell out my sister's name. "Are you sure you want to go?" It's the day she's been counting down to for basically her entire life.

"Of course," she says. "Don't you?" She's watching me with a funny expression on her face. It's almost like she's challenging me.

Maybe if she'd asked me an hour ago when we were sitting by the water, I would have said no, that going to Splash Land at Paradise Island was the last thing on earth I felt like doing. But now I remember how Muna reacted when I assumed she didn't want to go swimming the day after the bombing. *They don't own me,* she said. She wasn't going to let her fear of the Boys control her life anymore. I look at Sam, and I see the same sort of thing in her, and I hear her say, *I want that day back.* Tomorrow is the last day at Sam's before I go stay with the foster family. My last day with the Maisha girls. Am I really going to mope around here feeling sorry for myself? If they can be brave in the face of their worst fears, can't I go to a water park?

"Yeah," I say, starting to smile. "Let's go swimming on doomsday."

PARADISE ISLAND is swarming by the time we get there at eleven o'clock. We join the line of cars waiting in a hot haze of exhaust for a parking place. Steady waves of foot traffic are being swallowed through the outer gates. I don't know if it's just because it's a Saturday or because people are doing Christmas shopping, but it's like all of Sangui City has descended on the shiny new mall.

"There aren't enough spots," Sam says, inching the car forward into the lot.

It's the first time she's looked anything but euphoric all day. I woke up to the sound of her singing (really badly but with enthusiasm) and the smell of something burning. When I rushed out of my room, I found, to my shock, that she was *cooking.* She gave me a triumphant smile and slapped down a tower of what she called her "world-famous silver-dollar pancakes." They were mushy on one side, burned on the other. They tasted terrible. I ate the whole stack.

"Why don't you go ahead?" Sam says. "I'll park and be there in a minute."

"Are you sure?"

She grins, like she just can't contain it any longer, and hands me some cash, waving off my protests. "Go! Have fun! I'll be in soon."

As I hurry toward the mall, my nerves start to jangle. I was such an asshole to Muna and Alice yesterday. I wouldn't be surprised if they didn't want to talk to me ever again. For a second my steps falter. Maybe it was a bad idea to come here after all. Maybe I should go back to Sam, tell her I've changed my mind and ask if we can just go back to her house and watch *CSI: Miami*. But then I tell myself, *No, today is not the day for running away. You just have to apologize to them and hope for the best.*

Once I finally make it through the line for the metal detector at the entrance, a rush of air-conditioning ushers me inside. Clean blocks of light filter down from the high reaches of the cavernous, sky-lit ceiling. I follow the signs pointing toward Splash Land, which is in the opposite direction of the food court, where we went last time. As I make my way through the crowds, I'm struck again by how huge this place is. Between the store windows full of plush fabrics, the white marble tile and well-dressed shoppers, it feels like the court of some modern palace.

There's another long line for Splash Land, and by the time

I pay the entrance fee and finally make it through the park's doors, it's almost noon. I keep looking back over my shoulder, but if Sam is in line, she's way back there.

I pass under the Splash Land sign into heat and noise. Huge squiggly shapes fall out of a fake hill: tubes and slides and pools, everything in bright blues and yellows. The sun shines hard, and there are people, so many people everywhere. Children shout and splash and run and come hurtling out of tube slides into the water. Parents lounge under red-and-white-striped umbrellas, and kids my age huddle to gossip and flirt near a grass-roofed hut selling snacks and drinks. There are at least three pools. It is huge and loud and *awesome*. No wonder the girls were so excited about coming here.

Aiming for the deck full of lounge chairs and tables, I scan for familiar faces. There are lines for everything—the slides, the food, the bathrooms. They snake through the crowds and between high screens of palms, creating human mazes to weave in and out of. It takes a hell of a lot of effort to not get distracted and stare at what the girls my age are wearing. Or what they're *not* wearing. It's a different world in here, I realize. Most of these girls don't wear bathing suits like this on the public beaches, or at least not that I've seen, but they've paid good money to come to Splash Land, and it's a safe, contained space. The old rules don't apply. There are a few Muslim girls wearing long, form-covering suits and headscarves that make them look like scuba divers, but they're the exception.

I walk by a shallow pool for little kids where water cascades off plastic umbrellas the size of small trees. Past a winding staircase cut into the fake rocky hill that must lead to the top of the long slides. Finally I spot them, twenty or so Maisha girls sitting under umbrellas near the deep end of the pool. I see Alice, but where's Muna? For a moment I think that maybe she hasn't come with them and my heart sinks. But then I hear a familiar laugh coming from the pool.

And there she is. I didn't even recognize her. She's wearing a new suit, not just her normal clothes like she would swim in the ocean with. It still covers everything, down to her wrists and ankles, with a sort-of dress over top, but it doesn't hide how beautiful she is. But that's probably because she looks so happy. She floats on her back, her belly an island in front of her. For a moment I can barely breathe. I can't do anything but stare at her with a fierce kind of joy in my heart and a big dopey smile on my face. She's swimming. In the deep end. I did that. Or, well, I helped.

She waves her hands in circles underwater, keeping her chin up like I taught her. After a little while she rolls over on her stomach and shouts something at Adut. They both laugh. She dog-paddles over to the edge. Not gracefully, but comfortably. The water is nothing to be afraid of.

Suddenly a blur of bright green bathing suit comes hurtling from one side as Alice leaps over Muna, pinches her nose, and jumps in feetfirst, making a huge splash. Muna and Adut squeal, and the wave gets them both. Muna comes up sputtering and laughing, while Adut shoves off the wall toward Alice, ready to splash her back. Muna watches them, but then, like she can sense me, she turns her head and looks straight at me. I freeze. The corners of her mouth turn down.

My smile fades. My heart begins to hammer again. *Just go apologize,* I tell myself. I take a deep breath and make my way over. Muna swims to the ladder and slowly pulls herself out. She grabs a towel off a chair and wraps it around her shoulders as she totters over. Her belly looks almost comically large, like it's ready to jump off her frame and run away on its own. How much longer does she have? It must be only days.

"You came," she says, when she's finally in front of me.

"Yeah," I say. My hands feel floppy by my sides.

"We thought you were gone for good."

Some of the Maisha girls have noticed me. They bend their heads together and whisper.

"Can I talk to you?" I ask. "Alone? Please?"

She pulls her towel tighter around herself. "Fine," she finally says, and leads the way to a table behind some plants that's at least half hidden from the stares of the other girls.

"What I said yesterday, before I ran off . . ." I hang my head and look up at her, hoping she'll understand.

She crosses her arms over her chest and waits. She isn't going to let me off that easily. So I take another deep breath, and before I can lose my nerve I blurt, "You're right, I was a jerk. I'm sorry. I'm really, *really* sorry. I didn't mean any of that about not wanting to do lessons and you being a bad swimmer. You're a great swimmer. I don't know why I said all that. I mean, I guess I do. I think . . . I think I wanted you to feel as bad as I did, which is horrible, I know. I found out yesterday morning that I'm leaving to stay with a foster family. I was really mad about it. But it's no excuse. It was wrong to say all that stuff, really wrong, and I know that now, and I— Well, I'm just sorry."

I should probably leave it at that, but now that I've started talking, I can't seem to shut up. "I'll understand if you don't want to talk to me anymore, but I hope you'll forgive me. Because I think you're really great. You're a really cool girl, Muna, you and Alice both, and I just . . . I want you to like me too." I wince. That last part didn't come out right. "What I'm trying to say is that you're the only friends I have. You and Alice. And I don't want to lose that—I don't want to lose you. I'm sorry."

My face is on fire. The silence between us is so awkward that I have the urge to do something crazy—jump in the pool, turn a somersault—just to break it.

Muna takes a deep breath and lets it out very slowly. "You really hurt my feelings," she says finally.

I grasp for her words like a drowning man grabbing at a rope. "I'm so sorry, Muna."

"You have to apologize to Alice too." She presses her lips together and frowns, in a way that makes me wonder if maybe Alice took what I said even harder than Muna.

"Yeah, I will," I say eagerly.

"And I don't know what she'll say. She doesn't trust boys to begin with, and the way you talked to her . . ."

"I know, I know," I groan. "I'm a jerk."

She doesn't say anything for a minute. I want to melt into a puddle right here where I stand. How could I have messed this up so badly? I start to open my mouth to try again, but she stops me. She has something in her hand that had been hidden under her towel. She holds it out to me.

My yo-yo.

She must have gone and found it after I threw it over the wall.

I take it from her. My eyes start to burn, and I have to swallow before I can speak. "I'm sorry, Muna."

She sighs. "I know. It's just . . . you can't throw things away and expect them to always come back."

"I won't. Ever again."

I see the start of a tiny smile at the corner of her mouth. "Now go find Alice before she sees—"

But the rest of her words are sucked out of the air.

There's an instant when there is nothing but the absence of noise, like a vacuum. The air thickens, expands in my ears, and becomes something else entirely. Not sound, but blistering, brain-piercing pain.

I find myself flying toward Muna, flailing and bracing my arms, terrified I'm going to land on her stomach. I end up sprawled over her, my back pelted with what feels like rocks. We stay hunched over and frozen until everything goes still and horribly silent. I look up, blinking. Muna's saying something to me, but I can't hear out of either ear now. They both feel like they're plugged with clay. Dust as fine as flour fills the air and makes us both cough.

"*Are you okay?*" I ask when I can get a breath, barely able to hear my own voice. Muna nods, shaking. Little bits of rock or concrete fall off of me as I push up and turn around to the pool deck to see what's happening. My vision starts to slide sideways.

The park is unrecognizable. I can see only half the deck through the haze of dust and smoke. A crater looms on the edge of the pool where the cafe stood. Now there's only a black and burning absence, smoke chugging into the air. Figures rise, pale with dust, limping or crawling in slow, jerky movements. With everyone nearly naked in their bathing suits, the water and the fire, it looks apocalyptic. I hear Sam say the word in my head: *doomsday*. I can see a body half in, half out of the pool. Red clouds seeping into the blue water. The stark wail of a baby somehow pierces the ringing in my head.

And then I see them.

Five figures moving through the chaos in tight formation like knife blades.

Their guns bristle out. Their eyes sweep the scene.

A low moan escapes my lips.

It's them. The Boys.

I'm both shocked and not surprised at all. It's like a dream, a nightmare, where you know the monster is coming, and when he finally catches you it's almost a relief.

But I'm not prepared for what happens next.

One of them turns our way, and I see his face. Even half covered under a *keffiyeh*, I would know him anywhere.

Because he's my brother Dahir.

FIFTY-SEVEN

For a second I can't move. I can't do anything but stare.

He's *alive*. My brother is alive. Joy and relief swell inside me for one brief moment. And then everything else comes smashing back into focus: the Al Shabaab uniform and gun he wears, the bloody chaos he's helped create.

Muna stirs, trying to get up. I move quickly to help her.

"What happened?" she asks. I can hear her better now out of my good ear. "Was it a bomb?"

"I think so." Was there just one explosion, or did I hear another? Gunfire pops from deep inside the mall. I peer past an overturned table and through the plants that hide us from the Boys' view. We haven't been noticed yet. I don't think so, anyway. The Boys have come inside and they're moving through the pool deck, nudging at limp bodies to see who is alive. I can't tell who the other Boys are, not from here, not with their faces covered. But I see one of them grab a woman up by the arm, pull her to her feet. Something in the way he handles her is familiar, and I'm suddenly positive that the Boy is Nur.

"Oh my God, they're here. They're here."

I turn back to Muna. Her eyes are wide, her breath coming in short, jagged bursts.

"Shh," I tell her. "I don't think they can see us from here. But we should be quiet."

She nods, shivering. Her face shows everything that's going through her mind. Everything she lived through. The possibility that it could all happen again.

The Boys are fanning out. One of them will come this way and find us soon. Can we hide? Where do we go? Is there a back exit? All I see are the high walls topped in barbed wire.

A gunshot cracks close by, making us both jump.

"If they come over here, you have to pretend to be dead, okay?" I whisper.

"One of them is heading this way," she says, going very still.

I turn and catch my breath. It's Dahir.

He's kicking scattered lounge chairs out of the way, nudging at bodies. One of them responds with a whimper, putting up a trembling hand, and Dahir stops. For one horrible moment I think he's about to shoot the man, but then my brother tugs his scarf from his mouth, making a *shh* motion with his finger against his lips. I stare. Is Dahir . . . trying to help him?

He looks over his shoulder toward the Boys, then motions

396

for the man to lie down. The man seems confused, but sinks back to the ground, flattening himself. It's only then that I notice the man's got a small child held tightly against his body.

Dahir walks on, still moving toward us.

I lick my lips. Is it possible? Is he trying to save people? He must have orders to kill survivors, or take them hostage. But he isn't. What does that mean? Blood pulses in my ears.

I scan the deck, but the other Boys are busy with their own searches. Where are the security guards? How long until the police get here? Will they send the army? Are those sirens in the distance? I can't tell. Another Boy comes out of the mall. He hurries to the Boy guarding a group of hostages and says something to him.

How many more of them are there inside? Smoke pours from the mall roof. There must have been another bomb. They must have taken the whole mall, otherwise they never would have made it out here, so far from the main entrance. With a lurch I suddenly remember Sam. Where is she? Did she find cover? She would have been right in their path, standing in line to get into Splash Land.

I swallow past the thought. I need to get Muna out of here first. Then I'll see about Sam. If the Boys came from inside, we can't go that way. There's no way out. No escape.

Unless . . .

I swivel back to Muna. "Do you trust me?" I ask in a whisper.

"What? What are you talking about?"

"Please, Muna, do you?"

She nods, her eyes still wide with fear.

"Don't scream," I tell her. I take a deep breath, and crawl carefully out from behind the plants, until I'm sure my brother can see me.

"What are you doing?" Muna whispers hoarsely behind me. "Get back here!"

But I don't. I just pull myself up to my knees and look at Dahir.

Who has seen my movement.

Who is now staring at me like he's seeing a ghost.

My heart pounds. This is it. Either he'll help me, or he'll shoot me. I raise my hands to show they're empty.

Dahir blinks. Stares, doesn't move. And then I see his chest rising and falling, his nostrils flare. He glances to his left and right, and then slowly starts toward me, not rushing, like he's still just continuing to sort through the living and the dead. He pushes a body with his toe, but doesn't actually look to see if it responds.

"Abdi, what's happening? What are you doing?" Muna asks, still hidden behind the plants. I can't look away from Dahir to answer. We've locked eyes, and I feel like if one of us looks away, some bond holding the universe together will break.

He's only five meters away. He closes the distance faster now, and I can see the hollows in his cheeks, the darkness under his eyes. He is skeletal, a shadow of the brother I last saw. Did the gunshot wound do that to him?

He sidesteps an overturned table and then he's right before me. Flesh and blood.

I hear Muna's breath catch, her feet scrabbling to push herself away.

I'm still on my knees looking up at Dahir. He can't see Muna, but I'm totally helpless. He just stands there. And then with a noise like he's choking, he collapses to his knees. He grabs me, pulling me into him. And I wrap my arms around his back, feeling every bone. He's shaking so violently, it's almost like he's convulsing.

He clings to me. "I thought you were dead," he says.

"I thought *you* were dead," I reply, and we push off each other, as if to check one more time that each of us is real.

Then Dahir takes my head between his hands and bumps his forehead to mine, like my father used to do. "I'm so sorry. I'm *so, so sorry,*" he gasps.

I don't reply; I just keep holding on to him.

"Abdi?" I turn to find Muna staring at us, horror-struck.

I wipe my wet cheeks and whisper, "Muna, it's my brother."

She doesn't move.

"It's okay. He's . . ." My eyes rake Dahir's face. "It *is* okay. Isn't it?"

He knows what I'm asking. "I won't hurt you," he tells Muna. His shoulders start to hitch with silent sobs and his head falls into his hands. "I don't want to hurt anyone anymore," he says through his fingers. It takes him a few seconds before he can go on. "I only came here today to run away. But then it—it all started too fast. I didn't know what to do. If I try to stop them, they'll just kill me too."

I check over his shoulder. None of the Boys are headed toward us, but we can't stay here much longer. Dahir keeps talking in jerky bursts, barely seeming to realize where we are or what's happening. "After what happened—when I thought you died, after I got shot—I fell apart. It was like a veil was lifted and I could finally see what was going on. I had come this close to killing all those people. How could I . . . ? I just— And the General thought I had helped you. He locked me up, tortured me, trying to get me to confess . . . I thought he was going to kill me. I don't know why he didn't. I don't even know why I'm still alive."

He goes limp, and I shake him by the arm. "Dahir, look at me." He's so thin. Insubstantial, like he could melt right through my fingers. I want so badly to trust him. So badly. But I hesitate. "You're really done with all this?"

His eyes beg me. "*Wallahi,* I swear it!"

I search his face, like if I look hard enough, I'll be able to see inside of him, read what might be written on his beating heart. Is he the old Dahir, who used to preen in the mirror and tease me? Or Khalid the warrior? I try to find some sign of one or the other, but it's like the boy in front of me has been stripped down to his core and there's someone totally new looking back at me. He's neither Dahir nor Khalid.

"Please," he says. "You have to believe me, Abdi."

And then I remember what Bashir once said: *I'm tired of not trusting.* My brother is finally here before me, desperate for a second chance. And I remember Dahir sitting on the wall, making a decision to save me. I realize we could easily be in each other's shoes. It could have been me who got taken three years ago, me begging my brother to believe me now.

"Of course I do," I finally tell him.

"Thank you," Dahir says, sagging with relief.

I look around again, trying to pull myself together. We're still in danger. "Can you help us get out of here?"

"I'll do whatever I can."

"Can we get out that way?" I ask, nodding at the mall.

He shakes his head. "We took the whole building, all the main entrances. The police are outside, surrounding it, and the army will probably be here soon, but we have hostages in the front in clear view, so no one has tried coming in."

"I'm not going with them." Something in Muna's voice stops me cold. I turn to look at her. Her eyes are wide, her pupils black like she's in a dark room. A little trickle of blood is coming from a gash on her forehead.

"No, we won't let them hurt you," I tell her.

"Not going with them," she repeats. She winces, puts a hand to her middle.

I frown. "Are you okay?"

She doesn't answer, just stares at Dahir.

I turn back to him. "There's got to be some other way out."

He nods rapidly. "The blueprints we studied show a service door over there. A small one, not well marked." He points toward a far corner of the park. "There will only be one Boy guarding it. I can . . . take care of him."

"Okay," I say, but I'm worried that Dahir won't be able to take care of much of anything right now. He looks like a strong breeze could knock him over.

Muna is breathing hard, sweat standing out on her face. "Alice . . . Mama Lisa. All the other girls—they can't take them."

I look out into the haze. The Boys are still sifting through the dead and the wounded, but they're getting closer to our hiding spot, and closer to where the Maisha girls were sitting.

"Maybe I can get to them," I say.

"You can't go out there!" Dahir says, grabbing my arm. "The three of us can get around to the door without being noticed. We can hide behind those slides and the toilet block. But if you go that way, they'll see you."

"You and Muna go ahead. I'll be right behind you."

"Abdi, no! Not everyone thinks you're dead. You don't know the sorts of things they've said they'll do if they find you."

He doesn't need to elaborate. I know. Dying will be the least of my problems.

"What's he talking about, Abdi? They know you?"

I wince, force myself to meet Muna's eye.

Her look of confusion turns slowly to understanding. "You . . . you're . . ."

I reach out. "Muna, I . . ."

She recoils from me. "You're one of them," she says, her voice barely a whisper. She looks from me to Dahir. "You lied to me."

And what can I say? She's right.

I say nothing. And it says everything.

In the damning silence an army helicopter roars in over us. Gunfire rattles toward it; one of the Boys shoots from near the mall entrance. Muna covers her head and her belly as sparks fly off the chopper's underside. It soars out of sight.

"Please, Muna," I beg. "I was one of them, but I'm not anymore. I'm still me."

She doesn't move from where she's curled up. She's not looking at me; something terrible is unraveling behind her eyes.

"Look," I say, "you can hate me. You should hate me. But later. Right now, you have to let me help you get out of here."

"You're one of them. He's one of them," she says, her voice oddly flat. She repeats, "I'm not going anywhere with them."

"No, Muna, please! He's not with them anymore. I'm not. We're done with them. Please, we're going to get you to a safe place. Muna?"

She doesn't answer. Something is wrong. Something has snapped inside her, I can feel it. I know that look in her eyes. It's what I must have looked like when the police tackled me at the roadblock yesterday. My hands start to tremble.

"I think she's in shock," Dahir says.

I try to make my voice as calming as I can. "Please, we won't hurt you."

She doesn't look at me. I don't know if she hears me or not.

Dahir nudges my shoulder. "Look, the Boys are going

inside. Taking cover. They must be worried about the helicopters."

I turn to see four Boys push the huddle of shivering, dirt- and blood-covered hostages through the doors into the mall. One of them pauses at the threshold and scans the deck again. I know he can't see us here, but I sink back anyway. Is he looking for Dahir?

"Now's our chance," Dahir says. "We have to go."

I take a last look toward the Maisha girls, and then reach for Muna again. I'm afraid she won't let me touch her, but I'm able to pull her to a crouch.

Dahir stands slowly, checks the deck to make sure all the Boys are gone. "This way," he says.

Half carrying, half dragging Muna, I follow. It's like she's sleepwalking. Dahir leads us around the back side of bright blue slides that are still gushing water like nothing has happened. We weave through overturned umbrellas and tables and chairs that look like mangled animals, staying out of sight of the mall doors. Our cover is decent, but with her belly, Muna can't walk bent over. We're obvious and the going is slow. I can't tell whether the Boys have stationed a lookout at the mall doors behind the reflective glass. I put myself between Muna and the place where the Boys disappeared, my whole body tensed for a bullet. Finally we reach the wall separating us from the beach. I don't see the door, but Dahir motions for us to stop, and we take cover behind a table.

"It's just around that corner. Wait here." He looks around and then straightens, fixing his *keffiyeh* on his face and hefting his gun over his shoulder. Suddenly he looks fully like an Al Shabaab soldier again.

Muna stares at him.

As he rounds the corner, I tell her, "It's okay. He's not going to let anything happen to us."

"Alice," she mutters. "Mama Lisa."

"Yes," I say, grasping for her hand. Maybe the shock is wearing off. "We'll get them out too."

She stares at me blankly. Then suddenly she doubles over like someone's hit her in the stomach, a dry moan escaping her.

"What? What is it?" I whisper. "Shit." I look around stupidly for help. I can't see Dahir. I can't see anyone.

Muna's breath is ragged again. Sweat runs down her face. How badly did she hit her head? Is this the shock? Or is the baby coming? Dammit, what do I do?

"Mama Lisa," she repeats. "I need . . ."

A figure swims out of the haze above us and I lurch to shield Muna.

"It's just me!" Dahir says.

I look at him. I didn't hear the bullet. Did he . . . ?

Dahir sees the question on my face. "I knocked him out, but I don't think he'll stay that way for long. We have to go." He looks at Muna, his brow pinching. "Is she okay?"

Muna pants. Dark circles have appeared under her eyes. "I'm not leaving them. The Boys will kill them. They'll . . ."

For a second none of us moves. Then I stutter, "I—I'll go back and get them, okay?"

"Abdi, no!" Dahir says.

Muna stares at something on the ground, her body rippling with fear and pain.

I start to back away. "You have to get her out," I tell Dahir. "She needs a doctor. I'll be right behind you."

"Abdi, you can't!" he says.

"She needs them. I have to!" I say, almost shouting, my throat starting to close. I don't have time to explain why. I'm not entirely sure I know, myself. All I know is that I owe Muna this. I let girls like her get hurt before and I'll never make that right, but right here, now, I can do something. I can try to make sure no one else she cares about suffers.

Dahir looks at Muna, and then he looks at me, and he suddenly appears much older than nineteen. He gets it. He doesn't need me to explain.

"Just—" I take Muna's hand and place it in his. "Please don't let anything happen to her."

For a second I think he's going to argue again, but then his shoulders slump and he says, "I won't. Be quick."

He starts to lead Muna away. She's gone back to acting like a zombie. But she'll be out of here soon. Someone will get her to the hospital and she'll be fine. Just fine.

They turn the corner and they're gone.

Swallowing the urge to run after them, I look toward where the Maisha girls were sitting. I force myself to focus, to try to find some sign of life. Something twitches behind broken furniture. To get there I'll have go through an open stretch of deck. I'll be completely exposed. The only other way is around the kiddie pool, which will triple the distance I have to cover.

Just go, Abdi, I tell myself. If the Boys have left anyone standing guard, they'll see me for sure. But I know from experience that it's harder to hit a moving target. I take off in a jerky sprint, dodging between whatever cover I can find. Finally I dive behind a couple of upturned lounge chairs. I hit something squishy and hear soft screams. I've landed on a huddle of people.

"It's okay, it's okay," I say, raising my hands. "I won't hurt you! The Boys went back inside."

I scan the faces, recognizing a couple from Maisha.

Then I hear, "Abdi? Is that you?" Mama Lisa's face emerges from behind a chair.

Relief floods me. She's covered in grit and has spots of blood on her shirt, but seems mostly okay.

"I know a way out," I tell her. "Come with me."

Alice is suddenly right next to me. "We can't leave! Muna's missing!"

"She's safe," I say. "She's with my brother."

Mama Lisa gives me a sharp look. "Your brother?"

"I'll explain later," I say, avoiding her eye. "He's taking her out now. Something's wrong with her—I think she's maybe going into labor. Let's go, before any of the Boys come back."

There's a scramble and soon about a dozen people—some Maisha girls, some I don't recognize—are up and following me as fast as we can go. I hesitate, and then decide to lead them around the kiddie pool. It kills me to drag our escape out, but several of the people are injured and can't run across the open deck like I did. This way the cover is better. The last thing I want is for someone to get shot because I'm trying to rescue them.

"Did you see Sam?" I ask Mama Lisa as I help her support a girl with a bleeding leg.

"No. She was here?"

"I came in first. She was going to follow me after she parked the car. I don't know what happened to her." I glance at the mall, half expecting the Boys to pour out again like some nightmare horde. But it's dark and still inside. They must have cut the lights. One of the glass doors is shattered. I just have to hope Sam found somewhere to hide. There were stores all around. Maybe she ducked into one.

We weave through debris, picking up other survivors as we go, and by the time we reach the exit, there are maybe twenty people following me.

But they balk when they see Dahir and his gun at the door. The Boy who was guarding it lies at his feet, bound, gagged and unconscious. I choke a little when I see it's Gari, one of the Boys from my old unit.

I whisper hurried assurances. "He's my brother, he's helping us. Please, we have to hurry."

For a second no one moves. Mama Lisa gives me a long, hard look. Finally she says, "We can trust Abdi. Come."

Something untwists in my chest. I give her a grateful nod. "Thank you."

"Abdi," Dahir says, coming around to stand by me as the survivors rush out the exit. "I couldn't stop her."

My head snaps to him. "Stop her?"

He presses his hand to his head. Blood runs through his fingers. "The girl—she ran away. She's gone."

FIFTY-EIGHT

NOW: DECEMBER 16
SANGUI CITY, KENYA

"She hit me with something while I was busy tying Gari up," Dahir says. "Hit me *hard*. I must have blacked out for a second, because by the time I could see again, she was gone." He presses the wound on his head with his scarf. "I'm so sorry, Abdi!"

I scour the Splash Land wreckage, but there's no sign of Muna.

"What's the matter?" Mama Lisa asks.

"Muna ran away," I tell her. "She must have panicked. She—she wasn't thinking straight."

Because she was scared of me. Of Dahir. I feel sick.

"I should have gone after her," Dahir moans. "But I didn't know which way she went, and I didn't want to leave before you came back."

"I have to find her," I say.

Dahir grabs me, starts pulling me toward the exit. "No, Abdi. You can't save everyone! We need to get out while we can."

Mama Lisa looks pained but determined. "He's right, Abdi. Go. I'll stay and look for her."

The three of us are the only ones left; worried faces peer back through the door.

"No," I say. "You can't. The other girls need you."

"Abdi—" she starts, her voice authoritative.

"Please, you know I'm right."

"Mama Lisa," one of the girls says. "Hurry."

"Maybe she already went out," I tell her. "On her own. She could be with the police already. You have to check." I look to Dahir for support.

"Yes, maybe," he says, but I can tell he doesn't think so.

Mama Lisa starts to argue again, then stops. I don't know what she sees in my face, but it must convince her that she's not going to win this one. She takes hold of my bad hand and squeezes my three fingers. For a second I see something like fierce pride in her eyes.

"Be careful," she tells me, and hurries through the door.

"SHE DIDN'T go out," Dahir says, once everyone else is gone. We start back toward the mall, ducking behind chairs and tables, scanning for Muna. All my training comes back naturally, like I'm right back in the scrub around the Fort, doing drills, ducking behind stumps and bushes.

"How do you know?"

"There's a dead bolt on the inside of the door. It was still fast. She wouldn't have been able to lock it again if she were on the outside."

We decide to split up. I look behind deck furniture and fake rocks, in slide tubes and toilet stalls. I keep waiting for a Boy to spot me, the gunfire to rip into my chest as I dart from hiding spot to hiding spot, but none comes. I find other scared, shaking survivors and tell them about the exit. Some of them go. Some of them cower from me, and I'll bet Dahir has an even harder time persuading them to leave, since he's still in uniform, still has his gun slung around his shoulders.

I find three dead people, one of them a kid no more than ten.

I don't find Muna.

The search doesn't take that long, but by the time Dahir and I circle around to meet behind some fake boulders near the mall doors, dread has pooled in my limbs like poison. She's not out here.

"What's the plan?" my brother asks.

For a second I'm startled. Commander Dahir is turning to *me* to lead? But he just keeps looking at me expectantly, so I decide I'd better figure it out.

"She must have gone into the mall," I say. "There's nowhere else out here to hide." I look up at the huge building. "You don't have to come with me."

He just shakes his head like I'm crazy. "It's my fault she ran."

I sigh. It is and it isn't. It's my fault too, and it isn't. But blame doesn't matter right now. Right now I have to think. I have to figure out what to do. "I don't even know how we'll find her in there," I say. "Too many places to hide."

"There are at least fifty stores, and stockrooms behind them," Dahir agrees, frowning. "And what if they've taken her hostage? Sorry," he adds, seeing my face.

I shake my head like I can fling the idea out. "No, there's no way. She's hiding."

No one's luck can be that consistently terrible. Dahir opens his mouth like he wants to say something, but then closes it again. He knows exactly how bad some people's luck can be.

"Dammit," I say, hitting the fake boulder with my fist. I barely feel the skin rip from my knuckles.

"She's hiding," Dahir says. "Definitely. But we'll check, just in case. The plan is for everyone to meet back at the food court. We'll go up in the balcony above them and look. The Boys will never even see us. Once we make sure she's not there, we'll fall back, hide, and wait for all of this to be over."

I almost can't bear to ask the next logical question. "And if she *is* a hostage? What are they going to do with them?"

He licks his lips and when he answers, I can tell he's trying to keep his voice as calm as he can. "There are boats waiting out there at the docks near the food courts. That's how we came in, and it's how they'll escape. The Boys will take the hostages with them."

I force myself to breathe. "Where will the boats go?"

"There's a ship five miles offshore where we're supposed

to rendezvous. Once we're aboard, it will be nearly impossible for anyone to take the hostages." He forces himself to keep eye contact. "They'll be ransomed from there."

I take a shuddering breath and say, "She's hiding. We'll just go check." I force myself to go back to my training. What do we do next? "Are there lookouts in there?"

"There should be one at the door," Dahir says, "but I feel like he would have spotted us by now. He must've already gone to join the others."

Or Muna stumbled into him and he took her hostage too.

Dahir says quickly, "Let me go first, just in case."

He's about to move, but I grab his arm. "Wait. What if there *is* someone there? Won't he wonder where you've been? Won't he make you go back with him?"

Dahir doesn't answer, but before I can stop him, he's slipped out of my grasp and is walking toward the door, back to acting like an Al Shabaab Boy for anyone watching through the window. He's acting brave, but I know he's doing this for me. I watch him go, everything in me wanting to shout at him to come back. If I have to watch him get shot—again—I'm not sure what I'll do.

I don't breathe until he's at the door, signaling for me to follow. He's right; there must not be a guard there anymore. I run for the door, not bothering with cover. When I step inside the mall, the world goes dark. Only red emergency lights flash in the gloom. There's glass and blood and shopping bags spilled across the floor. It's a totally different place from what I walked

414

through less than an hour ago. Like maybe the busy mall was just some impossible fantasy world that never even existed except in my mind. It doesn't seem possible that it was ever anything more than this shadowland of broken glass.

We make for the sound of distant shouting, our feet crunching on debris. The air smells like burning plastic. Potted plants are overturned, spilling black earth across the white tile. We slide between columns and kiosks. Every once in a while I hear muffled noise coming from within the stores, crying or frantic whispers. I look for Muna. Eyes peek out and then disappear when they see two young men. I realize I'm still hearing gunfire echoing from somewhere deep in the mall. Some sort of alarm is going off in the distance, making it hard to think.

Once I catch a glimpse of a Boy inside a shop and freeze, my heart jackhammering. It takes me way too long to realize I'm looking at Dahir's reflection in a mirror, and even then my heart keeps pounding like it's going to explode. I have to force my legs to move again.

When we get to the staircase, we slink up to the second floor without speaking. The Boys' shouts grow clearer. *Keep quiet! Sit back down! No talking!*

I can't help but think of Jones. Surely he knows all of this is happening right now. Will he be part of the ransom negotiations? Or is he too black-ops for that? I wonder if he'll be surprised when he hears about the attack, or if maybe he was expecting it. Maybe that's why he didn't look happy that night after capturing the Doctor. Maybe he knew Mogadishu wasn't the end of it. Maybe this was the sort of thing he was worried about all along. Not one more suicide bombing in Somalia, but an attack on a mall full of rich Kenyans and ex-pats.

We skirt the body of a security guard lying halfway inside a candy store. Tiny red footprints lead away from his form, like a child tripped over him before hurrying on. Overhead another helicopter thunders past, casting a brief shadow through the skylights like a giant hunting bird.

We slow as we near the food court, careful to remain out of sight. There's more smoke here; the plastic smell mixes nauseatingly with burned cooking oil. Shouts and muffled crying float up to us. I slip behind a column to get a better view of the wreckage below. Dahir takes up a position behind another column to my left.

About thirty hostages huddle in a circle in the middle of the floor. Tables and chairs lie scattered, pushed out of the way. Two Boys train their guns on the group, and the others mill in front of the glass doors leading out to the patio where Sam and I once sat and ate pizza.

My breath catches. *No.* For a second I just stare, trying to will what I'm seeing to be a mistake.

Muna. She's here. Among the hostages.

And not just her; they both are. Muna and Sam.

They're together. Muna is curled on her side on the ground and Sam is hunched over her, shielding her from the Boys with their guns as best she can. Even from here I can see that Muna's gotten worse. Her face is gray and her bare toes curl and clench like she's in pain. There's no way she can get on a boat right now. Surely the Boys see that. She's about to have a baby right here on the food court floor.

Dahir mutters a silent curse when he sees Muna. "Who's the woman?"

"A friend," I say, thinking of Sam's calendar. Maybe it is doomsday after all.

Sam's eyes are red. Her shirt is ripped and spattered with blood, but I don't think she's badly hurt.

"All right, we go!"

The shout comes from one of the Boys at the window. More Boys emerge from under us, wrapping their *keffiyehs* back around their faces and checking their weapons. I almost don't recognize Nur. His scarf doesn't entirely hide a new scar he has across the bridge of his nose like he got slashed.

I slide over to where Dahir is crouched. "How many are there?" I whisper as the Boys begin prodding the prisoners to their feet.

His mouth moves as he counts. "There were fourteen of us, including me. I see ten."

Where are the other three? Outside, out of sight, right behind us? I cast a nervous glance over my shoulder, but the hall is empty.

"Five prisoners to a man!"

At the voice, my shoulders hunch up around my ears. "You didn't think to tell me the General was here?"

Dahir winces. "Make that fifteen. The General is here."

The Butcher himself. He steps out of the dark, as huge and terrifying as ever. With a gun slung over one arm and a big red gym bag on the other, he watches imperiously as the prisoners are distributed between the soldiers. For some reason the gym bag catches my attention. There's something odd about it. It pulls his shoulder down, like it's really heavy. I try to make myself concentrate on figuring out what to do now, but my eye keeps dragging back to the bag, like someone is physically turning my head. What's in there? It could be extra ammo, or maybe another bomb, but wouldn't he make one of the Boys carry it in that case? It's not like General Idris to do the hard work himself.

"Where is the rest of the team?" the General asks.

"Gari hasn't reported from his post yet, sir. Abdullahi went to go get him. We're not sure about Liban either."

"And that cur Khalid?"

Dahir tenses beside me.

"He hasn't been seen since we were outside at the pool, sir," one of the Boys says.

The General's nostrils flare in vindication. "Because he is a coward!" he says, stepping over debris and coming fully into the light. "He's deserted! Just like I knew he would. Just like his traitor brother! See what he's done with the chance I've given him to redeem himself today? I told you he would turn tail and run." He spits. "Now you see him for what he really is, a deserter and a traitor. And what happens to deserters and traitors, Boys?"

"They die like dogs, sir!" the Boys shout. The prisoners

flinch. They may not understand what's being said in Somali, but they know it's not good.

A mix of fear and fury passes over Dahir's face. He swallows, grips his gun more tightly.

I start to say something to him, but then I hear Sam's voice. I lean back around to look and see her pleading with a Boy.

". . . leave her, please! She's in labor!"

All the other prisoners are on their feet, but Muna's still hunched over on the floor, gripping Sam's arm. She looks so awful, so in pain. Don't the Boys get that? Surely they'll show a little mercy. But then I see who Sam's begging. The new, pink scar across Nur's face gleams as he wrinkles his lip in disgust. He makes like he's going to hit her with his gun butt, and Sam shrinks back. "Get her moving!" I hear him shout.

For one blinding second I'm ready to grab Dahir's gun and waste Nur. It would be easy. I have a clear shot. It's not like I haven't killed before. But as soon as the thought lodges in me, I feel a wave of nausea. Suddenly I'm not sure it would be easy at all.

"The boats are ready, brothers!" the General shouts, interrupting my thoughts. "There are helicopters and probably snipers stationed all around. Keep your guns aimed at the prisoners. If any of us are shot, we shoot a prisoner in return, got it? We don't want anyone thinking we are not serious." He switches from Somali to heavily accented English. "Any of you prisoners tries to run, you get shot dead!"

Someone sobs.

"Translate!" The General gestures at the helicopters droning outside, and one of the Boys moves to the open door. He repeats the message in English through a bullhorn for the benefit of the police outside the walls.

The General's plan is so horribly simple. Cause chaos, grab prisoners, use them as cover to get away. Unlike the mission in Mogadishu, there's no need for suicide bombers who might get cold feet or go rogue. If any of these Boys has second thoughts, there are ten more who can take his place. No big deal if you lose one or two guys. But what's the point of it all? There are no political targets here, just civilians. Is it some statement against Western commercialism and decadence? That sounds more like a plan the Doctor would have come up with, but no one seems to be trying to get the message across to the prisoners or police or whoever else is watching all of this unfold out there. It's more like a military operation than a religious one. Or even just a robbery-kidnapping. I look again at the bag on the General's arm and remember what Bashir told me, that the General was siphoning off money from the Boys. There are banks in the mall, jewelry stores. Is it loot in that bag?

"Move out!" General Idris yells.

It doesn't matter what's in the bag, I tell myself. *Concentrate. How are you going to save Muna and Sam?*

The first group of prisoners is shoved through the patio doors, hands raised high. I tense for gunfire, worried the helicopters will mistake them for Boys, but no shots rain down.

"How far away are the boats?" I ask Dahir. "How much time do we have?"

"Not long. They're just out there in the shallows."

I curse again. What do we do? We can't just rush down. We've only got one gun. We're totally outnumbered. We'd be dead before we were off the second floor. There's no way Muna can make a run for it. Should we at least try to signal to Sam? Let her know we're here?

I watch, getting more desperate by the second as the next group of hostages is pushed out the door. I strain, listening hard for the sound of rescuers, but no shots are fired, no word comes back that anyone is stopping the Boys from getting to the boats.

Could Dahir take me out as his prisoner and trade me for Sam and Muna? Try to convince the Boys that he was still on their side? But it sounds like there's too much suspicion on him. They're just as likely to shoot us both on sight.

The fourth and fifth clusters of hostages are leaving. Now it's just the group with Muna and Sam left. The General and another Boy take up the rear. I can't signal if the General is right there. And besides, neither Muna nor Sam is looking up. Over the drone of the helicopters I can hear a Kenyan voice shouting through a bullhorn, something useless about putting down weapons, but it doesn't seem to faze the General. He hefts the gym bag up on his shoulder.

"Let's go," he says, and then he's following the last of the prisoners outside.

I look around, as if I'll magically find a solution in the wreckage. Food and blood mix on the floor among broken cafe tables below. Up here on the balcony it's all smashed glass and smoke. People have dropped shopping bags, shoes, purses as they ran. A phone.

A phone.

An idea starts to form out of the chaos. I creep over and grab the mobile.

"What are you doing?" Dahir asks.

I touch the screen, praying the phone's not broken, that there's no security code. It works. I dig in my pocket for my wallet. "Call this number," I say, pushing the phone and the white business card Jones gave me into Dahir's hand. I have no idea if he'll be able to get through, or if anyone will even answer. After I bailed on Jones, he could have written me off entirely. "You'll need the password—it's *lightbulbs*. Tell them everything. The whole plan, where the Boys will take the hostages, anything that might be useful."

"Who is it?"

"Someone who can help."

"A friend?"

I hesitate. "More like an enemy."

Dahir starts to ask another question, but I cut him off. "Please, just do it! Hurry!" I stand up, ready to run.

"But— Abdi! Where are you going?"

I look to where the hostages have disappeared outside. He

knows where I'm going. "I can't let them take Muna and Sam. I'm going to try something."

"Let me help you!"

"Make the call. That's what I need."

"Just wait, and I'll come with you!"

"You can't, Dahir. You heard the General. They'll just kill you straight out!"

"But—"

"Stop arguing with me!" I say, close to tears again. "I'm not letting you get captured again—or die—because you're trying to save me!" I try to shake his hand off, but he won't let go.

"You don't understand how angry they are!" he says, his voice cracking. "They'll make you pay for what you did to the Doctor. You'll die a thousand deaths before they let you be with God, you know they will. *Torture* is too nice a word for it! Or . . . we can get out of here. Right now. We can walk away! You and me."

He tugs my arm. It's like that day in the schoolyard all over again, but instead of jumping down and sacrificing himself, this time he's still on the wall, holding a hand out to me. *Come, we'll both go over and run as fast as we can,* his face says. *We'll get away. We'll both escape.*

For a moment I can't move. He's right. The phone number probably won't work, and what do I think I'm going to do out there up against all those Boys with their guns? If—*when*—the Boys catch me, all I can really hope for is a quick death. Right now I'm free, safe. My brother is here, finally ready to leave the Boys.

Dahir and I could slip back into the shadows. He could grab some clothes, look just like a normal teenager by the time we're walking out the exit door. We could disappear into Sangui's streets. If we were together, we might be able to figure out some way to get in touch with Aabo. Maybe one day we could make our way to Hooyo. We could find some way to all be a family again.

If I follow Muna and Sam onto the beach, there's a real good chance I'm throwing all that away.

But then I see Sam again in my mind, crossing off one more day on her calendar. I see the fierce lift of Muna's chin as a wave comes toward her during our swim lessons. I think about Bashir making the decision to trust me. About how he tackled Nur. I think about my brother, hanging on that wall, so close to safety. How he gave up his freedom and his future to protect me.

If I walk out there, I'll probably die. I know that. God chooses the hour, and maybe this is mine. But I'm tired of running away. I'm tired of letting the Boys make me feel like I don't even exist anymore. Maybe I'm not Da'ud, but at this moment I think I know how he felt when he stepped out of the shadows to face Goliath with nothing but a rock and a sling.

Afraid, but alive.

Dahir sees my face and makes a strangled noise. He knows he can't convince me to stay.

I pull my arm out of his grasp. "It'll be okay," I say. *"Inshallah."*

And then I go.

FIFTY-NINE

NOW: DECEMBER 16
SANGUI CITY, KENYA

I slip down the stairs into the empty food court and pick my way to the patio doors. My heart beating in my throat, I duck behind a table and look outside. The gate in the wall that surrounds Paradise Island is wide open, and the Boys are hustling the hostages through it. Another dead security guard lies faceup on the patio nearby. They're leaving through the same gate I'd thought looked weak when I sat here with Sam weeks ago. If only I'd known then how right I was going to be.

Above, two helicopters hover like furious angels, slicing the air with wings like swords. I can hear noise from the direction of the parking lot, sirens and engines and people shouting on bullhorns, which must be the police and maybe even army troops. I wait until all the Boys and hostages are out and then follow them, ducking between overturned umbrellas and tables. At the gate I stop again. I can see the beach from here.

The tide is high, and the Boys' boats are waiting in the shallow water just meters from the gate. I count six, all with oversized outboard motors. They're already being loaded with the first groups of hostages. Far down the beach, lights flash on police trucks and ambulances. They're all following the General's orders to stay away. Sam and Muna trail toward the end of the hostage group, Muna leaning heavily on Sam.

I scan the ocean. There are fishing trawlers and dhows farther out, but nothing that looks like rescue. Was Dahir able to reach anyone on that number? Even if he does, will they believe him?

I shift in my crouch. This is it. I have to act now, or watch Sam and Muna get in that boat and disappear. Maybe forever. I suck in a deep breath like I'm getting ready to plunge underwater, then stand. I'm in full view of everyone.

"General Idris!"

My voice sounds tiny and weak. I feel like it barely rises above the noise of the helicopters, but the General looks back. The guard next to him mutters something, raises his gun in my direction.

"Who is that?" the General yells.

I put my hands up.

Sam's mouth falls open. I see her lips move: *No, Abdi.* I keep my eyes locked on the General. I'm afraid that if I look at Sam or Muna directly, my knees will collapse.

For a second the General just squints, and then, as I hear shouts of recognition from the other Boys, a shark's smile spreads over his face. "It can't be! The traitor!"

The Boy next to him is ready to shoot, but the General waves him back. "Get the rest of the prisoners in the boat," he says, never taking his eyes off me. "We thought you were dead, Da'ud! Are you a ghost, little traitor?" He comes closer, the shark circling his prey.

My legs wobble. I just hope he can't see how badly my hands are shaking.

"No," the Butcher says, "I don't think you are. I think you are flesh. You've grown fat. The Americans must have paid you well." His teeth are knives, glinting as he shakes his head. "Da'ud, Da'ud. You were going to be the match. Isn't that what you promised the Doctor? Before you betrayed him? You were supposed to be the spark that set the whole world on fire."

"My name isn't Da'ud," I say. "It's Abdi. Let them all go."

The General chuckles. "Such big talk for someone so out-numbered. Why shouldn't I just shoot you where you stand?"

"You don't want me dead."

His grin strains. He's growing impatient under everyone's eyes—the Boys, the police, the hostages are all focused on us. "And what makes you think that?"

I swallow, choosing my words carefully. "Because you want to make an example of me. You want to take me back and pa-rade me, bloody and broken, in front of your troops. I'm the traitor. I helped the Americans capture the Doctor. I should burn. Let them go," I say, "and you can take me instead."

"What's to stop me from taking you anyway?"

My heart is beating to break my ribs. I look from the

General to the guard who has his gun trained on me. The other Boys are too far away to hear my words. "Come closer," I say. "You don't want them to hear what I have to say."

"I don't have time for games." The smile is finally gone. "Grab him," he tells the Boy next to him.

"I know about the money," I say quickly. I wait, every fiber expecting bullets to rip through me.

The General raises his hand again.

My blood pounds in my ears, and it feels like an eternity passes as he considers me. But the more seconds that pass, the more I can tell he's wondering. I might be crazy, but then again, I might know things. Things he can't afford to let the Boys hear. "I don't know what you're talking about," he says. But he comes closer.

I wait until he's right before me. Until I can see the gray grizzle of his beard and the lines around his yellowed eyes. I speak so only he can hear. "Let them go, and I'll give the signal to the men up there in the choppers. They have bullhorns too. If I signal, they won't repeat what I've told them about you."

The Butcher shows me his teeth again. "Repeat what, you little shit?"

"About the money you've been siphoning off to your bank accounts in Saudi Arabia. Money that's supposed to pay for guns and food to further the cause. About how whatever you've got in that bag won't make it to those Boys. That most of it will go into your pockets. Everyone will hear."

The General doesn't move.

"They'll announce all of that over their horns in about five minutes. Unless I signal."

"You have no proof," he says quietly, inching closer. "Why would anyone believe you?"

"Maybe they would, maybe they wouldn't," I say, and even though my brain is screaming at me not to, I move closer too. "Maybe I die right now on the sand. But once the Boys hear it, they'll wonder. They'll think about it. They'll talk about it." I pause. "Maybe they'll even ask themselves if it's possible *you* were the one who led the Americans to the Doctor."

"Lies," the General hisses. I can practically smell his fury.

"It doesn't matter," I go on. "You profited most from the Doctor's capture. With him gone, you're now free to rob the Boys blind. They'll put it all together. They're not stupid. Maybe they won't say anything to your face, but in secret they'll begin plotting your downfall. You'll never know again if they're with you or if they're secretly chipping away at your foundation, bit by bit. Choosing a new leader, deciding how to frame your death. You'll stay awake nights asking yourself which ones are the bootlickers, and which ones are planning to chop you up and feed you to the fish."

Seconds tick by.

"General, sir, we must go!" one of the Boys shouts.

He doesn't respond. From the corner of my eye I see Muna shudder with pain. Sam's grip is all that's keeping her from collapsing.

"I'm not giving up all my hostages," the General finally growls.

I swallow. It's working. He's taking the bait. "Just this group, then," I say, pointing at the boat with Muna and Sam. I'm careful not to look at either of them.

He narrows his eyes, calculating. "Fine."

He's going to do it! I struggle to keep breathing normally.

"But you're coming with me," he says. "That's the exchange."

I go dead still. I look back at the Boys and then I understand. The traitor for the hostages. This is how he explains giving up prisoners; he gets me instead. I'll be taken back and made an example of after all. My eyes dart to Sam and Muna. Muna's looking at me now, shaking her head almost imperceptibly, like she knows exactly what sort of bargain I'm making.

"Deal," I say.

The General grabs my arms and twists them behind my back. "Signal," he snarls into my ear.

"Free them first."

He pushes me toward the boats, jamming his gun into my back. He shouts up at the guard, "Free these ones!"

"But, General, sir—"

"Now!"

The soldier does as he's told, grabbing and shoving the confused prisoners out of the boat. They stumble through the shallow water, running once they reach the sand.

Go! I want to shout at Muna and Sam. They're out of the boat but not moving, just standing in the knee-high water like they're frozen.

In that moment of hesitation I see the General look at them. Look at me. Look back at them.

"Hold those two," he says.

"No!" I shout, before I can stop myself.

"You know them, hey?" he purrs in my ear, holding me close. "Put them back in the boat!" he shouts.

"That's not our deal!"

"Then go. Leave them with me." His voice is soft and horrible. "We'll take care of these women. I have men who are in need of wives."

I look from Sam and Muna to the Boys, the ocean, the police and army far up the beach. I'm weaponless, helpless. "I won't signal," I say.

The General tightens his grip on my arm. To his guard he says, "I changed my mind. Shoot the girl."

"No!" I cry. "Wait!"

The General holds up his hand to the guard. "Signal them," he whispers, so only I can hear. "Now."

I shake out of his grasp and look up at the helicopter. I wave my arms. I wave just one arm—the left. Then the right. The pilot and soldiers on board probably think I'm crazy. I can just hear them now: *What on earth does that kid think he's doing?*

Because of course, no one up there knows who the hell I am.

The General smiles. "In the boat, traitor."

"Abdi!" Sam moans as I'm shoved in after them. "What are you doing?"

"Are you okay?" I ask, reaching for Muna's arm.

Muna looks up at me in obvious pain, but the fog I saw in her eyes earlier has lifted. "I'm so sorry, Abdi! I don't know what happened to me. I got so confused, and your brother—"

"No, don't," I tell her. "You were in shock. I get it."

She starts to say something else, but before she can, the General grabs me by the collar and pulls me to my feet. The boat rocks.

"We have captured the traitor Da'ud!" he crows, shaking me at the Boys. "We know him well, do we not? He is the boy who sold our Hakim Doctor to the Americans for a handful of gold! What happens to traitors, men?"

"They die like dogs, sir!" the Boys chorus again, the throaty promise of blood in their voices. The rest of the hostages cower at their feet in the other boats.

"Move out!" the General calls.

Boat engines roar, and I'm flung to the hull as we surge out over the chop.

These boats' engines are strong, fast. We'll soon be out of the shelter of the bay and into open water. I look for the big boat Dahir said we'd make for. It must not be far, but I can't see it yet.

Muna gasps.

"The baby is coming?" I ask her, but she only moans. It's answer enough. "I'm so sorry, Muna! Please, just hold on, okay?"

"She's having contractions," Sam says, holding Muna until it passes. Then she looks up at me. "You shouldn't have come after us, Abdi! What were you thinking?"

The General is watching, but he's distracted by something on his phone.

"I couldn't just let them take you," I say. I look around, desperate for any sign of rescue on the horizon. "How much longer until the baby is here?"

"I don't know," Sam says, her voice tight with the effort of trying to stay calm for Muna's sake. "It could be minutes, it could be hours. I don't know what to do. She needs a doctor!"

"Just hold my hand," Muna groans to Sam. "My water hasn't broken yet."

I'm not sure what that means, but suddenly an insane idea comes to me. "Sam," I whisper urgently, "whatever happens, you'll help her, right?"

Sam's eyes go bright with fear. "What—"

"No talking!" the boat driver growls, interrupting.

We fly over the water.

It takes us less than ten minutes to reach the boat, but Muna has another contraction on the way. As we reach the big fishing cruiser, hull scabby with rust, our boats slow.

The General's brow wrinkles as he scans the deck. "Where are the sentries?"

We all look up. The boat seems empty, eerily silent.

"Something's not right," he says, glancing down at his phone again. "No one answered my call. Stop!" he shouts to the first boat, which is already tying up to the ladder. The Boy in it looks back. He's pulled his scarf off his face. I recognize him now. It's Yusuf, my old unit commander.

Yusuf turns to the General, and just as his mouth is forming a question, there is a dull *crack* and then Yusuf is flying out sideways, landing in the water with a limp splash. All he leaves behind is a spray of red on the boat's hull.

We sit agog for a second, until two more *cracks* hit the air, then more, and I'm watching other Boys fall, either into the water or slumping into the screaming hostages.

"Get down!" I shout at Sam and Muna as a Boy in our boat is hit. He pirouettes neatly before going over the side. The General drops too, but reaches for Muna. She yelps as he pulls her in front of him. He has a pistol now, and he's holding it to her temple, his eyes scanning the rendezvous boat for any clue of where the sniper shots are coming from.

I look too. Pilot's house. That's where I'd go. Up high, good cover, plenty of slots to shoot through. And down there, behind that container. There may even be three or four others, scattered over the deck.

Which means Dahir got through after all. Mr. Jones's men are on the boat.

Seven Boys are down, only four left, including the General. The Boys on the cruiser must have been taken out quickly and quietly. Did Jones send in SEALs? Did they scuba in like they did when they got the Doctor?

The General swivels to me. "This is your doing, isn't it?"

"You're surrounded," I say, trying for my toughest voice. "Let her go before they take you out too."

He shoves the muzzle at Muna's temple and spits, "She's the only thing keeping me alive, fool."

I look around. The other three Boys have grabbed hostages too, holding them like the General. So far none of the prisoners have been shot, though. Maybe the Boys are afraid that as soon as they do, they'll be taken out as well. They look at the General for orders, but he isn't paying attention. I see the first traces of fear in the set of his mouth. He knows his head is most likely in the crosshairs at this very instant.

"Put the gun down and maybe you'll live," I say.

"Shut up, boy," the General says, and stands. He keeps a tight grip on Muna, holding her up in front of him. She gasps.

"No!" I shout.

Sam starts to stand too, but the boat driver rams his gun butt into her stomach.

The General shouts in English toward the boat, "This girl! She's pregnant! You cannot kill me without killing her too!"

The big boat is quiet, save for the sounds of waves smashing against the hull, and the creak of metal and rigging.

Muna struggles. "Let me go, you bastard!"

"Please!" Sam begs, gasping for breath.

I tense, getting ready. No one is watching me.

"Give me one of these boats," the General shouts at the cruiser, "and I won't kill her!"

There's only one thing I can do.

He waits. "Answer me! Or she dies in five . . . four . . ."

But he doesn't get to three.

I have one last desperate weapon. I leap up, launch into both him and Muna. We fly in an arc over the water. The fall seems to last forever, long enough for me to see Muna's mouth open in silent horror and the gun flung out of the General's hand as he grabs at the air. I hear Sam screaming.

"Swim!" I shout at Muna as the water rushes at us.

We hit hard, suddenly a sinking, flailing mass of limbs and foam under the surface, cut off from noise and air. The General thrashes, his hostage forgotten. He grabs at me, at Muna. Not to catch us; he's trying to climb to the surface. He'll kill Muna in his frenzy to get there. What have I done?

He lashes out, kicking me hard in the head. For a second everything goes black, and when I get my vision back, I'm floating on the surface. I struggle back down, wedging myself between the General and Muna, forcing him to clutch at me instead of her, which he does, pulling at my shirt, grabbing my face. I fight off the panic he's radiating and push Muna away, toward the surface.

The General barely seems to notice when she's free. I'm face-to-face with him, and bubbles stream from his nose and mouth. He tips his head up to the surface, only a foot away, and reaches, clawing at it. He climbs me, pushing me deeper, and for a second his head clears the surface, and maybe he gets a breath of air, but it doesn't matter. By then I've latched on to him. I'm too heavy for him to resist. I've chosen my stone wisely:

A gym bag full of loot.

The strap is now wrapped around my ankle, carrying us down.

I hug his shins. He can fight, but he won't be able to get free. The surface is receding. The ocean around us is growing darker. It is so quiet. I look up to see Muna's legs slash out above. She is making for the boat, kicking hard and strong. She's a good swimmer.

And Sam will pull her in.

She's safe.

My mind clears, and all at once I am very calm.

I look back at the General.

I am not the match, I say to him in my mind. *I was never the match, never the fire.*

I am the water.

The weapon you fear more than gun or knife.

You, General, cannot swim.

I haven't practiced in a long time, but I'm not worried. My body settles into a drill it remembers well. I let myself sink, find a clock already ticking in my head. Only thirty-eight seconds have passed underwater. I will not need to breathe for a minute and twenty seconds more.

It's just the General and me now. I swallow, clearing my ears as we continue to descend.

The General kicks but can't loosen himself from my grip. His lips pull back in a grimace. He has no more air, I can tell. If he were thinking straight, he would try reaching down and pushing me off, but he's drowning; he isn't thinking. All he wants to do is claw for the surface.

By the time we hit the sandy bottom, his movements are jerky and slow. His arms float up to his sides. His eyes roll back. I start to let go, and they pop back open. He thrashes and flails, and I think he might even get away. I grab his leg, wrap the gym bag strap around it like an anchor. He kicks once, twice, and then stops, his mouth open and lungs full of water.

I have about fifteen more seconds. My head is starting to pound. But before I kick up, I take a good long look at him.

He is gone. Bubbles like tiny pearls cling to his face.

I let go and rise slowly to the surface.

SIXTY

NOW: DECEMBER 16
SANGUI CITY, KENYA

Someone has put a blanket around my shoulders, even though the sun is still high and hot.

Except for Muna and a woman who was maybe having a heart attack, all of the hostages have been taken to a big tent in the Paradise Island parking lot. We sit in plastic chairs and wait to be interviewed by the police. Muna was rushed to the hospital. All they've told us is that she's doing fine. They both are, Muna and her baby girl, who was born healthy, if almost on the hospital floor on the way to Labor and Delivery. Otherwise, we hostages are incommunicado. The tent is surrounded by army guys who keep the reporters and gawkers away. Everyone wants to get out of here and go home, but apparently our testimonies are "essential to the good of the nation's security." Or something.

I don't know where Dahir is, but I'm afraid to ask anyone about him. I mean, what would I say? *Excuse me, one of the Al Shabaab Boys got away and he's around here somewhere. Have you seen him?*

An officer comes to the tent doorway. He has broad circles of sweat under his armpits. "You," he says, looking at me and then a clipboard. "You are Abdiweli Mohamed? Come."

"I'm going with him," Sam says, standing up.

"No, madam," the officer says.

"He's a minor, and he's under my care."

The officer is unfazed. "It is a matter of national security. We must talk to him alone. Please sit down."

"But—"

"*Sit*, madam."

"It's okay, Sam," I say to her. "I'll be fine."

She sinks back into her chair. Her eyes are still red rimmed, and she looks both worn out and furious. "You don't have to tell them anything you don't want to. *Anything.*"

I understand what she's trying to say and give her the best smile I can manage. Ditching the blanket, I follow the officer out. But instead of leading me toward the police tent, where all the other former hostages were taken, he heads off in a different direction.

"Where are we going?"

"Someone thinks you are special," he grunts cryptically, and leads me to a bunch of army trucks and police cars parked under some palm trees. When we reach a black SUV, big as a tank and looking like something that a politician would ride around in, he stops. The door to the car opens and he nods me forward. I can't see who's inside, but I'm starting to have a hunch.

The interior of the SUV is dark, and it takes me a few seconds of blinking to adjust. Just like always, I find Mr. Jones tucked into the darkest hole available.

Across from him sits Dahir.

"Hello, Abdiweli," Jones says.

Dahir's hands are cuffed and he looks scared and confused, but it doesn't seem like he received any of the rough treatment I did the first time I met Jones.

Once I'm in, the police officer shuts the door behind me.

"Buckle your seat belt," Jones says.

"Where are we going?" I ask, one hand on the door handle, already trying to figure out how to get Dahir out of here. I hear a heavy metallic *chunk* as the doors lock.

"Relax," Jones says. "I'm taking you and your brother to a new apartment where you can lie low for a while. It's not too far away. I think you'll like it. It's a nice place. TV's all set up. Got some good movies for you."

The car is already moving. I look at Dahir, who blinks at me like, *You know this guy?* and think of Sam. She'll go nuts when I don't come back. As if reading my thoughts, Jones says, "Don't worry. We'll have a talk with Samantha."

"It's just Sam," I finally mutter, pulling my seat belt across me.

"I need to ask you and your brother some questions, Abdiweli." Jones pops open his briefcase and shuffles some papers inside.

"Take those off him," I say, pointing at Dahir's cuffs. I wonder how many questions Jones has already made him sit through. Maybe he's trying to see if we give him the same answers.

Jones makes me wait until he has all his papers in order, but then leans over and unlocks Dahir. Dahir's eyes are as big as saucers.

"I didn't expect to ever hear from you," Jones says.

"Believe me, you were a last resort."

A ghost of a smile crosses his face. "Nevertheless, I appreciate your brother's call."

"What's your question, Mr. Jones?" I ask, suddenly very tired.

"I'm afraid I have more than one."

I grunt. "Of course you do. Did you know I was a spy for the Americans?" I ask my brother bitterly. "Pretty fancy, huh?"

Understanding starts to dawn over his face. "Shit," he says.

"Yeah. Shit."

"Are you going to—"

"I'm not going to hurt you or your brother," Jones assures Dahir.

"Well, that's nice of you," I tell him. "Since we just saved thirty hostages and killed the Butcher for you."

Mr. Jones isn't fazed by my tone. "How long have you known about this attack?" he asks me.

"What time is it?"

He blinks. "Five o'clock."

"The attack started at noon? So about five hours."

Jones stares at me with infinite, infuriating patience. "Who organized the attack?"

"That would probably have been the dead Butcher. You're welcome."

"Have you been in touch with your brother since you came to Sangui City?"

"Kiss my ass."

Jones sets his pen down. "Maybe we should have this conversation tomorrow. Once you and your brother have had a chance to rest."

I lean back in my seat, surprised that he's giving up this easily. "Aren't you afraid we'll run away?"

"It wouldn't be in your interest."

I watch him, thinking. Is there anywhere we could go where he couldn't find us? Not likely. And on top of that, he still has me by the balls. He knows exactly where Hooyo and the others are. If I don't cooperate and answer his questions, all he has to do is snap his fingers and they're his prisoners again.

We turn down a side street and pull into a gated, nondescript apartment complex. After the car has parked and the driver has turned the engine off, Jones says, "I don't think you were involved with this attack, Abdiweli. But certain questions have to be asked."

I put a hand on the door handle.

"One last thing for today." He pulls out a photo from his briefcase. "I thought you might want to see this."

I take it with a sinking feeling in my stomach. It's going to be of my family. Or Muna. This is some sort of warning to both Dahir and me to stay put and do as we're told. I'm so focused on my growing anger that it takes me a second to recognize the two people the photo shows. When I do, I suck in a breath.

They're getting into a minibus. He tugs a suitcase in one hand, holds her elbow with the other to help her up. She holds her dress out of the dust as she looks over her shoulder at him, like she doesn't want to let him out of her sight.

One of his eyes is missing.

Even in the photo, you can tell her movements are stiff.

But they are real. They are alive.

Bashir and Safiya.

"It was taken a week ago in Kampala," Jones says. "Keep it."

I can feel a swelling in my chest, and suddenly the big car feels too small, too hot. I need to get out. I'm about to cry, and that's fine, but this moment is my prize, my win, and I'm not sharing it with Jones.

"Apartment number fifteen. Here's the key," Jones says, handing it to me. "I'll be back tomorrow. We'll talk."

"I can't wait," I manage to growl past the thickness in my throat.

I get out of the car. The warm evening swells around me, rich and humid and full of life after the stale, air-conditioned car. Birds call and dart between fever trees whose branches shine copper-gold in the setting sun.

Dahir hesitates, like he can't believe he's actually going to be let go, and then he slides across the car's seat and practically flings himself out behind me.

"You know how to reach me if you need anything before then, Abdiweli," Jones says.

I keep walking. Dahir catches up to me and we walk side by side, our shadows trailing out long and silent ahead of us. I hold the photo tightly in one hand, and put the other on his shoulder.

"It's just Abdi," I say. I don't look back.

SIXTY-ONE

DECEMBER 16, ONE YEAR LATER
THE OCEAN

Three figures stand waist-deep in the shallows: two teenagers, one child.

The girl lifts the child when the waves come in, and the child squeals with laughter. She knows her mother won't let anything bad happen to her.

The boy smiles. The little girl is going to be a good swimmer. She isn't afraid of the water.

On the beach a pale woman with a sunburned nose shakes out a blanket and lets it billow onto the sand. She tugs the corners straight and then pulls food out of a Kuku Express take-out bag. She arranges it for the picnic they'll soon have. This year's doomsday is better than the last. Doomsday will get a little better every year from now on, she thinks to herself. Maybe next year she'll ignore it entirely.

Later tonight, when the boy goes home to the little apartment he shares with his brother, they'll call their mother, whose day is their night, and tell her about their week: school, a soccer team the boy has joined, what they ate for dinner, a movie about fast cars they went to with the pale woman. They'll listen to the din and clatter of three siblings and a foul-mouthed grandmother in the background like it's the sweetest lullaby on earth. They'll all miss their father. In a far-off country, their father will miss them.

Before the boy goes to sleep, he'll say a prayer. For strength to bear what he's lost, to voice gratitude for what he's been allowed to keep.

But that's tonight.

Right now he is just here, in this place, in this time. He lets the sun warm his skin. He listens to waves shush and a baby laugh. He stretches his arms. He picks a point beyond the breakers where the reflected light shimmers and dances.

Then he dives under the water and starts to swim.

AUTHOR'S NOTE

Truth is undoubtedly stranger than fiction and, in most cases, much messier and more complicated than a good editor would ever put up with. This is my attempt to explain what in this story is real, what is not real and what lies somewhere in between.

First, Mogadishu, Somalia, is as accurately portrayed as I could manage, having never had the pleasure of going there personally. (One day!) The history and politics of Mogadishu and the country as a whole are complex and ever-changing, and this book only tells one story from one perspective, which is in itself still limited given who I am and who I am not. The story is not meant to cover or even touch on all the dynamics at work in Somalia, and if there are glaring mistakes or omissions, I take full responsibility for them.

Regarding certain details of the city: Yes, there really are secret tunnels under Mogadishu that have at times been used by Al Shabaab. However, they're nowhere near as extensive as I've made them here. (Probably.) There really is an underground prison known as the "Hole." Lido Beach is real, but the Ocean View Resort is not.

Yes, there really are Western military actors, a small number of Americans in particular, at work in Somalia. This isn't necessarily a secret, it's just not well known. Hopefully they are not as nefarious as I've made them out to be here. But on that note, yes, the US regularly carries out drone strikes and ground raids on Al Shabaab targets in Somalia, in partnership with Somali armed forces. According to the Bureau of Investigative Journalism, in 2017 alone, around 220 people were killed in US led or assisted drone and ground strikes in Somalia.

Al Shabaab is a real organization whose use of abducted children as soldiers, servants and wives has been extensively documented. They may have started out as a force for good, but the organization has become repressive and violent. It regularly carries out deadly attacks on civilian targets.

Maisha Girls' Center is not a real place, but is partially based on the excellent work done on behalf of girls at RefuSHE (formerly Heshima Kenya) in Nairobi, Kenya (Refushe.org). If you have been moved to help support girls who have been in situations similar to those of Muna and Alice, RefuSHE is a great organization to fund.

Sangui City is not a real place in Kenya, but this author's fantasy of what would happen if Nairobi and Mombasa got together and made a beautiful baby. There is, therefore, no

Paradise Island. However, some events in the book were inspired by the 2013 terrorist attack on the Westgate Mall in Nairobi.

The characters in the book are entirely fictional, though some are very loosely based on real people.

Somali spelling has not been officially standardized across the country. I have tried to stick to the simplest and most commonly used spellings, both for Somali and Arabic-based words used in Somali.

Lastly, a note on writing outside of my own perspective and community. This was not something I took on lightly, especially given the sensitive issues that are a part of this story. I still have mixed feelings about putting this book out into the world. In particular, I have the utmost respect for religious freedom and in no way wish to add to the ridiculous misconception that Islam is a religion that promotes hate and violence. My aim in telling this story was to make stories and perspectives like the ones I heard while interviewing Somali refugees accessible to a wider audience. I talked to many Somalis who had survived terrible abuses at the hands of Al Shabaab, and they would be the first to say that Al Shabaab in no way represents true, "correct" Islam. But with any story, it matters who does the telling. I realize that it is impossible to discount that I bring my own perspective and inherent biases. I had incredibly wise and patient people helping me along the way, and if there are errors and missteps, they are entirely my own.

GLOSSARY

Somali

Aabo — father

Al Shabaab — "The Youth"; Harakadka Mujahidinta Al Shabaab

Ayeyo — grandmother

Canjeero — spongy, sour, traditional bread eaten throughout the horn of Africa

Ciyaalsuuq — unruly kids, hooligans, the bad kids your mom warns you about hanging out with

Dirac — a traditional women's dress (usually worn on special occasions)

Doqon — idiot

Duqsi — Quranic school

Hooyo — mother

Guul — victory

Jalbab — a long, loose-fitting garment worn by some Muslim women

Kaalay — come (a command)

Kafir — an insulting term used by some Muslims for non-Muslims

Kac kac — Somali pastry similar to doughnuts

Keffiyeh — a traditional Middle Eastern headdress

Khaat — a stimulant (leaf) chewed in parts of Africa and the Middle East

Khameez — a loose men's shirt

Koofi — a hat worn by some Muslim men

Macawis — a traditional Somali garment worn by some men

Miswak — tree whose twigs are used as toothbrushes

Niqab — a face-covering veil worn by some Muslim women

Oday — elder

Sambusa — Somali version of fried triangular pastry filled with meat and/or vegetables

Technical — a truck used for battle, sometimes outfitted with a mounted machine gun

Xalwa — Somali-style halva, a sweet confection

Arabic used in Somali

Adhan — the call to prayer

Allahu Akbar — "God is great"

Alayhi as-salam — "Peace be upon him" (Mohammed)

Alhamdulillah — "Praise to God"

As-salamu alaykum — "Peace be upon you"

Ayah — a verse (within the Quran)

Eid — a Muslim festival (in particular Eid Al-Fitr: the holy day marking the end of Ramadan)

Fi amman Allah — "God protect you"

Hadith — the collection of statements and actions of Mohammed, or actions approved by him, that help guide Islamic practice

Hajj — one of the Five Pillars of Islam, a pilgrimage to the holy city of Mecca

Hakim — physician (honorific)

Haram — forbidden

Inshallah — "God willing"

Kaaba — The most holy site in Islam, and the focal point of hajj. Prayers are also directed toward the Kaaba.

Mashallah — "God has willed" (a phrase used to express appreciation, thankfulness)

Ramadan — the ninth month of the Islamic calendar, observed by Muslims as a period for fasting, spiritual purity and reflection

Ramadan Kareem — "Generous Ramadan" (a phrase used to wish someone a happy Ramadan)

Salat — the five daily required prayers: *Fajr* (dawn), *Dhur* (midday), *Asr* (afternoon), *Maghrib* (sunset), *Isha* (night)

Ummah — the (entire) Islamic community

Wa-alaykum salam — "And unto you peace" (as a reply to As-salamu alaykum)

Wallahi — "By God"

Kiswahili

Kanga — colorful, popular style of fabric worn in East Africa

Kijana — young (boy), youth

Muzungu — white person, foreigner

Pole pole — slowly slowly

Posho — cornmeal

Samahani — sorry

Sawa — good, okay (sometimes said "sawa sawa" for emphasis)

Twende — let's go

Initialisms and Acronyms

AMISOM — African Union Mission in Somalia

IED — Improvised Explosive Device

NGO — Non-Governmental Organization

RPG — Rocket-Propelled Grenade

UN — United Nations

Note: Somali spelling not standardized; Arabic words in English sometimes spelled differently

Turn the page to read an excerpt from

ONE

I f you're going to be a thief, the first thing you need to know is that you don't exist.

And I mean, you really have to know it. You have to own it. Bug Eye taught me that. Because if you do exist, you might snag someone's eye who will frown and wonder who you are. They'll want to know who's letting you run around. Where you'll sleep tonight. *If* you'll sleep tonight.

If you exist, you won't be able to slouch through a press of bodies, all warm arms and shoulders smelling of work and soap. You won't be able to take your time and choose: a big lady in pink and gold. You won't be able to bump into her and swivel away, her wallet stuffed down your pants. If you exist, you can't exhale and slip through the bars on a window. Your feet might creak on the floorboards. Your sweat might smell too sharp.

You might.

But I don't.

I'm the best thief in this town.

I don't exist.

I've been sitting in this mango tree for long enough to squish seven mosquitoes dead. I can feel my own warm blood between my fingers. God only knows how many bites I have. Ants are exploring my nether regions. And yet Sister Gladys, bless her, will not sleep.

Through the windows I see her bathed in the light of the common room's television. Her face shines a radiant blue, and her belly shudders with laughter. Feet propped up on a stool, her toes bend at odd angles like antelope horns. I wonder what she's watching, relaxed now that all the students are asleep. Old *Fresh Prince of Bel-Air* reruns? *Churchill Raw*? What do nuns think is funny?

I check the time on my phone and briefly consider coming back tomorrow and lifting that ancient television once and for all. Shouldn't she be praying or something?

Eight mosquitoes. My stomach growls. I clench it and it stops.

Finally, the sister's head slumps. I wait for the rhythm of her breathing to steady, then slowly lower myself over the wall that surrounds the school.

A guard dog materializes from the darkness and rushes toward me.

I put my arms up. Dirty leaps on me, slobbering all over

my face. "Shh . . ." I say to his whines. His wagging tail thumps my legs as I walk toward the washroom at the end of the dorms.

"What took you so long?" Kiki asks, pushing open a creaky window as I approach.

I wince at the noise and look around, even though I know there's no one in the tidy yard but Dirty. He leans against my thigh, panting happily as I rub the soft fur between his ears. Dirty and I are old pals.

"I think Sister Gladys has a crush on Will Smith," I say.

My sister grunts and pushes a white bun through the bars on the window meant to keep thieves like me out. It tastes sweet, store-bought. I give a bite to Dirty, who wolfs it down in one gulp, licks his lips, and whines.

"Everything okay?" I ask between bites. "The penguins aren't beating you up too bad?"

She shakes her head. "You?"

"No penguins up on my roof. Can't fly."

"You know what I mean, Tina."

"I'm fine," I say. "Hey, I brought you something." I rummage in my bag and pull out a pack of No. 2 pencils, still wrapped in cellophane. I slide them through the bars.

"Tina . . ."

"Wait, there's more," I say before she can protest, and fish out a notebook. It has a cartoon of happy kids on the front, and the words SCHOOL DAYS! in dark, emphatic capitals.

I push the goods toward her. Her eyes linger on the tattoos that cover my arms.

"The nuns will give me school supplies," she says. "You don't have to steal them."

"They'll give you the reject bits. You don't have to depend on their charity. I can get you better."

"But *you're* giving me charity."

"That's different. I'm family."

She doesn't say anything.

I step back, leaving the gifts on the windowsill. "You're welcome."

"Tina," she blurts, "you can't just live on the streets for the rest of your life."

I zip up my bag. "I don't live on the streets. I live on a roof."

Kiki's doing that thing where her brow pinches, and she looks like Mama. I see more and more of our mother in Kiki every time I come here, which hurts sometimes, but still, better Mama than *him*. He's most obvious in her lighter skin and eyes, in her loose curls. You can still see that we're sisters; I just wish it wasn't so obvious that we're half sisters. Not that I would ever call her that. I hate how it sounds. Half sister. Like half a person.

But there's no hiding that Kiki's dad, unlike mine, is white. Once she let it slip that the other girls call her "Point-Five," as in, point-five black, point-five white. I told her to tell me their names, but she just said, *They don't mean anything by it, Tina. It doesn't bother me, and besides, you can't go around beating up little kids.* But sometimes I see her looking at my dark skin, comparing it against her own, and I can tell she wonders what it would be like to fit in for once, to not be the "Point-Five" orphan.

Kiki squeezes the bars separating us, as if she could pull them apart. She's not finished. "You can come stay here with me. You know you can. Sister Eunice would let you. You're not too old. She let that other sixteen-year-old in. They've got lots of books and a piano and—"

"Shh." I put a finger to my lips. "Too loud."

She glances over her shoulder into the dark washroom. From somewhere I hear one of the other girls cough.

"Seriously, Tina," she whispers, turning back. "They could put you on scholarship, like me."

"Come on, Kiki, you know they won't. It's one per family."

"But—"

"Enough," I say sharply. Too sharply. Her shoulders sag. "Hey," I say, and reach my hand through the bars again to smooth down the curls that have escaped her braids. "Thanks for dinner. I've got to go. I have to meet Boyboy."

"Tina, don't leave yet," she starts, her face pressed up close against the metal.

"Be good, okay? Do your homework. Don't let the penguins catch you out of bed."

"You'll be back next Friday?" she asks.

"Like always."

I gently push Dirty off my leg and make sure my pack is tight on my back. Scaling the wall to get out is always harder than climbing the tree to get in, and I don't want to get caught on the barbed wire and broken shards of glass embedded in the concrete.

Kiki is still watching me. I force a grin. For a moment her face is still, and then it softens and she smiles.

For half a second, I exist.

And then I disappear in the dark.

ACKNOWLEDGMENTS

Writing a second book is probably a lot like having a second child. You think you know what you're doing—after all, you've done this before! And no one died! But then the second is nothing like the first and you're left desperately googling things you have no business googling at three in the morning, like "Can kids poop out rocks?" or "How do you write a book?"

Thankfully, I had a huge amount of help birthing and raising this book to maturity.

First and foremost, I owe an unpayable debt of gratitude to the thousands of refugees who trusted me with their stories while I was working in Africa, especially the troublemaker of Cairo, to whom this book is dedicated. You told me about your mother's sacrifice for you, and of your sacrifice for your siblings, and I will hold that story in my heart forever. I hope you are home now (wherever that may be) and are causing good trouble there too.

Some of the first people to give feedback on this book were the kids of the phenomenal writing and literacy center 826 Boston. Thank you to Nakia Hill for helping to organize a group of readers who were insightful, patient, hilarious and not afraid to rip into some pizza. Xukun, Saadia, Mohamed, Nasra and Ahmed, thank you.

I am so grateful to all the others who read and gave feedback in such kind, generous and patient ways. Thank you to Sadio Gurhan for your unique Nairobi perspective, Mariam Ismail for real talk over good coffee, Nazima Abdillahi for taking time from her busy writing and editing life to read, Jenny Pro for her unique insight on UNHCR, and most especially Ahmed Ismail Yusuf, a writer and poet of tremendous vision and talent, who helped me understand so much. I know all of you are incredibly busy, and I appreciate the time you spared.

I am forever grateful to the Associates of the Boston Public Library, who, through the Children's Writer-in-Residence Program, gave me the space, time and resources to discover what it really means to be a writer.

Thank you to RefugePoint (refugepoint.org), most especially the dedicated and compassionate staff at the Nairobi office, for giving me the opportunity to do the work of my heart. Thank you to RefuSHE (refushe.org, formerly Heshima Kenya) for the incredible impact you make on girls' lives.

One thousand million thank-yous to Faye Bender, agent par excellence. You are so wise, so unfailingly surefooted, and a true master of your craft. I am so lucky to have you in my corner.

I am so grateful to the one and only Stacey Barney: tireless, fearless, brilliant editor. Your attention to detail is only matched by your ability to see and understand a landscape that goes far beyond the page. I live for your check marks.

Thank you so much to the Penguin Random House team of professionals who make a book really happen, and happen so beautifully. Thank you for all the essential things you do that we authors don't even know about.

To my family, Jay, Renee, Rebecca, Dylan, Margot, Katie and Anthony, for encouragement and love, and for always reading like you mean it, no matter how many times I foist the same story on you. To Mom, especially, for crossing oceans to babysit so I could meet deadlines. (I changed the fish bones thing. Did you notice?) To Dez, for being the best distraction in the entire universe. You make life so sweet. And lastly, but never least, to Marty. Thank you for being the stubborn and steadfast axis of my spin.

NATALIE C. ANDERSON is an American writer and international development professional living in Geneva, Switzerland. Before moving into writing, she spent a decade working with nongovernmental organizations (NGOs) and the United Nations on refugee relief and development, mainly in Africa. She was selected as the 2014–2015 Associates of the Boston Public Library Children's Writer-in-Residence, where she wrote her debut novel, *City of Saints & Thieves*.

You can visit Natalie C. Anderson at nataliecanderson.com